I0700698

ELECTRIC FIELDS

Blue and gray forces collide,
smashing particles of mind and body,
that cascade into dank ground,
a macabre dance into Death's goodnight.
Smokey ghosts emerge,
inchoate souls from wormy bones
waft through midnight air
over ground trodden by gawking descendants.
Now more than a century and a half
the cost of unrequited death arises in the gloom
with bitter scores—unforgiven.
The ghosts remain restless,
hovering in nightly air
still putrid with graves gone cold.
What I know I cannot say.
Lost in riddles of the past,
I warn you: Death comes for those
who ignore whispers.
Who knew?
They knew.
You know.

GHOST

Published by Compound Press.
Printed in the United States of America.
First printing, 2022.
Cover and book design by Karen Sketch
www.jancthorpeauthor.com

JAN C. THORPE

IN 2011 I WAS VISITING ON THE EAST COAST and spent a few days in Shepherdstown, West Virginia, which was chartered in 1762, making the town thirty years older than the United States. Shepherdstown is also located in the heart of the Civil War Heritage Area. It is fifty-one miles from Gettysburg, Pennsylvania, four miles from Antietam where the bloodiest day of the Civil War was fought on September 17, 1862, and one mile up the Potomac River where 48 hours after the Battle of Antietam the Battle of Shepherdstown was fought.

Given its strategic location so early on even before the Revolutionary War, it is no surprise that there are multiple graveyards in Shepherdstown and in the surrounding area. I was walking around with a few friends from college days, and we wandered into a very old graveyard. The marble plaques and grave markers were slowly disintegrating, but if you looked closely, you could make out the names and dates. Many were dated just pre- or post-Revolutionary War, and some were before, during and after the Civil War. The grounds were not exactly neglected because it was clear that care was still given to the preservation of the graves. But the plants, wild grasses and over-grown bushes evoked an atmosphere of a time long ago. And of course, there was the ethos of spirits, or ghosts, lingering.

At the time, I had finished my first novel, "Ancestors," which dealt with the spirit world of African Voudou. I was wondering what I would use as the background for my second book that would include six of the same characters, including two Chow dogs, with my plots originating in Berkeley, California where I live. It was in that Shepherdstown cemetery that the plot to use a ghost from the Civil War hatched in my mind. I was still a long way from conceiving how my Zakariah Monroe ghost character would play out in a plot, but the seed was sewn. My first plot question was, how do I get from Berkeley, California to the Civil War in the east, and make it work?

At the time I was in Shepherdstown the country was into the first few years of the Obama administration. The division between the so-called red and blue states was growing. Historically I have always been aware that the writers of the Constitution of the United States, our Founding Fathers, left the issue of slavery up to future generations. And for good reason. Many of them, including George Washington, Thomas Jefferson, James Madison, Benjamin Franklin, Alexander Hamilton, to name a few, were slave owners. Slavery was a thorny issue that festered for another 79 years until the Civil War ended.

For most Americans we learned that the Civil War ended slavery in the United States. But what did not end was the racism that fueled slavery.

The Civil War apparently produced more ghost sightings than any other war. That fact propelled me to think about why. And here's what I came up with. It has been surmised that ghosts linger around the living because of unresolved personal matters. And what would these ghosts who fought in our Civil War tell us if we could listen to them? I decided that whether the ghost is a Confederate or a Union soldier, they want to believe what they fought for was at least for something important—preferably some kind of peaceful reconciliation between the north and south, white and Black America.

I decided to write about a microcosm of an immediate plot between real characters living now, and the macrocosm—the unfinished business of the Civil War that permeates all of us now.

As I wrote *Ghost*, Zak (Zakariah) became the warning voice for an immediate danger facing the character of Daniel Perry through Benjamin Monroe's festering vengeance, and the future danger of our divided world where neither side seems to have the capacity to listen to the other. That leaves all of us with the biggest dilemma of all: What and how do we tell our younger generations about who we are now?

– JAN C. THORPE, PHD

CHAPTER 1

"And while they slept the lazy, rainy breeze drifted through the East Woods and the West Wood and the cornfield and riffed over the copings of the stone bridge to the south, touching them for the last time before dead men made them famous. The flags were furled, and the bugles stilled, and the hot metal of the guns on the ridges had cooled, and the army was asleep— tenting tonight on the old campground, with never a song to cheer because the voices that might sing were all stilled on this most crowded and most lonely of fields. And whatever it may be that nerves men to die for a flag or a phrase or a man or an irrepressible dream was drowsing with them, ready to wake with the dawn."

CATTON, BRUCE, SEPTEMBER 17, 1862, *MR. LINCOLN'S ARMY*, NEW YORK ARCHER BOOKS 1862 ED., P. 260.

HE FLEW IN LOW, A LAZY, DAZED HAWK beneath the high canopy of Oak and Hickory.

A slow, steady rain pelted the ground in silence—a dark mist everywhere shrouding the outline of trees swaying in the breeze.

He spotted the orange glow on the ground before he saw them, four in all, hunched over the dying embers. *Why here? He must want to talk about something important.*

He landed on his feet and walked to the edge of the small clearing where the men crouched, rocking themselves for warmth. Not until he was right behind them, did he hear the low murmurings and occasional chuckles emanating from their huddle. Through the stillness came a clap of thunder—*a long way off*—but after the low-riding rumbles followed, he wasn't sure. The rat-a-tat of a stray mortar sent to warn of tomorrow's pending doom?

Each looked up, as if they too listened for the same distinction—thunder or mortar?

"Shit," someone hollered into the wild, "don't you Rebs ever sleep?"

Closer in, right next to his ear, he heard his four-great-Grandfather speak. "Those Johnny rebs don't have more than half a grain of good sense that God gave em."

Silence.

Then one of them added, "I used to own a mule who'd start hee-hawin' up a storm when he was tired after a long day's work, and I knew he'd kick me, and there wasn't anything I could do with him except let him head for the barn. He was the best mule I ever knew, but the stubbornest old cuss I ever met. Nothin' could stop him when he got a hankering in his blood. Like those Rebs out there. We might out-number 'em, but God help us." And then his metaphor, "and those damn mules they rode in on."

They chuckled.

His grandfather stood up.

"Where ya goin' Zak?"

"Back to the barn's where I'm going. Back to the barn. I'm just a stupid old mule too."

He stood waiting, knowing that his grandfather came.

He greeted him the way he always did. "Howdy, Tom, my boy."

"Hello, Zak. I assume you wish to speak with me about something."

"That I do, my boy. That I do."

Silence.

He watched his grandfather find a rock to perch himself on. He waited. He always had to wait. With ghosts, waiting was part of their game. Zak had explained during his first visitation when Tom was ten years old: "I have all the time in the world." Now at eighteen, Tom had been carrying on his ghostly relationship with his grandfather for eight years. So, this was old hat really. But he knew they only met the night before Antietam, when there was something really important to discuss. And when there was something that important, his grandfather made him wait. The small talk would be endless.

Finally, he spoke. "Your twice-great-Grandfather was a foolish man. His great Grandson, that uncle of yours you happen to be living with at the moment, is not so foolish."

I wonder what this has to do with Antietam. He only uses it as background when he thinks something big is up. Twenty-two thousand dead in one day.

This was the War that put all others to shame. What's up with the old ghost? He watched Zak take out his pipe and fill it with Virginia tobacco from a pouch in his shirt pocket. He knew he wouldn't smoke it. He never did. *He's a ghost for God's sake!*

"What's going to happen here tomorrow should have been studied by everyone and anyone who wants to understand human nature. But, like human nature, those who studied it focused more on the details rather than what it showed most about humans. Some understood, but not enough. And you're my kin. You need to understand."

He hated this kind of singling out that his grandfather did. Expecting him to get something so momentous about human nature based on history, and like the great ghost he was, his grandfather always made the kinship argument. *I just want to be myself, Tom. I want to be an average guy. But this old Zachariah ghost of an ancestor won't let me. Why me? What could he possibly think I can do about the world now? He talks as if he's been grooming me for something. Maybe I'm about to hear what.*

"Everybody thinks Lincoln knew, but he didn't."

Silence.

Oh, God. He's going to speak in riddles. "Didn't know what, Zak?" He started calling him Zak during one of their little chats about three years ago.

Zak went on, amused by his grandson's exasperation. "Lincoln spoke to ghosts, you know."

"I know. You told me many times. Did you ever speak to him?" They'd also had this discussion before.

Zak looked startled. "Hell no. I was alive then. A mere sergeant in the cavalry."

Mere sergeant, my foot! "Zak, maybe you should get to the point."

"A little testy this evening, aren't we?" He pointed his pipe over toward the men in the woods. "See those men over there?"

Tom knew he might be getting to the point. It would be roundabout, but he had begun. He knew this when Zak brought him into the ghostly tableau.

"They'll all be dead tomorrow. Piled up on that sunken road. Why not me? Stupid luck. Meaningless, stupid luck! My life was nothing but a long, monotonous road after that day. I believe I was to live for 45 more years for only one purpose, to remember and make sure they were remembered down through the ages. But, Jesus, Tom. Your kin are not very smart. Maybe educated, but I don't give a damn for any one of them. Except you. I like you. You've got the right kind of brain. You're a good mule. Let me tell you, boy, a good mule is the best animal alive, except maybe for a camel." Tom knew that was supposed to be funny. "Independent, yes. But the right kind of brain." He chuckled, pointing to his temple. "We don't grow camels in this wet, changing climate."

Ghostly humor. Tom knew Zak loved mules. His father used to tell him, "your five-great-grandfather was a master rider in the cavalry. He liked horses, but he loved mules. Sure-footed. Could take one anywhere." His father had an old McClellan saddle that he kept for sentimental reasons. He would point to it and say, "They were a cross between a Western and European saddle."

He never asked Zak about being a ghost. Somehow, he knew it wasn't the right etiquette. When his grandfather first came to him, he acted as if it was just normal, and it was clear that Zak approved of him right off the bat.

"Well, I've been thinking." Zak waved his pipe around as if to include the whole universe. Then he looked like he forgot his train of thought, as if he were going to fall asleep and disappear. He raised his big head of hair like a horse flipping flies with its mane and began in his meandering way. "Seems to me there's a whole lot of religiosity going on now in the world." He looked out. "But there isn't any substance my boy. No substance."

Tom waited. He'd heard this prologue before. Zac loved to talk about the South as if they had some kind of superior passion for God, perhaps misdirected, but of course anyone who'd read about old Robert E. Lee knew he was lit up with the aura like Jesus. Zac would say over and over, "We all loved him. Didn't matter whose side. He was a Virginian first. The land was sacred to him. Everyone understood that in those days."

Tom knew better than to interrupt, but this was always the point where he wanted to say "I get it. You were all passionate about your beliefs. You were willing to die for them."

"You're impatient, boy. I understand. But what we fought for in this Civil War has been forgotten and I can't let go of that. Hell, why would I hang around talking to you if there weren't something important I wanted to make sure you knew? Those things take time to understand. It's not about facts or even feelings . . . it's about what's worth fighting for. And if there isn't anything worth fighting for—well, hell—then you might as well give it all up now."

The trees dripped in the mist.

Zak opened his mouth as if he was going to bellow something, but what came out was soft as the rain. "Wars are no longer viable. Your generation amuses itself with them. The whole world has become a game. Nothing's serious. That's all gone. And religion's a weapon."

He knew his grandfather liked to speak in the vernacular of the Pennsylvania woods, but he had been a self-educated man. Like Lincoln.

Zak looked at Tom. "You're about to be challenged, Boy. You need to be ready. There's danger lurking near you and it will force you to either reckon with yourself or be reckoned with. How you play it out will define your generation. I'm sorry to put this upon you, Tom, but I want you to pay attention. Your uncle Daniel's smart, he'll help you, but this is something you'll need to grapple with in yourself. And it's all about what you believe deep down inside you. What's worth fighting for. Really fighting for. And not with weapons. In the small fights there's the lessons."

He didn't know what that meant, but he assumed that in the near future he was about to find out.

Zak looked down at the ground and swished it with his big brown boot.

An illusion? Zak often said, "It's all illusion."

Tom heard the whoosh coming, the sound like a tornado sucking all the air out of the atmosphere, and the scene was gone.

He sat up in his bed, covered in sweat. It was 3:00 a.m.

CHAPTER 2

*In great contests each party claims to act in accordance with
the will of God. Both may be, and one must be wrong.
God cannot be for, and against the same thing at the same time.*

ABRAHAM LINCOLN

LONG BEFORE DANIEL PERRY TURNED 60, he frequently vowed to himself that it would be possible to do something he'd never done before he turned 60—something momentous and challenging he'd always wanted to do but never had the time. Not that he intended to retire. He just assumed that by the time he hit 60 he should have the experience, the know-how, and, more important, a diminished capacity to care what others think—all adding up to an accumulated combination of achievements that would make some kind of bold step possible. But, strangely, when his 60th came and went a few months ago he couldn't remember any more what that challenge should be. Somewhere along the line—he didn't know when—he'd run out of steam.

He tended to boast about a lot of things to his friends. He always had. But as he sat at his breakfast table on this lazy Sunday morning, June 21, marking the beginning of summer, his mind was more blank than usual.

As he slumped over the table, propping himself with his elbows and cradling his cup in both hands, slowly sipping the lukewarm coffee, his oversized Maine Coon, Numi, slithered onto the table and made for the milky remains of his Special K.

Numi lowered his nose into the sugary, mushy milk as if to test its nutritious worth, but he didn't drink. Instead, he daintily dipped his paw, dabbing it several times before he swung it up to his mouth and closed his eyes as he licked the savory sweet goodness before he dipped it again.

"Numi, you're dripping it all over the table. Why did I ever think this was cute? Anna got you started." She giggled every time.

Anna, his wife, died 4 years ago after a 2-year battle with lung cancer. She'd stopped smoking a year before the diagnosis. Too late.

He had been teaching history at the University where he remained over the years and became head of the department and one of the most popular professors when he announced to his best friend and colleague, Richard Wilson, that one day he would teach a graduate seminar entitled *The Radical Possibilities of Multi-Faceted Historical Truths*. He liked the irony of the title. And now, commencing this summer, he was about to teach it. He mused how it would go, but he knew this would not be the watershed event to push the envelope of his experience. In fact at this moment nothing excited him, least of all in a couple of weeks walking into a room full of eager graduates awaiting his unique brilliance.

He didn't even like the title anymore, especially after persuading those friendly ladies in the registrar's office to print the whole title without much clarifying information. The only qualification he allowed was: "This course will cover how Americans thought about themselves leading up to the Revolutionary War, the Civil War and in today's divided nation how doctrines of the past have been skewed and manipulated to politicize present events."

Because of his reputation as a charismatic teacher, the twenty available slots filled immediately. Now he wondered, *what the hell am I really gonna teach? I don't even remember what I had in mind.* He'd assigned a reading list that he made up on the spot at the registrar's office just to satisfy the requirement. Some stuff on the early colonies, the Boston Massacre and what later became the Boston Tea Party, the development and writing of the Constitution, debates over slavery, and finally what led up to the Civil War and that war's aftermath into the 20th century. He boasted that he would require only original sources. Now he realized he would have to put together a syllabus. The thought made him tired. He vaguely remembered that he'd hoped the summer seminar class would launch a much broader in-depth course that tapped into the marrow of what and why Americans believe what they do. Why are we so gun crazy and zealous about fixing the rest of the world? Why so madly religious now? Why so anti big government? And finally, why so damn anti-intellectual? That sort of thing. Daniel liked juxtaposing opposite notions—equally true, equally paradoxical.

Now he simply couldn't remember what had gotten him so fired up. He tried to sort through the many late-night rants he and Richard had into the wee small hours after their wives had gone to bed. Sometimes they polished off a fifth of Jack Daniels in the process. Now Richard and his wife were divorced, and Richard was recently remarried to Rebecca Calhoun while he, Daniel, was a widower dating a woman who was also a widow and an academic. He sighed. *How life changes. How we forget.*

He stared out into his back yard from the kitchen alcove window as Numi continued to dip and lift his paw, brandishing it upward like a bear examining a stolen honeycomb. He reached for his notebook on the table he always kept close by, poised for any moment to record random thoughts, a pneumonic device he'd used since boyhood. He had hundreds of notebooks randomly stashed somewhere in boxes, file cabinets, closets, in the basement—all over—a squirrel hiding its nuts in the secret hollows of his tree. This was the one bit of hoarding Anna stayed away from. Or perhaps a battle she decided wasn't worth the war.

Their marriage had been happily tempestuous. They missed having children—no one's fault really, but just the result of being too busy with their work. Besides, they had plenty of children. Daniel's students used his home as if it were their own parents' house, and Anna, always welcoming, had her whales and dolphins and bears to protect. Saving the wildlife was her passion and work. It consumed her. She believed animals' rights were equal to humans.' Arguing otherwise with her was not even thinkable, and he didn't. Just before she died she had published her book, geared for children, on the amount of plastic and other toxic products consumed by the sea birds, fish and mammals in the ocean. She'd given up on adults. In her last years she started teaching kids at the science lab on Sundays about her universe.

She'd written and illustrated the book herself. His favorite watercolor was a pelican vomiting out a treasure trove of plastic, glass, tin, Styrofoam, all kinds of toys and daily products—an infinite array whose chemical make up included toxic phthalates, polyvinyl chlorides, lead, arsenic, mercury, and so on. She painstakingly drew the label on each vomited piece of detritus making it a kind of hide-and-seek game for children to find. Where's the coke bottle, the rubber ducky, the tennis ball, the dog collar, the plastic truck, the Hannah Montana heart necklace, the plastic backpack, the vinyl lunchbox, plastic picnic forks and spoons—all covered in Styrofoam that seemed to blend into the sand? All seemingly friendly products in use every day. She drew a panoramic, once bucolic, beach scene strewn with the contents of a pelican's belly.

He watched her obsess on the details and wondered if he had been her inspiration. She named the pelican "Samuel Adams." She made sure that the label on one of the strewn beer bottles was a Samuel Adams. She never bothered to explain that name to the children. Her theory was, "They'll get it anyway. Children don't need to be told that shit like adults do. Just point at it and look like you're going to throw up. Kids get it."

She made them guess at numbers, like how many billions of bottles and jars Americans threw away each year. "Kids like whopping numbers," she insisted. "Twenty-eight billion a year has yet to surprise one of my kids! It only surprises the adults."

He didn't argue with her that at least the adults could grasp that such a number was unimaginable. But her faith was with the kids, not the adults.

Somehow as the years went by they always seemed to be more than enough for each other. She tolerated his clutter for the most part and developed her own style of humor to deal with it. She was fond of putting her hands on her hips and announcing, "The only reason I married you was because cleaning up is my favorite thing to do. It's clearly in my DNA to organize a packrat in the same category of instinctive behavior as cleaning up the oceans. My species is called *Organauseum Repeatitus*. I am rare. An endangered species!" He smiled, remembering her fire. Her wit.

He opened his notebook. Flipping through to the first pages he saw they were dated nine months ago. Not many entries for this year. *Am I slowing down? Jesus, I feel old.* His 60th had come and gone. No entries around that time. No clues to help him remember the momentous occasion. After all, when he and Anna were young they expected to be dead by now—not that she would be and he wouldn't. He allowed his gaze to aimlessly wander over the scribble. He stopped at one page, written on the day she died, four years ago, March 21—the first day of Spring, one week after the Ides of March when the Romans believed the sea succumbed to chaos and the full moon brought high tides. He squinted, wondering why he'd written something to commemorate her death this year. He read it.

"Through all the living Regions dost thou move,
And scattr'ist, where thou goest, the kindly seeds of Love;
Since then the race of every living thing,
Obeys thy pow'r; since nothing new can spring

Without thy warmth, without thy influence bear,
Or beautiful, or lovesome can appear,
Be thou my ayd: My tuneful Song inspire,
And kindle with thy own productive fire;
While all thy Province Nature, I survey,
And sing to Memmius an immortal lay
Of Heav'n, and Earth, and everywhere thy wond'rous pow'r
display."

He'd circled this with a scrawling winding vine heart that he drew to look like the roots of a tree and wrote a note along the outside: "From Anna, March 1, two weeks before she died on March 21, the first day of Spring."

He couldn't remember writing it. A chill hit him in spite of the warmth of the kitchen. *Where was I when she died? Checked out. You knew I couldn't handle it. When did I get this from you? I must have copied it from something. Obviously, I thought it meant something.* He realized he was holding his breath.

Numi flicked a dab of milk on his nose.

He squinted cross-eyed trying to peer at the spot. He burst out laughing.

"You taunt just like she did. I think she knew, someday this would mean something to me. Not then. Should it now?"

Numi cocked his head. His whiskers had little flicks of milk that looked like tiny flowers growing on spiney vines.

For a long time nothing meant anything after she was gone. He kept himself busy because he'd always done that. Not until last year did things begin to change. He ran into an old friend, Melinda Mason, PhD in social anthropology, whose husband had also died of cancer. One night, in a moment like an out of body experience he picked up the phone and called to invite her out to dinner. She said yes.

Melinda was the opposite of Anna. Sensible. Pragmatic. Proper. A mother of three successful children. Intelligent, curious, an adjunct professor at the university. But no Anna, whose breathtaking moods laced with her saucy wit and sailor's mouth sent him over the moon—every time. Anna was also exhausting, but somehow she kept him on his toes. He never knew what she was going to say or do. One minute she could be crying over some sappy movie where the dog died or she was shouting epithets at the idiocy of so-called organic products encased in plastic wrappers promising no footprint. And she drove the ubiquitous Prius. "I know, I know . . ." she'd shout back at him on her way out the door to drive somewhere when he mentioned the fact that their town was full of rabid Prius drivers crowding every block. "I never promised you I'd make any sense. You knew that when you married me." And indeed, he did. She did drive him crazy. And he did miss her. Horribly.

Melinda was helping him to rejoin the living, which he knew he needed to do if only to give his friends like Richard and Rebecca a break. He had spent too much time with them over the last 4 years and the real problem was they never complained. How many times had he been over at Rebecca's house for dinner, including just after they were married a year ago? He must have been a third wheel, but he never felt that coming from them.

Anna's voice would warn him, "Don't abuse the rarity of friends who really care!"

One time, as he walked through his front door at 3:00 a.m., he heard her reprimand. "Fuck yoooouuuu!" he shouted at the empty rooms, causing Numi to jump out of his chair. He went to bed feeling much better, more like himself than he had in a long time.

Another flick of milk shot him in the neck and Numi decided he was full and hopped off the table onto the chair, hind leg straight up, vigorously attacking his long, bushy, striped tail with strident licks.

He stared at the words on the notebook page again.

"My tuneful Song inspires,

And kindle with thy own productive fire."

He wanted to call Melinda. She could ground him, make him think logically, steadily. She would want him to remember. She'd be interested. But he couldn't because she was back east visiting her oldest daughter and her son-in-law's family vacationing on Martha's Vineyard. He idly wondered when vacation had become a verb.

Her son-in-law came from an old family descended from one of the Puritan first families who originally settled in Boston. They'd come over on the Arbella, the same ship that John Winthrop and Anne and Will Hutchinson sailed on. It struck him, maybe he should have them read Winthrop's City on the Hill speech that Melinda's son-in-law's ancestors must have heard. His mind wandered.

Daniel was fascinated by minds that worked like Winthrop's. Like a lead Husky. Steadfast. Dogged. Protective. Vicious if crossed. The last line of Winthrop's speech came to him, the line that fascinated him the most. He'd written it down in one of his notebooks:

"Therefore, let us choose life, that we, and our seed may live; by obeying His voice and cleaving to Him, for He is our life and our prosperity."

As he stared at the words his landline rang in the hallway. On the fourth ring he picked it up, fumbling with the curlicue cord twisting itself even more into a tangled mess like a writhing snake. He resisted the impulse to wrench it out of the phone, cursing under his breath *fuck fuck fuck*—furious.

"This better be good. It's Sunday morning and I haven't read my New York Times yet so I can once again fathom the latest depths to which the human race has sunk."

Silence.

He started to hang up when a trembling high-pitched female voice cried, "Daniel?"

He stared into the hall mirror, the one Anna loved, with the frame encrusted with shells. He leaned into it, his face looming large, mimicking "Shit!"

He was in no mood to talk with his sister. A guaranteed one-hour conversation during which he would have to hear every last tedious detail about her blue-collar life in another world a universe apart in Ohio—the small town from which he'd escaped 42 years ago—never to return except twice to visit his sister and her rapidly growing family and simultaneously to attend his parents' respective funerals.

When he was a kid growing up there, he tried to wonder what life would have been like if his grandfather had stayed in rural Pennsylvania where the family originally came from. At least he would have had proper woods and rivers. Ohio has rolling plains. As a kid he liked random statistics about all kinds of things, so he knew that the highest point in the state was 1,550 feet. He read somewhere that Mount Whitney in California had an elevation of 14,505 feet. When he was ten years old, he told his friends at school that he was going to be a forest ranger in the Owens Valley and live in Lone Pine, California, and take people up the slopes of Mt. Whitney just to show them. He would add for extra flair that Lone Pine was near the Alabama Hills to the west named by Southern sympathizers to commemorate the victories of the Confederate ship *CSS Alabama*. That extra tidbit always got him increased panache.

He loved his sister, just couldn't abide her life in red state America.

Anna always corrected him on this. "It's a swing state, dummy!" but he didn't buy it. Besides, his sister didn't discuss politics. She was not a critical intellect like him. She was his one and only sibling, Carol Ann, and she was his opposite. Simple, kind, maternal to a fault he thought, pious, and unquestioning. She married Billy Cramer right out of high school and raised a burgeoning family of four children—three daughters and last, but not least, a son, Tom.

Carol Ann liked to call Daniel on Sunday mornings after church when she got home and there would be a lull in the household activities. Only Tom, their son, was still at home, but Carol Ann would soon be preparing the Sunday meal for at least several if not all of her daughters and their husbands and kids, now about ten grandchildren—he wasn't really sure anymore. She liked to call between noon and 1:00 her time, knowing that California folk are three hours behind and liked to sleep in. She knew he didn't go to church and her way of dealing with that mystery was never to mention it.

She had increased her attention on him since Anna died. Recently, when he reminded her that Anna had now been gone for four years, she replied, "Danny, you don't need to be brave for me. I'm your sister, remember? I'm here for you and you know you're in my thoughts and prayers every day. I know that Anna is with our Lord now."

He wondered if she thought he would be joining the Lord since she suspected his unmentionable atheism. Once he told her that he was agnostic really, and Carol Ann replied, "Danny, hon, I don't understand that word. I just know you don't really mean it."

"Danny, are you there?"

"Hey, Carol Ann . . . yeah I'm here. Just sort of got tangled for a moment in this . . . fuuu . . . um phone cord for a moment. Let's see here . . ."

He attempted to unwind it, but the more he tried the worse it got so he finally gave up and held the phone up to his ear as the tangled black mass hung heavily like a swinging squirrel on a bird feeder. He succumbed to the inevitable, looking around hopelessly for the little phone stool, and finally slumped to the floor with his back against the wall.

"I'm here. How are you doing?"

"Well, I'm ok. Went to church you know, and that always makes me feel better. But . . ."

She hesitated. "Could I talk with you about something?"

This was not like his older sister. Usually she would be brimming over with confidant chatter, "a little Magpie," as Anna affectionately dubbed her.

"Yes, of course."

"Well, you know something's come up you see. It's good . . . I think. Well, it's about Tom."

Tom was Daniel's only nephew, her youngest, and had three older sisters. Daniel realized Tom was about eighteen now, graduated from high school he assumed. Guilt struck. *Christ!* He'd forgotten to send congratulations. Or maybe he was supposed to go back or something? His mind raced. *I don't even know what you're supposed to do.* Anna had always taken care of these social matters. She'd sent every niece a card, and sometimes a gift, for every occasion, and there were plenty. Graduations, marriages, birthdays, baby showers, he couldn't keep up and never attended any. Anna managed to make it sound as if they attended in spirit, and that seemed to satisfy. Plus, she'd often take over these Sunday calls. He rolled his eyes heavenward.

"Tom's graduated from high school you know."

"Hey . . . well Yay! He must be pretty tall now. Last time I saw Tom was—what?" He made a stab at his memory. "Spring 1999? Sure . . . of course. What's he going to do?"

He hated his own hypocrisy, especially because he met Tom when he was ten and wondered how a kid who wasn't athletic, wasn't interested in football, didn't like guns, and seemed to be pretty quiet and intelligent was going to fare in his sister's chaotic, noisy female-dominated world with a father who was an ex-marine and a fireman.

"Well, that's what I wanted to talk with you about. He's been accepted at your university and that's where he wants to go. Unfortunately, I don't think we can swing the tuition along with room and board. We were wondering if Tom could come and live with you, which kind of made sense to us. You know, Daniel, Tom reminds me all the time of you when we were growing up. His nose is always in a book."

The realization of what she was asking crawled up his spine as his arms and neck broke out in goose bumps. The seconds started ticking to the new throb in his temples and he quickly moved his head up and down praying for speech.

"Danny, are you there?"

He cleared his throat and made himself cough, which turned into spasmodic choking as a piece of spittle got caught in his lungs.

"Oh, my goodness," she blurted. "Do you need a doctor?"

He managed to bob his head forcing speech. "Hey . . . I'm ok. Just got something caught in my throat. So . . . well, that's quite a decision. What's he planning to study?" He didn't know where to go with this.

"Well, that's just it. We don't really know. But, you know, he's so interested in the Civil War like you are, and since he's your only nephew, we thought this might be a solution. You could keep an eye on him, sort of be a mentor for him. Tom and Billy love each other, but, well . . . you know, they're so different."

He heard Billy shouting in the background over the Fox News channel that was always on if there was no football. "If he doesn't want to do it, Carol Ann, Tom can go to the State School here. Lots of people do you know."

He knew she was having trouble with this. She wouldn't want to admit that Billy and Tom weren't bosom buddies. In his sister's mind people were basically good no matter what. He always felt his sister belonged in another century when women could count on the protection of their husbands and quietly practice their pious homemaking. She was no Ann Hutchinson, but she was a truly good person—probably touched by grace, whatever that was. He secretly believed she deserved better, but Anna always said he underestimated Billy.

"You've never taken the time to get to know him. People are better than you think, Daniel." He remembered her remonstrating tone, "And maybe worse, too. You're such an academic, living in your head, seeing the world through your theoretical mind." Anna never hesitated to speak her earth-bound attitude.

Filled with sudden compassion he heard himself say, "Well, of course Tom can come live with me. How soon do you think he wants to come?" When he pronounced this, he was sure he saw a vision of Anna smiling down on him. He started coughing again and assured Carol Ann they would talk in a few days about the details. He managed to make a graceful exit from the call as she whispered her final "God Bless."

CHAPTER 3

In ancient times cats were worshiped as gods;
they have not forgotten this.

TERRY PRATCHETT

THE FOLLOWING SUNDAY MORNING Daniel knew that the elusive challenge he had yearned for would not be something he chose, but rather something that chose him. There it was, sitting across from him at the breakfast table—his nephew Tom.

He'd worked out with Carol Ann and Billy that Tom might as well come right away and spend the summer, perhaps do some research for Daniel, and audit the graduate seminar he was about to teach. He suggested that Tom could have an experience of what college classes would be like. The fact that it was advanced might be even better than a beginning class, if only for the shock value. He wanted Tom to realize what he would be in for. A common experience, he explained to Carol Ann and Billy was that students came out of their high schools where they were used to being the smartest kids in the class only to collide with the reality that every student at this university was a top student and many would be smarter than Tom. Carol Ann quickly effused "Oh, we understand," while Billy added, "He may surprise you," and Daniel said to himself, *Don't say I didn't warn you.*

His parents hastily packed him off and here Tom sat eating his scrambled eggs and toast, already feeding Numi bits of bacon. He hadn't asked if it was ok to feed Numi. He just did it. Daniel sensed it was best to say nothing, not even apologize for the fact that he and Anna had raised this feline monster. Besides, Numi did like almost everyone except Rebecca's Chows—Juno and Dido—and he'd immediately attached himself to their new guest, following him around as if he were the official welcome committee. Tom treated Numi as if he were an instant pal, clearly dispensing with any getting-to-know-you rituals.

Daniel knew Anna would have liked Tom right away. On the other hand, he felt at a loss how to talk with his nephew, and those same rituals between them so far weren't working. During their first few days they had spoken very little to each other. As he sat across watching him with Numi, he decided to try a different tack.

He chose as his opening salvo, "So, your mother says you're interested in the Civil War," spoken jauntily, he thought, something not too prying but then again approaching his interests—maybe some cross over to get them started.

Tom's big hand reached over to pet Numi's fuzzy head.

No reply.

Daniel waited.

"Yeah . . . I guess. I realize that's what Mom does think."

Nothing more.

He felt annoyed, irrationally perhaps, but annoyed nevertheless. He wanted to snap back, "Well, what the hell do you think?" but he resisted the impulse knowing it would most likely get him nowhere. He really didn't want to start off on the wrong parental foot in spite of the fact that this kid just plain annoyed him so far. He thought of Anna and how she had endless patience for baby critters, squirrels, raccoons, snakes, dolphins, lizards, spiders . . . she liked them all.

More softly, he tried again. "Well, I guess that's right, your mother does think that. I don't know . . ." he speculated, "the Civil War's a big subject." He drew it out as if he were talking to a six-year-old. "Did you know Shelby Foote—a great writer I might add—took twenty years to write his three volumes covering the whole war? He started out thinking he could do it in three years. Had no idea it would take him twenty." He hoped this bit of information might enlighten his guest a little, get him started, at least elicit a "Wow!"

Tom stopped petting Numi and looked out the window into the back yard.

"Yeah . . . I know. I read them."

This simply stated fact stunned Daniel. All his biases about his sister and her family—her choices to remain in that small town in the back of nowhere and to marry her high school sweetheart Billy and thereby joining the great American cliché—all came crashing in on him. He needed their silence to recover.

"Oh . . . wow! I didn't uh . . . realize . . . I mean . . . what am I trying to say . . . ?" he ran out of words.

"I know what you mean. You thought a backward know-nothing kid like me couldn't possibly have read all of Shelby Foote's Civil War."

Abashed and put in his place, he managed to squeak out "Yeah."

Tom smiled and returned to petting Numi, who looked over at Daniel, preening with his mouth—a Cheshire cat smirk: "I told you so!"

Daniel wanted to squish Numi and warn him that he was just a cat. Instead, he calmed himself down. "Well, all right . . . when did you find time to read all three volumes?"

The answer came quickly. "Last summer. My parents rented an RV for a month and left me at home alone. I didn't want to go, and they were fine to go without me. It worked for all of us. Only my sisters came over to bug me, but I gave them very little to do. I took care of myself and made sure there was nothing for them to do when they came over to snoop and clean so they would go away. I read about 7 hours a day . . . maybe more. Rented the books from the library." He added for good measure, "We do have a library you know."

"Ok . . . ok you got me. My apologies. Remember I grew up there too."

Tom nodded. "So, what was it like for you?"

He felt put on the spot. As if the tables had turned on him and he wasn't in control at all in this conversation. And to make matters worse, his memory was now blank concerning his teen years' experience. He replied meekly, "You know . . . I barely remember."

Tom continued to pet Numi. Daniel felt suddenly sad and decided to try again to regain some high ground. "So, . . . remind me . . . what has it been like for you?"

He hoped for confession time, some male bonding, some witty cynicism, the kind from his students he was used to. He smiled eagerly at Tom, nodding like a dunking duck to egg him on as if to say, "Man to man, son. Let's talk some truth." Hopeful, he could see Tom searching for the right words.

"Well . . . you know . . . I have to say for a kid like me it was close to idyllic."

Another showstopper. *What's with this kid? Christ! I can't figure him out.* He heard Anna's voice "Well, Duhhh!" *Shut up Anna. I really mean it. Shut up.* He was in no mood for her digs.

"How so . . . ? I mean how was it idyllic?"

"Well, I knew I wasn't like any of the other kids. Not like my sisters, not like my dad . . . not like anybody . . . so nothing much was expected of me. My dad knew I wouldn't play football . . . not even sitting on the bench . . . or any other sport he liked. I mean he tried to understand me, and then I guess he just thought the best thing he could do for me was to let me alone. My sisters gave my parents plenty to do, they were pretty tired by the time I came along."

"Yeah . . . but idyllic?" He was still hopeful that he was right that the real story would emerge if he just kept pressing him.

"Sure. When nothing's expected of you, that's real freedom. I could go anywhere, do anything. I got good grades, so what were they gonna wring their hands about? I had a dog, plenty of open space . . . I even learned to do my chores without being told because that bought me a whole lot of freedom. I wish I could write a little pamphlet on that for teenagers. I'd call it 'Common Sense for Teens' and sign it with my pseudonym 'Tom No-Pain.'"

It took him a minute to absorb all of this, including the little bit of humor at the end. He tried to picture it. *A boyhood of freedom.* He'd never realized it but his had really been much the same. Was that why Anna used to guffaw when he liked to catalog his grievances about his lowly beginnings? She'd tease him. "And how many miles did you walk to school . . . barefoot I bet . . . in the winter no less!" Then she'd really turn on the boo-hooing, producing snot and everything. She would even scare Numi. Then she'd laugh hilariously. *God she was crazily annoying sometimes!*

"Well . . . but I couldn't wait to leave. How about you? Why leave an idyllic life?"

"Because it was time."

This statement sounded final, ending the dialog.

Tom stood up and started clearing the dishes.

Numi stood up and stretched himself into a camel's hump, then yawned.

Daniel stood up scraping his chair on the tile floor almost knocking it over. "Hey, no. You're still a guest. I'll do that."

"No, I need to be useful. Let me know what else you'd like me to do."

Later that day he gave Tom the syllabus to look at. He sat in the living room on the sofa with Numi draped over his shoulder lazily kneading his neck and hair while Tom absentmindedly brushed him off with his head when the love claws got too intense.

Daniel left him alone and went out for more groceries and admittedly to get away from the strange kid in his house.

He pushed the cart down the aisles of Whole Foods, aghast at the prices, grabbing at everything, putting things in the cart, putting some back—unsure what an eighteen-year-old liked to eat. Certainly not Tofu. He'd never seen so many kinds of tofu. It made him gag. It didn't occur to him to ask Tom what he liked to eat. He just assumed that, like his sister, he should shovel food at him. Of course Anna would have known but where the hell was she now? Cavorting with the Lord? He knew he had to cut out the cynicism, but he couldn't help it. His mind had a mind of its own.

When he returned, he came into the living room to find Tom pouring over Anna's book that had been lying on the coffee table, the syllabus set aside. He was absorbed in the two-page panorama of the vomiting pelican. So absorbed he didn't even look up.

Daniel watched him. *Interesting kid.*

Then Daniel asked, "Why do you think she named the pelican Samuel Adams?" He'd never intended to ask her this himself, and now this kid was asking.

Tom looked up. "Oh, I think that's pretty easy." He stared at the painting. "I think Samuel Adams was the most radical patriot leading up to the war. He probably really was responsible for the first shot heard around the world. He sure riled the British. They were after Hancock too, but I think Sam Adams baited them the most. I think his most memorable line was 'It does not take a majority to prevail . . . but rather an irate, tireless minority, keen on setting brushfires of freedom in the minds of men." He never took his eyes off the pages.

This reminded Daniel that Anna said something in the beginning of the book: "It only takes a small minority to make a humongous change. And you kids have my vote." She liked the word humongous because it spoke to the kids—they seemed to understand instinctively how big "humongous" was.

He couldn't help it. He teared up and his throat constricted. He didn't dare speak.

Finally, Tom looked up at him and smiled.

He managed a wan smile in return.

Later, they had hamburgers and hotdogs—he cooked both on the grill outside—far too much for two people, thinking an eighteen-year-old from the mid west must eat a lot, even though Tom seemed pretty lanky.

He asked him if he'd looked over the syllabus, assuming he hadn't, ready to apologize for asking him to do too much right in the beginning.

Tom raised his finger, warning that he would have to finish chewing and swallowing a mouthful of juicy hamburger before he could speak. He gulped it down, took a swig of milk, dabbed his upper lip and then put his hands forward on the table as if he were about to make a momentous pronouncement, and said "I think you should add some excerpts from *Thomas Paine's Common Sense.*" Then he whipped out a small notebook not unlike the ones Daniel himself used. Only his was more expensive, the Clairefontaine one, bright yellow—spiffy. He flipped it open and read:

"As much hath been said of the advantages of reconciliation, which, like an agreeable dream, hath passed away and left us as we were, it is but right that we should examine the contrary side of the argument, and enquire into some of the many material injuries which these Colonies sustain, and always will sustain, by connected with and dependent on Great Britain. To examine that connection and dependence, on the principles of nature and common sense, to see what we have trust to, if separated, and what we are to expect, if dependent."

Now Daniel saw Anna smiling again like a Cheshire Cat. *She's not cavorting with angels, she's haunting me. How about that Your Lordship God Almighty! Huh!? How about that? Where's my peace and tranquility?*

Later in the living room Daniel sat across from Tom wondering how this could have happened. One week ago he was a little out of sorts, bored perhaps, but now he was looking at something bigger than himself. He couldn't wait for Melinda to return. She'd be home next week. He realized he felt tired and ganged up on. To end the dinner discussion, he asked "What did you like about that particular passage you read to me? Why choose that one?"

"I like it because it's easy to understand and, I don't know . . . I just think this country could use a little reminder about that right now."

That was the last straw. Daniel got up, strode down the hallway heading for his bed shouting, "Amen to that! Good night, Nephew. Welcome to the West Coast!"

CHAPTER 4

"Ku means 'rising upright,' Hina means 'leaning down.'"
The sun at its rising is referred to Ku, at its setting to Hina; . . . Together
the two include the whole earth and the heavens from east to west."

MARTHA WARREN BECKWITH, *HAWAIIAN MYTHOLOGY*, P. 13

SHE SAT IN HER FAVORITE GRUNGEY CAFÉ near the campus, way in the back at her usual seat on the bench in the darkest corner where she could be alone and drink her low-fat café au lait and try to calm the voices in her head. They weren't too bad today. She hadn't heard from Sugar Pie or that sanctimonious, Beth in at least a week.

Sugar Pie was the worst, never satisfied, always wanting more, pushing her into action when she just wanted some peace and quiet, and, most of all, blessed sleep, the rarest commodity in the world.

Last night she slept. She needed it because last week Sugar Pie kept trying to get her to flirt with guys.

A voice in her head: "That one's hot. Come on . . . come on," she'd whine, as if she had to pee, "just go say hello."

Whenever she told Sugar Pie to "Fuck off!" she pouted. That was the worst voice—like a hungry child.

Like I'm some kind of pimp, for God's sake. She just can't understand that's not my thing. I don't understand why she's such a necessary part of my little trio.

Normally, she kept her dark blue hoodie on with the Chinese celestial dragon on the back, which gave her a little privacy, but not today. Today she—the real Morrigan—felt like being more of her genuine outgoing self. Not outrageously sexual like Sugar Pie, and not demure and geeky like Beth.

Along those lines she had begun to wonder more and more what she would do when she graduated in a year and had to return home to the family compound up north, now their ten-year permanent residence in that northern forest—hot, dry earth where not much food could grow.

Except, of course, Benjamin Papa Cat never shied away from a challenge and managed to import tons of disgusting bat guano soil to fill up the rock-piled barriers he made her and the other kids build to grow vegetables and the almighty marijuana crop. Their "bread and butter," her mother liked to call it. She and all the other kids still had nearly permanent calluses on their hands from carrying those rocks one by one without gloves—Papa Cat said it was good to suffer—*slowly trudging back and forth from that rock pile spilled out from that frickin' huge, rusty dump truck that sped by, driven by freak, scrawny driver named Chewie, for God's sake, who looked like he probably ate insects for breakfast. Why brown lava rocks that looked like giant turds? Why couldn't he have gotten something pretty— like the granite? But thank God for Missy Tupelo and her money and may God rest her soul. I mean, who in hell calls themselves Missy Tupelo? Christ! How did Papa Cat ever find them?*

She knew he'd go on solo trips he called his "little scouting parties." She never knew what or who he would bring back, and always the night he got back after dinner he would whisper to the little ones in his high-pitched kitty-kitty tone of voice: "Guess what Papa Cat dragged in!?"

She did like Missy T., though, because she was so treacly sweet and innocent, a magnet for their sport, all wrinkled up like a little prune doll, which was what she got all the kids to call her behind her back. One time Missy T. whispered conspiratorially just to Beth that Tupelo was the town where Elvis was born and so was she. And that Benjamin Papa Cat had given her the name not more than a few minutes after he met her in that little café where she liked to go that was near her McMansion designed to look like Elvis's, now sold, of course, with the proceeds and her small inherited fortune subsidizing their growing commune.

Who knew?

He'd given her the name "Morrigan" one day not long after he picked up her and her mother off the street. He told her she was like Morrigan the Celtic Goddess of War, Revenge, Night, Magic and Prophecy and Queen of the Fairies and Witches. She remembered swelling with pride just at the sound of the name.

She knew she was good with the children and that's why she got to take care of them so much, and she did kind of miss making them laugh all the time. Ah well, whatever happened to Missy T, she hoped she was resting peacefully. She knew it was her money, along with the scholarship she got that sent her to the university. Papa Cat had said when he saw her off in her little VW bug named Ladybug, "Promises kept Baby M. Be good and remember, you owe me." He always called her Baby M., when he was feeling particularly close and affectionate toward her.

She didn't really miss any of them. Not Benjamin Papa Cat, not her mother, Peggy Sue, and not the kids, Jack Sprat, Jumping Bean, Lard—all of them—and definitely not any of the other old timers: Spaced-Out Sally, Little John—The Swede. None of them. And yet, she was tied to them in ways that could never be severed. Not ever. They weren't any kind of normal family. And she knew she owed them. She heard Papa Cat's voice in her head: *Morrigan oh Morrigan Pay day is a comin'.* The sing-songiness of that reminder made her think of Robert Mitchem playing the preacher in *The Night of the Hunter.* She wanted to try and enjoy the time she had left.

Benjamin would have been very angry if he knew how she really felt, but so far he couldn't read her thoughts and he didn't know about the others who came out inside her. He just thought she was very versatile and possessed multi-faceted parts. He liked that about her. Thank God he wasn't her real father, although heaven only knew who he was—and probably not even her mother knew. But he must have had a fairly big brain because she sure as hell didn't get her brains from her mother. That's what Papa Cat liked about her—her big, fat, smart brain. He was fond of telling her, "You're the brain in this family." That's why he wanted to educate her.

She was killing time before she would head for Professor Perry's graduate seminar, which she managed to get Sanctimonious Beth into even though she wasn't a graduate. Beth never could have done it, at least on her own. She didn't have the chutzpah. She'd learned that as long as you showed the registrar your money first—and they did like cash— that was distraction enough from looking further into your credentials. Besides, they loved Beth in the office because they had known she was Phi Beta Kappa material early on, even during her freshman year. They liked it when a non-Asian also showed some brain. They felt proud of one of their own, a real American, not some foreign student. Since they never met or heard from her parents, they kind of took Beth under their wing.

She could do whatever she wanted.

That was my doing. Ah. well—ours is not to reason why . . . and all that.

She had another thirty minutes to kill before she needed to wander over to class so she got up and ordered another café au lait.

"Hey, Beth, what's up!" Mitch behind the counter, a forty-seven-year-old long time college dropout, greeted her again.

She wanted to tell him her name wasn't Beth, but that would only confuse him. It was best he kept thinking she was that little geek with the good grades. But there were times she had the urge to show him her muscles under the hoodie and the tattoo around her belly button that said Ride the Wave of Vengeance.

He handed her the second café au lait and added "Just the way you like it. Low-fat and frothy."

"Thanks."

She went back to her seat under the eighteen-inch Monkey Pod Tiki mask hanging on the wall with its hole-boring eyes and glowering toothy mouth threatening to rip you from limb to limb if you crossed him. One time, when she was sitting around with a few of her own friends—not Beth's—under his stern gaze, to show off she poured her margarita into its mouth saying "Take that you impotent Ku Boy!"

Shrieks of laughter. Only Mitch didn't think it was so funny and made them clean it up.

She had to turn on her best charming self to calm him down.

"That wasn't funny," he chastised. "I'm from the Big Island and we take that stuff seriously. That Tiki mask embodies both Ku and Hina. Look it up!"

They all apologized and later she found him a little dark statue of Ku to put behind the bar up front. She made sure it was the right one because when she ordered it online, they all looked the same. It even had straw hair spewing out its head. That fixed it, and he gave her a free margarita the next time she came in.

She held the big white bowl of a cup with both hands, sipping it slowly, letting her mind wander. This would be her third class with Professor Perry. She really liked him. He wasn't pedantic like so many of the others and she got the feeling that he genuinely enjoyed teaching. She thought of his big bushy eyebrows expanding and squinting as he hopped around waving his little piece of chalk like a conductor that he was endlessly dropping and retrieving or looking for more. He wiped his pants to get the chalk off his hands but didn't notice the smudges on his pants. He was the quintessential absent- minded professor.

One time, he scribbled on one of her papers she—that is, Beth— wrote on the Lincoln Douglas Debates: "Interesting slant. Who knows, you could be right."

He gave her an A-plus.

The Little Scammer. Of course, that Goody Two Shoes, Ass Licking Beth wrote the paper. But who cares? She, Morrigan, could take the credit because she was the driving force. *Beth wouldn't know.* Beth didn't know about either her or that little trouble-maker Sugar Pie. What Goody Girl wrote about in her/their paper that got the compliment from Professor Perry was her thesis on what Lincoln was really getting at in his House Divided speech.

She focused on the two famous lines: "I do not expect the Union to be dissolved—I do not expect the house to fall—but I do expect it will cease to be divided. It will become all one thing or all the other."

Beth made the point that Lincoln knew that if Douglas' doctrine of popular sovereignty were to win there would be no end to slavery. Beth's point was that Lincoln was wily and understood human nature. He understood a moral imperative. It wasn't just the issue of slavery, and he had the depth to understand that. *Anything polarized breaks apart eventually. Slavery would polarize the nation and it would inevitably break it in two.* With one sentence—"A house divided against itself cannot stand"—he planted a moral imperative into the public consciousness in 1859.

She compared Lincoln's statement to Kant's categorical imperative, speculating that Lincoln must have come across Kant's Metaphysics of Morals, or if not, she speculated, he understood the concept that humans must treat each other according to universal laws and that deep down Lincoln knew that eventually slavery had to be abolished through such a moral imperative. She claimed in her paper that the one sentence was the seed placed by Lincoln in the consciousness of the country. He knew slavery had to end in the minds of the people, not forced upon them like some kind of religious dogma, but growing out of their own collective conscience.

Oky, Doky, she mused. Beth is a smart little critter, I'll give her credit for that. Professor Perry liked it, whatever she meant. Me? I read it once. Thought it was gibberish. In fact I erased it from her laptop. Moved it to trash. I know she was looking for it one night. Too bad! Gone gone! But I'm happy to take the credit. Can't let that little snot get too full of herself.

She gulped down the last of her café au lait and raced out the door slinging her backpack over her shoulder. "See ya later," she shouted at Mitch.

He shot her a high five.

In the history department building she walked down the linoleum-floored hallway heading for Room 4.

Suddenly, the headache came on and she veered over to the wall to brace herself, feeling slightly dizzy. She leaned against the coolness of the wall for what seemed a split second when she heard a voice behind her say "Are you all right?" Her eyes popped open, and she turned and saw an open, smiling face. He had large blue eyes, a high forehead, sort of unruly dirty blondish hair and a tone of voice that sounded immediately friendly, almost intimate, and definitely reassuring. She liked him instantly.

"Hey . . . thanks," she said. "I think I'm ok."

Both Tom and Beth headed for Room 4 and entered together, which made it natural that they would sit next to one another.

Instinctively, they both went for the back chairs. After all, he was just auditing, and she really wasn't supposed to be there.

But somehow she got in because the registrar sent her the confirmation. She rationalized that Professor Perry wanted her to take this summer class. It was a small classroom and any student who wanted to escape notice would have trouble. All you could do was hide behind the first row already filled with eager beavers waiting for Professor Perry.

After a pleasantly brief introduction, Professor Perry opened an old, well-worn leather book to one of the multiple, bright green Post-it marked pages. He read the part of Lucretius' *Ode to Venus* that Anna had given him in a card two weeks before she died. He had copied it into his notebook when he found it several days after that momentous morning several weeks ago when he sat on the edge of his bed letting the waterfall of tears flow as he remembered and read it over and over.

He passed out copies of the entire *Ode to Venus*, including the part he had read, so they could have the complete text in front of them without reference to the author. As he read it, hoping to do it justice, they listened and followed along, but there was clearly a subatomic ripple of perplexity waving through a few of them as they stole glances at each other and shrugged.

When he finished the last line with a flourish, he allowed the pregnant pause to infect them with even more doubt and curiosity, and then he repeated: "My tuneful Song inspire, And kindle with thy own productive fire."

Silence.

"All right folks . . . who wrote that?"

Shrugs all around.

"Come on . . . think! Who would have written that? Think Roman poets."

Beth raised her hand tentatively.

He pointed at her. "Beth. Tell us."

"Lucretius. He wrote a poem to Venus. Botticelli's painting Primavera—Spring was inspired by it."

"Yessss . . ." he bellowed, stooping low and swooping his half inch of chalk up to the blackboard and scribbled in bold flowery cursive: De Rerum Natura. For good measure, he drew a few little flowers, birds and bees like an experienced Disney cartoonist.

"Yes. Lucretius. Nothing of his survives except a 6-volume poem written in hexameter verse—same as the *Iliad* and *Odyssey* and *Aeneid*. You have before you an English translation from the Latin of his opening hymn, his *Ode to Venus*. And yes, he's describing Spring. In fact, it got lost for over a thousand years along with anything else Lucretius wrote and then was found in the 14th century and was later published in Europe. Just so you know, I mention here that Thomas Jefferson owned at least five editions of this poem in Latin. So, . . . ok. Why do you think I read this to you?"

Silence.

"Come on. Come on. There's no right answer. Take a quantum leap. Someone. Anyone."

He called on a student in the front row, a slouched, long-haired young man with his hand cupped over his mouth, frowning, trying to look smart and thoughtful. His name was Neal Viner.

"Well . . . ok . . . I'll try." He sat up straight and looked around behind to make sure his audience was listening. "I think you dropped a hint by telling us Jefferson had five copies, which means Jefferson must have liked it. And since the poem argues against fear of death . . . well, I gotta say . . . that's not very Christian. The poem argues . . . let's see here . . ." he squinted at the writing, . . . "here, yeah 'All Nature is thy Gift; Earth,

Air, and Sea: Of all that breathes, the various progeny, stung with delight, is goaded on by thee . . .'" He read it with no feeling, none of the passion the poem demanded. "Well, he's deifying Nature, not some anthropomorphic God."

Daniel didn't like this student, Neal, particularly because he was so full of himself and always was the first to speak even though he pretended to hold back. Daniel knew he would go far in academia, but Daniel preferred the more tentative, humble ones.

"Okay . . ." Daniel nodded, unsure where Neal was taking this. "Say what you mean by "not very Christian.""

By then three more hands shot into the air and he assured them they would have a chance.

"Well, I think the Puritans who came in the 17th century were all about controlling each other with instilling a fear of Hell for those who didn't meet their standards of what they wanted a good Christian to be. They all believed in Hell for the damned non-believers. The reward of Heaven was waiting for those who qualified as good Christians. It was all about instilling a fear of what would happen in death. Heaven or Hell. I mean, in Salem they called those women witches and burned—I think about nineteen of them—at the stake. Of course, there were plenty of burnings in Europe, but they did it here as well."

He paused, and then quickly added, seeing that he had lots of competition, "by the 18th century I think those guys we call the Founding Fathers like Jefferson did not believe in scaring people, through Christianity into being good citizens. They were over all that. They wanted only separation between Church and State. People could worship any way they wanted."

As the rest of the class got more and more excited, it started pouring out of them: The early Colonialists used their literal interpretation of the Scriptures to control each other; poor John Winthrop got trashed while Ann Hutchinson was raised to celestial heights.

They forgot all about Lucretius, but Daniel's reading of the poem got them going and they were excited. Only at the very end did he notice another hand go up, one that had not gone up before. It was Tom's. He'd forgotten to tell Tom he couldn't be part of the class discussion because he was only auditing. Besides, it didn't occur to him that Tom would be prepared to say anything at all.

He pointed to Tom and nodded.

His voice was a little frail at first, then he cleared his throat. "This poem makes me think of quantum mechanics. The poet is talking about the natural world as if what goes on is unseen, subatomic, based on physical laws invisible to the naked eye and no one really knows how or why it works, but it does, and death-rebirth-death are part of the natural process, like particle wave theory—not really understandable, but predictable and mysterious."

The room was quiet.

Daniel looked at Tom and held his gaze for a few seconds then burst out "That's very interesting young man. An interesting observation."

Tom had enjoyed the banter and admired the way his uncle got them all fired up. This atmosphere was new to him. The sizzle and crackle of ideas zinging around the room.

He looked over at Beth's notebook and saw she was writing something.

He couldn't help trying to read it.

She was doodling. She'd drawn a big face with eyes, nose, mouth, ears with a large forehead. Inside the head she wrote on the left "Mind" and on the right "Spirit." Next to it she put an equal sign pointing to the same head, now collapsed down like a sunken balloon with 2 little kites with long tails wafting up and away. One kite said "Mind", the other said "Spirit". She slowly circled the collapsed head and wrote over it "Dead Head?" Then she drew arrows all around the first head pointing in on it with a word on each arrow. Pain, Sorrow, Loss, Torture, Damnation, Eternity, Certainty, and so on. Across the bottom she wrote a line "Death=Death=Death=Death." Somehow, she made it look like grass.

"All right everyone," Daniel bellowed. "Good class. See you all Thursday. Do your reading."

Tom and Beth walked out together. Out on the common she headed off and he watched her go. Then she turned and shouted, "Interesting comment" and she waved goodbye, "See you in class."

"Bye," he waved back.

As he ambled across the grass in the opposite direction, he allowed his mind to think about her. *What a strange girl. I could swear something weird was happening to her when I came up to her in the hallway. She didn't seem to realize that she'd slumped down, and if I hadn't propped her up, she would have sprawled on the floor. When she came to she acted like nothing had happened, or she didn't know that something had happened. Weird. So was that picture she drew.*

That night, Morrigan woke up in her room with a start. It was windy outside, and she heard the blinds knocking back and forth on the window she liked to keep open at night for the fresh air. She reluctantly got up and shut the window. She flopped back on the bed, tossed the quilt off and puffed up the pillow under her head. She threw her arms out behind her head and stared at the dark ceiling dancing with shadows of the trees from the window. As she lay there trying to close her eyes, she started to get the creeps, as if someone or something were in her room. She sniffed the air and smelled the sickeningly sweet smell of patchouli oil and knew instantly he was there. She rose straight up like a gymnast and saw his dark form sitting across the room about 10 feet away in her chair.

"Jesus Christ! You scared the shit out of me."

"Hey . . ." he drawled lazily . . . "I didn't mean to scare you."

Yes, you did you frickin' maniac.

He used to do this a lot before she left. Just come and sit by her bed at night and watch her sleep.

She hated that.

"I was just passin' through and thought I'd drop in and see how you were doing? Everything ok? Got everything you need? We haven't heard from you in months. Your mother was worried. I told her I'd check in on you and just see how you were doing."

Everything out of your mouth is a flaming lie. Mother is worried, I like that one. He liked to talk about the family as if they were just as normal as the Waltons. Using the nicknames accentuated their normalcy.

Only of course, it didn't in her mind. It only made everything all that much more sinister. *You're probably down here looking for some more old ladies. I'd feed you my nosey landlady, but she's not rich, and between the two of you, she might win. She's like that Kathy Bate's character in Stephen King's Misery. You and she'd get along real well.*

"Well, I'm fine. Been busy." She knew he needed more. "I started that guy's class today . . . Perry's class? You know the guy you want me to set up?"

"Good."

He waited.

How'em I gonna get rid of him? He wants something. He always does. She wondered if he'd had sex with Sugar Baby. *But I'd know if he had. No, that's not what he wants from me. He spared me that for some reason. He wants my brain.*

"Guess what? Professor Daniels has a houseguest living with him. His nephew. Name's Tom."

She could tell even in the dark that got his attention.

He sighed. "How do you know?"

"Just do. You know me. I have my ways."

"I wanta know how you know."

"Ok . . . look, it was easy. He sat next to me in class. I asked him his name. That's all. Then I got this intuitive hit that he and Perry knew each other. He's young and nervous . . . not one of the regular students. So, then I looked up some background on your professor there and found out he had a nephew named Tom. His sister's son. He's enrolled in the nniversity for the fall so I put two and two together and figured he's living with his uncle. Viol'a! QED!"

"Good." He stood up and headed for the door.

She was relieved.

"Want me to do anything about the nephew?"

"No. Not now. But good work Baby M."

He quietly slipped away, and she fell back on the bed with her arms sprawled out—exhausted.

CHAPTER 5

*While many reliable reports of the supernatural emanate from all over
the battlefield of Antietam, the singular experience of the students of
McDongh School remains the most credible account to date.
In the "landscape turned red" of Antietam memory of the valor
of the valor of the Irish Brigade lingers on—in more ways than one."*

CHRISTOPHER K. COLEMAN, *GHOSTS AND HAUNTS OF THE CIVIL WAR*,
FALL RIVER PRESS, 1999, P. 57.

TWO NIGHTS LATER, Tom woke up startled out of his dream.
As he sat up all he could remember was stormy sky, dark clouds, trees
swaying—the Antietam atmosphere.

Then he felt Zak's presence.

Oh, no. Not now. Please Zak. I'm tired.

He couldn't see him, but he heard him.

"Hey Tom Boy. Meet me in the back yard."

He knew he had to go. It was moonlit, probably around 2:00 a.m.
When he pulled himself out of bed and stepped into the hall, he heard
Uncle Daniel's muffled, rhythmic snoring behind his closed bedroom
door at the end of the hall. Long breaths in and out like waves of the
ocean.

Good. At least he's asleep.

He made his way down the dark hall into the living room, guessing
where to avoid knocking into furniture, and crossed into the kitchen.

Numi was right behind. He could feel his tail swishing against his
bare ankle.

By then his eyes began to adjust to the dim light.

The moon was almost full. *Zak probably picked tonight because of the
clear skies and brilliant moon,* and it was unusually warm, still about 65
degrees.

He wondered. *Do ghosts do the weather thing? They must. Zak likes to comment on the moon every time I see him.*

He wanted to ask him, but he knew he couldn't.

Trying not to make any noise, he slid open the glass door that opened out from the kitchen onto a back deck, then out into the yard. He left the door ajar.

Numi perched himself half in, half out, the way cats do according to their equivocal natures.

The grass felt cool on his feet.

"Over here, kid! Come sit over here."

He couldn't see him in the dim light, and the trees surrounding the yard made a dark canopy over the ground. He knew he must mean the carved teakwood bench from Indonesia at the far end of the yard.

"Anna's bench" Daniel had explained when he first came over three weeks ago and was showing him around. "She sat out here every day, rain or shine. Mostly neither. We get a lot of fog in the summer. Not like your hot, muggy Ohio summers. She said she liked the view looking out at the yard from under the giant Coast Redwood."

She'd planted lots of sorrel and ferns under the redwood so that in the daytime the bench looked cuddled in green around the rest of the yard. It wasn't big, but an irregular half circle that surrounded the back of the house with a high canopy of trees.

Tom could barely make out Zak's presence. It looked like something was shimmering on Anna's bench. *He picked her bench for a reason. He's setting the stage for something, and he wants Anna's presence there when he tells me what's up.*

"She liked to plant natives," Daniel had explained. Whenever he suggested they already had enough, she waved him aside with, "Never enough. They all work together—they take care of each other and figure it out."

He didn't bother to suggest that some of the ornamental ivy was like the brown snake of Guam, climbing up and into anywhere it could go. She responded the same to any criticism, "It's all beautiful, all meant to be."

Tom loved the feel of the place the moment he arrived. *This is a long way from that scrabble pit my parents call a yard.* As he came closer, Zak looked relaxed and yet somehow poised as if he could spring into action.

He patted the bench beckoning Tom to sit.

Wild roses grew up the fence, with wild blackberry bushes hanging over one part. Ceanothus, California buckwheat, poppies, bulbs, grasses, wild strawberry groundcover ran wild. Her own vibrant primavera. The setting seemed to fit the moment—both calm and wild, befitting Zak's calmed immediacy.

Tom sat out there every day now. He wished more and more that he'd known Anna. He liked Uncle Daniel, but for some reason had concluded it was Anna's influence that had humanized his uncle. And humbled him.

Anna's here, too. Thank you, Anna, 'cause the old ghost really seems up to something this time!

Tom thought that when his uncle was younger, he may have been insufferably arrogant and sure of himself. *Maybe he had to be. But he found a good partner in Anna. He probably never realized it, but Anna I think, was a lot like my mother.*

He sat and waited for Zak to speak. In the silence he remembered something from a few days ago.

In the guest bedroom where Tom slept, he had come across a small, academic press copy of a book Daniel published when he was 30, entitled *The War That Never Ended*. He loved the first two paragraphs:

"We Americans love our legendary heroes. We carve them on mountains, build over-sized statues and monuments, erect buildings, bridges, freeways, parks, and anything else you can imagine that will enhance the instant iconic recognition of their all-American names. Like Robert E. Lee—great general, Virginia gentleman, southern aristocrat, descendant of George Washington, refined manners, affectionate husband and father and lover of animals. He had a deep bond with his horse Traveler, and a pet hen that went with him during all his military campaigns. His tent flap was always open so she could come in every morning and lay an egg under his cot. When they withdrew from Gettysburg, they couldn't find her, and Lee wouldn't leave until they did, so Lee also joined the search and when she was safely ensconced in the headquarters wagon, they departed.

To truly understand this man—the South he fought for and the deep contradictions at the end of the day we are all still grappling with, we need to pull Lee and all the others including Lincoln down off their monuments and pedestals and all the myths that have been written and grown after them to understand the human, flawed men they were. For someone so pure to sacrifice so many, for someone so devoted to the South and yet did not agree with slavery, for someone so honorable to have fought for secession despite his fervid belief in preserving the Union, and finally, for someone of such delicate sensibilities to have thrown his beloved army into the jaws of death—how can we understand this man behind his image? I have no answers, but I propose to offer the questions with which future generations will need to grapple."

Daniel dedicated his book: "To Anna, a Seeker of the Truth."

Tom looked over at Zak. There was always a holographic quality to him. Even though he had the urge, Tom never dared reach out to touch him.

"So," Zak began, "You're finally here at your Uncle Daniel's in sunny California. Not real sunny from what I can tell."

"Yeah, I am. Uncle Daniel's strange. Not at all like my mother, but you know that."

"Well, I suppose I do. Does it surprise you that two people can come out of the same parents and be so different?"

"I don't know. I guess not."

"What surprises me," Zak ambled on in his seemingly lazy have-all-the-time-in-the-world way, "is how humans don't notice what's right in front of them. Most of the time unless they're forced to, they see what they want—that's what they see."

"You mean wanting kids to be the same who come from the same parents?"

"Something like that."

Zak was not ready to get to the point.

"Well," Tom decided to play along, "most people don't really understand the unpredictable side of genetics—mutating genes. My mother still doesn't accept Darwin's natural selection theory and, if she did, she'd have to accept how chromosomes work. She can't do that. To my mother it's all just one great big mystery and only God knows. She's comforted by not knowing. And yet unlike her brother, Uncle Daniel, she is the most accepting person I've ever met."

Zak rubbed his chin. "Well, a lot of people just don't pay attention. Never really did. You've got a good brain boy, not like your mother's, no offence. I suppose that's genetic too."

Tom didn't want to argue. He knew this was preliminary chatter. He was tired and feeling unusually self-conscious. *What if Uncle Daniel hears me chatting with a ghost?*

One time at home his mother told him that she'd heard him talking to someone out in their back yard during the night.

This didn't upset him at all because it was his mother. He explained, "I was speaking with my four-great grandfather Zachariah. You know, Mom, the one who fought at Antietam."

"Not just Antietam," she corrected. "He was in another battle after that. Can't remember which one, but that's when he was shot through his right calf. Lost that leg below the knee. My grandmother Matilda used to say 'landagoshin! Your ancestor Zachariah lost his leg in that terrible war. Why, those limbs stacked up like your granddaddy's woodpile out there.' Isn't it nice, Tom, that you now commune with God's children like that?" Tom never had the heart to tell her he didn't think that Grandpa Zak was necessarily cavorting with angels, since he knew Zak hated religion. His God was no anthropomorphic wise old white man with a long flowing beard floating above in the sky. For a ghost, he was a pragmatist. *Perhaps an Epicurean?*

"So, Tom, how's life with Uncle Daniel?"

"Well . . . it's different. He doesn't really have much of a routine. Some days he's busy, gone all day and then he rushes home like the White Rabbit loaded with bags of groceries he really doesn't know what to do with. You should see his refrigerator. Most of the stuff is long past its sell-by date and he doesn't even know what that is. So, I've kind of taken over the cooking because he's terrible at it. He seems to barely notice that I do that now."

Silence.

Zak looked like he was sniffing the air.

Tom wondered if ghosts could smell. He took the silence to mean that Zak wanted him to go on.

"Uncle Daniel just grunts what I think is some kind of approval, and once I heard him mumble under his breath something like 'Thanks Anna.' He still talks to her."

Zak looked up at the trees. "Yeah. Thought so."

Tom noticed he was rubbing his right calf, which did look kind of peg-legged.

"But don't get me wrong. I'm glad to be here. He's got a huge library all over his house and I can lounge around and read all I want. He loses everything, so I've started to take over a little where Anna left off, I think. I've learned where he drops stuff, and his piles of paper have a system— sort of. Anyway, I know better than he does now where he puts his stuff like his reading glasses sitting on top of his head, or his wallet he threw behind the groceries wedged up against the toaster on the counter in the kitchen. When I walk right to it and hand over whatever he's lost in the moment, he looks at me as if I've performed a miracle, but then he's sort of begrudging at the same time about it. I can only imagine how Anna put up with it."

Zak nodded, then suddenly shifted his attention. "There's something I want you to do for me."

At last, he's getting to the point.

"What is it Zak?"

"Daniel's in danger."

For Tom, this felt like an ambush. *How can he just drop this on me?*

"Never mind why right now. But he's going to need your help."

Tom felt a chill crawl up his spine to the base of his neck and he massaged his neck involuntarily. "Come on, Zak. You gotta give me some explanation. You can't just dump this on me."

Zak waited as if considering something, weighing the need. "Daniel has an old enemy. Someone from his distant past. They were in graduate school together. Squared off on a difference of opinion—well . . . really . . . a different philosophy about the Civil War, what it was all about." Zak started to rub his peg-leg as if it was still there.

He went on.

"Daniel's research used a letter written in 1863, that he got from a friend. That letter was important for Daniel's thesis. Only Daniel's rival, that old enemy, claimed different."

"Oh . . . you mean like forgery?"

"Exactly." Zak stared up at the moon.

Tom waited.

"So, . . . this rival of your uncle's filed a formal accusation against Daniel and accused him of forging all, or most of his material. Daniel had some other stuff from way back—some letters, diaries, and such, written by runaway slaves who made it to freedom, you know, before the war when the laws changed, and those slave owners went after anyone who looked like a runaway and brought 'em back. Daniel's rival got hold of those documents, so when Daniel went to find them, they were gone.

No copies."

Zak leaned toward Tom. "He was just as absent minded in those days as now!"

Tom nodded. "So, he made it look like Daniel was guilty, especially when it came to that one letter that no one had ever seen because it was never sent. It had stayed in his friend's family for generations—unsent. But it was an important eye witness account," Zak pointed to his eye, "of an event Daniel thought was important for his work." Zak moved his head up and down. "Catch the drift, son?"

This annoyed Tom, but he wanted Zak to get to the point. He felt put upon. *Why me? Why does he think there's something I can do?*

"So, what happened?"

"Daniel was let go from the university pending an investigation. Then things dragged out. His rival managed to convince a lot of people that Daniel had cheated in other ways, that Daniel had it in for him because he was jealous, and so on."

Tom felt as if he were free-falling. Like the time he had jumped from a 30-foot ledge at the old quarry where the kids used to swim. He had to do it at least once. It was a rite of passage. But the feeling of free-fall didn't exhilarate, it only terrified him. The same way he was feeling in the moment.

"Well . . ." Zak went on, "things went from bad to worse as Daniel was expelled while his friend got awarded that Ph.D."

Zak went silent as if that explained everything.

"What happened?" Tom prodded.

"Daniel came back with a vengeance. He went to find the source of the letter that had belonged to his friend, Ephraim Winslow Brown. It was Ephraim's great grandfather who'd written the letter to Frederick Douglas, but never sent. Ephraim's great grandmother kept the letter and passed it down through the generations until it came to her four great Grandson, Daniel's friend Ephraim. That letter was a major piece of evidence Daniel had that those documents he used in his dissertation were original."

Is this why the old ghost has been meeting me all these years? To tell me this? Tom decided that jumping off that ledge thirty feet down into cold water was nothing compared to this. He heard his mother's voice. "It's all in God's plan." Sometimes his mother made sense in her own way. In the moment, he also thought of Anna. Was she smiling?

Zak went on, "Daniel tracked down Ephraim, who'd joined the Peace Corps and was far away in the rainforests of Zaire. It took some doing, but Daniel went there to bring him back to testify on his behalf that the letter originated from his family. It took several years, but finally Daniel was reinstated and finished with honors while that rival of his was kicked out and divested of his degree and lost his job—black-balled from academia everywhere." Zak winced and leaned over to rub his fake leg some more.

"What happened to that guy?"

"He disappeared after that. No one has seen him since."

"What was his name?"

Zak waited a long time.

"Benjamin. Benjamin Monroe."

"So, what's this Benjamin got to do with Uncle Daniel? If he'd disappeared for forty years, what's he got to do with anything now?"

"He's back!"

Tom had looked away for a moment at the moon, and when he turned to look at Zak, nobody was there.

He sat in the moonlit garden for about twenty minutes trying to absorb what Zak just dumped on him. He felt Anna's presence even more in the moment, which helped him move. All he could muster was to make his way back to bed. He slept past his morning class with Daniel.

No one had awakened him, not even Numi, who normally was a reliably annoying alarm clock, kneading his claws into Tom's head at 6:00 a.m. But not this morning as he was also sound asleep, sprawled across the foot of Tom's bed.

CHAPTER 6

"A pyramid fire is popular with novices who enjoy watching a big blaze."
RICK (AT) KUDU.NET

THAT SAME EVENING Daniel and Melinda climbed the steps to Rebecca Calhoun's house in the nearby hills.

Rebecca, a 55-year-old psychotherapist, had recently married Daniel's old college friend, Richard Wilson, a cultural anthropologist, and former head of the University's Department.

Richard still taught part time and now was spending his semi-retirement years writing, teaching graduate seminars, cooking, gardening and generally enjoying life with 'the woman of his dreams,' as he liked to refer to her, together with her two cinnamon Chows, Juno and Dido, "The Queens."

Now that Daniel had found Melinda, who could at least distract him from his obsessive devotion to Anna's memory, the four had become close and often shared long dinners mostly at Rebecca's, cooked by Richard who took great pride in his new-found culinary talents. Dinners were often a forum for Rebecca, Melinda, and Daniel to come up with more adulation than before to congratulate Richard's efforts. They shared an inside joke among themselves at how eagerly Richard accepted their praise, never suspecting some of it was tongue in cheek. They all knew they had to keep Richard stoked to keep it up, because none of them cared to take over the business of cooking for the group. Melinda and Daniel contributed by searching for the best wines they could possibly find—under twenty dollars—a feat they all agreed was pushing the envelope.

On occasion, Gertrude Lerner, Rebecca's 82-year-old mentor who continued her psychoanalytic practice out of her nearby home, would join them. They all loved Gertrude for her wit and wisdom. They also loved Gertrude for her desserts—she did desserts like no other. Even though she waved aside their praise they all knew she spared no expense putting together only the most fresh and extravagant ingredients. She would make profiteroles from scratch that rivaled anybody's little old Dutch or French pastry chef. One Thanksgiving, Gertrude arrived with a giant, *choux a la crème* pastry "Bossche bol" filled with whipped cream and covered with a Dutch chocolate glaze. She insisted that it was traditional for them to eat it with their fingers, which they did, giggling like a group of preschoolers, talking with their mouths full and pretty much getting chocolate all over themselves. Only Gertrude seemed to know how to eat it and not spread it on herself like finger paint. Now they referred to that occasion as "the night we consumed Gertrude's 'baseball' home run dessert." But on this particular night, Gertrude would not be joining them because she was in Washington, DC visiting her grand-daughter and, to add diversity to the usual status quo, Rebecca was cooking.

Melinda held a bottle of 2009 Barbera d'Alba, and Daniel a bag of doggy treats for The Queens as Richard opened the front door, arms wide, bellowing "Buono notte mi amicis!" As the Queens rushed forward, tails wagging like flags, checking out Daniel's pant cuffs for smells of Numi, as odors of tomato sauce, basil and garlic greeted them. Richard rubbed his hands, whispering "She's nervous. It would be good to give her all the encouragement you can."

Melinda rolled her eyes and entered the kitchen to greet Rebecca, whose hair was pinned back with multiple clips in an attempt to tame it, and when she saw Melinda she took off her Wonder Woman apron. The large bouillabaisse on the stove simmered, awaiting the piles of mussels, hard-shelled clams, shrimp and turbot.

"He warned us you're nervous."

"He's nervous that it might be just fine. The sauce needs to simmer. The clams and mussels and all that other stuff from the sea" she gestured to the counter, "go in at the last minute. Let's go outside."

Rebecca opened the refrigerator and retrieved a chilled bottle of Sauvignon Blanc and lead Melinda out to the back porch. It was still warm enough to sit outside.

Daniel and Richard made it as far as the dining room, where they stopped to give the Queens their snacks and to discuss the issue of biofuels for the military that had been in the news.

Rebecca and Melinda sat back in the green wrought iron chairs around a low, redwood table and toasted their glasses.

"So how are things going with Daniel these days?"

Melinda set her glass down and popped a cherry tomato into her mouth. Chewing and nodding, she smiled. "It's going pretty well. He's a bit of a hand-full, and I find myself sympathizing more and more with Anna . . . but so far we're having a lot of fun."

"I understand his nephew is living with him. That must be a switch considering he and Anna never had children of their own. Richard and I have yet to meet him. We've been away so much this summer and haven't had the chance."

"Well, I've met him. Briefly. My impression is that he's polite . . . in a good way. Not programmed, if you know what I mean."

Rebecca agreed. "Manners are best when they come naturally."

"Yes, well, it seems to come more from a natural sensitivity to others. I think he speaks directly, says what he thinks, and he does it with tact. Unusual in an eighteen-year-old."

Rebecca couldn't help being the therapist. "How do you mean? What did he say or do that made you come to that conclusion?" *God, I'm still doing it with my friends. Asking for examples.*

"Well, I came by the other morning hoping to catch Daniel for coffee and maybe a walk before his day took off. You know how he is once he's off and running."

"Yeah," she laughed, looking toward both Richard and Daniel who had now made it into the kitchen and were pouring themselves a glass of red wine.

"So, I popped in as I do, and came to find no Daniel, but there was Tom. He was squatting down and pouring Numi milk in a little saucer, patting his head, talking gently to him while Numi preened and drank. Tom looked up when he saw me standing there . . . I guess I was smiling . . . he didn't act surprised as you might expect. You know, here's this intruder—he could have demanded "Who are you?" because I'm sure Daniel forgot to mention how I do pop in from time to time. But his smile was like the sun coming out and he jumped up and said "Hello, you must be Dr. Mason." He came right over to shake my hand. Good, strong, friendly handshake. Right away I told him to call me Melinda."

At this point Richard and Daniel joined them, and after a while they went inside and made a great fuss over Rebecca's fine dinner.

Richard was so effusive Rebecca began to feel suspicious. *Methinks, he protests a wee too much*. But she let it go and made up her mind to take all the praise she could get.

After they'd finished, they retired to the living room. The fog had rolled in, as it does in Big Sur, taking the temperature down fifteen degrees. Richard had laid a fire. He struck a match and lit a small twig that stuck out from the kindling underneath the larger logs piled carefully into a wigwam. After about four seconds it burst into flame as Richard's face radiated the joy of a kid who just set off his first successful cherry bomb.

"Wow! Richard, were you an Eagle Scout?" Melinda teased holding her hands out to the crackling flames.

He chuckled modestly. "No, I flunked out of the Boy Scouts. For my first real merit badge I chose wilderness survival. I had to demonstrate my survival skills, so I thought I'd show off to my scout leader, an ex-Marine, Mr. McKinley, who fought at Guadalcanal. I built a fire out on the weed patch called a yard at our den mother's house. I didn't tell her because I wanted it to be a surprise. Actually, I wanted to build a teepee from my 1912 edition of Ernest Thompson Seton's book on woodcraft that my grandfather had given me, but I didn't have time to do the teepee. I knew how to set the wigwam fire because Granddad had shown me how to do that . . . only I decided to help it along by putting one of my tiny firecrackers, left over from the Fourth that year, inside the kindling . . . you know, just to help it along. I actually sacrificed for kindling my little meadow mouse nest that I'd kept in my room from a camping trip. You know . . . to show them I knew what I was doing. That's where I hid the firecracker. Just a teeny, little thing," he reiterated.

His audience listened—spellbound. Richard was twelve years old.

"Well, so when Mr. McKinley arrived to observe my skills the den mother and seven other boys in the troop all came outside where I'd set up my demonstration and, well, I guess it didn't go so well. It lit up just great. Um . . . too great. The kindling and my little mouse nest spewed everywhere and, well . . . he wasn't amused, so you can guess the rest. He said I had no instincts for survival." Richard looked at the fire, reliving the moment.

"My mother was on my side. She told me," he imitated his mother, 'Richard, that was misguided, but your survival skills just need a little adjustment.'" He waited a moment, then added "Bless her heart."

He looked at Rebecca.

Always the therapist, "What did your Dad think?"

"Don't remember."

They sat in amused astonishment. Richard finally rescued the moment by pointing at his fire. "So, I still build that same fire. The wigwam. It burns the brightest. Not great for cooking, but if you want a thrill, this is the fire. Only now I leave out the pyrotechnics."

Juno was asleep half under the coffee table emitting little whiffling sounds as her paws twitched.

Richard watched her. "Get it girl. You can do it." He looked up. "Maybe it's a rabbit."

They nodded together.

Dido stretched herself in the dining room and wandered in sensing where their attention had gone. She went over to Richard who rubbed behind her ears.

He looked up. "So, Daniel . . . how's it going with that nephew of yours?"

"Tom." Daniel smiled. "I'm glad you brought him up. Now that I have all of you in the same room together feeling fat and satisfied with that wonderful dinner," he looked over at Rebecca who smiled, "I was so glad we were getting together tonight because I want to talk with all of you about him."

They waited for Daniel to collect his thoughts.

"Please do" Rebecca encouraged.

"Tom's a real surprise. First, I have trouble even imagining how he came from my sister and Billy. Seriously, that's no joke. They're fine in their way . . . but, well, you know . . . my sister's kind of simple, and Billy . . . well, he's a good ol boy." He stopped abruptly as if he'd just run up to the edge of a cliff without realizing. And then, like Richard, he was lost in his memory.

"And then there's Tom." He looked frustrated, as if he'd gotten off on the wrong note somehow and couldn't find his way around what he'd just more or less blurted out. Even though these were his closest friends, he wanted their respect, and he didn't like himself very much when he put down his sister and her husband. He also knew Anna disapproved of any disparagement of Carol Ann. He heard her voice. "Daniel! Careful!"

Rebecca chimed in, "The best way to tell us is not to worry about whether it makes sense. Let us worry about that."

He looked like a boy whose mother had just taken him by the hand.

"Ok, ok. He's very smart . . . and well-read. But it's more than that. There's something about him I just can't explain. Anna could've, I think. I'm sure they would have connected."

He sat forward on the couch staring down at his hands intertwined—palms up. "Well," he looked at all of them, "he talks to a ghost. At night. Out in our yard, or maybe I should still say Anna's yard. Long talks. Calls him Zak. The only Zak I ever heard of was my three-great- grandfather Zachariah who fought in the Pennsylvania 8th Regiment Calvary for the Union during the Civil War."

A minute went by. Richard started filling wine glasses.

"Did you see the ghost?" Richard asked, as if that were the obvious next question.

"No. But I saw Tom talking to him last night, and . . . well, I just couldn't help believing he . . . I mean Zak . . . was really there."

"Did you hear the conversation?" Rebecca asked.

"Some. From Tom's side."

Rebecca leaned forward, obviously thrilled. "What did you hear?"

Daniel leaned back on the couch staring into the calmed-down fire to which Richard was adding another log. "Ok. First, I woke up the other night about 3:00 a.m. and I was pretty groggy but heard a voice—or voices—coming from the yard outside. Out by Anna's bench. So, I went out to the kitchen to the back door and there was Numi, sitting in the half-opened doorway. He was alert, the way he looks when he's hunting . . . you know, crouched for the mouse. I remember squatting and petting his head and for a second he looked up, but then back at that part of the yard where I heard Tom's voice." He stopped for a moment, remembering.

"I heard Tom say something like 'Come on Zak you gotta give me some explanation.' Then the other, I mean the ghost, spoke. I couldn't hear, and by then I saw Tom sitting on the bench looking at someone, only I didn't see anyone. Tom asked something like "You mean accused him of forgery?"

Well now, let me tell all of you, there's only one person in the world who might know what that could be about other than me, and that person's here in this room." He looked at Richard who agreed.

"Honest, Daniel, I'm not having secret rendezvous with your nephew behind your back."

"I know, I know . . . that's not my point. My point is how could this entity, this ghost, be talking to Tom about something that happened forty years ago and, as far as I know, no one except Anna and Richard really ever knew about that. It's ancient history. Even I haven't thought or talked about it in years.

Rebecca asked "Did you hear anything else? Anything that might explain at least why this ghost—whatever it is—was talking to Tom about something that happened forty years ago?"

"Well, I remember after he listened for quite a while as if he was being told a story Tom asked 'What happened to the friend?'"

Both Daniel and Richard exchanged knowing glances as if this explained something.

"And then," Daniel continued as if he were getting to the denouement. "Then," he held his finger up as if he were in class, "Tom asked the question that convinced me he was learning something real. He asked 'So what's this Benjamin got to do with Uncle Daniel now? If he disappeared for forty years, what's he got to do with anything now?'"

They all looked at one another.

Melinda finally spoke. "I think you should call his mother. Ask her about this."

Daniel turned to her and smiled. "Well, I did. This afternoon. And you know what she answered?"

They were all ears.

"You guys have never met my sister." He chuckled. Imitating Carol Ann's high-pitched voice, he went on. 'Oh Daniel. You know I told you he's different. Sweetie' . . . she calls every one 'sweetie' . . . 'Tom understands there is more than just one dimension here on God's earth. And you know he's been communing with our Grandpa Zak for about eight years now.'" He looked upward imitating his sister's naïve, wistful countenance. "'He started when he was about ten. They like to meet out in the back of the house . . . you know, out under the peach tree.'"

Richard got up and offered everyone more wine, coffee, tea. They all took the wine and sat for a while sipping.

Rebecca broke the silence. "Daniel, if you'd be willing, or think it could be useful, I'd like to meet Tom."

Daniel smiled. "I was hoping you'd say that."

Rebecca continued. "Not because I automatically think there's something wrong, or pathological, but as your sister says, "he's different and understands there is more than one dimension to reality. Not everyone is a charlatan. There are people who see beyond this two-dimensional world we think we all agree about."

They were all looking at the fire, absorbed in their own thoughts about this.

"Where I might be of service would be to offer him a safe haven just to talk about it. I bet his mother who, obviously accepts this part of her son without question, but . . . well, she's his mother. Her acceptance without question might not be enough right now. And keep in mind your sister has sent him to live with you. It might not be just because you are connected with the university."

Daniel seemed to wake up out of a stupor. "Yeah, but I'm his uncle . . . his kin. And I'm related to Zak as well. Why wouldn't I be the safe person for him to confide in?"

Rebecca nodded. "I can't be sure, but that's just my point. He's kept this a secret for the obvious reasons. You're an academic Daniel. Tom might not want to risk what would be a reasonable fear that a reaction from you might be disbelief, thinking he's crazy, or just a high level of intellectual skepticism." She looked away searching for the right words. "And well . . . the latter reaction might be the worst. Nothing like intellectual rationalism to kill the spirit."

They all looked at Daniel, who put on a mock expression like a kid who just fell off his skateboard after showing off. "Yeah, but . . ." he was grasping for a defense . . . "come on . . . I lived with Anna all those years. She talked to the weather for God's sake." He looked at their quizzical expressions. "Seriously. She'd throw out her arms and call to the wind . . . or rain . . . or fog. Whatever!" He sounded desperate.

Richard came to the rescue. "Daniel, we know. We all loved Anna. But that's not the point. Rebecca's talking about Tom's point of view. You're his academic uncle. He admires you. Telling you he talks to ghosts might just be a bit of a reach he's not prepared to make with you. Not just yet."

Daniel fell back into the couch sighing. Melinda patted his knee. "Ok. So how do I get him to see you, Rebecca? What do I say?"

"Well . . . let's see." Rebecca frowned. Then brightened "Why don't we arrange an outing of some sort. On a Sunday, and make it a picnic. That way I could meet him and perhaps find myself walking with him. Get to know him."

"Maybe we could get Gertrude to come," Richard chimed in.

They all liked the idea. They decided on the botanical gardens, on a Sunday, two weeks later.

CHAPTER 7

"Killing must feel good to God, too. He does it all the time."

HANNIBAL LECTER

AT 4:00 IN THE AFTERNOON HE DROVE NORTH out of town on Interstate 80 pushing the blue 1990 Vanagon camper to do 60, its outer limits. He was thinking he should have been happy after his visit with Morrigan. But he wasn't—not at all. He was losing his hold over her. *Well, shit . . . she's growing up. It's to be expected. Normal. I'm the only father she's known. She loves me, depends on me. She'll do what I want.*

But something nipped at him. *She's growing away from me. I should have expected it. Maybe I did but I didn't expect it so soon. That mind of hers. Where did it come from? Not her ditz of a mother, that's for sure.*

Lost in thought, he didn't notice the sleek, champagne-colored Audi W12 passing on his right, a little too close for comfort, doing at least 80. He'd been driving in the left fast lane near the concave barrier not realizing that he probably should have been over in the slower lane. He wasn't paying attention, lost in thought over his recent visit. But testosterone took over and he flattened the gas pedal, forcing the Vanagon to wheeze and buck. He looked to his right into the grinning face of a 20-something with his girlfriend bobbing her blond ponytail back and forth, eyes closed, ear-phones—no difference between her and the rock concert in her head. He was forced to brake as the Audi veered closer.

The leering face became the Joker from Batman. "Get off the road old man!" The Vanagon shimmied.

He knew what to do to slow down, only there wasn't time to gradually ride it out. It had happened before, but this time his rage betrayed him and in seconds the van was climbing up the break wall, sending him over into a 360 degree roll, landing upright across three lanes into the right.

He woke with a flashlight in his eyes and a highway patrolman asking "Sir, can you hear me? Can you follow the light?"

All he remembered later was thinking "For Christ's sake . . . doesn't anyone have any brains anymore?"

They made him get into the ambulance. He knew he needed to go with the flow, so he relaxed and let the young paramedic fuss with him, taking his vitals, looking important with his dangling stethoscope, reminding him of kids at camp showing off their lanyards, as he cleaned Benjamin's forehead mumbling about a possible concussion.

"You were very lucky, Sir. I'm not sure how it happened, but the other driver said you tried to ram into him. He said he'd done some race driving so I guess he thinks he knows. We think his girlfriend may not have been wearing her seat belt and she almost went through the windshield. So it doesn't look too good for her."

Benjamin's eyebrows climbed up his forehead. The paramedic interpreted this as a look of concern, but it really indicated he was delighted they would be at the same hospital. His appetite for revenge knew no bounds. Once he was bit with the bug there was nothing that could stop him. Even as a young boy he knew this about himself.

The first time he remembered being humiliated was in kindergarten. His teacher, Miss Swanson, told him in front of the others "Benjamin, when was the last time your mother washed your hair? Doesn't she know about lice?" She had little thin, twiggy legs, skimpy hair, wore long wool skirts, black rimmed glasses and, in dramatic contrast to her New England spinster look, she sported a large diamond on her left ring finger.

Later, he learned she was married to a distant off-shoot of a wealthy family. *Playing at being a teacher for a few years.* He vowed to get back at her. *Stupid old teacher. Just you wait.*

The following year, when he was out of her class, he collected some bedbugs that his friend gave him who knew where to find them in old box springs at the dump. He especially liked finding out from his friend that when bedbugs bit humans and sucked their blood they turned red. He went home that night and, with his new set of colored pencils he'd gotten for his birthday, he drew a scrawny stick figure with a parade of little bugs with greedy smiles heading for her and crawling up her legs, adding the detail of making the bugs bright red, coming out all over her hair. He was proud of it and showed his friend whose admiration for him soared to new heights.

He went to her class, and into her little closet he dumped them out of the baby food jar into the pocket of her loud plaid coat. He was certain he saw her a week later out on the playground scratching the back of her calf with her other foot.

They made him stay in the hospital overnight to keep an eye on him. He consented because he was too tired to argue, and since his van was totaled, he would have to take care of it. That would require some energy he simply did not have at the moment.

They put him in a room with a cranky old man they called Mr. Mendosa. He had coughing and choking fits that sounded like he would croak any second while he compulsively plunked his buzzer for a nurse, who would rush in and try to calm him down. But Mr. Mendosa refused and continued coughing as if he finally had a chance to get back at the world.

Benjamin's night nurse, a young African American gay man named Arthur, promised to check on him every hour or so. "Don't you worry, my Man, no one dies on my watch!" whatever that was supposed to mean. He lay flat with his head bandaged, feeling old. He blinked his eyes to let Arthur know he appreciated him. Which he did not. *Snoopy little bugger. I'll have to watch out for him.*

Benjamin's mission was clear. Between Arthur's scouting parties to check on him, he needed to find out where they were. Especially the girl. He'd already figured out that the guy's daddy was rich. He knew cars and that Audi was brand new and expensive and the kid was no entrepreneur geek with his own start-up. He was a party boy probably on his way up to Tahoe and the casinos for some fun.

As he lay there listening to Mr. Mendosa snore, he came up with a bright idea. These little epiphanies in a crunch were his genius. He smiled at the ceiling and allowed himself to rest.

At 12:00 a.m. Arthur came in and took his limp wrist in his soft velvety hands and peered at his watch.

He pretended to wake up and smiled.

"All's well," Arthur cooed. "Resting heart rate 60 right to the minute." He fussed a little, tucking in the sheets, and patted the skimpy over-washed white coverlit, as if to rid it of crumbs or dust mites that weren't there, at least not visibly.

Benjamin knew that the real bugs in hospitals, the microscopic

Superbugs called names like MRSA or Steno, were the real killers and he had no intention of sticking around to attract them.

Just as Arthur was leaving, he stopped him. "Hey, Arthur, maybe you could help me with something?"

"Sure. What do you need? Want the TV on, or something to drink?"

They both heard the old man move and groan.

Arthur shrugged. "Can't do much about him."

Benjamin would have loved to take care of Mr. Mendosa, but he knew he had bigger fish to fry, so his normal tendencies had to be curbed in the service of the greater good. And now he needed to know what that kid's name was and where his girlfriend was napping.

"Well, Arthur, I'm having trouble sleeping because I don't know what happened to that nice young couple who were in the other car. I'm lying here thinking how lucky I am to have survived that horrendous accident, and yet I don't know if those two are all right." He turned on his sweetest Papa Cat cooing voice that he used with the little ones back home. As he talked, he imagined licking them all. That fleeting image pulled him back to reality. Imagining licking Arthur was another thing entirely. Maybe Morrigan, but not this guy. For some reason he just never was attracted to nurses. *Not my type. Too co-dependent.*

"So, I'm wondering if you could just reassure me on that, and I promise I will lie here like a tired old lamb."

Arthur giggled, then turned conspiratorial. "Well, patients' names and records are confidential . . ." he glanced out the door down the hall . . . "but . . ." he put his index finger to his lips . . . "I'll look around and see what I can find out."

Benjamin sighed a happy, child sigh. *My charm never fails me. It's like my faithful friend.*

He allowed himself to close his eyes, and just when sleep might have returned, he was jolted awake by the old man's coughing. He could hear him jabbing the buzzer, muttering as he coughed and choked with no regard for the reality that it would be impossible for his nurse to appear like the Fairy God Mother. He lay there keeping his eyes closed, imagining getting out of his bed calmly and standing over Mr. Mendosa. With one finger he would slowly jam his windpipe. Watch his eyes fade out. Just like Missy Tupelo's had, down by the river.

As he thought of her, he was jolted by the expanded memory that Morrigan may have witnessed that little episode. He'd heard something about ten yards away and as her body sank like a deflating party balloon he went to investigate and found Morrigan with two of the young ones collecting blackberries. When she looked up at him, he couldn't help the nagging thought that she had seen something.

The old man's nurse came with reinforcements. One held him down while the other gave him a shot. Presumably to sleep. *Good, you old Fuck. Go to sleep forever.*

Finally, he drifted off again. He woke at 1:30 with Arthur gently taking his pulse. His eyes opened and he beamed gratitude and curiosity. "I found out that she may have a broken neck. They're not sure, of course. Her boyfriend is ok. Name's Drexel. Drexel DeWitt, III if you can believe that."

That pleased him. *Who names their kid Drexel these days? This is good. He's got to be insecure with a lineage like that. Well, Drex, I'm looking forward to meeting you.*

"He's sitting in the waiting room," Arthur explained, proud of his reporting skills. "I saw him. He looks like he's about to jump out of his skin every time he hears someone come in. He's scared. I think maybe she wasn't wearing her seatbelt. Poor kid. I think she'll be in traction for some time."

"What's her name?" He wanted to know before he paid her a visit.

"I think her name is Julie. Can't remember the last name. Sorry. Didn't get everything, but like I said you can call the hospital tomorrow and maybe find out."

As he sidled to the door, Arthur started looking a bit nervous, since he'd just told a little too much

"Oh, hey, thanks Arthur. I suppose there's some family coming?"

Arthur sighed and added quickly, "His parents are coming in tomorrow morning, back from some cruise they were on. Don't know about her." He looked at his watch. "You take it easy now. Nothing you can do for them. Just be grateful you're fine. Get some rest."

"Will do. Will do. Thanks." He closed his eyes letting Arthur know he intended to abide by his good advice.

Eyes closed, wide awake. *Perfect. Now all I need to do is pretend I'm in the bathroom.* He slid out of bed, found his clothes in the closet, and dressed, wondering if he should go barefoot, but decided his vans wouldn't make noise.

Better they think I'm a visitor rather than a patient. He peeked out the door down the long-deserted hallway. All was quiet except for the suction and metal trolley sounds from distant wings that permeate hospitals, an invisible beehive of patients coming and going. He headed for the nurse's station.

He wasn't sure what he would say to the nurse on duty. Allowing a certain spontaneity in any plan of action was part of his daily routine. He turned right, down the corridor and as he approached she looked officious, an old timer who'd seen it all. *Good. She won't mind me.*

"Oh, hey . . ." he cooed in a respectful whisper, "I just got released from emergency," pointing to his bandaged forehead. "Say . . . I was just wondering if I could find out what happened to that nice young couple brought in from that accident. I was in the other car he rammed. I understand she hurt her neck or something?" He paused, to emit a pained expression. "I'm not surprised because just before he side-swiped my van I saw her in the passenger seat . . ." he rolled his eyes "and would you believe? No seat belt."

She pulled her glasses down to the bridge of her nose, as far as they would go.

Her stare made his head hurt. He liked her. He knew exactly how to play her.

"You know . . ." he cocked his head, "swear to God, you remind me of my first high school girlfriend. She'd probably look just like you now. Elegant, smart. I always knew . . ." He glanced at her nametag that said "Marilyn.". . . "Merrill would really make it someday. I still think about her."

He observed with his hawk-eye focus as her seasoned skepticism twitched ever so slightly and the faintest blush revealed her inner world.

"Ok . . ." she snapped. "What's this about? You know you're not supposed to be here." She glanced at the clock on the wall. "It's 2:00 a.m."

"Oh, hey . . . I'm heading out of town right now and I wondered if you could just tell me how she's doing."

"Don't know. She's resting. The doctor will see her in the morning. You can call the hospital in the morning around 10:00. Her boyfriend is in the waiting room, asleep I think. He's ok."

"Oh, great." He feigned relief. "Thanks."

He plodded back the way he came, trying to look like he was not in a hurry, and passed his room where Mr. Mendosa coughed and choked.

When she said "she's resting" she nodded her head down his corridor.

It took three peeks into each room before he found her. He knew right away. Her neck was in a big, white brace, the rest of her draped in a sheet. *A snow queen.* She was alone in the room. Her face was bruised but he could see that she was beautiful. *Stupid little empty-headed nitwit! I'm doing you a favor. Now you won't have to live out a meaningless existence going from one man to the next. You have no idea what families like boyfriend Drexel's can do.*

Five minutes later he was in the elevator gliding down to the third floor waiting room.

He sat in the chair across from him as he lay sleeping on the beige vinyl couch with his sweatshirt under his head for a pillow. He had on a blue t-shirt with "UCLA" scrawled across it in bright white. He looked about 23 but he couldn't tell for sure.

He guessed she was younger, maybe much younger.

He had tousled, sandy hair with a face that could be construed as cherubic when he was small, but Benjamin detected the signs of wear and tear already. *Skin that didn't like the sun. Crinkles around the eyes. Lips that could curl if threatened. Girls may like you now but later it will only be for your money.*

He looked at the clock on the wall. 3:00 a.m. He watched him sleep the way he liked to watch Morrigan, and the others. His favorite moments. Secret. Elicit. Powerful moments.

When he was little, he hid in his father's closet and stole the change from his pockets. Sometimes he found paper money too but didn't always take it. That made him feel independent. Strong. He could take it or leave it. That was the game he played with himself. Should he, or shouldn't he? It was about the choice. That's what counted. He wanted Morrigan to understand this someday. Eventually, she would need to understand that moment when he took Daniel's letters. *The world is your oyster. That's my gift to you.*

When he decided to take Daniel's letters he didn't think. He just acted. Later, back in his room he began to fathom the full implications of what he had done and knew from that point on there was no turning back. It had to be total. His life was ahead of him, and it almost worked.

His father's words wormed their way through his memory: "I guess you think you're hot shit now. Professor and all. Well . . . la de Daaaa . . ."

He winced. Those words had not diminished with time, only grew louder. Sometimes he swam under water just to find the silence.

The only saving grace was that the old man died before total humiliation when the truth came out. Not long after, his mother followed like the good wife into the funeral pyre. *Not exactly Suttee, but close.* That's when he had his greatest epiphany. *Good and evil. What's the difference? It all ends in the void when the great noise is over. Parents reduced to powder.* He kept them mingled together in death as in life—not in an urn, but in a plastic baggy in an old shoebox.

Look at you now, Dad. Where did those years of working for the Man get you? Stuck with her in an old shoebox waiting at my whim for my decision to dispose of you as I see fit. I've had some ideas over the years—a toxic dump . . . in the garbage of your favorite restaurant McDonalds' . . . mail it anonymously and see where you go—naw! Nothing's been quite right. I'll know it when the right opportunity comes along.

Lost in thought, he didn't notice the startled eyes staring at him from six feet away

"Who're you?"

He doesn't recognize me. "Well that's a good question. I wanted to find out how Julie's doing." He was purring.

He sat up, pushing his body back into the couch—prey in the headlights. "Are you a relative or something?"

Wow! He has no idea. "No. But I have an interest in her."

"You're too old for her. Who are you?"

He turned on his sad, patient look. "Are you and she in love? Engaged to be married?"

Shock. "Hell no. I barely know her."

"Where'd you two meet?"

"Why?"

He shrugged. "Just curious."

Drexel stared at the disheveled stranger with the smoky voice. "We met in a bar. Last night. I have no idea who she is except she said she was from out of town. Is she ok?"

"Well, I can't exactly say that she is. Neck broke."

"What?!"

"Yeah. She'll be in traction for some time. Assuming there's nothing else broken . . . or paralyzed . . . like a spinal cord." *He's freaking out now. Big time.*

"Omigod!"

"Well, hey, don't worry. I understand your parents are coming in this morning from their cruise. I'm sure your dad will take care of everything from here on in."

He looked like a rabbit who'd just been shot at, quivering, nervous eyes scanning for his hidey-hole. "What do you mean, my parents are coming? What do you know?"

"Oh, I guess I didn't mention. Night nurse up there told me." He pointed at the ceiling as if that made it clear. "Marilyn. Nice woman. No nonsense if you know what I mean. I assumed you knew."

He sunk down. "I must've been asleep."

"Oh, yeah, well you need to rest. Big day coming up. I understand the car's ok. Your car that is. Minor scrapes. Lots to figure out I guess."

His look of terror even surprised Benjamin. "I gotta get out of here! Now! Get me out. Shit!"

He's more scared than I thought. I bet his old man has had it with this errant son. He's sizing things up in his mind. Just as I thought, he's no chip off the old block. No interest in following in the old man's footsteps into the wondrous world of Capitalism. Why should he? He'll inherit plenty. He's probably like the mother—looks without the brains. Now he's screwed the pooch big time and he's scared. Chances are he wasn't supposed to use the car. It didn't even have the new plates yet. Time for me to lend a helping hand.

"Hey, my name's Benjamin. What's yours?" He held out his hand.

Drexel's manners clicked on. He held out his hand, but didn't say his name.

Benjamin smiled. "Why don't I buy you a cup of coffee?" He glanced at the clock. 3:30 a.m. "I think there's a vending machine down in the cafeteria first floor . . . near the garage." He'd checked out the marquis. He hoped that Drexel knew where his car was and, in all likelihood, it would be in the hospital garage.

Drexel stood up. "Ok." He shrugged and dove into his pocket to pull out the car keys. "I can check on my . . ." he hesitated . . . "my car. Might as well."

He doesn't want me to know it's his dad's car. Perfect.

In the cavernous elevator going down Drexel pointed to his head. "What happened?"

Oops! He's getting suspicious.

"Oh God . . . yeah. That happened yesterday. Fell off my bike. Motorist side-swiped me."

"Huh."

He's starting to think. He'll want to know how I knew to ask about her. He knew he would have to think fast. *Choices, choices. Is she a distant cousin? Could she have called him? Had the nurse call him?*

"Ya know . . ." he began, "I came in about 5:00 this evening to have this checked" pointing to his head, "and just as I came in they were bringing her in on a stretcher. She was awake. Looked scared, though, I'll tell you. So, I'm standing there and for some reason they left her alone for a minute . . . I guess to alert the front desk they were bringing her in. She looked at me. Pleading kind of. So, I went over and took her hand and told her it would be ok, that she was in the hospital, and I assured her all would be well. She looked a little confused and then as they wheeled her away, she said 'Tell him. Tell him I'm here.' So, I'm guessing 'him' is you."

Drexel looked ever so slightly skeptical.

"Yeah, so, well . . . it took a long time for me to get this looked at and I had some dinner here in the hospital and then had some time on my hands, so you know, I looked her up later. I asked about her. And that's when I talked with Marilyn and found out where she was, and she told me you were in the waiting room."

"It sure took a long time for you to get looked at."

"Well, they also sent me down to x-ray to rule out a broken collar bone. Which I don't have. You know how doctors are these days. Multiple tests, mostly unnecessary." *Now he's bored. I've said enough.*

They sat on a bench outside the cafeteria drinking hot chocolate that seemed like a better choice than the so-called coffee in the machine that offered numerous choices with or without cream, meaning that powdered shit, and then an assortment of flavored sweeteners that were surely cancerous.

That was when he made his pitch. He found out that indeed Drexel was in a lot of hot water with his parents, especially his dad. Disinheritance was on the horizon. With this new wrinkle—the girlfriend under-aged as it turned out since she was seventeen, the other guy in the car he knew might be a problem, he'd already gotten two DUI's, flunked out of UCLA—the list went on and on.

Benjamin was only interested in one thing. *Did the kid have his own bank account?* He had access to his trust fund, but he was sure his dad would put a block on that as soon as he got to the lawyers. Benjamin knew they had to hurry.

The out he offered Drexel under normal circumstances would never have flown. But he knew the kid was completely cornered and that any plan, any way out, would sound good.

Within half an hour they were driving on the Freeway heading back north.

Only Benjamin was driving, and the kid was sleeping. *Home Sweet Home.* They would be there in a few hours. Plenty of time to hatch a plan.

CHAPTER 8

*When first I encountered her, I was aware she was made up of three
individual goddesses, but I saw her very much as a single being . . .Today
I tend to look at it as a kind of godly multiple personality disorder and hive
mind akin to something you would see in science fiction.*

STEPHANIE WOODFIELD, *PRIESTESS OF THE MORRIGAN:
PRAYERS, RITUALS & DEVOTIONAL WORK TO THE GREAT QUEEN*, P.

EVEN THOUGH BETH DIDN'T KNOW ABOUT
MORRIGAN, Morrigan knew about Beth. She knew that Beth liked
Tom and for the first time in her life she felt the same.

After the last summer class together, their third, Beth and Tom went
for coffee. While they were talking, Beth left for the bathroom, and
Morrigan made her appearance on her return. She sat down across from
him and turned on a big grin.

He responded smiling, with curiosity.

She leaned forward across the table close into him about to share a
secret.

He waited.

"Are you up for some fun?"

He looked quizzical, considering her.

She knew he noticed something different. *He's feeling it but he can't
put his finger on what it is. Obviously.* Sanctimonious Beth was gone and
here Morrigan was, the stronger of the two—well three—if you seriously
considered Sugar Pie. Which she did not.

Sugar Pie was actually a spawn of Beth's, not Morrigan's. Beth and
Sugar Pie needed one another, and they both needed Morrigan.

Morrigan giggled her infectious giggle, the one when she played
Tickle Rip with the little ones back home, or back at Yahoo Ranch, as

she liked to call it. The game grew out of the stories she read to them, like Gulliver's Travels and Rip Van Winkle.

Any time the others came back home from afar they brought books for the children, and she liked the classics, the old tales, because they were much more imaginative than the politically correct moderns that wanted to teach children how to think. No one was as wild as Gulliver and Rip.

Morrigan would start the game by yawning, and announcing "I think I'll just have a little nap here in the Catskills. Wake me in a hundred years, please."

The children would whoop and holler announcing they were Lilliputians and climbed all over her trying to tickle her awake.

She would hold out as long as she could playing fast asleep, even snoring. When finally, she'd erupt awake, they'd all scream in terror as she chased them all to tickle them back. No one was spared.

Hannah, the three-year-old, loved the game the most and would be the last to get caught. She was small with stocky legs that could climb like a cub and run like a little pony. She loved to play hide and seek, so when she wanted to, she could disappear. But Morrigan wouldn't give up and eventually Hannah would scream when Morrigan got too close, giving away her hiding place.

After hesitating, he said "Ok. What kind of fun?"

"You'll see."

Benjamin allowed her to buy a 1978 VW bug. She rarely used it. He wanted her to have the possibility of coming home any time she wanted, which she never did. But she loved the little rattletrap and called it Ladybug. Occasionally, she took it for a drive just to get out of town into the country.

"Follow me."

He followed. Tom appeared to be an introvert, at least reserved, while his true nature was up for anything. It was as if his personality was simply in readiness for the next adventure or what could seem like an adventure. After all, who could calmly accept a relationship with a ghost?

He was not like his mother who gravitated to all things paranormal, because such occurrences demonstrated the Lord's work. She truly believed that Zak's appearances to Tom were really Jesus dressed up as a Union Cavalry soldier. She would look out the window with that faraway gaze and tell him "He chose you Tom. You! For a reason." Why he never bought that little bit of true belief, even when he was young, he never knew. He just knew that he didn't. But he did accept—from the first visit when he was ten—that it was the ghost of his four-great-grandfather Zachariah, and that Zak knew a lot of stuff he didn't and there was a purpose behind the visits. He also realized that the only other person who knew was his mother. And that made her special.

Morrigan took him to the garage of the house where she rented a room and invited him to get in Ladybug.

He threw his backpack into the back seat and got in beside her.

He felt no reservations. In fact, he continued to notice that she seemed different, almost as if she'd shifted into another person. This one was more interesting and exciting. He automatically reasoned that Beth had more to her than he'd first realized. And that was a lot, because that first Beth was very smart, the smartest he'd ever met. And this expanded, the other Beth was awesome.

They wended their way up and over the hills behind the University, out through rolling yellow and green hills.

She drove with confidence, gliding easily into second when it got steeper, took the turns just right without breaking. After about forty minutes' drive she turned into a dirt road that had a Regional Park sign and pulled into a parking lot where there were only two other cars.

"Come on," she instructed.

There was a wide trail at first that narrowed as they started to climb up into the hills. Within twenty minutes they were in a high chapparal with Coast Live Oaks and Toyons and a few Big Leaf Maples.

He was amazed at how faraway it seemed from about an hour ago sitting across from her in the coffee shop and she'd asked "Are you up for some fun?" This wasn't his idea of fun. It was better, and he was pleasantly surprised.

When they reached a plateau, she pointed down into some heavy brush that had formed a dense Scrub Oak tangle with sinewy vines and clumps of Mistletoe—suddenly, she disappeared into a curtain of bramble.
He tried to follow but didn't see where she had gone.

Then he heard a rustle and she pulled back some branches warning "Look out for the poison oak. Come on. In here." She disappeared again.

He ducked down and pushed his way through, trusting the scratches and possibly torn shirt had a purpose. And there she was, standing in a clearing about twenty feet in circumference almost completely enclosed within this inner circle with blackberry bushes. The ground was covered with green grasses with some tiny wildflowers still in bloom. It was sunny and warm like a secret garden.

She held out her opened hand with three chubby blackberries beckoning him to take them.

He held his hand out and she dropped them into his palm. He ate them one by one as she watched, silent, waiting for his reaction. He smiled.

"Wow!" She threw out her arms. "Welcome to my blackberry market."

In the quiet, he began to detect the sound of tinkling water.

She pointed into the bushes. "A little stream. That's why they're so big and juicy." She plopped down on the carpet of grasses, and, on her back, she looked up at the sky.

He did the same, beside her.

They lay there for what seemed like a long time. Silent. Staring at the sky, watching a red-tailed hawk glide overhead hunting for rodents, listening to the hidden creek and the buzz of wasps near the Oaks, smelling the over-ripe berries.

She spoke first. "Where are you from?"

He wanted to talk, to tell her about himself. "Ohio. Originally from Pennsylvania."

"Your family moved from Pennsylvania to Ohio?"

"Yeah. In the 1920's. After World War I. My great-great-grandfather Jacob moved his family to Hamilton, Ohio, to work for the new tractor plant. First of its kind. He was a farmer who thought like an engineer, so when he heard about the idea of motorized tractors, he wanted to become part of making and selling them. Henry Ford and his son Edsel opened the plant just after the war—the first plant to be hydro-powered by the local big river. In fact, Ford got the farmers to work in his factory and he used their water source to run his plant. They sold Fordson Tractors at $700 each, and every farmer in the country wanted one."

She listened. Quiet.

"So, your people have been there ever since?"

"Well, I guess. How about you? Where are you from?"

She sighed. "Don't know."

"Seriously?"

"Seriously. I don't know. My mother moved all over. She met my Stepdad—I guess that's what he is—when I was three. I've lived with him and her and some others ever since."

He looked at her. For whatever reason, he couldn't think why, he believed she was not holding something back. She really didn't know where her people were from.

"Well, where do they live, the others . . . I mean, whoever you live with?

She grinned. "It's a secret."

He looked away. "Ok, it's a secret. I have quite a few myself."

She did tell him she lived out in the country on a communal farm and that there were five little kids from two and a half to six with an assortment of seven adults, some parents. She didn't tell him details about any of them and she only mentioned that her Stepdad was named Benjamin—nicknamed 'Papa Cat'—and that he owned hundreds of books and that's how she educated herself. Enough, anyway, to make it into the University.

He told her that he was the youngest in his family with four sisters. He explained that he liked his father, thought he was an ok guy, but they just couldn't relate. "My Mom . . . well, I suppose she'd seem very unsophisticated out here, but I think she's really different . . . in a way probably even she doesn't understand." He thought about that and added, "Not at all like her brother, my uncle."

"You mean Daniel Perry?"

He looked surprised. "You knew?" He rolled over on his elbow to stare at her.

"Well, yeah," she laughed. "I mean, you and he have the same ears . . . sort of shaped like large lima beans. Dead giveaway, that stuff."

He rolled back and stared up again.

"What's he like by the way? I mean he's so popular around campus, but what's he really like?"

"Well . . . let me think. What would I say about him? First, he's a little arrogant, but I don't think he means it. I mean, he tries not to be, but when he sometimes encounters the amazing fact that he doesn't know everything he thinks he knows . . . well, then he's really funny. He gets this absolutely stunned look on his face, which is almost a cartoon. I mean, he doesn't try to defend himself like most adults. He just looks like a kid who got caught at something."

She grinned. "Yeah. That's good." She liked the description.

"How about Benjamin? What's he like?"

"Oh . . ." she seemed startled by the question. "Ah . . . let me think." She was quiet. She turned up on her elbow. "Benjamin's a wacko. He's smart . . . literate, I guess . . . but he's warped. Don't know why. I have no idea about his background. I do know he has a lot of books on the Civil War."

Tom came up on his elbow. "So does Daniel."

"Well, yeah" she laughed. "That's his area of expertise."

"Yeah" he agreed. "But there's something personal for Daniel . . . it's not just academic. And I'm not sure what that is."

She lay back down. "One time Benjamin told me something. It was a really strange thing to say, and trust me he says a lot of strange things but this one I never forgot. It was somehow different. Maybe I thought for once he's telling the truth."

"What was it?"

"He said, 'For me there was only one important war and that was the Civil War.'

And then he said, 'And don't kid yourself. That war's not over.'"

"What did you think he meant?"

"Well, he said something else, I guess it has to do with that . . . he said, 'the South lost their right to live how they wanted and that's all that matters.'"

"Forgetting that little bit about slavery that made their nobly free way of life possible? Not only on the backs of the slaves but in the sale of slaves? How can a way of life be justified when that's what it was built on?"

"Yep," she agreed. "Forgetting that little bit. Benjamin thinks personal freedoms trump all. I guess he believes that thing Voltaire supposedly said. 'I do not agree with what you have to say, but I'll defend to the death your right to say it.'"

"Uncle Daniel claims Voltaire didn't say that. And remember" he looked at her with a big smile "Uncle Daniel knows everything."

"Yeah, well, who cares? The truth is an elusive fiction at best, don't you think?"

"Not sure." He looked at her, wondering who she really was. That brainy girl in class, or this little renegade lying beside him who finds secret giant blackberries in the middle of an oak grove?

He sighed. "Sometimes I agree with that. Who cares if some guy living in the 18th century actually said that, or like most of history, it's someone's composite of what he said. Voltaire was a wordy guy. Maybe there's no real distinction between truth and fiction. Maybe the truth is always somewhere in the middle. And that makes even the idea of truth very complicated."

She giggled. "Yeah. Maybe lying here in this secret meadow isn't real." And then she added, "And maybe there really are ghosts."

This seemingly throw-away remark jolted him. He shot her a glance, but she was lazily chewing on a long piece of sour grass, as if that last comment hadn't meant much at all, hadn't been a bull's eye right to his core.

They lay on the grass in silence looking up.

He wanted to kiss her, but something warned him that he shouldn't. Not now. He didn't want to risk spoiling the mood.

Half an hour later when they decided they had to leave and were standing brushing grass and nettles from their clothes he told her something he'd never told anyone except his mother. "I talk to a ghost." She looked at him.

He could tell this piece of information about himself pleased her immensely.

They made their way back to Ladybug and she drove him to Daniel's.

It was 6:00 o'clock. He realized Daniel might be wondering where he was.

They said goodbye.

He told her it was the best time he'd had since he'd arrived in California.

"I'm glad." She smiled. "Me too. See you in class."

He opened the front door and heard the mild thud Numi made when he jumped down off his couch where he often slept, lounging across the back like King of the Mountain. Tom picked him up, a heavy sack, and draped him over his shoulder. Numi kneaded his back carefully, clawing just enough like little pin-pricks that could mean business if he wanted.

Daniel was sitting in the living room as Tom strolled in with Numi. He'd been waiting for Tom, beginning to realize that his nephew was starting to have a life of his own while living with him. Even though he could tell Tom was not a typical 18-year-old, whatever he thought that was. Back in the day when he actually taught them at the University, they all seemed like eager beavers. But as the semester wore on, they began to break off into different groups.

Anna warned him not to pre-judge, and "try to remember when you were 18," but he couldn't.

He judged them—period. There were the eager beavers, basically trying to think like the professor, hoping for a good grade. There were the C students who made some effort, but just didn't care really, and then there were a few brilliant ones who came along. What passed for brilliance for Daniel was when they thought for themselves. Came up with new theories and connections, especially ones he hadn't thought of himself. They asked questions and were skeptical of answers, never satisfied. He thought Beth Monroe was one of those. He liked her. And now, he wondered if Tom was one as well.

He'd noticed that the two of them sat together in class and he remembered earlier today that they left together talking shoulder to shoulder. He wondered. And then he heard Anna's voice. "Welcome to parenthood!"

Tom broke his reverie.

"Hey, Uncle Daniel. Have you been sitting here waiting for me? I thought you were having dinner with Dr. Mason . . . I mean Melinda."
"Well, I was, Tom Boy, but she cancelled on me, left me in the lurch so to speak."

He sounded like Zak. Uncannily like Zak, who was the only one who called me Tom Boy.

"Sit down Tom. Let's chat."

He sat.

"So, how are you liking it here so far?"

Tom nodded. "It's fine." He realized Daniel might want more. "Well, it's great. Very different and I'm getting used to being here. It's beautiful and for me the amazing, varied landscape with mountains and ocean on either side feels like freedom." Then he added for good measure "I appreciate your having me."

Daniel smiled. "So, listen. I'd like to introduce you to a few of my friends. Richard and Rebecca. He's an old friend from my early graduate school days. Rebecca's a psychotherapist. They're recently married. And Gertrude Steiner. She's 82 going on 45 or thereabouts. An analyst. We're planning a picnic next weekend and I'd like you to come along. And of course, Melinda. So what do you think? Are you game to meet some old folks?

He could tell Daniel was a little nervous so he suspected there might be an agenda here. *Psychotherapist? Analyst?* He decided not to ask, not to appear suspicious. "Sure, I'm in."

"Good! Good! Well, let's eat. Are you up for a steak on the barbi?" he asked jauntily in a very bad Aussie rendition.

Tom didn't have the heart to inform Daniel that he did eat other things, but not tonight. Tonight, he was up for another steak.

She lay on her bed, hands behind her head, staring at the ceiling. She was already inside the dilemma, feeling it close in on her. Benjamin would be creepily happy that she'd infiltrated Daniel Perry's camp, sidling up to his nephew so soon. *He'll shake his head laughing, telling me I'm his bright baby girl.* She didn't know what was between Benjamin Monroe and Daniel Perry. She only knew that it was intense and had a pretty good idea what Benjamin was capable of. *So, what's the rub? I like him. A lot. And I like Daniel. If I turn on Benjamin and don't do what he wants . . . what happens to all of us? And what's most strange . . . I have to protect Beth. Because what the fuck does she know about any of this?* She calmed down into her big brain mode. *I know what's happened. I've never liked the Beth in me. But maybe now I need to let her in. Or at least try.*

With that, she fell asleep.

CHAPTER 9

He is brought as a lamb to the slaughter.

THE BIBLE, ISAIAH 53.7

AS BENJAMIN DROVE UP THE NARROW, DIRT ROAD he took more care than usual to avoid the potholes, to protect the new Mavis tires. He had already imagined the new paint job. Jet-black, suited for the moments. He would design his own new plates. Maybe call himself "Papa6." His friend, SammyO, ex con from Folsom, and now, a convenient neighbor and marijuana grower, he could make anything. *Maybe add some artwork.* Well, he had plenty of time for that.

Drexel slept the whole way. Like a baby. Benjamin concluded this was his emotional developmental age. He looked over at him slumped down in the passenger seat. *The character part of you Drex is a tad wanting, but that's good. You should fit right in.*

He swung the Audi around in front of their tilting veranda porch.

All was quiet still.

He looked at the digital clock on the shiny new chromium paneled dash. 6:30 a.m.

Suddenly, a flock of children burst out the door—a screaming babble of five with Midge, who jumped at the car—a large, loping big-paw Golden Retriever puppy that Benjamin had brought home from his last trip. He cringed, already feeling the pride of ownership, but then reminding himself not to worry. The new paint job would cover any scratches by the bouncy dog. Benjamin's big weakness was children and pets. The rest were dispensable.

Drexel snapped awake dazed from sleep and stared blankly at the marauding children as Benjamin carefully emerged from behind the wheel, since he was still a little sore, and began hugging them.

He picked up Arlo, the two-year-old whose swelling diaper squished and sloshed as he carried him inside, leaving Drexel to figure out whatever he cared to. He hadn't told him where they were going. He'd only said, "My place," and Drexel nodded grateful for someone else to do his thinking, which Benjamin assumed was his usual style when not on impulsive mode.

They were still at the long, black oak banquet table. They looked up, used to Benjamin arriving home whenever, and often he brought guests. They were all sitting on the benches, the table covered with plates and the leftovers from breakfast.

All seven adults: Cassi, mother of Morrigan and Hannah (his and Cassi's child); Angel and Manuel, parents of Arlo and Rose; Cloe and Stormy Carl, parents of Ziggy and Lennon; Luna, their youngest and most recent family member who was sixteen; and then Blanco, nineteen, their in-house Geek.

Cassi rose from the table and came up to him. She was dressed in her purple Moroccan caftan, and her long black hair, mostly gray now, tumbled down around her shoulders, wet from having just been washed. It was her hair that attracted him in the first place, and it still was. Her daughter had the brains. Maybe Hannah had his brains too. He considered Morrigan Cassi's gift to him.

The others waited expectantly.

"Ok everyone, we have a visitor."

"And a new car," Ziggy the seven-year-old shrieked. "Really cool too." Benjamin nodded patiently. "That's right. The Vanagon's been in an accident. Not sure it's salvageable, but we'll see. We needed a new van, anyhow. Now listen up!"

He switched to his formal leader Papa Cat role. "We have a new house guest. He won't be here for long, but as long as he is here, I want you all to give him our best treatment because he's a special guest. This will all be new to him," he swept his arms wide, "and he won't be used to our ways, but you know the drill. Keep him pleased, occupied and watched—POW. Now he's probably gonna come in that door pretty soon and I want you all to clear out except Blanco because we have a little business to attend to."

Like dutiful, respectful children they all got up, cleared their dishes and disappeared through the kitchen door, quietly closing it.

Blanco stayed seated at the table. He was nineteen and had been with them four years. A runaway from his last foster home. Benjamin found him on the streets of Los Angeles living under a freeway pass with a group of street people. Blanco was the youngest of the group. Although he and his clothes were glued together with grime, Blanco was a maestro with the computer. How he got hold of a 15-inch Apple Macbook Pro with Retina Display Benjamin didn't bother to ask because under Blanco's Midas touch, he could hack into any bank account anywhere in the world. And what was even more miraculous, he didn't do it for money. Blanco never had any money. He had high standards. He did it if he believed in the cause and the cause could be anything from something he read in the newspaper to how he was feeling in the moment.

Benjamin took Blanco under his wing and turned him into his creature, his Mastermind, just as he'd groomed Morrigan for the Final Act that was approaching.

Blanco sat at the table watching and waiting for Benjamin's direction. When he was nervous or feeling a little edgy, he cracked his knuckles, which he started to do. It was better than chewing off his nails, especially since there was never much nail growth to work with. They called him Blanco because of his carefully spiked hair that looked like a bleached agave plant. He appeared almost albino. To enhance the look, he circled his eyes with black grease paint and when it smeared, which it mostly did, he looked like he had just emerged from a Viking war party.

Cassi helped him maintain the length of his hair that worked for this hairdo, and she taught him how to use globs of hair gel to keep the points sharp.

Benjamin recognized that Blanco's hairdo was his strength, like Samson's. One time when they'd run out of the gel Blanco had a meltdown that took him a week to recover.

Benjamin went out himself to Costco a hundred miles away and bought a huge carton of the stuff.

The clerk at Costco asked him if he was a hair stylist, to which he replied, "How perceptive you are. Have you ever considered College?"

The clerk didn't know what to make of that response, and as Benjamin wheeled his shopping cart out the door he looked back and saw the clerk was still scratching his head.

"Ok, Blanco. Get your laptop. We've got some business to conduct with our new guest."

Blanco reached for his backpack under the table and pulled it out, set it down and flipped it open like a blackjack dealer.

As if it were rehearsed, Drexel hesitantly pushed open the screen door and peered in.

Benjamin opened his arms. "Welcome to my castle Drex!" He explained to Drexel that they were a family of dropouts who lived in a secret forest. He made it clear that no one had ever found their little collection of cabins that were protected by the heavily forested terrain all around. "We're off the grid. My Grandpappy owned this land," he lied, "and he was a logger from way back. We're surrounded mostly by red-neck renegades, and if you know how to behave and you come from them, they not only leave you alone, they'll protect you." The truth for Benjamin had always been an expedient that trumped any need for meddlesome details that muddied the waters.

Once a visitor entered their portals he or she was inevitably led into the scenic world of Benjamin's endless imagination and ability to keep reality conjured like a circus performer. He would lead people around singing in a low voice, "The magical mystery tour is dying to take you away, dying to take you away, take you away."

Once Luna served Drexel some fresh coffee he looked reasonably ready to pay attention.

Benjamin observed Drexel's wandering eye as he assessed Luna's chest.

"Ok, Drex, this is how I see your options."

He waited for Drexel to signal he understood.

"First, we get into your account and move most of the money into another, so your Dad can't track it."

Drexel looked completely bewildered, but wasn't dumb enough to ask how because he'd sized up Blanco and watched him stretch and position himself like an acrobat, cracking his fingers one at a time, and then lacing them together to make one big noise like a firecracker

After all, Drexel had spent some time in a college dorm, the hot house breeding ground where these Uber Geeks grew. He might not be one of them, but he imagined they were what his father used to make the wheels go round and round. And one day, they would be working for him.

He came to his senses. "What're you gonna do?"

"Well, good question Drex. So, here's the plan."

Benjamin kept it simple. "First, we need all the information you can give us. Names, bank accounts, trusts—all you know about your family finances."

Drexel turned pale and shifted his eyes around looking for an escape hatch. It came out barely more than a whisper, "Not much."

"Well . . ." Benjamin cooed, "not much is all this little genius needs." His arm draped over Blanco's shoulder like a pelt.

Blanco stared at Drexel, making his lips rise and fall—an attempt to smile, showing his front left cuspid missing.

After an hour of frustrating interrogation, they learned enough about the father's business holdings, that he bought and looted companies for profit, some of the banks he did business with, and that Drexel had a trust fund with approximately two million in it, but he wasn't sure because he didn't have access to any of the principal. What Drexel had was a credit card that gave him a spending limit of $3000 a month that was paid off by the trust. If he went over the limit he would receive a call from the trustee, Mr. Tauser, who worked for his dad. Drexel let it be known that he hated Mr. Tauser. "He's an A-hole!"

Benjamin studied Drexel. *Sophisticated thinking, this boy. Simple is as simple does.*

Benjamin was patient with Drexel as he displayed his vast lack of knowledge about his own money and his father's financial empire, a lack that accompanied a bit of shame on his part, but not enough for him to notice Blanco's thinly veiled contempt.

Blanco knew to keep a neutral expression, but every so often he flexed his head from side to side and cracked his neck, itching to get going. This had the effect of making Drexel even slower with the flow of information that was not plentiful in the first place.

Noticing a drop in his mood from wide-eyed curious to sullen, Benjamin whapped Drexel on the back, producing his Santa Claus happy-wow face, and invited Drexel to follow him into the kitchen to help make some breakfast.

The kitchen was large and modernized with two sub-zero refrigerators, a Wolf stove and miles of smooth concrete counters mushed as if they'd been finger-painted to look rock-like.

Benjamin retrieved a dozen eggs carefully perched in a wire basked. "Get 'em from our own hens," he smiled. "Mostly Rhode Island Reds. We breed our own, all from our matriarch—Henny Penny. Know anything about chickens, Drex?"

It was clear that Drexel was still in a state of shock. He watched Benjamin hop around the kitchen like a circus performer, while he remained silent and wide-eyed.

Benjamin chatted as he expertly cracked the eggs with one hand, whisking them with the other. He grabbed an omelet pan from the rack and with the dexterity of an experienced chef produced three perfect omelets with sour dough toast with homemade blackberry jam. As he added sprigs of parsley he started to hum under his breath "You Are My Sunshine." Pushing open the door back into the dining hall, balancing two plates, he tossed his head back. "Hey Drex, bring the coffee pot my man. Let's chow down."

Drexel obeyed, carrying the pot and third plate for Blanco, placing them on the table and looking around.

Benjamin produced coffee mugs, napkins, and utensils.

He and Drexel ate listening to the clickety-clack of Blanco's fingers dancing over the keys.

Blanco's omelet remained untouched.

Drexel wondered if he'd even noticed it.

Satisfied, Benjamin pushed his plate to the middle and refilled their coffee cups. "So, tell me Drex . . . what do you think your Old Man's worth?"

Drexel frowned.

He doesn't like that question. I shouldn't push it. Benjamin put his hands behind his head feigning interest in nothing. And then it popped out.

"He's a billionaire."

That even stopped Blanco for a second. "Yeah Ben . . ." he echoed "this guy's worth a shitload. Interests everywhere. Does a lot of business in Saudi Arabia. Accounts everywhere. Not much here in the U.S. . . . but some. Drexel's money is here."

"How much have I got?" he asked Blanco.

"Shit, Dude. Don't you even know?"

Drexel was getting over his shame. "No, Dude. Money's not my thing."

"Well I can see why."

"Yeah?" Drexel was really curious.

Blanco shot him a look that sized him up. "Well, yeah." He looked at the screen. "You'll never have to work for it, so why would you be interested?"

That seemed to stop Drexel for a moment.

Blanco continued the clickety-clack, peering in and out of the screen like a pecking bird.

Drexel seemed to decide to stop being so clueless. "Hey. Are we planning to steal money from my father?" A seemingly rhetorical question. He looked at the wall alongside the dining hall decorated with the children's crayon art but he wasn't seeing it. Fear made his complexion sallow, his jaw hurt.

"Hey Dude. Chill. We're just reconnoitering for the moment."

Benjamin returned from the kitchen where he had gone with the breakfast plates to plunk them into the large aluminum sink. "Tell me something Drex. Does your old man treat you well?"

Even Drexel knew where this was going. He looked down.

Blanco kept working, presumably not listening, but Drexel suspected Blanco could type and follow the numbers as well as listen to another conversation, and this did not reassure him—on the contrary.

"All right . . . Let me paint you a picture and you tell me if it's accurate." Benjamin thought for a moment as if trying to figure out exactly how to paint the picture. "Your Dad will be none too happy when he gets to the hospital. I'm afraid the worst has happened. I just called to see how she was doing, and the nurse told me she passed away during the night. A blocked windpipe. Happened suddenly. They're not sure, but think there was some sort of object stuck in her mouth when she hit the window, sort of lay there dormant or something, then she swallowed it, I guess, and it got stuck."

Benjamin was jolted and overjoyed to see that Drexel bought this load of bullshit hook, line, and sinker.

He stared, uncomprehending. He wrapped his arms around himself and began to rock slowly.

"Ok . . . so you're here now Drex. No one knows where." He gestured with his arms. "We're in the middle of nowhere. The car's in the barn. You haven't used your credit card. No one knows where you are. You're safe here." He waited for this to sink in, to sooth.

"So, here's the situation. Your father will go berserk . . . of course. She was in the passenger seat of your . . . I mean your father's, car without a seatbelt. And she is . . . sorry . . . was a minor. So that's child endangerment right there. And, well now, that's she dead I think that might make it a felony. I'm no lawyer but you know . . . you were wearing your seatbelt and you came out unharmed. So was the car pretty much unharmed, but she hit the dashboard and broke her neck." He waited for this to sink in.

"Did you try to get her to wear her seatbelt?"

Drexel looked like he was trying to remember. "I didn't notice. We were pretty high, just on Marijuana. Nothing major. They put me through a breathalyzer, and I was ok."

"Then there was that other driver. What happened to him? Do you think he's going to say nothing?"

"Who is that guy? I didn't see him after it happened. Was he taken to the hospital, too?"

Benjamin knew this might be taking him too close to home, but he had to make sure there was no chance that Drexel might remember him. That would complicate things right now and he wanted to avoid that. Keep this simple. "Did you get a good look at him?"

"No. It happened too fast. They took her in the ambulance and me in the cop car behind her. Honestly, she seemed ok. I mean, she wasn't going to die or anything. I don't know who drove my car to the garage at the hospital, but after they checked me out, they let me wait there in the hospital and told me I could go to my car if I needed to get my jacket or anything. So that's how I knew where the car was. I sort of thought she and I could just leave the next morning."

"Who contacted your parents?"

He shrugged. "The police, I guess. They probably got my dad's name from the registration in the car." He stopped to think. "They must have asked her or found out how old she was. She told me she was 21."

"Ok. Well, so your dad, the police . . . a lot of people are looking for you right now. But I assure you . . . you're safe here."

One of Benjamin's first rules with any guest was to impress them with how isolated they were, and, therefore safe from the outside world. Reassurance for someone in a state of shock, or even for someone who just wanted to escape, was an important strategy to keep them calm and to begin the process of building trust.

Drexel bent over holding himself, taking in the reality.

Benjamin approached and cradled his head against his thigh. "So, listen up, son. Here's the plan."

CHAPTER 10

Yorkies are a playful and spunky bunch.

GRUMBLE DOG

THEY CARAVANED IN THREE CARS. Daniel, Tom, and Belinda in her new Escape hybrid with Pixie, her Yorkshire Terrier, her topnotch tied in a pink bow that exaggerated her impish "I'm the center of the universe" expression.

When Tom climbed in the back seat Pixie dove straight into his lap. "Hard to believe," Belinda said over her shoulder as she pulled out of Daniel's driveway, "In the 19th Century England they were bred to catch rats. She chased one once, but when she tried to bite it, the rat squealed so loud she let go and retreated very fast."

"Now they're bred to be spoiled," Daniel teased.

Belinda ignored this.

Pixie draped herself on Tom's lap, letting him massage behind her ears, a sensual experience she expected from any human. Tom learned instantly that if he became distracted for one split second her paw would shoot out a warning signal in spite of Belinda's admonition, "Pixie, you behave yourself." It was clear that Pixie had no intention of behaving herself. As far as her worldview was concerned, humans were her pets, not the other way around.

Daniel speculated when he first met Pixie, "Hey, Pix, we're your rats now aren't we?"

Belinda invariably chose to ignore these little jabs, just as she'd learned to tolerate Daniel's self-centeredness that rivaled Pixie's any day.

Rebecca and Richard were already at the Botanical Garden holding down their favorite picnic spot, a table under a panoply of coastal Oaks looking out at White Dogwoods. They set out drinks with chips and salsa. Richard brought his New York Times just in case there was a lull in the day.

Rebecca was used to his mild crankiness on Sundays if he didn't have time to read it.

While they waited, he sat at the end of the table reading the book reviews, and Rebecca went over to the grass knoll and stretched out under the sun.

The Queens were not there.

Pixie didn't like sharing her center stage with them, while Juno and Dido ignored her existence altogether.

None of the humans wanted to add possible friction to what they intended to be a harmonious day.

Daniel, Belinda, and Tom arrived next.

Rebecca and Richard got up and approached them, especially to greet Tom who stood in their midst, clearly unused to so much adult attention. Pixie, on the other hand, ran around underneath them, leaping and preening about their feet, stealing center stage.

They all sat down at the picnic table commenting on the glorious sunshine, hardly a constant, living near the Pacific Ocean in northern California, especially in summer, and waited for Gertrude.

Soon they heard the melodious call . . . "Hallooo, here I am."

Tom clambered out of his seat, dumping Pixie on the ground, and loped toward the tall granddame carrying a large picnic hamper.

She wore black pants and a flowered linen chemise with a straw hat that looked like an old friend had perched it on top of her white bale of hair, un-thinned by age.

"Well, hello young man." She handed him the hamper and took his arm as if they'd known each other for years.

"Look at her," Richard murmured under his breath to Rebecca as they approached the group, looking like a royal entourage about to be introduced to their people, "the old operator, smooth as silk. She's already won him over."

Rebecca gave him a look that said, "Well, yeah!"

Tom placed the hamper on the table and escorted Gertrude to the end of the bench, so she didn't have to climb over. She patted the seat next to her and he hopped in.

Pixie, who had been restrained for the moment in Belinda's grip, broke free and hopped on the table, trotting daintily through drinks and Tupperware to greet the new guest.

"Hello, you little monster flirt." Gertrude leaned in and allowed Pixie to lick her cheek, while looking at Tom, winking. "She's spotted my basket full of treats."

"Be careful, Gertrude," Belinda warned. "She's a little trickster."

"Oh yes, my dear, I know about tricksters." She leaned over and opened the hamper lid and reached in for a baggy of dog treats. As she unzipped the baggy, Pixie, like the Tinker Bell she was, planted her front paws on the edge of the hamper and quick as a flash retrieved a cube of yellow cheese. She gripped it in her mouth, backing toward the edge of the table across from Gertrude as the adults watched—all aghast.

Belinda started to get up, but Gertrude warned her off. "Let me handle this, my dear. It takes a trickster to out-trick a trickster, now doesn't it Pixie?" She kept her eye on the cheese as Pixie emitted a low growl, shaking her prey slowly, suggesting her rat-chasing genes weren't completely bred out of her.

"Well, well my little thief" Gertrude chirped as she took a bacon bit treat out of the bag and held it up over Pixie, who eyed it both with suspicion and covetous greed, trying to figure out how she could have both. Gertrude watched her beady little eyes narrow and widen, sizing up the possibilities, growling her displeasure at being confronted with both objects of desire. The standoff was on.

They all watched Pixie's dilemma: *if I drop the cheese I can get the bacon bit, but if I take the bacon bit, I might lose the cheese.*

Gertrude held the prize over her, speaking softly. "Pixie, I trust you to make the right decision. After all, a smart little dog like you with your bouncy step and quick little ways is a force to be reckoned with. Believe me, I think you shall live a long and happy life among us humans, as we are your mere handmaidens at best."

Pixie heard the friendly, soothing voice and started to drop the cheese, but suddenly suspicious, gripped it again, growling her response. But her dilemma wore on.

Finally, after a minute of indecision, Pixie dropped the cheese and seized the bacon bit as Gertrude simultaneously, and with the dexterity of a magician snatched back the cheese.

"Thank you, Pixie. You made the right decision."

After gulping the treat, Pixie, unaware that she'd been out-maneuvered, sniffed around the table for her cheese, which had been tossed into the hamper, a little worse for wear, and the lid shut.

"A few teeth marks, but perfectly edible," Gertrude announced. Then to Pixie, who had settled back down in Tom's lap, her head on her paws, her final salute, "The web of our life is of a mingled yarn, my dear. Good and ill together."

"All's Well That Ends Well," Richard echoed.

He and Gertrude smiled and nodded communing in their like-mindedness.

"Well, Pixie," Tom soothed, "I think you've met your match." He looked over at Gertrude. "You knew she'd drop the cheese."

"Well, it was a gamble." She looked up at all of them. "My dears, you know the story of the Fox and the Crow?"

"No" they all chimed in, knowing that they were about to hear.

She began in her sonorous voice:

"Well, a Fox once saw a Crow fly off with a piece of cheese in its beak and settle on a tree branch much like this Oak we're under now.

'That's mine,' said the Fox, and he walked up to the foot of the tree.

'Good day, Mistress Crow,' he cried. 'How well you are looking today: how glossy your feathers; how bright your eye. I feel sure your voice must surpass that of other birds, just as your figure does; let me hear but one song from you that I may greet you as the Queen of Birds.'

The Crow lifted her head and began to caw her best, but the moment she opened her mouth the piece of cheese fell to the ground, only to be snapped up by Master Fox.

'That will do,' said he. 'That was all I wanted. In exchange for your cheese I will give you a piece of advice for the future: 'Do not trust flatterers.'"

"Aesop," Rebecca announced.

"Exactly, my dear. You know the tale."

They unpacked the picnic lunch and spent the next hour and a half lazily stuffing themselves with Gertrude's typical southern picnic fare: deviled eggs, southern fried chicken, buttermilk coleslaw, homemade lemonade, and strawberry cake.

Her knowledge of southern cooking came from her husband, Charles Reynolds, now deceased for 23 years. Gertrude was 15 years younger than her husband when they met in 1950 and married less than a year later. Unlike so many of her peers who took their husbands' last name,

Gertrude kept her own. In the 1950's that was almost unheard of. He was from Charleston, South Carolina, and she, born and bred in New York City. He, a southern gentleman banker with family money and a lineage that went back to the early 1700's, and she, a young Jewish analyst in training, a first generation American.

They met at a cocktail party held at the Museum of Modern Art. Both were standing in front of the newly acquired Jackson Pollock's No. 1, painted in 1948. Both were transfixed with the painting and neither had really noticed the other.

As Charles stared at it, he said out loud to no one in particular: "I have no idea why I love this painting. But it is magnificent."

And Gertrude responded by saying, "I love it because it makes me imagine what my life will be about."

They looked at each other, and he invited her to dinner. The rest was history.

They moved to the west coast in 1965 with their five-year-old daughter, Margot, who long ago had moved back to New York and, like her mother, married, also with one daughter, and had an analytic practice. Charles had his own investment company and when he died in 1990 at the age of 94, he and Gertrude enjoyed their later years giving money to worthy causes.

She enjoyed her work, which was why she did it. "It keeps my brain on the right track," she liked to explain.

But everyone knew Gertrude's brain didn't need any stimulation.

"It's the little-big engine that can," Richard liked to call Gertrude's brain.

They started to walk around the gardens, and Rebecca sidled up to Tom. "Hey, Tom, tell me . . . how do you like our world so far?"

Thoughtful, he nodded. "I like it."

She rooted around in her mind to find something to say other than, "So how's school?" But that's exactly what popped out, as Tom simultaneously laughed and said "Fine."

"You knew I was going to ask that." She looked at him.

"Yeah, I did." He smiled. Then he asked her, "What would you really like to know?"

This question—right back—took her off guard. *He's smart. Fast. Wow! I'm impressed.*

She stopped and stood still, looking around with her hands on her hips. The others were ahead, out of earshot. She turned to him.

"Your Uncle says you talk to a ghost."

He shoved his hands in his pockets and looked around.

"So, Uncle Daniel heard me out in his back yard a few weeks ago when the moon was full."

"I think so. Yes."

He looked down at his feet, as he drew a little circle in the path with his right foot. "Ok. He's been coming and talking with me for eight years. Started when I was ten."

"What do you think he wants?"

"He's been leading up to telling me something. He told me that last time. He said Uncle Daniel's in danger."

"Why?"

"Well, it goes back about 40 years. When Uncle Daniel was writing his dissertation on the Civil War. A friend of his . . . well, I guess he was a friend . . . was writing on the same subject, the war. They had a falling out. Big time. The other guy . . . Zak calls him Benjamin . . . accused Uncle Daniel of making up something, I mean, forging a letter with a friend. A letter he used as an original source in his dissertation. It was an eyewitness account of something important that happened toward the end of the war."

He let this sink in and waited for her to ask questions, but she didn't, so he went on.

"This Benjamin's accusation was taken seriously enough to cause Uncle Daniel to be expelled from the University and that guy became a professor. So, Uncle Daniel spent the next five years or so finding his friend, who was in Africa at the time, and finally he cleared himself and was reinstated."

"What happened to this Benjamin?"

"Yeah . . . well, then he got expelled and completely disappeared."

"Tell me . . . who's Zak?"

"Oh. Right. Sorry. Zak's my great-great-grandfather. Zachariah Winslow Perry. He's the ghost."

"Tell me about him."

He shrugged. "Well . . . I used to think he was just in my dreams. Seriously. I thought I just dreamt him sometimes and that's how I didn't let it freak me out. But now I know he's not. He seems to have a real purpose. I mean, he really wants me to know something. He didn't use to talk about anything, really . . . I mean, I thought he just wanted to impress me. But now he's really warning me that Uncle Daniel's in danger. By that guy, Benjamin."

"He actually named the danger 'Benjamin?'"

"Yeah. That's who he said."

"You know, Tom, most people will think all this is pretty far-fetched. I know there's a lot of ethos about ghosts of the Civil War, but most ghost-chasers are . . ." she hesitated.

"Nuts?"

"Well, yeah, I guess. I mean I know there's a lot of paranormal research going on, but to tell you the truth it's mostly pretty boring stuff, detailed to the point of ad nauseam. Not like your Zak, an ancestor who actually engages you in a real conversation. Mostly ghosts are just about random sightings."

He looked off into the treetops. "All I can say is I do think something's about to happen."

"You know what?" She looked at him. "I do too."

They both stood still, staring at the ground. "How would you feel . . ." she began tentatively . . . "about coming to see me at my office next week?"

"You're a shrink, right? Sorry, but that's what people I know call you guys."

"Yeah." She laughed. "I'm used to it."

"Well . . ." his voice was tentative . . . "are you saying I need psychological treatment or something?"

"No. I think you need someone you can talk to about this, sort of help you figure out what's going on."

As they stood in the path, Gertrude left the group and approached them.

Tom smiled at her.

It was obvious to Rebecca that he liked Gertrude. *Well, everyone likes her. She exudes ancient wisdom. And she's funny and modern and sharp. All ages want to get close to her. I used to be jealous, a little, but thank God I'm over that. Gertrude belongs to all of us. She's not the mother I always wanted. No. She's the Delphic Oracle we all yearn for. Only some of us don't know it. But I think this young man knows it.*

All three stood together in a huddle, and Tom didn't hesitate to tell Gertrude what they'd been talking about. As if he knew she already knew.

"A ghost . . ." Gertrude clapped her hands together gleefully. "We've been needing something juicy and interesting to discuss."

Rebecca explained to Tom that she would be consulting with Gertrude and possibly Richard as well. "Richard's got the Library of Congress's conveyor belt of storage marching through his brain. Ask him a question and trust me, you'll get an original, data-filled answer." This was a situation where a team approach would help.

His response was positive, and so Tom and Rebecca set a time to meet in her office the following Tuesday, day after tomorrow, at 3:00 p.m.

CHAPTER 11

"Captain, my religious belief teaches me to feel as safe in battle as in bed."
STONEWALL JACKSON

BENJAMIN LEFT BLANCO AND DREXEL to continue their research finding bank accounts.

The plan was to leave Drexel's trust account alone because any monies taken from that would be noticed immediately. Instead, several offshore, and not so offshore, accounts belonging to the father, William Dewitt, III, were located and incremental amounts of ten thousand were moved that would take some time to notice.

There would be a manhunt for Drexel, and Benjamin prided himself on his ability to provide a safe house for people to disappear. He bought cell phones by the carton to be used in emergencies.

Blanco's laptop was fire-walled by the little genius himself. "Discovery is impossible," Blanco would brag. "I's the Mannnn! In my world," he referred to a network of fellow hackers around the globe, "I'm 'Titus'— short for Titanium."

Blanco's buddies were the extreme underground of crazies, the hackers for whom not a single value conformed to the norm, any norm, except one. Loyalty to each other. None of the secret services in history—not even the inner sanctum of the Freemasons—could come near this group's underground inscrutability.

"That's 'cause we don't stand for anything, and we need nothing. That's real freedom," Blanco once explained to Benjamin, and so Benjamin told Blanco, "You are my archangel from under the bridge."

Blanco was flattered.

Benjamin took up his backpack and headed down the path into the woods about a quarter mile, before he descended down a steep ravine with switchback trail, through sprawling Manzanita and low shrubs. It was hot with the sun directly above, heading past midday. His head started to pound with the pain. He stopped, and stood in the shade of a tall ponderosa, lowered his pack to take out his canteen, jiggling it with the ice to make it cold. He reached in his pocket and pulled out a small plastic vial, popped the lid and dumped three Vicodin on his tongue. He didn't like taking it because the medicine could slow him down, but he needed it. *I can take a nap when I get there. No hurry. They'll watch him. I have his wallet and the car keys. Besides, I disconnected the carburetor, and something tells me ol' Drex doesn't fix his own cars.*

He continued to make his way down to the river, the South fork of the Trinity, stopping periodically to wipe his forehead with his yellow bandana, waving his hat to dry off some of the sweat mixing with the sunscreen that was irritating his eyes. He reached the river, smelling the algae on the rocks in the sun, sucking air as if he couldn't get enough.

The sound of the river always soothed him from childhood, and the long summer days of camping on the river with his grandfather.

He sat now on the rocky beach to rest, about a mile down river from the same campsite with his grandfather and watched a pair of hawks hunt along the high chaparral on the other side, gliding lazily, poised to dive for some innocent rodent hiding under the fir and ponderosa pine.

He felt like dead weight sitting on the beach at the river and wondered what it would be like if he just stopped breathing. This might be the spot. But he summoned himself with a clarion call to duty. *There's work to be done.* He recited the last stanza to rouse himself. *'The woods are lovely, dark and deep, But I have promises to keep, And miles to go before I sleep, And miles to go before I sleep.'*

He crossed the river, choosing each rock as the next stepping-stone, balancing himself with care. On the other side, he looked up, knew it would be a while, and spurred himself on confident that Drexel's money was going to speed things up. He was feeling the pressure for closure after so many years. He tried to think how many. *Thirty-five years?* There was a time when he almost decided to let it go. But then he had a dream.

He's standing in a forest filled with smoke. The mortar fire from the cannons pounds in his ears—boom after boom after boom. Through the poisonous atmosphere he hears the moaning. Paralyzed, he watches three buzzards squabble over a pile of entrails. He looks up and sees him. The old Stonewall himself, iconic sentinel, holding up his right arm. *He's confused. I know he's dead, but there he is.*

A lone rider comes up on the left and Stonewall doesn't move. The rider looks at him, and he feels scared by the grin that spreads over the rider's face, that becomes a clown. He recognizes Daniel as he raises his hand and pushes Stonewall, making him fall over on the ground like a rag doll. Daniel grins some more and rides off.

He woke shaking with rage hearing his own voice declare, *"Vengeance is mine; I will repay, saith the Lord."* The rage felt like cool water in a parched throat.

It took him two more hours trudging slowly up the steepest side of the river, following the ducks he'd placed years ago, because even he could get lost in these woods. No one as far as he knew had any idea about the cabin that had belonged to Cal Gates, an old geezer who died back in 1971.

During the summers from 1955, when Benjamin was nine years old, until 1960, he'd camped on the south fork of the river with his grandfather, Joe Wheelright—'Mighty Joe,' who could throw an axe from 30 yards and never miss. There was a small shack back in the woods, but close to a beach on the river's edge used by some of the old-time loggers who used it for their fishing gear. In those days, there were plenty of wild steelhead in the river.

Cal's father had come to the area during the Goldrush and built his cabin higher up from the side Benjamin now climbed, well hidden in the forest. He would come down some evenings to their campsite and bring some sort of homemade brew, strong stuff. Benjamin would listen to their stories as they sat around the campfire. Sometimes, Cal brought his old, battered guitar and he'd sing country songs like *Red Headed Stranger* and *Tumbling Tumbleweed.*

One time, his right hand was wrapped in bandages. As Benjamin stared at it, Cal said, "Com'ere boy. Let me show you something."

He unwrapped the gauze layers while re-wrapping it around his right hand, taking care to keep the ends even, raising his eyebrows in mock surprise to draw out the suspense. What came unveiled was Cal's thumb, the size of a squash and the color of eggplant.

Benjamin retreated—repulsed.

"It's one thing to not trust a rattler alive, but let me tell you, son, their fangs are just as lethal when they're dead, maybe more, 'cause when they're dead, you think you're safe and don't expect it. I killed this one the other morning, a big sucker about three and a half feet long, and when I slung it over my fence his mouth caught on my thumb just as if he was alive and goin' for me. Damned if that ol' bugger didn't bite just as bad when he was deader than a doornail." Cal held out his thumb.

Benjamin backed away.

"There's your proof, son."

He listened to their stories. His grandfather was originally from North Carolina, and so was Cal. Both had grandfathers who fought for the Confederacy in the Civil War.

Cal's grandfather was born in 1840 in Charleston and grew up in Mississippi on a farm. "He could ride a horse through any obstacle and shoot a target right in the bullseye at a full gallop. Nobody could outshoot my grandpap, Abel Gates. Known in every county far and wide. When the Civil War broke out General Forrester asked Abel to join his Escort Company. Best cavalry unit in the war. Only soldiers Grant ever really feared."

He learned that his own ancestor, Joe's grandfather, also named Benjamin, fought for the South, also in the cavalry, but not as elite as Abel's unit. Over these summers these heroes grew larger than life, and listening to Joe and Cal reminisce a portrait of a saga filled out.

Southern men were great warriors fighting to preserve a way of life that was about to disappear forever. In Benjamin's mind General Forrester was a flying God on his charger, whirling his carbon steel saber, a lightning bolt cast from the heavens above. Hearing of their exploits at Shiloh dazzled him. Whenever they talked about the aftermath of the war, he could feel their grief seep into his bones.

During those summers his imagination created a reality that became his calling in life. He would redeem the South, he would become Forrester, Joe and Abel, and Benjamin all in one, one for all. He would redeem their memories, a majestic rising as a tribute to their South that was taken away. His motto: "The North won the war, but the legacy never dies."

Later, during his graduate school years, long after Cal and Joe were gone, his studies of the Civil War convinced him more than ever of the superiority of the Confederacy's sublime cause. *A race of elitists, divinely driven.*

The fact that Forrester had not only owned slaves, but also traded in them as well, only meant in Benjamin's mind that he was a man of his time. The fact that he was the first Grand Dragon of the Ku Klux

Klan—disputed by many—only served to reinforce the man's mystique of zealotry, something Benjamin wanted and needed for himself.

Benjamin did not concern himself with the issue of slavery. On the contrary, he did not consider himself racist at all. In his child's mind the issue didn't exist. In his adult mind, the issue paled in comparison to the ideals of freedom and the right to defend a way of life that was heaven on earth.

One time, when a fellow graduate student told him, "Benjamin, you can't ignore the horrors of slavery," he imagined wearing a great bear skin over his head, draped down his back, sitting on his horse. Then his reply. "Slavery was never the issue. It would have died of its own accord."

That was it, his rationale. Truncated and swift—like the steel blade of his imaginative sword.

He arrived about 3:00 in the afternoon. The cabin was covered in grapevines that Cal had planted a century ago. Benjamin kept the slanted roof and siding shingled, and weather-proofed.

From the outside it still looked abandoned, but inside the floor was tiled and sealed. He used carpenters from the little town 25 miles away who had known about Cal and knew never to reveal its location. *Never.* Cal left the cabin and its half-acre to his grandfather and when Joe died in '77 he left it to Benjamin, and it was his sole inheritance, since there had been nothing from his parents.

He worked the code—4141861—the day Brigadier General P. G. T. Beauregard took command of Fort Sumpter. Also, the day the first soldier of the Civil War died, an accident from a gun powder discharge during the 50-gun salute Beauregard set off after taking command from the Union Major Robert Anderson. That day no one had any idea, neither North nor South, what was to come.

Inside the cabin it was cool and dark. The new bed he put in last year looked inviting beyond his dreams. But he couldn't indulge in a nap. Not yet. He had work to do. He opened the backpack on the table and put the supplies in the screened cooler that Cal had made.

Anything left in the cabin—the slightest edible—would be found by the Black Bears. He'd never been on a bear hunt with Cal and his brother, Jim, but Joe had.

Benjamin ate the bear meat when Cal would bring it down to the camp to barbecue. He expected it to be tough, but it wasn't. Not much different from beef, only greasier and a kind of sickening sweet taste to it.

He didn't like its strong flavor at first, but he also didn't want Cal and Joe to think he was a sissy, so he learned to like it.

When Cal and Jim headed out with their hounds, they'd stay out until Jim shot their bear with his Winchester 1890.

Benjamin heard more than once how to field dress a bear. The first time, he had to leave and throw up in the woods.

Cal and Joe waited until he returned so Cal could describe it from the beginning.

"After we got our bear we'd bleed it by cutting its throat, then cut from the breastbone to the neck area just below its jaw, cut through the ribcage muscles to expose the windpipe and gullet, break the breastbone which took two axes, slice open the stomach, separate the genitals from the abdominal wall and cut the skin all the way down to the pelvic bone, separate the anus from the pelvic canal, pulling it out with the bladder, intestines and the rectum, being careful not to let them or any droppings touch the meat, and, finally, separate the diaphragm and the ribs, pulling the esophagus and the windpipe through the chest, and, lastly, remove the heart and lungs. We had to do all that quick because bear meat spoils. Biggest bear we ever got, and I mean trophy size, was in the Spring of 1910—more than 500 pounds. Got his pelt on my cabin wall."

On the wall looking like the Rorschach card was the huge pelt. His mammoth head hung downward, his jaw open still, with shiny white molars indicating he had been a young male, in his prime.

Cal called him "Jimmy" after his brother, who died before Cal.

Benjamin liked Jimmy, who was now a hundred years dead. He thought of Jimmy as a talisman, a protective icon. Benjamin wasn't normally sentimental and only wanted to own what was essential, but some things were just special, and that was Jimmy.

He unlatched the back door, pushed it open and went down the path to the natural spring that seeped up out of the ground far below into a rock-lined pool that Cal had built, and Benjamin maintained. He took the old tin cup off the Manzanita branch and dipped it into the cool water and drank, thinking this is nirvana . . . cool water. As he drank, he heard Cal's voice singing the first stanza, substituting his brother's name for the original name of Dan:

"All day I've faced a barren waste

Without the taste of water, cool water.

Old Jim and I with throats burnt dry

And souls that cry for water."

Cal had built the cabin so he could be near the spring.

Benjamin pushed his canteen deep into the pool, letting it fill. Back in the cabin he sliced some bread and cheese and sat down into the old, rickety, leather Morris chair with another cup of the water. He gazed out at the trees and sky—chewing, drinking, listening.

He wanted to sleep, but he didn't let himself. He got up and walked over to the old roll-top desk, the one piece of furniture Cal prized just as much as Jimmy.

He sat in the old oak, high-back swivel chair and pulled the chain around his neck over his head and rubbed the little key between his thumb and forefinger before he inserted it to open the inner drawer. He cupped the papers and envelopes in his hand and set them down on the desktop. He took a clipped bunch of papers from the middle and laid them on the top. He fingered through until he came to the one page he wanted to read again. It was the last page of the last chapter of Daniel's dissertation. The last time he read it was ten years ago. He didn't want to read it ever again, but he felt he had to. He sighed deeply, and then read:

"If it were not for the extraordinary bravery of the black soldiers on June 7, 1863, at the little-remembered Battle of Milliken's Bend it is more than possible, as I have explained, that the War would not have ended after the fall of Vicksburg but would have gone on.

"Had the Confederate troops prevailed with their plan to re-take the west bank of the Mississippi and get in contact with Vicksburg and drive cattle across the river into the starving city, General Grant's position on the Yazoo might have been broken by Confederate."

General Johnston, and the force west of the river would have been in contact with the Vicksburg Garrison. As I quoted in the beginning of this dissertation, it all came down to Lincoln's own words, The key is Vicksburg. What has been lost to history, except for a few notations and one book on the subject, of the 1,410 troops left to defend the garrison, 1,250 were contrabands, all former slaves, who had been mustered on May 22, 1863, just 16 days before they were to go into battle with the seasoned, Confederate Division of 2,500. Texans known as Walker's Greyhounds. The raw contraband troops made up the First Mississippi and the

Ninth and Eleventh Louisiana.

"This encounter was one of the most bitter, hard-fought and bloody actions of the Civil War, ending in hand-to-hand combat with both sides fighting with bayonets and musket butts. The black contra-band troops proved not only that they could hold their own with the seasoned Confederate troops, essentially, they saved General Grant's ass. Sadly, this most ironic piece of history, which should be the source of stories and legends down through the ages, is a little. known footnote of the war.

"I will end with a quote from the letter I have referenced in a previous chapter, a letter never sent, never published, never before read by the general public, written by Ephraim Winslow Brown to Frederick Douglas: 'And so, Mr. Douglas, I pray that you will acknowledge and thus in some way make certain that what I experienced and saw on this fateful day of June 7, 1863, will go down in the annals of the history books as a most extraordinary and gratifying occasion for the Negro race. Although it has been our fate as a race to be so demeaned as to the point of being enslaved, it has also from this point forward been our fate to win a battle that must and will come to be acknowledged as the true end of the War on slavery in these great United States. The time has come for the white races to acknowledge our bravery and equality.'"

Benjamin didn't think of it as a grudge. This was a vendetta, and he was its martyr. He wanted Daniel dead. But dead wasn't good enough. He needed Daniel to face his life of idealistic and utter liberal stupidity, to face his lowly self. *For a self-centered autocratic academic to face the legacy that he got it all wrong would be the same as hell on earth. No one cared about Milliken's Bend. It was forgotten by both sides, North and South. And for good reason. Who would believe that just one incident could undo the will of God?*

I will believe to my dying day that Daniel wrote that letter himself. He got his friend to collude. Good forgers can authenticate anything. The ink can be reproduced, like the paper. I will never forget how he behaved when I accused him. He said nothing. I read the guilt all over his face. He thought he could get away with it. One stupid letter is proof of nothing. Yes, the battle was won by the contrabands. I never denied that. I simply called Daniel on his forgery. That's the liberal fakery. I hate it, and will stamp it out wherever, whenever I can.

At times, over the years, he wondered whom he was doing this for. *Me? The South? Posterity? No. I'm doing it for Mighty Joe, Cal and Jimmy.*

He looked at Jimmy's dead eyes. "You're my muse, Jimmy. On the night I finally kill Daniel Perry you, dormant these one hundred years, will be resurrected. I shall wear you and build you a mighty bonfire out of his flesh and bones that will illuminate the heavens. And all those great warriors shall see and hear my war cry hymn that lets them know tomorrow is a new day."

He had worked himself up. His heart was beating. He needed to calm down. Sifting through more pages he found the notes he'd written to himself in preparation for his own concluding page. His preliminary notes were more vivid and to the point than the actual last page.

"Lincoln was an old trickster. Odysseus had nothing over him. More wily than a cat, he was a shapeshifter, if ever there was one. Frontiersman, my foot! Lincoln was a study in urbane manipulation. He understood people and how to use them. Love the people? He wanted them to love him. Now he's a legend all over the world filled out with half-truths and simplistic homilies. A great warrior-general while McClellan has been demonized into oblivion as a coward. Except McClellan understood what Lincoln never could. A negotiated peace would have spared 600,000 lives—all those boys who walked into the fray to become cannon fodder . . . and for what? The war was a slaughterhouse to preserve a predator industrial North that killed a way of life people can now only dream about. There are remnants, but the real South was killed by Lincoln and his cronies.

"I never condoned slavery. Neither did Robert Lee or Stonewall Jackson, and many true Southerners. Slavery would have ended just as it did in England and the rest of Europe—of its own accord.

"The relationship between those Southerners and their Blacks was not always how its depicted. No one talks about that. No one mentions Thomas Jefferson and his black mistress and their children. And yet, it is one example of thousands.

"The blending began long before the Civil War.

"Racism was just as rampant in the North as the South, as many examples show, only the racism in the North came out in even greater ignorance, born of a more total unfamiliarity.

"My thesis: The Civil War could have been prevented and the peace that ensued out of reconciliation would have risen out of a familiarity between the Southerners who knew and understood the need for slavery to end and it would have ended without the sacrifice of 600,000.

"Note: Daniel forged the letter. He is a bogus liberal, like all of his ilk. Thoughtless. Insensitive. Self-centered. I will have him expunged."

Those words were 45 years old. He hadn't read them in a long time, but they rang true now as much as ever. He sifted through some more pages and found a scrap of paper with the quotes he now needed most.

"Always mystify, mislead, and surprise the enemy; and when you strike and overcome him, never let up in the pursuit. Never fight against heavy odds if you can hurl your own force on only a part of your enemy and crush it. A small army may thus destroy a large one, and repeated victory will make you invincible."

And then his eyes dropped down to the bottom of the page. He was more than ready for these words. He read them aloud to Jimmy, who continued to stare lifeless these hundred years.

"Let us cross over the river, and rest under the shade of the tree."

It was always Stonewall's words that soothed him.

CHAPTER 12

*It's the middle of the night. The air is filled with the sounds of battle—
the roar of cannons and the screams of soldiers.
The shadows of phantoms in blue and grey lurk in every corner.*

FRANK SPAETH, *PHANTOM ARMY OF THE CIVIL WAR
AND OTHER SOUTHERN GHOST STORIES.* LLEWELLUYN PUBLICATIONS, 1997, P. 1

THAT EVENING, THE DAY OF THE PICNIC, Richard and Rebecca lounged in their living room with light snacks since they had stuffed themselves with Gertrude's picnic. They were both unusually quiet, and even the Queens slept—Juno with her back legs spread out behind her, chin on front paws, and Dido curled around Richard's feet as he sat in the big, overstuffed chair.

Rebecca took a sip of her wine, looked at him. "What did you think of Tom?"

"Nice young man. Daniel should feel proud. Even some of his features reminded me of Daniel."

"Yes." She agreed. "He speaks directly. No guile. He seems to have none of that angst that plagues so many teenagers, or he's grown out of it. He's so humbly smart. That's not so much like Daniel, who is not what I would describe as humbly smart. Daniel's humbly arrogant, know-it-all smart. There's a difference. But I agree, some of Tom's gestures certainly are reminiscent of his uncle."

She leaned over to pick up her glass again, and as she lifted it, she put it back down. "He's telling the truth you know."

"Yes, I agree. I think he is too."

"Well, ok, Mr. Know-It-All, tell me . . . how can this happen? How can it be real? He's talking to a ghost for heaven's sake!"

The rheostat shifted dramatically from calm to a level of passion they were used to when a real discussion was about to begin.

This was the point that Richard, if he still smoked a pipe, would be reaching for his tobacco pouch, eyebrows furrowed. Instead, he reached over and put some soft cheese on a cracker and popped it into his mouth.

This roused Dido at his feet, which in turn roused Juno. Both dogs stood to watch Richard chew. They weren't beggars, but their behavior was a game to see which one could spot a stray crumb that might fall on the Persian carpet. But this morsel of food was being crunched whole.

For Richard, chewing was a form of deep thinking.

"Did you know that there are so many ghost hunters out at night in the Gettysburg cemeteries with their flash cameras that they've literally become a public nuisance for the locals?"

"No. I didn't know that."

"Well, I'm not sure of the statistics, but I think the Civil War has spawned more ghost stories than any other war in history." He brushed a cracker crumb off his knee. "And perhaps that's because there's still so much unfinished business around our Civil War that haunts the nation."

She petted Juno's head. "That's an interesting fact, but it's not answering my question."

"You're wondering how a normal kid like Tom—normal and intelligent—could be doing something so completely abnormal."

"Yes. I am wondering. Aren't you?"

"Well . . . not as much as you are."

She took a deep breath. "Richard, it would be nice if you could be a little less oblique and try to remember that we mere mortals cannot always connect the dots of your inner mind."

As she said this, she knew he would take his own sweet time anyway. He enjoyed the visual process of his own thoughts, and this kind of dialog, especially with Rebecca, was a pleasure for him, and he intended to draw it out.

He laughed. "I know you'd like the bottom line, and I'm not your man for that, so . . . may I proceed at my snail's pace? I'll try to make it an interesting journey, and I promise . . . if I'm making no sense, you have my permission to interrupt."

She leaned back into the couch pillows, curled up her legs, droped her sandals, picked up her glass of wine, and bowed her head forward. "Proceed, Mein Herr Professor."

"Thank you," he nodded. "Although the "Herr" wasn't necessary." His eyes twinkled. "Ok. The latest neuroscience confirms what I believe many in your field assumed all along . . . and that is our ancestors live on in our DNA. Instincts are hard-wired. Of course, it's also true that the brain allows us to lose our accumulated and distilled experiences of thousands of previous generations in a single lifetime. We lose the wisdom of previous generations when cultural customs are dropped. And here in our own country, even though we espouse family values . . . we've pretty much adopted the umbrella value of the nuclear family and the cult of individualism. Children are now raised to be special individuals, not part of a community, where being special is not so valued. But some pockets of individuals retain the memories."

As he spoke, she looked out the window at the fog coming in. She knew he was starting on a roll, and it occurred to her that the fog was now a perfect metaphor. Moving slowly, inexorably—retaining its density. He would follow his mind like a hound, not editing or caring whether it was completely accurate, or made total sense. Richard's intuition would lead him inexorably to an interesting and unique conclusion.

"Genetics does not weed out the instincts of our forebears after several generations as some believe. Instincts and customs of behavior become hard-wired in the brain. Take these Chows for example . . . you always know they're Chows, not just by their appearance," he looked at Dido's great halo of reddish hair as she leaned forward to attempt a slurpy lick on his face . . . "but Chows are not particularly interested in other dogs. They're aloof. They instinctively know the difference between friend and foe and behave accordingly. If a stranger walked through that front door," he nodded at the door, "without our permission, they'd attack. If Daniel . . . no, let's say Tom, whom they've never met, just walked through that door they'd instinctively know from our tone and response to him that he's a friendly. They'd get up and tentatively wag their tails."

"Yes. Ok. You're right. I have a lot of thoughts stirring, but do go on."

"Well, we humans have that too. Our emotions are pretty much hard-wired, based on instinct. We're a little more complicated genetically, but not by that much."

She smiled. "Ok. Are we going to get to the ghosts?"

"Oh yes, we will." He slowly spread more cheese on another cracker. His appetite was whetted now. "Let me present you with a 'what if' scenario . . . and then I'll circle back and offer some science . . . since you're so impatient." He offered her a cracker.

"No thanks."

"What if I told you that Tom is psychic, and what I mean by that is his brain is perfectly attuned between his right and left hemispheres. His logic mind and intuitive mind are in perfect harmony. And that means neither side dominates the other. He is completely open to all his experiences . . . he doesn't edit or pre-determine by thinking he knows what's going to happen, or why. Most of us by age 16, or thereabouts, probably think we've got it all figured out, so not much learning happens after that. Too much doubt has crept into the creative imagination, and the plasticity of the brain has hardened. Thinking has become more concrete." He paused to sip his wine.

She could feel her impatience rising as she watched him swallow contentedly. *I've got to learn patience. He's following a train of thought and I know him . . . he'll come out the other end of the tunnel with something I never could. This is why I love you, Richard . . . and my God how you try my patience.*

He smiled as if he read her thoughts. "Ok, so far?"

"I'm listening." She smiled sweetly.

"And then there's the whole business of the ancestors. Those folks we descend from. Most Americans don't really pay much attention to that topic. The ancestry of our country is only little more than a few hundred years old. Where we all came from before that is of little interest for the most part. We project great status on those who came over on the Mayflower, or thirty years later on the Arabella, and their descendants. But in the rest of the world, a few hundred years is nothing."

He stopped for a moment to pet Dido's head.

"And then, of course, we pay little attention to our own original people . . . many of whom were here thousands of years, some up to 30,000. Now that's ancestry for you. And many of the tribes retain their ancient ways through religion and rituals. All over the world . . ." he waved his arms, once again rousing the dogs . . . "there are countries whose people still hold onto their ancient ways."

She agreed. "Yes. Like Africa, Asia, Europe . . . Australia, New Zealand."

"Yes. Like all those continents. Much, much older civilizations—and more intact. Of course, everyone who came here in the 17th and 18th centuries came from one of those civilizations."

"So, Richard, are you claiming that we all carry within our DNA . . . how shall I put it? . . . memory of our ancestors, only as a culture Americans don't take that very seriously?"

"Well, yes. That's putting it simply. Neuroscience is catching up with that notion."

He sipped his wine.

"Your ancestors are what we Americans call Scots-Irish. You carry some of their racial traits. You may not realize it."

"Like what?" she asked, a little too quickly.

He laughed, knowing he was treading on precarious ground. He started with the positive traits. "Well, you're passionate, adventurous, hard-working and spiritually oriented." He waited for her reaction. She maintained a neutral gaze that he recognized came from her professional training.

But it didn't fool him. "And . . ." he plunged ahead . . . "you're also impatient, a bit stubborn, a little bellicose when aroused . . ."

"Bellicose!" she burst out.

"No, I mean . . ." he searched frantically for the right words . . . "when threatened you do not back down. You'll fight back. That's one of your many traits I love. You're not easily intimidated."

"And you think I'm different from others?"

"Well, take Gertrude. She's German American. Viennese parents. Came here to escape Hitler. Gertrude's got a calm, analytical, poetic mind. She's like cool, calm water. You're wild, like volcanic fire. Gertrude's Athena. And you're Artemis."

"Ok. I'll go with your analogy for the moment."

"All right. I know Daniel's ancestors are from Scandinavia. Norwegian, I think. So that means Tom is too, at least on his mother's side. Just in passing, the Norwegian Vikings landed on our east coast about 400 years before Columbus. So, where was I? . . . oh yes. So, I'm not sure about Tom's dad. But I remember at our dinner a few weeks ago when Daniel talked about his sister, he said she didn't blink when Tom told her about Zak . . . the four-great-grandfather who fought at Antietam."

Rebecca remembered. "Yes, but what do you make of that?"

"Well, I'll make a giant leap with that. Tom and his mother share a genetic trait. The fact that he speaks to a ghost who's one of their ancestors does not surprise either of them. They just accept that. Now, think about the Norwegian Vikings . . . what comes to mind when you think about them?"

She frowned but decided to play the game. "Well . . . I'm pretty sure they were clannish . . . you know, family came first. They weren't afraid of death. They believed they joined their ancestors when they died. And, oh yeah . . . I think honor was a big deal to them."

"All right . . ." he agreed. "Then let's suppose Tom and his mother, without realizing, have retained some kind of connection to their ancient past. And if we throw a little modern science into the mix, there is a connection, an energy field between the past, present and future. And keep in mind, the belief in energy fields—our nuclear physics—is ancient. The belief that all humans are connected within a subatomic field. And we humans have 100 billion neurons in our individual brains. Interconnected neurons, half of which are up in the cerebral cortex . . . all that gray matter up here." He pointed to his head. "Neurons contain the DNA, which is our hereditary, our genetic material."

A memory came to her. "I remember when you and Daniel went through your Epicurean phase. You were both fascinated with the idea that the ancient Greeks actually understood modern quantum physics."

"Yes. Well, let's take all that a step further and, as I said, I'd circle back to the question about why I'm not so surprised that Tom speaks to a ghost."

"Please do," she urged.

Well, so we have two ingredients necessary for connection to the ancestors. A completely open mind to any experience, and an assumption that we humans are all connected—past, present and future—in a subatomic energy field. Now, there needs to be a third ingredient."

Ah . . . he's coming to the point at last. The denouement of his pursuit. A third ingredient. "So, what's the third?"

He scooped up a handful of mixed nuts, studied them in the palm of his hand, picked through them for the cashews first, and then one by one he ate and chewed. When he was done eating the nuts, he brushed his hands to get rid of the excess salt.

"Ok." He slurped some wine. "Here's the third. The battle of Antietam produced one of the bloodiest days of the whole Civil War. That was September 17, 1862. Many believe it is almost inevitable that Antietam has become associated with the ghosts of the combatants. Twenty-two thousand were either killed, wounded, or missing on that day."

He paused, as if he were actually experiencing the pain of a memory.

Then he went on.

"On that day the worst of the fighting happened along what they called the sunken road, which later was called 'Bloody Lane.' Later the slaughter there was regarded by veterans as probably the worst day of the war. At that site, the veteran 'Irish Brigade' from New York lost two thirds of its men—about 600. The Confederates fared almost as badly. The dead lay four or five bodies deep in the Bloody Lane."

She thought his eyes were tearing. She felt the spell of the horror as he described it. He seemed almost in a trance.

And then, suddenly, he snaped out of it. "So, Bloody Lane is a hot spot. It's an especially powerful spot. A majority of ghostly or supernatural phenomena have been encountered there."

"Is that the third ingredient you're talking about? There needs to be a hot spot?"

"Yes. And that one's perfect. The bodies of the powerful Irish Brigade. Piles of corpses. Both Confederate and Union soldiers. In bloody conflict. And with no resolution. The war should have been over after that battle, but it wasn't. It went on for two more years. If there is such a thing as a restless soul, a soul that can't leave its earthly attachment . . . what better than such an unresolved, bitter conflict than that war . . . epitomized by that day on that road . . . at that particular time, and place?"

"So, when Tom meets Zak . . . somehow Zak transmits through that energy hot spot?"

He looked at her. "Something like that. If you can imagine it, then it could be true."

She nodded. "Yeah. It kind of makes sense."

At this point, they both decided that they'd gone far enough into this gray matter area and decided to take the Queens for a walk.

Later that evening, just as she was falling asleep, Rebecca realized how much she was looking forward now to really talking with Tom.

CHAPTER 13

All bodies of matter are in motion. To understand this best,
remember that the atoms do not have a place to rest,
and there's no bottoms to the Universe since Space does not have limits,
but is endless.

LUCRETIUS, THE NATURE OF THINGS, PENGUIN BOOKS, 2007
BOOK II: THE DANCE OF THE ATOMS, PP. 38-39

THE FOLLOWING DAY, MONDAY, was Daniel's fifth class for the summer, with three more to go. He and Tom would have a break for a month before Tom started classes in the fall and Daniel would continue to work with his graduate students.

He decided it might be good to take Tom north for a few weeks to show him the rest of northern California—up the coast to the Giant Sequoias, and then perhaps back down 395 that separates the eastern Sierra escarpment from the desert lands to the east, stopping at places like King's Canyon and on through the Owen's Valley, so he could at least gaze up at Mt. Whitney. He imagined they would camp most of the time. Death Valley was too hot in the summer, but he could tell Tom about it, and they would sit around the campfire in the evening. He could teach him about basin and range, and perhaps even talk about ghosts.

He knew Tom would see Rebecca soon, and he hoped that with both Rebecca and Gertrude, somehow more light would be shed on the mystery of Tom's ghost. He already knew Richard's theory. He didn't completely disagree, but he and Richard had a long history of enjoying their debates on any subject from the Civil War to which brand of under fifty-dollar single malt scotch was best—Glenfiddich or Glengoyne. Since they both liked both, sometimes they forgot which side they'd each last argued for. They debated like puppies, enjoying the sport of growling and biting, as if they were continually in training for the real thing. Underneath the bites and snarls was mutual respect.

Tom ran into Beth just before class started. They sat together, this time closer to the front.

Daniel made his entrance a few minutes late, as usual, hair untamed, and Tom noticed that one sock was blue and the other closer to a shade of pale green. Maybe an effort was made to match up two socks as best he could. Probably not noticeable to most, but Tom had gotten to know him.

He told his mother on the phone the day before, "Mom, Uncle Daniel needs a wife. He can't even tie his own shoelaces."

Carol Ann, always the one to point out the positive elements in any situation, said, "Well, hon, Daniel was always the smart one in our family. And you know how smart people can be . . . they don't pay much attention to these smaller things in life. Why, I remember when we were growing up, he would almost always forget something when he got to school . . . you know, like his jacket, his lunch, his homework . . . you name it."

"But your grandmother—God rest her soul—would drop it off for him when the principal called. Miss Lyon was her name. She'd tell your grandmother, 'I'm afraid Daniel needs such and such and would you mind bringing it on over,' and your grandmother would stop whatever she was doing and take it over to the school. She never complained. That's just the way it was. She'd say, 'Carol Ann, he's a genius. Not like the rest of us.'"

"Well, Mom, I don't agree with Grandma. Out here at the University, he's one of many." He paused. "And, Mom, just for the record, I want you to know you're just as smart—only in a different way."

"Bless you, Tom. And you know what I really think?"

"No, what?"

"You're smarter than all of us. You have heart, Tom. And without that I don't put too much stock in plain ol' genius. His heart really is in the right place—most of the time. He's just a little rough around the edges, and without Anna . . . well, I think he's sort of lost. I understand he has a new companion, and she sounds very nice."

"Yeah, she is. But I think she doesn't want a baby on her hands. I like her, and I don't think she wants to coddle him."

"Well, I understand Tom, but you know me . . . that's what I do. So, for me . . . please take care of him."

"Ok, Mom. I miss you. Tell Dac they play football out here too."

She laughed, and they hung up.

Daniel wrote across the blackboard with bold strokes as if he wanted to punctuate his point by using up the entire little bit of chalk.

"Contrabands. Carpetbaggers. Civil Rights."

He whirled around and jumped right in, a technique Tom decided that Daniel developed to catapult them into the central issues before they could scratch their heads or think very much.

"Let's connect the dots. Who wants to start?"

He panned his leering smile across them, especially catching the ones who averted their gaze, hoping he wouldn't notice them. As usual, silence was their first defense, until some brave soul would take the plunge, knowing they would be rewarded with Daniel's eager-beaver grin, accompanied by "yes, yes, yes . . . keep going," even if the plunge was only into shallow water.

They knew Daniel liked the Socratic style of picking out pieces of the puzzle, letting them grope their way into making their own sense of things. Open-ended questions elicited all kinds of responses, but Daniel had a knack for piecing it all together in the end, making it look like they'd already come up with the theory or answer he'd had in mind. Their reward was being told that they knew it all along, only they didn't know they knew.

Twenty seconds ticked by. Longer than usual.

Then Neal Viner in the front row cleared his throat, a prelude for his oratory, which usually propounded more form than substance.

"Yes, Mr. Viner," Daniel bellowed. "Do begin, and allow us all to breathe a little easier."

"Well, General Benjamin Butler coined the phrase in 1861, I believe. At Fort Monroe in Virginia, he refused to return three runaway slaves to their masters, and instead declared them to be 'contraband' of war." He stopped there, perhaps the extent of his knowledge, or perhaps not wishing to venture further into connecting the dots until he'd heard more clues from the others.

Another student raised her hand, and Daniel gestured his permission.

"We have to remember that the Fugitive Slave Act of 1850 was the law of the land in 1861. So, claiming that fugitive slaves were actually the contraband of war changed the whole deal. By deferring to a higher court of international law that claimed all property of an enemy might be seized quickly became a counter play to the South's use of the Fugitive Slave Act, where none had been there before. So, the Union started holding the slaves as contraband goods and refused to return them to the enemy's country, which was the Confederate states, and turned those contrabands into soldiers."

"Yes," Daniel explained, "under the strict law of nations, all the property of an enemy might be seized, and under the Common Law, the property of traitors is forfeit. That's all correct. So, tell me, what was Lincoln's response to this stand, precipitated by General Butler?"

Silence.

"Come on . . . think. How would Lincoln and his cabinet have responded to this upstart General?"

Neal raised his hand. "Not you Mr. Viner."

Daniel pointed at a young woman in the back. "Miss . . ." he couldn't remember her name.

"Laurel Greene," she smiled.

"Tell us Miss Greene . . . what do you think Lincoln's reaction was?"

"Well . . ." she hesitated, but after Daniel shrugged as if to say any answer will do, she plunged in. "I'm sure Lincoln was mostly concerned about doing anything that was contrary to the Constitution, while also worrying about upsetting some of the border states who might be pushed into more sympathy to join the Confederacy. At that point, Lincoln and his cabinet were still hoping then for some kind of early, peaceful settlement to the war. They still had no real idea about the ferocity of the South and what was to come."

Daniel smiled at her. "Well put."

He looked around.

"Yes, remember my friends, Lincoln was a consummate political tactician. In 1861, he did not, and I repeat, did not wish to piss off the South any more than he had." He paused, always aware of the time and knowing where he wanted to drive them to their conclusions.

"Ok, what's the upshot here? I mean from our historical perspective. We know that in 1861 Congress supported Butler by passing the first Confiscation Act in August 1861, and then in July 1862 passed a Second Confiscation Act expanding the rights outlined in the first. This meant those contraband slaves could be used to fight in the Union army, which later they did, honorably and without much acknowledgement."

"But let's move on. Connect some more dots."

He tapped his chalk on "Carpetbaggers." "Let's start weaving some threads."

He pointed to another young man who had rarely spoken. He knew his name. "Mr. Baker . . . Carl, tell us what you think." He knew Baker was smart but rarely spoke, out of shyness. Choosing him at this point was a strategic move on Daniel's part.

"Ok. The term 'carpetbagger' is an intentional insult Southerners used to describe Northerners after the War who traveled south to try to make money off the impoverished South. It's a term that has come to describe any outsiders who move into some new place in order to take advantage of the local people." He spoke softly and carefully. "Some of my family members still live in Georgia, and they still tell stories about the damn Yankees coming down to run their state governments. I think the link between the Contrabands and the Carpetbaggers puts perspective on what it must have been like for those proud Southerners, not only to tolerate the shame of having the rest of the country force them to do the right thing, but then along came the carpetbaggers to rub it in even more. The hatred by 1865 was so extreme that the end of the Civil War was just the beginning of a more insidious, underground war fueled by memory, resentment, and rage . . . that still rages on today. My Grandmother liked to quote Mark Twain who said '. . . in the South the war is what A.D. is elsewhere; they date from it.' My grandmother was a librarian and for some reason she talked a lot about Twain's writings about the Civil War. She told me that Mark Twain understood the contradictions in this country better than anyone. How the original democratic ideal of states' rights was completely killed by Federal troops in the South during the ten years of Reconstruction, and when it ended in a standoff . . . well that ushered in an even greater polarity between the whites and the blacks."

He paused to see if he was on the right track.

Daniel liked this student. He was connecting some dots. "Let me remind the class, in case you've forgotten, Samuel Clemens was a Southerner. Born in Missouri. "

"Carry on Mr. Baker."

"Well, I just think my grandmother always had a point. The Civil War made imperialists of Americans. I mean, she said that Twain understood the contradictions inherent in using Federal control over states' rights that robbed the South not only of being able to regain its dignity on its own, but precipitated a backlash of even more hatred and polarity between the races. And when she told me that, it was when she was telling me about the death of Martin Luther King and the Civil Rights Movement in the sixties."

"Good. Now we're getting somewhere."

Daniel looked around. "What good came out of the Civil War? Everyone. One-word answers. Let's hear them."

"Saved the Union."

"The Emancipation Proclamation."

"Produced the greatest president we've ever had."

"The 13th Amendment making slavery illegal."

"The 14th Amendment stating that all people born in the United States are considered natural citizens with the same rights as all other Americans."

"The 15th Amendment protecting the voting rights for African Americans."

They started to peter out. He knew they would.

"What bad has come out of the Civil War?"

There was another long silence.

He looked at Beth and Tom.

She started. "The crushing of the South under Federal law created an even greater backlash than would have happened if the Federal government had not intervened."

Tom added on to Beth's statement. "I read Mark Twain's *The Gilded Age*. From 1870 to 1900 the industrial economy driven by the North exploded. There was vast wealth, which created a greater divide between rich and poor."

Others chimed in.

"Yeah, but industrial growth improves our lives."

"But not everyone shares in the wealth. Like now. There are the mega-rich and let's face it—the mega-poor—and never the twain shall meet!" They all laughed at the pun because the student hadn't realized she'd made one.

Daniel jumped in. "Ok. Let's summarize. The Civil War ushered in major changes—all supposedly for the moral good of the country. But look what happened. An inherent contradiction, that is the use of Federal power to force the southern states to keep in line was a breach of the original ideals those guys we call the Founding Fathers believed in. All of them, some more, some less but they all wanted states to retain their right to govern themselves. That was the democratic ideal. But the backlash against big government opened the floodgates for economic predators to exploit those very freedoms that were taken to be self-evident. No one understood the natural inclinations of human beings when all restrictions are lifted. The African Americans had to fight for their rights for the next hundred plus years. The Civil War amendments gave them their ammunition. And now we have a black president. But we still have a lot of the same inflammatory ingredients we saw in the thirty years after the Civil War. A case can be made that our Civil War never ended."

He stopped with that statement.

"Ok, everyone. You know what we'll discuss next class. Parallel threads. Are we any better, or worse—developmentally speaking—between now and 1870? Ponder that question. I'll see you next week."

After class she invited Tom for coffee at her café where Mitch worked. He wouldn't know it of course, but she was Morrigan—not that sanctimonious Beth—and she enjoyed the class

After coffee, outside on the sidewalk, he started to wave goodbye and turned away when she called out, "Hey, do you want to see where I live?"

"Well, I saw where you keep your car, isn't that where you live?"

"Yeah, she laughed. I'm inviting you to come in, really, see where I live."

He shrugged. "Ok. I don't really have any plans. Sure. Show me where you live."

They walked through the streets, occasionally bumping shoulders, discussing what had been said in class.

When they got to her house, they climbed the outside stairs that led up to her second story brownstone, a house converted for students. She unlocked the door, and he followed her in. It was a large room with dormer windows that looked out over a somewhat neglected, but once well-groomed, garden—still green and watered.

She dropped her backpack near the desk. Her double bed against the wall looked out at trees and sky.

"Make yourself at home," she said. "I've got my own bathroom too." She disappeared behind the door. He sat down in the old leather chair that faced the bed and looked around. A fairly typical student's room with small desk, laptop, a few CD's, some books, a coffee cup full of pencils and pens. She had one photograph on the wall—an Ansel Adams photograph of a moon just coming up over a rocky escarpment.

He liked that one, too.

She had a vase of peonies on the side table by her bed. The room smelled like fresh air.

He closed his eyes and felt at peace. *Daniel's class had been stimulating. Actually, over-stimulating.* He wanted to rid his mind of it long enough to create some distance, to get some perspective on what he really felt. Something Zak had said once played in his mind.

He never knew whether he actually fell asleep or not. But when he opened his eyes, he thought he'd been dreaming, when he heard the voice say his name.

He opened his eyes and saw her sprawled across the edge of the bed wearing short shorts and a pink undershirt. Her legs dangled out over the bed. Clearly, she'd changed her clothes from cargo pants, sweatshirt and tennis shoes to what . . . something a little more comfortable? She didn't look like herself, but he couldn't exactly put his finger on what was different. She leaned on her side, cat-like and grinned at him.

All she needs is a lollipop. The only book of Nabokov's that he'd read that summer when his parents were gone was *Lolita.* He remembered looking forward to reading more of Nabokov and when he learned what his books were all about, he felt embarrassed that the only one he'd read was *Lolita.* But here she was. In the flesh. Lolita!

Embarrassed? Yes, he was. Confused? More so. Scared? Absolutely.

"Wanna have sex?"

He wasn't sure he'd heard correctly. But he stayed cool and said nothing. From his childhood book came the line from Uncle Remus. "Brer Rabbit? He lay low."

She held his gaze, toe to toe.

He blinked first. "Beth, I really like you. But I admit, somehow, you're scaring me."

She held his gaze like a laser beam into his eyes.

And then, suddenly—she cracked. Her laughter was a high-pitched giggle.

He stood up slowly, as if she were a python poised to strike. He went to her and pulled her head to his thigh and kissed the top of her head.

As he headed for the door, he turned to her. "See you in class on Thursday."

She'd pulled the pillow over her head.

He wasn't sure, but he thought she was crying—softly, deeply.

CHAPTER 14

Now I know what a Ghost is. Unfinished business, that's what.
SALMAN RUSHDIE

SHE SLEPT FOR THIRTEEN HOURS, waking only once. In the dream he came at her in the dark. No face. But she knew it was Papa Cat all the same. He was a giant and could have held her in his hand, but she hopped around like a little bird, skittering under the bed into the deeper dark. He sang the hymn in his sing-songy bass voice, sounding just like Robert Mitchem in *The Night of the Hunter*. He had taught her the alternate version of the refrain, the one he liked better:

"Leaning on Jesus, leaning on Jesus, safe and secure from all alarms;
Leaning on Jesus, leaning on Jesus, leaning on the everlasting arms."

She made herself tiny, backing up against the wall hearing the pull of the melody—its hollow trust in the Lord. That's how he seduced them all with his haunting refrains, and this was the one he taught her.

His big hand came searching under the bed moving like a crab sideways and back—she heard the melody with different lyrics: feeling, feeling to do everlasting harm. Just as his fingers stood up looking like legs coming toward her with searching eyes, she gasped awake.

She didn't think that she'd been screaming, but she was pretty sure she'd been trying to, and nothing came out. But, then again, she wasn't sure. She didn't want anyone knocking on her door asking if she was ok. She got up and sat on the toilet, head in her hands, rocking.

That wasn't the first time she'd had the dream. Each time he sang the refrain and each time she made herself small to get away. He was after her in that slow, methodical, reassured way he had. It wasn't like precision, but more like sleepwalking, but it was always mesmerizing and sometimes she was amazed that she was the only one who noticed.

Her mother was completely blind to any danger. Her blind love was pathetic, made more so by the fact that he regarded her with veiled contempt, invisible to all except her. She could never tell her mother. *You can't explain to a blind person something they can't see.* She wondered if he knew she knew. *He probably did.*

She knew Benjamin was a creepy type of genius. *Probably really is like Jesus, who must have been quite a creep himself hanging out with his fringey crowd of true believers, all waiting around for some kind of miracle like it was money. No wonder so many sects or cults looked like that. Well, Benjamin had his bag of tricks too.*

People would come to live with them periodically, and then would disappear without a trace. *And no one asked any questions. That was some trick.*

Her head throbbed and finally she put herself back to bed curling up into a fetus, the quilt covering her like a protective tent.

Five hours later, she woke up. It was a little after 9:00 a.m. Her head still hurt, but she was too exhausted to get out of bed to look for Tylenol. She lay there, staring out her window, glad the fog was in, cocooning her mood that bordered on hysteria. She knew how to calm herself to stave off the panic. She felt Tom's lips on her head, which brought on the tears that relieved the build-up of shame that could boil over any moment into panic.

She didn't remember what she'd done. But the skimpy, white shorts and pink, huggy t-shirt told her that Sugar Pie had made an appearance. Her face burned with rage. I'm going to annihilate that little Bitch! She knew that Sugar Pie was losing her edge and would be the first to go—unlike Beth, whom she needed. But not for long.

For now, her concern was her headache first, and then she needed to remember: *what the fuck happened? Did we have sex? Somehow, I don't think so. Sugar Pie would never have packed it in so early. Once the rumpus starts, she won't quit until the last drop is drunk and the poor guy—whoever he was—pled for mercy.*

Still, she never intended Tom would meet Sugar Pie. Never. And now she knew he had. The damage was done, and she had no idea if it could be repaired. *How to find out?*

She closed her eyes and mercifully fell asleep again.

This time, in the dream she was walking along a narrow trail. On her left were grassy meadows with Poppies and Lupins—brilliant orange and purple. The rolling hills of California in the Spring. She couldn't take her eyes off the beauty of it, and yet a roaring sound on her right pulled her away. She looked down where sixty feet below was a raging surf, waves spewing over the rocks and crashing on the narrow, craggy shore. She felt the conflict between her left and right landscape not wanting to move and yet pulled along the trail as if on a conveyor belt, as though some force was going to make her experience this horrifying contrast. Until she came to a path that took her inland, up to a little cottage.

The landscape once again became serene. The front door was open. She climbed up the steps to the porch and walked in. She felt at home, safe. He came in from the other side. Tom. All smiles. His arms open.

She woke up about noon. The headache had subsided. It was still there, but she knew it would wear off.

She crawled out of bed and found her cell phone and texted him. "Hi. I slept mega-long. Just wanted to say 'hi.'"

She went into her bathroom and took a shower, washing her hair over and over. She came out with her head furled upward in a blue wrapper, her body cloaked in her Hawaiian Plumeria towel, and flipped the switch on her hot water kettle. When it boiled, she waited and then poured it slowly into the small carafe before pressing the plunger. She forced herself to slow down and be patient, but she was worried. Sipping it from her thick white vintage mug she dared to look at her phone. Nothing. She went back into the bathroom and started to comb her tangled hair. Looking into the mirror she winced as she impatiently pulled at her snarls making herself tear up with the pain. She felt hurt and angry and betrayed. *So, what else is new? I have taught myself not to care, and look at you now, you fucking little wimp.* She leaned into herself in the mirror and it was then she heard the "chirp." She tried not to rush, but she couldn't help it. She looked at the phone.

"Hi you too."

She felt the adrenalin leave her body, not realizing how tense she had been.

Then she heard the second "chirp." The adrenalin rose. *My body's a fucking roller coaster.*

She looked. "You ok?"

Grabbing the phone, she tapped too fast and typed "I'm nine" instead of "I'm fine." Her fingers on automatic tapped "send." Jerkily, she corrected it. "Oops! I meant fine."

He responded, "Good. See you Thursday in class."

His response threw her into a mix of emotions. *He's being nice, maybe even condescending. He doesn't want to get together. He's embarrassed and wants to avoid me.*

She couldn't stop the obsessive speculation. She almost wanted to conjure Sugar Pie, as if she could, and get her to do something. *The little tramp!* But Sugar Pie knew how to handle men.

She consoled herself, something she'd learned to do. Maybe it meant he didn't think her behavior was really as bizarre as it was. She knew that some guys like the erratic, sexual stuff. She shivered. She wanted to think Tom wasn't like that. She concluded, for the moment, *I really don't understand this romance thing. I've never had a boyfriend. Never cared. Not interested in women either. I left all of that to Sugar Pie. Now I hate Sugar Pie. She may ruin my life.*

She dressed and went out to the café with her book, *Shaara's Killer Angels*, that Tom had recommended.

"Hey, Mitch," she greeted him, wanting to sound normal like her old self. She needed to feel normal.

"Howya doin?"

The good thing about Mitch was that he was always the same.

"The usual?"

"Yeah. I'll be in the back."

She found her table under the watchful eye of the Ku Tiki and started to read the first sentence of the first chapter. "He rode into the dark of the woods and dismounted."

At 2:40 that afternoon Rebecca sat in her office contemplating her meeting with Tom. He was due at 3:00. Her conversation the night before with Richard played through her mind. His comment at the end about epigenetics left her wondering. When Richard went off on his tangents of interest she often felt left in the dust.

But he knew she could be hooked eventually.

That night he'd come out of the bathroom brushing his teeth and, with a mouth full of toothpaste, he said something about a study of changes in gene expression above and beyond the assumed underlying DNA sequences that might explain Tom's inherited proclivity for ghosts.

Her mind wandered. *Was it possible that both Tom and his mother,*

Carol Ann, had the same predisposition to psychic phenomena? Passed down through centuries of perhaps random environmental events, all through an ancestral line? She thought of her own mother, now dead for many years. Whenever Rebecca thought of her mother these days it made her sad. No matter how she chose to look back at her mother, one view predominated. *Mom, you were afraid and anxious most if not all your life. You saw me as needing to learn how to be more passive, or more accommodating, like you. You honestly thought I would have an easier time of it if I could be more like you. But I just couldn't find myself in you. Not any part of me. And I guess I rebelled the whole time. I had already evolved into someone too different from you.*

It was now 3:00 and her signal light went on.

She found him sitting in the waiting room, backpack at his feet, dressed in khacki pants and a blue shirt. He'd tried to tame his tousled hair. He was already steeped in a National Geographic article on the Alaskan pipeline and fracking. He was so engrossed that he didn't immediately look up.

"You can keep that if you want."

He looked up. "Oh, sorry!" He stood up like a boy scout and put the magazine back in the rack.

"I mean it. Take it. You can bring it back if you want. Come on in." He grabbed the magazine and followed her into her office.

They spent the first 20 minutes talking about his family back in Ohio.

He described his parents, his sisters and their husbands, his nieces, and nephews. He described them by telling anecdotes for each. His sisters married guys they all knew in high school. They could still break into their school football team, chant, in unison, waving their arms as if they still had their pom-poms.

"They'll do it anytime, anywhere. I think they need to do it now . . . just sort of to remember a time when they were still young and free. Now, they've all had babies and their high school years are fading away. This is their way of staying in touch."

"My Dad's kind of in hog-heaven with three daughters, married to football guys. He plays golf now, but he follows football like a religion and has three sons-in-law to do it with."

"How about your Mom? Does she love football too?"

"Well, she never loved it, but she supports him. When my sisters come over, which is pretty much all the time, our house is like a pre-school. Little kids, all sizes and shapes. That's my mother's element, little kids."

"Do you have any favorites?"

"I think Harry's my favorite. He's four. He jumps in the air when he catches a ball and clamps his arms around it and then he just runs in any direction. It's hilarious. He's like a little mouse running under all these big cats swiping at him and it takes a while to tackle him. And when you do tackle him, he hunches over the ball just hugging it to beat the band and I swear to God, it's hard to pry him from that ball. My Dad loves him."

"Sounds like you do, too."

"I love his passion. He won't quit. And the size of his older siblings and the adults doesn't faze him a bit. He's fearless."

They both laughed.

"Are you a bit like Harry yourself?"

He thought about that.

"Maybe. But Harry's already a gifted athlete. I'm not."

"Well, I was thinking more about the fearless part."

He smiled. "Perhaps."

He knows I'm thinking about the ghost. She waited, not wanting to spring the subject on him and yet she felt she needed to. It was as if he read her thoughts. "You're wondering how I can be so calm talking to a ghost."

"Yes. You read my thoughts."

He nodded. Looked down at her Kurdistan carpet. Serious. "Well, I think my mother's really the psychic one. But maybe I am too. A little."

He waited.

She knew he wanted to add something. Like most people who boast about being psychic, this one did not.

"I'm not sure why . . . but I'd rather not think of myself that way."

"In what way? I don't ask out of surprise, but I want to make sure I understand what you mean."

"Well, let me put it like this. I've never met . . . and probably never heard about . . . anyone who claims to be psychic whom I respect. So, I guess I just don't really relate to the idea."

"What about your mother? Don't you respect her?"

"Oh . . . well . . . right." He chuckled. "You know, if you met my mother, you'd understand. She almost always has an apron on at home, she's in her kitchen most of the time, and maybe when she's taking her muffins out of the oven, she'll just sort of stop mid-stream and say something like . . . he imitated her . . . 'You know Tom, I've been thinking. Maybe your Grandpa Zak has something on his mind. You know . . . he lived a long time after that war, and I think he chose you because you're so level-headed. He's got something he needs to talk out.' She says stuff like that right in the middle of passing you one of her bran and apple sauce muffins, and the next thing she'll say, 'Try this. Let me know if it's over done . . .' which her muffins never are . . . and then she'll just rush off to pick up a child and sort laundry, as if she forgot all about what she said. Like it was just a passing thought. And you never know when she'll bring it up again. Those statements come out of nowhere."

He likes his mother. He's lucky. So often parents are just the luck of the draw.

"How about your dad? I mean . . . does your mother say those kinds of things to him?"

"Well, my dad just really accepts her the way she is. I'm not sure he distinguishes much between the muffin talk and the other. But yeah . . . she says whatever comes into her mind pretty much to anyone. He likes her, though. Honestly, my dad's a simple guy, but he knows who he is and knows what he thinks about things. And I'm pretty sure he thinks he's lucky to be with my mom. He never talks about her as if she's anything other than . . . well . . . normal."

Rebecca was satisfied. "And you and your dad?"

"We're ok. He thinks I'm like Uncle Daniel. A brain." He made a face. "What do you think?"

"Well, I'm getting to know Uncle Daniel. He's different from my mom. I think he thinks she's a little simple in the head. But she's not."

"Does that bother you . . . that he thinks that?"

"I think it did. Yes. But now that I'm getting to know him better . . . well . . . first, his wife Anna . . . my Aunt Anna who I only met a few times and now she's dead, so I won't get to know her directly . . . but I really get to know her through him. She's with him, you know. I mean, he says things to her. Not always nice. I heard him tell her to shut up once. 'Shut up, Anna!' He yelled it. He was walking down the hall to his bedroom. But he was very dependent on her."

He paused. Thinking. "The fact that he has this relationship with Aunt Anna makes him less of a brain. More human. I think Dr. Mason is helping." He corrected himself. "Melinda. He's absent-minded. He comes across as arrogant, but I'm beginning to think he's not so much. Maybe he's more like my mother in some way more than I thought. Sort of unaware in a way I can't quite explain."

Rebecca indicated she understood. "Do you think your Grandpa Zak has a purpose talking to you?"

"Yes."

This startled her. She wasn't expecting such an emphatic answer.

"Can you say what it is?"

He told her what Zak had said to him at their last meeting, out in Anna's back yard on her bench. Zak had warned him that Daniel was in danger. "He said the guy's name was Benjamin."

Rebecca thought about this.

"So, Benjamin was a former graduate student, a colleague who got Daniel kicked out of the University and divested of his degree by accusing him of forging an original document given to him by a friend, and then Daniel came back a few years later to prove his innocence and got Benjamin, a rising star in the University by then, kicked out, and Daniel was reinstated. This was back in the 70's."

"That's pretty much it."

"Does the name Benjamin mean anything to you other than what Zak said?"

He waited a few seconds as if holding his breath. Then it came out. He told her about Beth, meeting her in class, the hike in the hills to her secret blackberry patch. "I told her about my family. She didn't say much about hers, only that her stepfather's name was Benjamin."

Rebecca took this in.

"What more do you know about Beth aside from the fact that she's a brainy student?"

He told her about the episode in the hallway before he even met her on their way to the first summer class, how she seemed to swoon, and he caught her before she seemed to slowly collapse against the wall. Then he told her about the night before. "It was as if she changed into a completely different person. In class she's shy and studious. At the berry patch she seemed tough and wild. But last night she seemed like Lolita."

"Lolita?"

"Yeah. You know. Nabokov's *Lolita*."

"Ohhh . . . When did you read *Lolita*?"

"Ummm . . . I think it was last year. I spent a summer at home by myself more or less while my parents went on a road trip . . . except when my sisters came by, which was often . . . and just read whatever I wanted.

Our librarian . . . Miss Bernard . . . said I should read Nabokov. So, I read Lolita."

"What did you think of it?"

"I think he's a great writer and I'm going to take a course on him."

She asked him more questions about Beth and her different moods.

This young man is very observant.

When the session was over, they decided to meet again.

She asked him to continue observing Beth, not sure what the mood changes could mean, but she decided it was worth paying attention.

When Benjamin returned from his cabin across the river, he checked on Blanco who was having fun stealing money from Drexel's father.

"It's like taking candy from a baby. Seriously. This guy is mega-rich, and he likes multiple accounts. And it looks like he sort of lets the money just sit there in lots of them. It's ridiculous."

"Ok. Remember, don't overdo it. We don't want him noticing. Besides, he's probably got his scouts out looking for his wayward son. By now, they've figured out he left in the Audi. And by the way, where is our new little guest?"

"He's being quiet, sort of wandering around. Following Lily. Just seems to be taking it all in."

"Do you think he's fitting in? At least for the time being?"

"Ahhh . . . yeah, I guess. But methinks he's going to get bored pretty quick. He was looking for his cell phone. I don't think he'll last too much longer without it."

Benjamin scratched his three-day old beard. "Ok. I'll take care of it."

That afternoon he found Drexel sitting alone on a rock, looking lost.

When he saw Benjamin, he almost exploded with anticipation. "Hey Dude! Where you been? Say listen, I need my cell phone."

"No can do, Drex. Remember, I told you, your Dad's looking for you. If you make a call on your cell, he'll find you . . . and the rest of us."

Drexel looked not only disappointed, he also started to look impatient and annoyed.

Well, Drex. Time's about up. "Hey, come with me. I want to show you our mighty river. You'll like it. Come on. Follow me."

Drexel followed. Like the little lost lamb he was.

CHAPTER 15

. . . ghosts and ghost sightings bring in some eternal, somewhat scientific questions as well: about the nature of time; about the seemingly inviolable laws of energy and physics; about existence and life after death; about the nature of life itself.

MARK NESBITT, *GHOSTS OF GETTYSBURG: SPIRITS, APPARITIONS AND HAUNTED PLACES OF THE BATTLEFIELD.* INTRODUCTION, P. 13.

THE FOLLOWING DAY REBECCA MET WITH GERTRUDE. Every two weeks she consulted with her, but this session was scheduled sooner than usual. She called Gertrude and left a message. "I think we need to meet and talk about Tom and his ghost. I don't know what concerns me the most, but I need to talk it through."

Gertrude called back and confirmed 11:00 a.m. the next day. She trusted Rebecca's instincts. They had worked together for many years, and she thought of Rebecca like a daughter—different from her own daughter, who was an established analyst, married with one daughter, living in New York City with her husband. In Gertrude's mind, Rebecca was instinctive and creative while her daughter was academic, steeped in classical literature, more like her father. Rebecca was a free spirit and intuitive; her daughter was careful and analytic. Between the two they covered both sides of the brain.

Sitting in Gertrude's soft leather couch in her office was as familiar and comfortable to Rebecca as her own home she shared with her husband Richard. She was glad to be there on the day after seeing Tom, so that he was fresh in her mind.

She already felt close to Tom, but she was perplexed and worried about the ghost's latest, intentional message. Part of her wanted to chalk up the ghost to an interesting and rather benign delusional disorder.

But she couldn't. It was because of Tom himself. Everything about him suggested not only a mature eighteen-year-old, but an old soul. *He just was.* She knew it was a bit new-agey to think that, and Rebecca tried to steer away from her own 70's indoctrination, only because that era had become satirized, and the butt of too much misunderstanding by the younger generations. Even though in Rebecca's and Richard's minds the music, the philosophy of living closer to the earth, and not caring so much about money, and a strong ethical sensibility about the environment got lost in the overriding cloud of the Vietnam War and the 'tune in, drop out' flower children—*those crazy hippies.*

Rebecca's own daughter, Margo, would invariably wrinkle up her nose at the mere thought of Rebecca smoking marijuana. Which she had done because everyone did. You couldn't get Jesus Christo to a party without marijuana being passed around. For the seventies, it was de riguere.

Her mind was filled with questions about Tom. Rebecca attributed her ability to accept a broad range of phenomena to the development of her sensibilities in the seventies. Even to her experimentation with psychedelic drugs, which was done in her circle of friends—not to go to raves, but to experience the expansion of one's mind.

How to understand Tom's ghost? Was the ghost real? If so, how could that be? She needed Gertrude's always wise and broad perspective.

"So, tell me, my dear . . . don't think . . . what worries you the most?"

"Well, ok . . . I'm thinking that this warning from his ghost, his four-great-Grandpa Zak, is real."

"Yes. It certainly is real to Tom, isn't it? So that must be our task . . . to understand what he experiences about this ancestor of his who has been speaking to him for . . . I think you said eight years now."

"Yes, I'm sure Zak is real to Tom."

"But we have no details about this present danger. That is, how is Daniel in danger now?"

"Only one clue."

"And what is that?"

"Tom put it together. He's become friendly with this student in Daniel's class."

She told Gertrude about Beth.

"He remembered that Beth told him her stepfather's name is Benjamin . . . nicknamed 'Papa Cat,' that he owned hundreds of books, and that she lived with seven other adults and five children, including her mother and five-year-old stepsister, Hannah. She described this Benjamin as a 'stormy and worrisome man,' who is very smart. Literate, but warped. Knows all about the Civil War and apparently told Beth that the Civil War wasn't over."

Gertrude emitted the sound she often made when she was thinking deeply . . . blending groans with periodic "ah ha's."

Rebecca liked these moments. It was like submitting her riddle to the sphinx who digested the data and soon would make her pronouncement. They were both used to each other's long silences. And this was a long one. Finally, Gertrude looked up. "All right, my dear, let's connect some things that we know first. Then we speculate."

"Of course. Connect away."

"One—both Tom and his mother accept as real the ghost as their ancestor from the Civil War who speaks to Tom."

"Two—what he tells Tom makes sense to Tom. I mean the communications are pretty straightforward, aren't they?"

Rebecca confirmed this.

"Three—this ghost told Tom some old history about Daniel and this man, Benjamin. They both know a great deal about the Civil War . . . as does Tom himself . . . and there was bad blood between Daniel and Benjamin some forty years ago when they were both in graduate school, working on their dissertations. Do we have any reason to doubt the veracity of this history?"

"No. I remember some time ago Richard mentioned this about Daniel. They've known each other for many years, and I believe Richard was able to be supportive of Daniel during the time he was expelled from the University."

"Good. So, let's move on."

"Four—Zak tells Tom . . . with no equivocation, that Daniel is in danger now from someone named Benjamin."

"Five—Tom shows up this summer to live with his uncle and meets a student who happens to be in Daniel's class this summer with Tom, whose background sounds . . . well, let's just say, a little 'fishy.' But, she's very bright. And she has severe mood changes, or she appears to manifest three different personalities all of whom Tom has met, the third one just recently."

"And six—last but hardly the least and perhaps the most important, is that her stepfather, the ominous sounding character we mentioned is named Benjamin."

"So, what have I left out?"

"Well, nothing really, but let me add something that might be of interest." She told Gertrude about Richard's theory of how Tom's brain seemed evenly balanced between his left and right cortex and his theory of epigenetics. "I don't really understand it, but he seems to think it's a new field of neuroscience that studies the possibility that certain genes can actually carry and pass down generationally an expression of personality traits. We can also lose certain inherited traits when the rituals and the cultural norms are dropped, but we can also gain traits through certain genetic expressions through new experiences. All of this Richard thinks somehow might explain Tom and his mother's proclivity to accepting and actually talking to ghosts."

Gertrude leaned back and made her hands into a pyramid tapping her fingers, bobbing her head. She laughed. "Well, I must say, I do love that husband of yours. He doesn't hesitate to toss the pieces around to see where they should land."

"No. He doesn't. What do you think?"

She rocked her head. "Well," she leaned forward, "he may just be right."

Rebecca knew that would be all Gertrude would say in the moment on that subject. She waited her to elaborate.

She continued to tap her fingers looking out into space. "Okay. Let's speculate. I will tell you what I think so far. There may be a real danger here. I don't know why or how, but I think there is. This young woman who has taken up with Tom very well may hold some sort of key to the mystery. His description of her makes her sound like a possible dissociative disorder and if that's the case she has suffered some kind of serious, early trauma. This stepfather of hers named Benjamin cannot be overlooked, since someone named Benjamin seems to be the culprit. There are too many coincidences. Tom's arrival, Zak's warning, Beth in the same class whose stepfather is named Benjamin, her unknown and rather mysterious background, her family of seven adults and assorted children sounding like a cult, and lastly, this Benjamin knows all about the Civil War, as does Daniel. Too many coincidences."

She made her final pronouncement. "I think not."

She tapped her fingers some more. "So, these are some pieces of the puzzle. And now, the questions. Who is this young woman named Beth . . .

really? Who is her stepfather and mother and where do they live? Is this stepfather the Benjamin from forty years ago? Is he the danger? What does he want, or more to the point, what does he intend? When and how?" She stopped here, always aware of the time.

She looked at Rebecca. "I think you may have to do some sleuthing. Find out what Richard knows about the episode long ago. He and Daniel are still close friends. Both you and Richard should talk with Daniel. Ask him what he thinks about all we have discussed here. See if there is a way to find out more about this student, Beth."

"That should get you started."

They stood up, and as Rebecca was leaving Gertrude warned, "Oh, and be careful."

That evening after dinner he sat in his small office behind the kitchen staring out at the Ponderosa pines. The air outside was still, no breeze after the temperature rising all day. It was 10:00 p.m. and no relief yet from the heat.

He refused to install air conditioning in the main house because the more improvements they wanted always invited the outside in and risked exposure. He liked to keep the carpentry and fix-it stuff in-house.

Dinner had been quiet. Even the children were subdued.

No one asked about Drexel, and he mentioned casually that he had gotten Drexel a ride into town where he could catch a bus. "He's on his own now," he explained to their passive, unquestioning faces.

Only he knew that he was getting careless, but that was because the end was near. He didn't intend to survive. And after it was all over, they would be on their own as well. Since they were a band of sheep, perhaps they'd follow Blanco. He, after all, was the only one with any brains. Well, except for Morrigan. He didn't want her to come to any harm. Not really. But as he sat there in the silence, he couldn't imagine a way out for her. But he knew she was resourceful. Sometimes too much so, but he regarded her as a survivor, like Blanco. He pushed the problem out of his mind, as if he were clearing a table in one fell swoop.

He reached in his small desk drawer for one of his cell phones and pecked out her number.

"Hello . . ." It was her batty old landlady.

"Well, hello Mrs. Bellfry, this is Beth's father." He knew she called herself Beth at school. He assumed she did this to preserve her anonymity, which he thought was astute of her. He had no idea there was a divide between Beth and Morrigan, much less a third in the form of Sugar Pie.

"Whooo?" she demanded in her chronic, high-pitched, shrill tone of voice.

He sighed. *I'd love to take you out, Lady, really, I would. It'd be doing the world a favor.* "Beth's father," he repeated patiently in his sing-song Papa Cat voice. "How nice to hear your pleasant voice."

She heard that. "Oh . . . well, I guess you want Beth."

"Yes, if you would be so kind. Beth speaks so highly of you and well she should. You provide such a lovely home away from home for her." *I shouldn't lay it on too thick. She might get suspicious. On the other hand, these old bats are all the same. Enough sweet talk is never enough. They're starving for it.*

"Oh . . . well . . . yes. Ok. I'll see if she's in."

He heard the clunk of the receiver on the hall table. He remembered it had a crocheted doily on it and he'd wondered why anyone would put an old, stained doily under a dirty antique telephone, the landline for all her boarders. He knew she wouldn't move quickly and that she had to haul her fat carcass up the rickety stairs to Morrigan's room. He could hear her groaning and the creaking of the stairs as she made her way up.

While he waited patiently, his thoughts wandered. *I wonder if she has any money. She's a slumlord, for God's sake. They all have money stashed under their mattresses. They prey on needy students and wealthy parents.* The more he thought about it the more appealing the idea became.

This was how it went with Benjamin. An idea took hold and could quickly ratchet up into an obsession. He bit down on his tongue to make it hurt enough to stop the flow. There was no time to deal with Mrs. Bellfry. At least not in this lifetime.

Finally, he heard some voices. "Your father, dear. What a nice, polite gentleman. I hope you appreciate all he does for you, dear."

He didn't hear Morrigan's response. He realized that was because she apparently had none. Irrationally, he had hoped she would respond in kind, with something like "Yes, thank you Mrs. Bellfry. He is a great Dad." But nothing.

"Hello." Her tone sounded neutral, but he detected that little rivulet of irritation that crept into her attitude toward him since she'd been away at school. It didn't used to be there. She always treated him with genuine respect. At least he thought so.

"What . . ." She stopped herself, not wanting to finish her sentence, but he knew just the same what the rest of it was. She wanted to demand "What do you want?" But she stopped herself. *She's being careful with me, and I'm not sure why. Is this a good sign? . . . then again, maybe not.*

He decided to skip the daddy talk and get right down to business.

"I need you to do something. It's important."

He heard her sigh.

He decided to get tough. "Listen up!"

She snapped to. "I am. I've just been a little tired lately."

"I know." He softened. "Listen, Baby M., I'm going to need your help implementing some plans of mine. Remember I talked with you about that?"

She didn't know what he really had in mind, she just knew it had something to do with Daniel Perry, her professor.

"How's the relationship going with that nephew of Daniel's?"

She hesitated for one second too long.

"What's the matter? I thought you were getting to know him. That was all I asked of you . . ." He was instantly furious.

"Wait. Stop. I am. I am. It's just that . . ."

"What?"

"I don't want anything to happen to him. Tom. I mean his nephew."

"Whatever gave you the idea that something would happen to him?"

"I don't know. I mean . . . it's just that . . . her voice sounded hoarse, as if she were tearing up.

He was shocked. *Omigod. She cares about him. Well now, you little tramp, because of you something probably will happen to him.*

"You weren't supposed to care about him."

"I don't. Honest. I could care less." She knew she had to recover herself. "Besides, he is just a kid. Not too smart. I feel sorry for him. He has to live with his uncle and, well . . ." she needed to convince him . . . "he hates him."

"He hates him?"

"Yeah. He hates him. Daniel's mean to his mother . . . you know . . . she's Daniel's sister. Tom feels protective . . . and thinks Daniel puts down his family. So, . . . honest . . . there's no love lost there."

Her heart was pounding. She wanted to force him to be distracted from the scent. She knew how he could be.

"All right, all right. He's just a pawn here anyway. Nothing's going to happen to him."

He needed her to believe that. He knew she was protecting this kid and he didn't really care why, he just didn't want her in any kind of sentimental mode. Morrigan was only useful to him because she was tough and unsentimental.

"Here's what I need you to do. After Daniel's last class next week, I want you to distract the kid. Keep him away from his uncle's house . . . all night, if you can. I have some business to conduct with Daniel and I don't want any distractions."

"That might be difficult."

"Make it happen."

He hung up. No goodbyes. No pleasantries. She needed to obey. He was sure she would because she was smart and knew when to be afraid.

CHAPTER 16

The Constitution cannot be made easy. It was never meant to be easy.

SHE CLIMBED THE STAIRS, each foot a lead weight, concentrating on making it back to the safety of her bed, where she collapsed and stared at the ceiling. *What's he planning?* Her fears seeped up. *He's going to kill Daniel Perry.* She didn't know why or how she knew, but she knew.

Back home in the family, even though they didn't call it the family because that sounded too cult-like—she had always known they were a cult. She'd looked up the definition—'a relatively small group of people having religious beliefs or practices regarded by others as strange or sinister.'

There were times she wondered what he believed in. *Certainly not a benevolent god.*

Her mind went home—her mother Cassi and her half-sister Hannah—Benjamin and all the rest—Angel and Manuel and their two children, Arlo and Rose, and Cloe and 'Stormy' Carl, Ziggy and Lennon. Then Luna and Blanco.

She could see each of them, especially the children playing their games and following her around when she was there.

The denial was seamless. There were only a few times she approached her mother with the question, "Where does he go when he disappears? How do we pay for things?" And then, "What happened to Missy Tupelo . . . and all the others who came and went?"

Cassi's response was always the same. "Shush, Morriegan! Benjamin knows what he's doing. He takes care of all of us. He loves you. But don't question him or you'll bring trouble down on all of us."

Then her mother would rush off as if she had too many chores to do. *Which was true. She did. Because she lives to serve.*

She'd been away from them for two years, returning only briefly when she felt she had to put in an appearance.

She knew her power with him was her quick mind. He valued that above all. She feared the only reason her mother had special status was because of her, the daughter.

One time he told her, "Don't worry Morrigan, your mother's safe, as long as I have you. He didn't want her sexually; she was pretty sure.

She didn't trust Sugar Pie. She was convinced he didn't know about her—or Beth. *They don't come out when he's around.*

She remembered something from long ago. He came upon her one day when she was fooling around with an old guitar and singing a poem to the children who were dancing and whooping around. She crooned,

"The Owl looked up to the stars above,

And sang to a small guitar . . ."

The children burst out shouting and dancing around like little wild sambos.

"O lovely Pussy! O Pussy my love, What a beautiful Pussy you are, You are, You are! What a beautiful Pussy you are!"

She was laughing.

His looked stopped them in their tracks.

He walked away quoting to her, "A little learning is a dangerous thing; Drink deep, or taste the Pierian spring."

Why did he want to stop their fun? The quote sunk in like an unwelcome intruder. She took it as a warning. *Showing pleasure or having too much fun pissed him off. Better not to feel. Need to shut down. Back to reality. I need to get a grip.*

Whenever she made a plan, some kind of strategy, even if impractical, she felt better. She kept feelings out of her scheming, but now she couldn't. She liked Tom. She couldn't help herself. It wasn't that he was so good looking, or smart—which he was—it was that he possessed an openness she'd never encountered. He appeared to be without guile and didn't seem to need to please or be pleased.

Her emotions about him continued to take her by surprise. She felt young and inexperienced. Vulnerable because of it, but she couldn't stop. She had known for as long as she could remember that she couldn't afford that luxury—to feel happy. It led to bad places.

So, what's the plan? She let her mind wander, while focused, something she'd taught herself to do. Ironically, Benjamin had taught her that. "Focus on the problem, and then let your mind wander," he used to tell her. She tried it and it worked.

He wants me to somehow get Tom out of the way, the night after the last class. That's week after next on a Thursday night. He must be planning to go to Professor Perry's house. And do what? Whatever it is, it can't be good. People disappear when Benjamin's around, so I'm guessing Tom's uncle is about to disappear. Why? What can I do?

Her memory traveled back six years. She was with the little ones in the blackberry patch down by the river. Hannah was on her back in the carrier and Rose and Lennon were picking the berries.

She smiled at the memory, because their lips were smeared with blackberry juice. She told them they had to stop eating them and put some in the basket because otherwise there wouldn't even be enough for one pie.

It was then she heard the noise. Just faint grunting sounds. Possibly a bear? She walked about ten yards down to the river and saw him standing there. He looked at her. She'd startled him. She noticed he was eyeing something in the bushes. All she could see was a shadowy bundle. She backed away. He said nothing.

She rounded up the kids and hustled them back.

She told her mother they couldn't find any more berries.

"But Benjamin wanted blackberry pie tonight." Cassi was more upset than she should be. Later at dinner, Cassi told Benjamin there weren't enough berries for a pie, so instead he got a bowl of them all to himself with cream.

He didn't complain. He smiled at me.

She shook herself out of the memory.

Her eyes closed. The basic plan was simple. She would tell Tom about Benjamin . . . and all the rest . . . and they would figure things out together.

That same night he fell asleep early with Numi draped over the edge of the bed. After three hours, at midnight, he awoke with a start, as Numi leapt up and skedaddled out the door down the hall to slither under the living room couch, green eyes staring out into the dark.

"Jesus, Zak! You scared me."

He was perched on the end of the bed, surveying the room while leaning down to rub his leg.

"So, this is where you repose. The cat doesn't like me. They're psychic you know."

Tom sat up, rubbed his head, propped up the pillows and leaned back. "No, I didn't know that Zak." He didn't want to be rude, but he was bone tired and not in the mood for small talk or innuendos, like pieces of a puzzle he couldn't quite put together.

"Don't worry, Son. I'm not here for long." He kept looking around as if he wanted to find something.

Maybe something familiar? Who knows with Zak.

"He's on the move."

Tom wasn't sure he heard correctly. He said it almost as an aside from other more important matters. Tom decided in the silence that he'd heard him correctly.

"Who's on the move?"

"Benjamin."

More silence.

He sighed. "Okay . . . can you help me out here a little? Is there any more?"

"Nope. That's it. I'm just the messenger. Get some help. Don't know the details." Then he looked at Tom. "Kid, you can do this."

"Zak . . ." he was frustrated. "What can I tell anyone? How can I expect anyone to believe me? Should I try to warn Uncle Daniel?"

"That would be a start."

Tom reached over to the bedside table to get his glass of water. When he turned back to answer, Zak was gone.

"Shit!" He rarely swore, so it felt good. Fatigue hit him hard, and he closed his eyes slumping back down in the bed wondering if Zak had actually been there, actually warned him.

In his dream he stood at the edge of a river. The water was swift, heading down as if the ground were at an angle. He held his hand over his forehead to block the sun as he scanned along the other side, covered with large boulders and pines. He was calling out. "Uncle Daniel . . . where are you?" Nothing. Only the sound of the rushing water. Soothing, but urgent at the same time. The sun started to go down in slow motion and darkness crept over the other side and crossed the river. A moving shadow coming toward him. He knew he couldn't make it to the other side. He saw a darker shadow, something moving on the other side, as if it were pacing, looking for a way across. Leaning forward to get a better focus he realized it was a giant black bear.

He woke with a start as Numi dabbed his cheek with his paw.

The next day, he was five minutes late for class.

She'd saved him a seat, this time in the back where they sat the first time. She smiled.

He sat next to her, and as he opened his notebook, he realized he had not smiled in return. For the first time. The Lolita business a few nights ago had rattled him more than he realized.

Daniel was standing in front of the class looking at him. "Nice you're able to join us, Mr. Cramer."

That was the first time he'd ever heard his uncle say his last name. The tone was unmistakable. *Daniel is pissed.* The whole mood of the class felt out of sorts. He wasn't sure why, but he'd noticed that for the past few days Daniel seemed a little more distant than usual.

He thought it was because he had his mind on something, and Tom had decided not to take it personally. Living in a large family, not taking things personally was a high priority coping strategy. Only his mother hadn't learned it very well and as a result she felt responsible for making everyone feel good. And, apparently, doing that made her feel good.

She told him once, "Tom . . . I was born this way. Taking care of your father . . . and all of you is all I've ever wanted."

He'd grown into believing that she really meant that.

As he watched Daniel preening in front of the class, he couldn't help feeling a little resentment toward him. *When they grew up together was there ever any room for my mother?*

"Ok, Everyone. I asked you last time to think about ramifications of the Civil War. Who are we now, in these United States . . . based on the long-term aftermath of that war? I'm asking for thoughts."

Tom thought he shouted the last word just a decibel too loud, more a challenge than a question.

Daniel added, "I don't want hum-drum, dogmatic, derivative responses. Use your original minds." He pointed to his head, as if his own was the icon of originality.

Neal Viner raised his hand. "Ok, Mr. Viner . . . go ahead. Lead the way."

Viner hesitated, even though he had the floor, as if his thoughts had not caught up with his desire to lead the discussion in a direction that would make him the most thoughtful.

"Come, come, Mr. Viner. Just speak what's on your mind."

"Reconstruction . . ." he blurted . . . "is difficult to analyze. So much of what we know comes from biased sources and different eras in different contexts." Sensing Daniel's impatience, he got to the point. "But my first thought is that the Northern Republicans quickly lost interest in the cause of equal rights. Had it not been for the ratification of the Fourteenth and Fifteenth Amendments any progress for equal rights might have been lost. Perhaps forever. Because reconstruction turned into a free for all, a northern exploitation of the crushed South, polarizing our country for the next hundred and fifty years."

Daniel approved, egging him on.

"Well, we're certainly divided now." As Viner said this, he looked around the room, hesitant.

"Go on, Mr. Viner. Complete your thought. You're among friends, open-minded citizens."

"Well, President Obama is pushing for more like a centralized government, while . . . well, there are strong opinions that centralized government threatens our civil liberties while a more decentralized government . . . that is, allowing the states to govern themselves, maintains individual liberties."

Daniel stared at Viner. "Well, Mr. Viner, you've set the stage. Good thinking."

Hands shot up.

Tom got the impression that with those hands going up Daniel's mood improved.

His face lit up. He picked students at random from one side to the other, as if he were conducting a choir. When one student looked particularly eager, he would choose the student right next to them. Daniel didn't let any one student take over. If they tried, he would cut them off, waving his piece of chalk around so it would land on someone else.

A chorus of comments commenced.

"I think it's important to remember that many of the Founding Fathers owned slaves. Jefferson, Washington, Madison . . . just to name a few."

"Wasn't Jefferson a paradox?"

Daniel piped up. "How?"

"Well, he owned slaves, but he's the one who said, 'All men are created equal.'"

"Ok. A contradiction. How do we think about that?" He scanned the room and pointed at a young woman who never spoke. "What do you think?"

She was startled, but rose to the occasion, gratifying Daniel.

He knew some of them hesitated, but were thinking just the same.

"Well . . . I think . . . um . . . yes, it's a contradiction, but in a way not really. I mean . . . we're looking at them from our perspective . . . almost two centuries later. They weren't perfect. 'All men are created equal' was an ideal. I mean, something to strive for. It wasn't going to happen overnight."

"Do you mean to suggest that in 1780 men like Jefferson understood the contradiction, but somehow lived with it?" His gaze bore down on her, nudging her to go on.

"Well . . . yes. Not exactly lived with it as in accepted it, but they couldn't resolve it either. They thought slavery would resolve itself . . . with future generations."

"Ok." He spun around, pointed to a male student who seemed anxious to speak.

"King George III wanted his American colony to continue slavery because it was economically advantageous. Jefferson and the rest of them knew it was wrong. Some of the original states began abolishing slavery, like Pennsylvania in 1775. In 1807 Thomas Jefferson signed the Act Prohibiting the importation of slaves into Federal law in the US. It took effect in 1808. That was the earliest date permitted by the Constitution." He paused to let that sink in. Then continued using a tone for dramatic flair. "But it wasn't enforced. Slavery continued until the end of the Civil War."

"So, what are you saying? That the issue of slavery was an important issue after the Revolutionary War, and it continued up until the Civil War?"

"Yeah. It seems like it was always the issue. And after slavery was abolished, the issue didn't go away. It turned into the civil rights movement . . . still with us today."

"Ok, who doesn't agree with that?"

A few tentative hands went up. Daniel pointed at random.

"I think people have plenty of civil rights. We now have a black president. I'm not saying there still isn't racism because there is, but people do have rights. I think the problem of a divided country has now become a problem of a divided world. The carpetbaggers are now global corporations. My grandmother used to quote my great grandmother who went through the Depression. She said we'd become a country of 'haves and have-nots.' My mother told me that was all over now, that our country had learned its lesson. She really thought the banks couldn't fail. She was wrong. And I think we're more divided than ever."

Hands shot up.

Daniel was in hog heaven.

A prissy, articulate young woman spoke up. "Well, I'm confused. I don't know how we got from slavery to the banks failing. All I know is I want to believe that the Civil War was really about our country's beginning. After all, Lincoln did save the union . . . and without that, where would we be? Who would we be? I can't imagine it."

"Look guys . . ." his gaze panned the room, "let me say something about confusion. Your brains," he pointed to his own head again, "contain 100 trillion connections between 12 billion neurons, which means that your brains are equipped to handle non-linear, chaotic thoughts, or systems. Chaos theorists argue now that there is a conflict between the spontaneity of young minds versus the rigidity of the forced structure of the industrial age paradigm of learning. Ok?" He looked around daring them to argue.

Tom watched. *He's kind of doing what he just said not to do.*

"Let me explain. Chaos theory suggests a hands-off approach to learning—that the non-equilibrium associated with confusion will lead to innovative thought. The order that arises out of chaos. So, carry on with your confusion."

I guess he didn't notice that he delivered that with the industrial age paradigm. But maybe I'm being too hard on him. I don't disagree with him.

The room was still.

Daniel stood in front of them like a bedraggled warrior when more hands shot up. His chalk flew up as if a new round was to begin. He chose another young woman, who rarely spoke.

"If we're more divided than ever, then the Civil War is still with us. I don't understand the parallel."

"Well if the banksters are like carpetbaggers they take advantage of people who are in trouble. It's like a bunch of professional gamblers playing with amateurs."

"Yeah, well, you shouldn't play the game at a table where you don't belong."

"There are no rules, and anyone can play. We live in a free capitalist society. At least that's the idea."

"Freedom is a privilege, and it has rules. That's what our Constitution's all about."

"Rules get broken all the time and nobody cares."

"People care, but they lose commitment. They're afraid."

Finally, a student in the back, who never spoke, bellowed, "Are we still talking about the Civil War? Or is this class now just like some kind of free for all? Let's get back to the subject of history and I thought the Civil War."

Daniel weighed in. "We're talking about what discussing the Civil War has triggered in your minds. So . . . to answer your question," he looked at the student who sounded disgruntled . . . "yes, we're talking about the Civil War and who we are now."

"I'd say we're confused. We're all over the map. Definitely chaos reigns."

Tom had enjoyed the banter. And finally, he spoke. "President Lincoln did not want to punish the South after the Civil War. He wanted reconstruction to be about forgiveness. Had he lived things might have turned out differently. The bullet that killed him happened to strike his heart and so that bullet set in motion a chain of events . . . kind of like the flutter of a butterfly's wing that set in motion a tornado in Texas. Instead of forgiveness there has been vengeance on both sides . . . and well, here we are a hundred and fifty years later."

Daniel held out his arms like a preacher. "We've gone five minutes over, Guys. Let your minds tussle with the chaos and confusion. See you next week for our last class."

As everyone started to pack up and leave, he shot Tom a smile and disappeared out the back door of the class.

Outside, Tom walked across the grass heading for the student union. He didn't hear her come up next to him until she was there. He stopped and turned to face her. She looked her old self. Tough. Confident. He could tell she was very tired.

"Look, I know the other night was weird. I'm sorry. Please . . . can we go somewhere to talk?"

He shifted his weight, still not feeling like talking.

"We have to talk. It's an emergency. I have to tell you some things."

They went to her table under the Tiki God and she told him everything.

Two hours later they knew that her Benjamin was the same Benjamin Zak talked about.

CHAPTER 17

There's something delightfully intimate about the relationship between predator and prey.

THAT AFTERNOON REBECCA SAT IN HER OFFICE waiting for Tom, who was due in ten minutes. She picked through what she had learned so far. *He talks to a ghost, he calls his four-great-grandfather "Zak." He's not delusional. But then again, delusions can be compelling. Believable when you hear them. There's always that disconnected feeling you get later when you start to think about what was really said. The mind levitates over what seems true, only can't quite connect the pieces strewn all over the ground. A jigsaw missing its last piece.*

She stared at the Rothco print. Stained yellow, field with floating forms—the thinnest orange-red hovering over doom.

Only I didn't get that feeling after I saw him.

She drifted to Daniel.

Then there's Tom's mother—Carol Ann—Daniel's sister. He never really mentioned his sister, much less Tom, until he showed up on his doorstep. And Daniel, like Richard, only respects what he considers the truth based on facts. Richard said Anna wasn't like that—at all. And neither is Carol Ann.

She remembered Richard described Daniel's marriage to Anna as comfortable with contradictions. "That's why they got along."

She asked Richard what he meant by "why they got along."

He gave his Cheshire Cat smile. "I've never trusted toadstools, but I suppose some must have their good points."

She knew to ask no further, and muttered as she walked away, "You've gone quite mangy, Cat . . . but your grin's a comfort."

He muttered under his breath, "That's why we get along!"

Daniel seems attracted to the occult. Like Richard, he pays homage to logic, but yearns for the outer darkness where he searches for the real answers.

She moved on to the girl. The student—Beth, or Morrigan. Her strange behavior. *The name Benjamin. Same name the ghost kept mentioning to Tom.* She knew she needed to resist the assumption that they were one and the same. But she couldn't. She closed her eyes, then stared again at the red-orange band. *He's Morrigan's stepfather and Daniel's long-ago friend who betrayed him. I'm sure of it.*

Her little red light flicked on. She got up to greet Tom in the waiting room.

He walked quickly past her, head down.

He's worried.

He laid his head back into the couch and closed his eyes.

She waited.

"I'm glad I'm here."

She smiled. "I'm glad you are too. But tell me . . . why . . ." she shrugged . . . "are you glad now?"

He stared at the black and white photograph on the wall of the Glastonbury Tor. A ruin of a twelfth century church sitting on an older Pagan site. Cirrus clouds overhead.

"I just had a long talk with Morrigan after class today."

He repeated the whole story. How Benjamin found Morrigan and her mother living on the streets in Los Angeles when she was five. He took them to live in the mountains, where she grew up. Others came, some stayed, and some disappeared. The kids were home-schooled, after a fashion. She didn't know why Benjamin trusted some and not others. He came and went. They were all used to it and no one questioned when, why and where he went. There was money, she didn't know how much, but enough to pay for what they needed. Her little sister Hannah came as a surprise and that made Benjamin happy. And finally, she told him about Beth and Sugar Pie.

Rebecca realized she was doing what Gertrude did when she was thinking and concentrating—dabbing her fingers together. She rested her hands in her lap.

"So . . . it was Sugar Pie you met the other night."

He leaned forward, elbows on his knees. "Yeah." He leaned back and sighed.

"What are you thinking now?"

"That she's got a multiple personality."

"Yes . . . well we don't really call it that anymore." She was relieved to be able to take a moment to ground herself by explaining something. "We now call it Dissociative Identity Disorder. That means, within the same person there can be one or two, or even more, separate and distinct personalities. They're called the alternates. The host personality uses them to escape reality when the situation becomes too stressful."

He nodded and waited for her to explain more.

She shrugged. "I'm sorry, but it's complicated and I'm not sure how much we should get into all that right now. The important part for our purposes is that anyone suffering from a serious dissociative disorder has been severely traumatized early on."

She stopped to think about how much more she wanted to say. "Most often the person doesn't remember the trauma. A diagnosis is never a one-dimensional thing. It varies from person to person and depends on a lot of factors. It sounds like Morrigan is very bright."

He indicated his agreement.

"That'll help her."

He looked at Rebecca. "How?"

"The more she can understand by using her intelligence the better chance she has for treatment."

"What if she doesn't want treatment?"

"Well, maybe it's never been offered to her."

He understood, waiting for her to go on.

"So . . . I assume that you believe what Morrigan has told you."

"Yes."

"Ok. What do you think we should do?"

"I was hoping you'd have some ideas." He added, "Morrigan is willing to see you."

She did what she always did when she wasn't sure. She waited. She could hear murmurings from the office next to her. A door opened and shut. The elevator hummed through the walls, stopping with a jolt. Its door clanged shut. She wanted to speak with Gertrude, but reigned herself in.

"It's now pretty certain this Benjamin is the same person Zak and Morrigan refer to. Daniel's in danger and this is not a situation for the police."

"I know."

"Ok. I would like to call a meeting for tonight . . ." she glanced at her clock . . . "in a few hours from now with Gertrude, Richard, you . . . and Morrigan. We need level heads and a plan before we speak to your uncle. I would also like Gertrude to meet with Morrigan separately before the meeting . . . if possible. Do you think she would agree to that?"

"Yes. She knows she needs help, so I think at this point she'll agree to just about anything."

"Good. Go see her now and set it up for tonight at 6:00. I'll arrange this with Gertrude."

He got up. "Where will we meet?"

"My house."

It was 5:00 a.m. when he backed the Audi out of the garage for the first time since it had been repainted three weeks ago. Jet black. Sleek. New plates. New registration. *SammyO's a genius. Amazing the skills you can learn in prison with only time on your hands.* The license plate read PapaC6 and he'd added a small wildflower—Forget-Me-Not. Blue with yellow center, five petals.

All was quiet. As usual no one knew he was leaving, except Blanco.

At 4:30 Blanco's eyes popped open when Benjamin stood over his bed.

"I'm leaving for a while. Keep the money flowing."

Blanco understood.

There had been times in the last week when Blanco was tempted to take more than the ten thousand increments. He considered opening his own account with a secret stash. Just for a rainy day. After all, it had been so easy. But his denial about Benjamin was not so sealed shut as the rest of them. He was pretty sure what Benjamin was capable of. He didn't believe that Drexel had taken a bus out of there. *Not for one second. Drexel was a loose cannon. Benjamin snuffed him. He likes me because I'm so useful, but if I weren't . . .* his thoughts trailed off . . . *I'm pretty sure I'd join Drexel . . . wherever he is.*

On the other hand, as Blanco continued to lay awake, his thoughts followed an instinctive trail. *He's up to something. Something more than usual. And it's big. I can tell. He was out of breath, his nostrils flared and I'm sure he'd been up all night. Gone to the river. That's where he goes when he's planning something. He knew he couldn't just sit around and wait like the rest of the sheep. I've gotta protect myself. He'll never find out. How can he? I'm the computer whiz. He's a Baby Boomer idiot . . . pickled by the nineteenth century and his romance with the Civil War.*

He was feeling more awake. He got up and pulled the laptop out of his backpack and sat up in bed opening the lid to reveal the stage. His stage. His world. Where everything was under his control. He stared at the keys, cracking his knuckles. He had a last thought just before he went into the Ethernet. *And I'm pretty sure where he goes when he crosses the river.*

The Audi easily navigated the narrow, winding dirt road that used to serve the logging trucks piled with the big trees from the virgin forests that sped down the mountain, hell-bent for the mills. Even Benjamin couldn't imagine what would happen if a lone car climbing up met one barreling down.

As Cal explained when he was a boy, "Those suckers stop for nothing. Brakes probably wouldn't work anyhow. You better be prepared to meet your maker, Boy, if you encounter one of those Big Rigs heading for the barn and you happen to be in the way." He remembered the stories. In those days the loggers were heroes who fell the giants with one or two-man saws using picks and axes. They showed off their skills like Paul Bunyan at the County Fairs. One man could cut through a three-foot diameter log using a crosscut saw with blades as sharp and lethal as any Tyrannosaurus.

He'd seen the old photographs with 16-foot saws and men posing like bathing beauties inside the hand-cut wedge where the giant would fall. He knew the heroic logger myths perpetuated the slaughter of the native forests. A bygone era. He remembered the slogan "You Don't Know What You've Got . . . Until It's Gone" over one of the photographs of a Sequoia that must have taken a thousand years to grow . . . about to come down. When he saw that he did feel a pang. Just for a moment. He wouldn't allow himself to indulge in sentimental losses. For some irrational reason . . . he sided with the loggers. He liked them and felt bad they were no longer the heroic lumberjacks they once were.

The Audi swung smoothly onto the four-lane highway doing 80mph. *No need to rush. I'll stop for breakfast.*

An hour later he pulled into a truck stop. An old loggers' hangout. There were always a few old timers in there shooting the breeze, drinking Folgers . . . cup after cup . . . reminiscing about the old days, telling their tall tales. He felt at home among them even though he'd never really gotten to know them.

The waitress wore her uniform. Black skirt, too tight. White blouse. Sensible black shoes. Ponytail. Chewing gum. He'd never seen her before. He assumed she was new. Probably just out of high school.

"Howya doin?"

"Good." He nodded, smiling. "Two over easy, hash browns, wheat toast. No bacon. And how about a fresh cup of coffee . . . with milk."

She didn't write it down even though she held a pad and pencil. She nodded at the window that opened out on the parking lot.

"Your car?" She grinned and popped her gum.

He looked out. Hesitated. He flicked back and forth landing on the conclusion that she was harmless.

"Yep . . ." he drawled. "All mine."

"Cool. Neat license plate. 'PapaC6."

She disappeared and reappeared in three minutes with a vintage Sterling China desert tan mug of fresh Folgers. She set it down in front of him as if it were her mother's fine china.

"Whereya headed?"

"South. On business." He sighed.

"Somehow I wouldn't have taken you for a businessman type." Teasing tone.

He shot up to red alert. Calming himself, he inquired, "Well, what type do I look like?"

"Dunno." She studied him. "Someone who's been disappointed."

He zapped her a look.

She met his gaze.

If he weren't so busy, he might take three days off. Have some fun. He chuckled, "Well . . ." he looked at her nametag pinned to her lapel, "Flora, you're a perceptive girl."

"Thanks." She was pleased and disappeared again, returning in ten minutes with his eggs.

He looked at the plate and gestured his thank you.

"Anything else?"

"No thanks."

He picked up his knife and fork realizing she hadn't moved.

"I've got it. You're one of those genius CEO types who just lost a fortune—and you're traveling incognito."

He was swallowing coffee on top of his first bite of toast. He started to choke and grasped for more coffee to force the lodged piece of toast down his windpipe.

"Hey . . . I'm sorry." She laughed. "I was just kidding."

He continued to cough up phlegm while nodding that he would be ok.

"But you know how it can be working in a place like this. Ya gotta have some fun. And with a license that says PapaC6 on it I kinda assumed you had a humorous side." She waited for him to recover. "You ok?"

He pretended he was OK, but he wasn't. *She was just the type. Stupid . . . but smart—like a fox. Maybe I do have some time to kill after all.* The pun did not occur to him.

He made himself laugh nonchalantly. "When do you get out of here?"

"Me?" She considered his invitation. "My shift ends at noon. I only work breakfasts so far. Just started here last week."

"Well, listen, Flora . . . I've got an errand to run before I head south. If you wait outside at noon . . . what the heck . . . I'll take you for a spin in that old buggy of mine out there. Would you like that?"

"Really?" she squealed.

"Yeah . . ." he agreed, laughing. "Really."

He left her a $5 tip and as he headed out waved at her, and lip-sinked, "Nooon."

She waved back, smiling.

CHAPTER 18

*Animals are ever so psychic. There are some people who just can't
come in here. The cats particularly I seem to know. You can fool everybody,
but landy M deary-me, if you know what I mean.*

SHE RODE HER BIKE TO REBECCA'S HOUSE instead of
driving Ladybug, arriving just before 6:00 p.m. She'd pedaled hard,
trying to alleviate her anxiety. *How had all this happened so quickly?* Her
feelings jumped around creating a mixture of dread, despair, and elation.
She wanted to conjure Beth to come forth. *Solid, smart Beth.* But she
wasn't there. Neither was Sugar Pie, who could bring the manic, to-hell-
with-the-world highs. Both would be a refuge for how she felt now. The
thoughts that circled like a pack of wolves were the ones she was most
certain about. She knew what he would do to someone who betrayed him.
And she was about to do just that.

Rebecca met her at the front door with a flurry of Chows who encircled
her, with sniffing and wagging of flowy tails.

"Hi, I'm Dr. Calhoun." She held out her hand. "These two are Juno
and Dido. They're friendly. Come on in."

She followed.

"Oh, by the way . . . call me Rebecca." She led the way into the living
room.

Morrigan was relieved to find Tom already there.

He was standing and came over by her side as if to show a united
front.

"Tom, why don't you introduce Morrigan to Dr. Lerner."

Gertrude was sitting on the couch. She smiled and held out her hand.

"Tom and I are going to head out and pick up some food. We'll be back in an hour or so. Give you two a chance to talk."

Gertrude nodded and patted the couch next to her.

Morrigan took the cue and dropped her backpack on the carpet near the coffee table.

Juno came over and as Morrigan held out her hand to pet her head she flicked her velvet, black tongue up into her palm.

Gertrude sighed. "I know this can't be easy."

"No."

"Well, I'll tell you what. I'm here to listen, not to judge. So . . . just start wherever you want and tell me what you would like me to know."

Her voice was soft and clear. Even though she spoke in a hushed tone, Morrigan could hear her perfectly and was comforted.

"Take your time."

Tears welled up. She tried to calm herself but holding back the tears just made her throat constrict. She choked.

Gertrude produced a box of Kleenex out of thin air.

Grateful, she snatched up three and held them over her face.

Gertrude remained still.

Dido sighed in her sleep.

She took a deep breath. "I live with crazy people."

Gertrude indicated ever so slightly that she understood.

"I mean, my stepfather . . . I guess that's what he is . . . has this place up in the mountains. Isolated. Where my mother, half-sister who's five now, seven adults and four more children live." She looked up for a moment. "I think Luna's 18, but I'm really not sure."

Through stops and starts Morrigan managed to cover the highlights of the last fifteen years.

Finally, Gertrude spoke. "When did you meet Beth and Sugar Pie?"

She blew her nose and looked for a place to put the used Kleenex that had piled up.

Again, out of nowhere came a tiny rattan basket.

Juno stood up wanting to sniff the basket. Morrigan giggled and patted her head. Dido woke up, but stayed put on the other side of Gertrude, her legs sprawled out behind her, head resting on her front paws.

"First there was Beth. A year or so before I left for college. Then Sugar Pie. My freshman year."

"Does he . . . I mean, Benjamin . . . have any suspicion?"

"I don't think so . . . but honestly . . . Benjamin has a way of knowing pretty much everything. He watches everyone, and no one knows it." She paused to reconsider. "At least no one lets on they know anything. That's the way with our family."

"Except you," Gertrude added.

"Well . . . yeah. I suppose so."

"I wouldn't ask if it weren't important. What's your hunch about whether he suspects?"

She waited a long time before answering. "I think he may suspect something is going on with me."

Both looked up as the front door opened with Rebecca and Tom carrying bags of Chinese food.

Ten minutes later Richard arrived.

They discussed the situation until 10:00 p.m.

Richard agreed that the police should not be called immediately because there was no crime to report. "And" he surmised, "we don't really know what this Benjamin is up to." He looked at Tom and Morrigan, who sat together on the couch. "Morrigan, I think you should stay here with Rebecca and me. Just for a few days until we can figure things out. I'll drive you over to your apartment to pick up your things and we'll come back here so you will be safe.

She felt both relieved and anxious. "What if he goes to my place? He'll wonder where I am. Should I bring my car?"

"No, don't bring your car. Leave it. Tell your landlady you're staying with a friend for a few days. She won't know where you are and at least if he does show up this will stall for time. He won't suspect immediately."

Tom looked concerned.

"Tom, you go home tonight. After I take Morrigan to her place to get her things we'll swing by Daniel's and I think it's time we brought him in on what we've talked about. If he's in danger, he should know about it. Also, I'm going to call my friend, Leonard Whitmore. We call him "Bear." I think he can help."

Gertrude and Rebecca both looked pleased. They liked Bear and remembered how helpful he'd been in the past when they had another dangerous situation.

He turned off the highway at the exit that would take him to the street where Daniel lived. He checked the clock on the dash. 5:30 p.m. *Made it. Just in time. She wasn't as easy as I thought.*

He glanced at the scratches on his arms and, for the fifth time at least, flicked the sunshade down to gaze in the mirror, hoping his left eye wouldn't shut completely. She'd torn at it. It was swollen and would be turning shades of blue and green before morning. He just didn't want it to shut.

He slowed to 20mph and passed the address, leaning over to look out the passenger seat to confirm that it was the right house. He'd driven past it before. He remembered, because he saw the wife flounce out the front door, big purse flying over her shoulder, and sped off in her blue Prius. He remembered her hair. Graying, but still long and full. Morrigan later informed him she'd died. He sighed.

Morrigan. You've been my eyes and ears for so long. How special could that nephew of his be? He's just a kid. Well, we'll soon find out.

He drove around the block looking for a place to park. Nothing looked right. He also realized a car like the Audi might seem out of place parked on the street. These houses had driveways and garages. He circled back to the house hoping something would present itself. Ideally, he wanted to park right in front. But that might be a little awkward. He chuckled to himself. *Daniel will hardly suspect whose car it is.* Certainly not mine. He decided to park under the neighbor's elms, counting on the increasing shadows of evening. *Who knows when he'll be back?* He prided himself on being able to take chances and win, enjoying the high it gave him to brush close to exposure and not get caught. *So far so good.* He sighed again.

As he approached the house, he glanced at his watch. Almost 6:00. He ducked into the driveway and stood under a canopy of Redwoods. No sign of anyone. He headed for the side gate that he assumed would lead him into the back. As he crept slowly, he spotted Anna's bench at the back of a lawn that wound around bushes and large pots. *No golf course here!* It was shaded. Out of the way. He headed for it, and gingerly sat down to peer into the sliding glass doors about thirty yards away from him, leading into what looked like a kitchen.

As he focused on details, in spite of his swelling eye, he realized he was staring at a very large tabby cat on the inside of the doors. At first, he thought it was one of those realistic sculptures people put in their yards— until it moved. Raising its back into a camel's hump and emitting what was certainly a long, sustained hiss, it bolted into the interior.

I'm thinking you don't like me, Cat. His attempt to brush it off didn't quite work. Benjamin was just superstitious enough to take the cat's reaction as a bad omen. To stave off the feeling, he thought of Jimmy on his wall. *Jimmy would eat you, kitty kitty . . . in one swallow.*

Leaning back into the bench he took in the garden. *Someone cared for it.* He assumed the dead wife. Somehow, he didn't take Daniel for a gardener type. *Probably pays someone to keep it up. Homage to her. He always was a sentimental fool.*

Twenty minutes passed as he considered his next move. *No rush, really. He'll come home eventually . . . if only to feed his creepy cat. Big fuzzy coat like that needs tending. I bet he produces some major hairballs.* He chuckled, then looked down at his right hand where she'd clawed him. Deep scratches. He felt a twinge of regret. Not about the life he'd snuffed out, but it'd taken longer than he thought, causing him stress, which had not been in his plan for the day. He wanted to arrive in a calm mood. But he wasn't calm.

He'd dumped her over the embankment into the bushes near the river. He heard the thump of her limp body in the thicket of Chinquapin.

What he didn't realize was that she wasn't quite dead. Unconscious. Almost asphyxiated. But not dead.

An hour after he was long gone, her left eye opened. The other one was probing the dirt and dead leaves under the bush where he'd tossed her. She knew nothing. Couldn't move. She saw thorns on a twisted branch. Little white flowers, browning in the sun as the blackberries withered. A bee hovered, still hoping for some syrup. The sun was still overhead, just past mid-day.

After twenty minutes, she managed to crawl out, stinging all over from the nettles mixed in the bushes. Aching. Hearing the river, she managed to crawl down to the edge. After a while she sat up and pulled herself into the cool water. She drank, cupping her hand into the water over and over, and wrapped her hands around her neck to sooth her raw, reddening skin. She sprawled her legs out like a small child in her bath.

An hour later, two boys who'd come down to fish, found her.

Within the next hour she was at the hospital. Judging from the neck abrasions the emergency doctors determined that she was suffering from cerebral hypoxia.

The on-call doctor told the nurse as they were wheeling her into the ICU, "Another hour and she would have been dead."

Flora's mother, Jenny, was a single mother and also a nurse at this same hospital. It didn't take long before she was identified as Jenny's daughter.

By early evening Flora was in a hospital bed hooked up to numerous tubes and oxygen.

Her mother sat in the chair next to her bed, waiting and praying that her daughter would wake up.

A co-worker friend came in. "Jenny, take a break. Go get some coffee. I won't leave her side."

She hesitated but agreed because she wanted to call someone. The police had already interviewed her at the hospital and all they knew was that Flora left work at noon. No one had seen her. Usually she went for a run, then to the animal shelter where she volunteered to walk the dogs, and would normally be home by 4:30 or so.

"She's pretty routine with her habits," Jenny told the police. "No reason for me to wonder where she was."

"Any boyfriends?" they asked.

"Not at the moment."

Jenny knew her daughter was a dreamer. She also knew that she wanted to leave their small town, and, in an impulsive moment, might have jumped at some kind of opportunity. But this situation was beyond Jenny's comprehension. Her daughter almost strangled to death? No way.

She went outside into the parking lot for better cell reception, and after lighting a cigarette she dialed his number with one hand, as she took a long drag wincing from the brilliance of the setting sun through the trees.

He picked up on the second ring. His name was Leonard Whitmore. He was ex-CIA Special Forces turned private detective who lived in the northern woods of Oregon below Seattle with his Basset Hound, Bessie. His nickname was "Bear."

He and Richard met at the University of Chicago getting their degrees in Political Science and Anthropology. One went into the military, and one went into academia.

Bear had three marriages and many girlfriends over the years but had recently settled down to one—Susan. They didn't live together, and perhaps that was their secret, because she had now lasted the longest. Over six years. None of his marriages had lasted that long.

"Thank God you answered."

"Hey, long time. How are you?"

She broke down, rubbing her snotty nose into her sleeve, still holding onto the cigarette and pressing the phone to her ear. He stayed quiet until she recovered enough to tell him what had happened.

"It's Flora. She's been hurt . . . I mean . . . O'migod . . . I think someone tried to kill her. The police are doing what they can, but until she wakes up there's nothing to go on. She was found next to the river . . . left for dead . . ." She broke down again and mashed out her cigarette, pulverizing it into the gravel. "I need you. Please come."

"I'll leave right away. Susan can take care of Bessie. I should be there in a few hours, by 6:00."

Bear and Jenny dated seven years ago when Flora was twelve. It was Jenny who introduced Bear to Susan because they were friends. Jenny and Bear parted amiably and all three of them had stayed in touch, and they all loved and worried about Flora—her sweetness, smartness and fast mouth. They all knew she could be impulsive and wanted to "leap over the fence rather than walk through it," as Bear put it. "Just get her through her twenties and she'll be fine." What none of them bargained for was the possibility she wouldn't even reach her twenties.

He arrived at the hospital at 9:00 p.m. He met Jenny down in the cafeteria for coffee out of a machine. "It's not coffee really, but at least it's hot."

"So, tell me all you know."

At 10:30 p.m. Bear's phone rang. It was his old friend Richard Wilson.

CHAPTER 19

Vengeance is mine, and recompense, for the time when their foot shall slip,
for the day of their calamity is at hand, and their doom come swiftly.

DEUTERONOMY, 32:35

HE FELL ASLEEP ON THE BENCH, slumped down with his head
on his chest, when he heard a car door slam and the click from the locking
door. At first, he couldn't remember where he was. He squeezed his eyes
shut, and popped them open in an attempt to jumpstart his memory. It
worked.

He's home.

He had no plan beyond finding the house. Usually, he allowed things
to unfold in the moment. Knowing the best strategy took into account
that almost nothing proceeds as planned. For him there was no such thing
as luck, there was only being in the right place at the right time. But still
. . . this time was a little different. *Maybe I should've taken into account
that Daniel might not be alone.* He erased that thought.

*And here I am at last, after 40 years, lounging in his back yard. He's in
there with that crazy cat of his.*

He squinted, in order to peer through the darkened glass doors, and
saw it still hissing indignation, and then it disappeared into the darkened
house. He actually liked cats. They reminded him of little girls. *Cute, sly
and screechy. Morrigan was a cat. Only she's a panther.*

After ten minutes he got up and walked briskly around the side of the
house, stomped up the front steps and pushed his whole weight against
the doorbell. Chimes played, sounding like church. He looked up for a
bell tower somewhere.

I bet she had that put in. He's not musical.

He recalled that Daniel liked the usual 60's stuff. Bob Dylan. The Beatles. Joni Mitchell. He, on the other hand, liked Wagner. And he'd learned over the years to appreciate good country. Willie Nelson, Johnny Cash.

He waited. No sound from inside. After several minutes he might have concluded that no one was home, except the blue Prius was there now where it wasn't before. Looking a little shabby with a few dents and probably not washed in . . . well, who knew how long? Not all shiny spick and span like the one he saw her get into six years ago. But the bumper sticker was still the same. A pelican vomiting words that looked like garbage tumbling from its bill loosely spelling Catch of the Day.

He pressed the bell again as if he could make the chimes louder and longer. Stepping back while looking up, he was startled when someone snatched the doorknob and yanked the door wide open.

"What the Sam Hill . . . !" He leaned out. "Do I know you?"

"Daniel, I'm hurt."

He narrowed his gaze to study the stranger standing in his doorway. He heard Anna's voice. "Calm down, Danny. I think you know him."

Benjamin stepped across the threshold and walked confidently into the vestibule where the landline was perched on a spindly table under the seashell mirror. He pointed. "Interesting object. Did someone make that?"

Recognition dawned. It wasn't his looks, it was his voice. Haughty, aggressive with those little ambiguous barbs that threw others off guard just enough to hesitate, while not knowing how to respond. He waited. He looked into the interior. "So, Daniel, aren't you going to invite an old friend in?"

Daniel stepped aside and ushered him into the living room, gesturing toward the far couch.

He sauntered over and slouched back with his arms akimbo, legs wide apart—grinning.

"What're you doing here, Benjamin?"

Ah . . . he speaks. "Well, I happened to be in your neck of the woods and thought I'd drop by for a little chat after how many years? Forty?"

He kept grinning. "You're looking well, Daniel. And prosperous I see." Without turning his head, he allowed his eyes to survey the room, which was cluttered, but comfortable, with an attempt to welcome "wayward travelers," as Anna referred to her numerous and highly diverse set of friends.

Without being too compulsive about it, Daniel tried to keep things exactly the same after her death. Even Melinda's recent presence on the scene couldn't change that and she didn't try.

"Say, Daniel, would it be possible to have a cup of coffee? I don't want to trouble you, but it would sure hit the spot. I'll be on my way soon. Just wanted to pop by and say hello, you know, for old times' sake."

He's wary. Maybe he'll calm down if he thinks I'm leaving soon.

Without hesitation, Daniel disappeared into the kitchen to make the coffee. He stood at the counter peering out into the darkened yard, mulling over his uninvited guest. He had to control the urge to order him out of the house. Buying time seemed the best tack, but his fear was rising.

He's up to something. But what? After all these years what could he want?

She whispered. "Be careful. Be nice. Bide your time."

Benjamin took in the ambience of the room. He spotted the book with the pelican and read the title with her name. *A Pelican's Progress*, by Anna Taylor-Perry. He flipped it open to her large drawing that spanned two pages.

It was then he heard the long, low growl.

"Well, well, kitty kitty. You're here. Maybe under the couch?" He leaned down to peer between his knees but couldn't see under, as he felt a twinge of pain from the blood rushing to his eye.

Numi hissed his answer.

He chuckled. "Don't worry pussy cat. I've got enough scratches on me for one day." He winced and gently tapped beneath his eye to feel the pillowing skin.

Daniel returned with a tray of mugs, creamer, and coffee pot.

"Help yourself."

He sat across from Benjamin on a smaller couch draped with Anna's great grandmother's hand knit afghan.

Benjamin reached for the creamer and daintily poured a dollop into his mug, adding the coffee slowly. He looked to his host for a spoon.

"No spoon."

Daniel poured his coffee first and then dumped in the cream and took a sip, staring across at the blotchy stranger whom once he called a friend. The idea of that just wouldn't sink in. The scene felt unreal. He noticed his swollen eye. *I'm not going to ask. I know it would be a lie and I don't want to hear his tall tale.*

Benjamin smiled. "Thank you, Daniel."

"You look a little banged up, Benjamin, if I do say so."

Benjamin nodded at the book. "Your wife's creation?"

"I'm a widower, Benjamin. Somehow, I think you know that."

His eyebrows raised in mock surprise. "I'm sorry to hear that. You must miss her." He pointed at the book. "Why'd she name him Samuel Adams?"

"My nephew says it's because Samuel Adams was the most radical patriot of all, responsible for the first shot hesard around the world."

"Your nephew? Where is he?"

"He's living with me this summer. My sister's son. Smart boy. Starting classes this fall at the university."

Red alert. Benjamin gulped down his coffee. "Oh, didn't realize you even had a sister."

"Why are you here, Benjamin?"

"Is your nephew coming home tonight? I'd like to meet him."

Daniel realized he longed for Tom to walk through the front door. His presence might diffuse his growing panic, since he still had no clue what this old nemesis was doing in his living room—his and Anna's sanctuary where they spent so much of their marriage—making pretentious small talk as if they were old friends. *His presence defiled her memory.*

"Don't know. I don't keep track of his whereabouts. He could return any time, sooner or later. Certainly, some time tonight."

Benjamin yawned and stretched himself, scratching his tangled hair. "Say, Daniel, mind if I use the facility? I've got a long drive ahead of me and time's a-wasting."

Maybe he really is leaving. "Down the hall on the right."

The bathroom was feminine, completely tiled in different colors, with seashells displayed on the counter next to the sink with what appeared to be a child's rendition of the pelican. It was roughly hewn, about 5 inches high, bursting with the character that emanates from a six- or seven-year old's sure hand before self-consciousness sets in.

He leaned into the mirror and studied his eye, deciding it might not shut. He stood up straight, puffed out his chest, took a deep breath and walked back down the hallway, keeping his eye on Daniel's tousled, peppery hair. Coming up from behind he pulled the ether-soaked rag out of his back pocket and swung it around in a wide arc pulling back over his nose.

He struggled, but Benjamin's approach created an advantage that Daniel couldn't fight.

Out like a baby. Nothing like the right time and place.

He knew the next part wouldn't be easy, moving him as quickly as possible to the trunk. He loped for the front door and maneuvered the Audi a few feet from the front steps. Legs flopping like a rag doll, he dragged him over the carpet holding him under his elbows, but had to lift him down the steps. He staggered with the weight coupled with the insane but humorous thought that the nephew might show up, because he could sure use the help. Humor, Benjamin had also learned along the way, was an aphrodisiac for pain.

He stuffed him into the trunk, arranging him on the blanket, removing his shoes, which he threw into the back seat. He lowered the trunk door and pressed it shut.

Suddenly, he had to pee and realized he'd not gone a few minutes ago when he had the chance. He bounded back down the hall.

Just as he was leaving the bathroom he grabbed the child's pelican and stuffed it into his pocket. He'd always taken what he coveted, a habit from childhood he never bothered to break. As he shut the front door, he thought he saw the cat dash across the hall. For some reason this made him uneasy. He wasn't all black, but . . . Benjamin always had the thought that cats were furry spooks.

The Audi glided down the tree-lined street and was back on the highway in ten minutes. He looked at the clock: 8:00 p.m.

An hour into the drive he was ravenously hungry and decided to stop at the In-N-Out Burger. He pulled up to the microphone.

A high-pitched, girly voice chirped through. "May I help you?"

"Well, yes, darlin' . . . you can," he drawled. "Let's see . . . how about a nice juicy 3 by 3 with the cheese'n onions. Oh hell, give me the works. And, oh yes, a large coffee with milk. And if you don't mind," using his treacly tone, "pour the milk in first, then add the coffee. It's better that way."

"Anything for you, Sir. Pull on up and get it. Ready in a jiff."

She handed him the coffee first, pre-mixed with the milk, then the tray with burger and fries.

He settled it down next to him and handed her a $5 tip. "Keep the change."

She smiled.

He winked.

Back on the road as he bit into the burger he couldn't help remembering that Missy Tupelo liked In-N-Out the best, too.

They dropped off Morrigan first at 9:30 p.m., and then Richard drove to Daniel's, pulling up next to the blue Prius.

"Looks like he's home."

"Yep." Tom climbed out, then leaned in. "Should we meet with Uncle Daniel tomorrow?"

Richard nodded. "Yes. He needs to know that he might be in danger. He'll take some convincing, but I've known your uncle for many years. He knows about you and Zak. Trust me. He'll get it."

"He probably thinks I'm crazy."

"Don't worry. Your uncle's at home with the spirits. He always has been. You know he still talks to Anna. I mean . . . he really takes her seriously. As if she's right there with him."

"Yeah, I know. He even yells back at her."

They laughed.

Tom looked toward the house. "See you tomorrow."

Richard drove down the road as Tom opened the front door and stepped into the brightly lit house. Usually, Daniel left a dim light on in the foyer, but tonight he left all the lights on. *Absent-minded as usual.* He turned out the lights and headed down the hallway to his bedroom, flicking on the little lamp on his bed stand, to find Numi curled up on his pillow.

"Hey, my man." He petted his head as Numi swelled into a hump and pushed his head into Tom's palm demanding affection. Tom rubbed his head and chuckled. "You're certainly very friendly tonight. Didn't Uncle Daniel pay you enough attention?"

He went into the bathroom to rinse his face and brush his teeth.

Numi followed.

Amused and curious, Tom watched him, never having seen him so needy. Normally, Numi played the aloof card.

They went back into the bedroom and Tom undressed putting on his pajama bottoms and tucked himself in with Numi cuddling up next to him on the pillow, purring his contentment, or relief that at least some one was home. Tom lay there with the light on for a few minutes. Then, for no reason that he knew in the moment, he tossed off the coverlet and went back into the bathroom turning on the light. He winced from the brightness.

Sure enough, it was missing. He liked to move it around on the counter, placing it in funny stances, imagining which one of her kids made it. Boy or girl? He wanted to think boy, but for some reason he concluded . . . probably a girl. He didn't know why. But girls at the age he guessed it was made were clever and unafraid.

The pelican had an expression that conveyed wise amusement. Definitely an expression he recognized from his three sisters. Like they knew secrets little boys just couldn't fathom. That was the only thing he envied about his sisters. Their camaraderie, as if they inhabited a nether world of their own with no boys allowed. This made him think of Morrigan. She was like that, a very smart sister living in her secret world that she'd allowed him into.

That thought startled him. *Who took the pelican?* He couldn't imagine.

Certainly not Uncle Daniel, who'd been dismissive of it when showing Tom around when he arrived. He'd pointed and explained, "One of Anna's kids made it. She loved that thing as if it were a precious relic."
He left the bathroom and headed down the hall to Daniel's bedroom.

Numi peeked out from Tom's bedroom.

He knocked on the door. Nothing. He knocked louder and put his ear to the door, waiting, and then cautiously opened and stared into the void. He walked over to the bed and by then could see that no one was there. Flicking on the overhead light the room lit up. No one had slept in the bed.

After searching the house, turning on all the lights, he saw the two coffee cups and realized someone had visited and Daniel was gone.

He called Richard who was still up.

He said he'd be right over.

While Tom waited, he went to the kitchen and pulled the door open and walked out to the bench. There was still some light from a quarter moon. He sat and stared at the house, then closed his eyes.

"Guess we were too late."

His body jolted. "For God's sake Zak. Are you trying to kill me?"

"Sorry about that. I forget you never get used to me."

Tom sighed. "I'm tired. I suppose you know he's gone."

"Well, I don't know everything, son, but you're correct about that."

"Was it that Benjamin?"

"That would be a fair assumption."

"Any ideas, Zak . . . before Richard gets here?"

"Well, I'm not here just for one of our little chit-chats. Don't know the details, but he is in danger."

"You know, Zak . . . I've always wanted to ask. Do you know . . . like everything, or just some things . . . or you know . . . how much about the world do you know? I mean, like centuries worth . . . ?" He let his questions hang in the night air.

"Well, son, it's complicated, and I'm not going to get into it now. Suffice it to say . . . and I do mean this literally . . . I only know what you know. That's what allows you and me to communicate. Your limits are my limits."

Tom looked up at the sky, as he knew Zak was fading away. He waited a few minutes in the silence. Before he headed back into the house he looked down at the ground and absentmindedly picked up a book of matches from the ground under the bench and dropped it into his back pocket.

Richard had let himself in. They looked around silently. He pointed at the coffee cups and Tom explained, "He must have had a visitor."

"Can you find some plastic bags?"

Tom went to the kitchen and returned.

Richard carefully covered the used cups with the bags. "Don't touch anything."

"I won't. I've seen Law and Order too. I also know the police won't do anything until someone's been missing for 48 hours."

Richard explained to Tom that he would call his friend, Leonard Whitmore. "Better known as 'Bear' to his friends."

But first, he called Rebecca, who would call Gertrude and arrange a meeting at Daniel's the following morning.

Richard spent the rest of the night at Daniel's waiting for Bear to arrive early the next morning.

CHAPTER 20

I John Brown am now quite certain that the crimes of this guilty land will never be purged, but with Blood.

JOHN BROWN, FINAL WRITTEN WORDS, DECEMBER 2, 1859

EARLIER THAT SAME DAY Axel Theodore Dewitt, II, sat behind his vast mahogany desk facing floor to ceiling views of Los Angeles swathed in grayish brown. His office was devoid of personal decorations except for a wooden plaque on the wall behind him depicting his Dutch ancestry's coat of arms, with "De Witt" scrolled in flowery script underneath, and on the wall by the entry to the outer room of his inner sanctum was the Dauna Whitehead photograph entitled 'City of Angels' depicting a yellow-orange LA.

From one glass wall at the far horizon the dark Pacific lay placid and serene, while out the opposite was the silhouette of the San Gabriel mountains.

As he stared at the mountains, he remembered that just a few weeks ago when things were still normal, someone named Drew from his personal account manager's office called and asked permission to lower the price for the Mt. Baldy property.

"What property?"

"You own a house in Mt. Baldy, sir? It's on the market for 2.8 million and we think if you're really interested in selling you need to lower the price. Right now, second homes aren't doing too well in this market."

"Does my wife use it?"

"No, Sir. I think your son, Drexel, has used it to take his friends skiing."

"Then sell it. I've never even been there. Must have been my wife's idea."

"Yes, Sir, I believe it was. Should I speak with her?"

"No. Sell it."

After he hung up, he looked out and tried to remember if he even knew she'd bought it. *She didn't ski. Only Drexel skied.* His wife, Florinda, liked the warmer climates for her vacations. *No one went to the mountains unless they skied. She went to their house on Maui all the time and probably bought the Mt. Baldy place for that rotten son of theirs.* With that thought he snatched up the phone and stabbed the button for his secretary, Monica, to pick up.

"Yes, Mr. DeWitt," she responded in her usual temperate tone. Nothing much ruffled her, and that was why she had worked for Axel DeWitt, II for so long.

He picked up the receiver. "Get me that Detective what's his name on the phone. Now!" He slammed down the receiver.

She never put the receiver to her ear when she communicated with him because he liked to slam his into the listener's ear when he was put out. *For such a bright man he's such a child.*

Two minutes later she buzzed him. "He's on the line."

He pressed the conference button.

An even-toned voice emanated from the sleek black landline with multiple uses Axel had never bothered to learn. "Hello, Mr. DeWitt, what can I do for you?" The sigh in his tone was barely perceptible. Detective Sanchez doodled on his small yellow pad: Call #38. He circled the number slowly with his pencil, then doodled hairy flames—the face of the Mexican sun god. Or a shield.

"Well, to start with you can find my son. It's been 12 days and so far, it's my understanding that LA's finest has come up with diddley squat. What the hell are you people doing?"

He drew stick legs under the face of the sun. Sanchez was used to the DeWitts of the world, but he did tend to bristle whenever he heard one of their favorite phrases—'you people.' He disliked his reaction because he knew it made him just a little more vulnerable than he wanted. He allowed a certain modicum of vulnerability because it kept him sensitive to what was going on, but more than a little was too much.

"Well, Sir, let me bring you up to speed. Our assumption that this was a kidnapping for ransom does not seem to be panning out for the simple reason we are long past the point of expecting to hear from anyone of that nature."

"So, what are you assuming at this point?"

"Ok. Well, we may have a small break just this morning. We've finally determined that your son, that is Drexel, probably left the hospital with the other patient, an older gentleman, who was driving the other vehicle when they both crashed. How or why they got together at the hospital after the accident is unknown. Now, as I mentioned to you earlier, we located the garage where his vanagon was taken and after a thorough search, and I do mean thorough, Sir, we determined that his registration was forged. No such person and no such address exists."

"Yeah, OK, you told me all that before. Now what?"

"Well, we did get a description from the head nurse on duty at the hospital where they were taken that night, and we now have a sketch of him. Remember, both vehicles were heading north, so we're confining our search to areas further north." He paused, adding quickly, "And we'd hoped some relatives of the deceased girl might come forward by now, but so far . . . nothing. We now have a sketch of her and we're taking it around down here, as well as trying to determine if anyone who knew your son also knew her. So far, that does not seem to be the case."

"North! You say you're looking north? Well, that's just swell. Listen to me Detective Sancho . . ."

"Sanchez, Sir . . ."

"Ok, San . . ."

"Chez, Sir . . . spelled with a zee, not an s."

"Chezzz," Dewitt drew it out. "You mean there are no prints from his, whadiya call it . . . vanagon . . . that you can't run through your fucking system? Jesus, I thought you people could find anyone these days."
Axel was heating up and knew he couldn't control his temper.

Florinda had taken to her bed after realizing that Drexel was gone. *Really gone. Not going to come crawling back any time soon per his usual behavior.* At first, she joined him in his anger, but now she was hysterical and practically living on the phone with her therapist, whom he hated, and once in an angry outburst had called him "a fucking runt," which only pushed her more into his protective arms.

This was getting old. Real old.

"Is there any asshole out there that hasn't been plumbed yet? Whadiya mean you can't find this guy?"

"Well, Sir, while that may be true most of the time, whoever this guy is he's managed to live off the grid for a very long time. He obviously didn't keep any personal property in his van that could be traced to anything. Pretty remarkable, really. Usually there's something, but in this case, Sir, there was nothing. And that does tell us something."

"What would that be?"

Sanchez knew he'd set himself up, but nothing clever came to mind. "It means he'll be hard to fine."

Axel picked up the receiver. "For Christ's sake. I need some answers." He slammed the phone down.

Detective Sanchez held the phone out from his ear and looked at it, as if he were staring straight at Axel DeWitt. "Sir, maybe you should fall off the grid."

Axel sat in brooding silence and then buzzed Monica.

"Yes Sir?"

"Who's that guy . . . we got his name last year . . . ex CIA, lives up north in the woods. Outlier, but smart, turned private detective. Get me his name and number."

"I'll see what I can do. I may have to look up the referral source, but I'll get back to you."

"I don't give a rat's ass what you have to do . . . just get me his number."

Arriving at the compound at 2:00 a.m., he rolled smoothly into the garage and shut the door, enveloping the Audi in darkness. Reaching in his daypack for his flashlight, he opened the car door, leaned out and listened. All quiet. He pulled himself from the driver's seat and felt the pain in his joint from sitting too long, not to mention the scratches and bruises and swollen eye that ached. He calculated that Daniel should be waking up. Leaning in, he released the trunk and heard the muffled clink, unlocking. The trunk door rose ten inches. He stood over it as if he were going to stare into a coffin.

Daniel lay in a fetal position, completely still. He pondered how to do this. Finally, he reached down and jostled his shoulder.

No response.

For a split-second panic seized him. *Jesus! Don't tell me you're dead!* But then as if in response he heard a low groan. No movement, but he read the telltale signs of an awakening. Again, he jostled him.

More groaning.

"Come on, Daniel. Wakey wakey! Rise and shine! The early bird's here to greet you!"

His eyes opened, but he lay still.

Benjamin wondered what he could be taking in. *Soon, he'll panic.*

As if on cue Daniel sucked in a huge gulp of air and sat bolt upright hitting his head on the trunk door. Dazed, he rubbed his head. "What the . . . !"

"Easy does it, Old Boy. Stay calm. You're ok." *He's still disoriented. Doesn't remember or recognize me.*

He reached down as if he were tending a waking baby and popped the handcuffs on.

Daniel looked down, uncomprehending, at his limp arms constrained at the wrists. It was then he looked up and stared at Benjamin. Recognition spread over his face. "What have you done, Benjamin? How do you think you can get away with this?"

"Come, come, Daniel. Let's get you out of the trunk and find you a more comfortable spot." He helped Daniel climb out. "Need a potty?"

"Shut up you sick freak. I always knew you were bent, capable of anything. And yes, I need a bathroom."

Benjamin opened the garage door and instructed Daniel to walk ahead. "Over there." He ushered him through the back door and showed him the tiny bathroom off the kitchen.

Daniel obeyed. "Don't shut the door on me!"

"I'll leave it open a smidge. Don't worry. Take your time."

As Daniel relieved himself, he began to take in the situation. *I've been kidnapped. He's brought me somewhere.* He turned his manacled wrists up so he could see his watch. 3:30 a.m. He sighed. The relief of urinating calmed him down momentarily. He heard a pan clanged on the stove. Benjamin was whistling. He looked for a sink.

"Sorry, Daniel ol boy. No sink. But you can use the one out here in the kitchen."

Daniel emerged and took in his surroundings. At first, he thought he might be in some kind of restaurant, but not quite. There were children's drawings magnetized to the huge refrigerator.

"Where am I?" He asked, not really hoping for an answer. "Just asking, Benjamin."

"Don't worry. Let's say you're far from the madding crowd. Remember once, you and I, how we discussed Thomas Hardy's work?"

Daniel walked to the large industrial sink and extended both hands to turn on the water. The cool water felt good, and he cupped it in his hands to rinse his face. Looking around, along the concrete counters he spotted a roll of paper towels and helped himself. Wiping his face, he responded. "I don't remember that." But he did remember.

Benjamin stood in the middle of the kitchen and, with spatula in hand, orated Gray's poem on which the novel was based.

"Far From the madding crowd's ignoble strife

Their sober wishes never learn'd to stray;

Along the cool sequester'd vale of life

They kept the noiseless tenor of their way."

Benjamin finished the recitation with a flourish of his spatula, took a bow, and turned back to his cooking.

"Remember, Daniel, we used to argue about passion. You argued that there had to be some pragmatism for love to last and I argued there needed to be enough passion to overcome whatever got in its way. Do you remember that?"

"No," he lied.

Benjamin pointed at the kitchen table with benches. "Have a seat over there." Back to the stove and the business at hand, he added, "Eggs ok with you? I'm starving."

Daniel stared, hoping some kind of bright idea would come. But nothing did. He was exhausted and yes, he was hungry. The scrambling eggs and sausages and toast smelled good. He decided he was not the type of prisoner who might go on a hunger strike. He needed protein to get him through whatever ordeal this was shaping up to be. Anna whispered, "Don't set him off. Be friendly."

"So, Benjamin, is this your home?"

Benjamin started to whistle Dixie.

"It's nice. Spacious. You live alone? Looks like there might be more." The whistling turned into singing. ". . . old times once forgotten . . . look away, look away Dixieland."

"Ok, Benjamin. You didn't bring me all this way just to cook me breakfast. We might as well chat. Like old times, ok?"

He opened the refrigerator. "Orange juice? Coffee coming up. Cream or sugar?"

"Just cream, thank you. It's going to be a little awkward," he held up his hands, "eating with these handcuffs on me. Any chance you could remove them?"

Benjamin put down the spatula and with three long strides arrived to take an old key out of his back pocket to unlock Daniel's left hand and deftly latched it to something underneath the table.

"A little awkward, but I'm sure you can manage with one hand. You always were a clever fellow, Daniel. Resourceful too. I admired you for that."

He continued to hum to himself and returned with two plates of scrambled eggs, toast, sausage, with a fork and napkin. "Coffee?"

Without reply, Daniel picked up the fork with his free hand and surveyed his breakfast. Benjamin was a fastidious cook. Eggs perfectly scrambled, sausages a dark candied brown, toast with plenty of butter melting, with a small white thimble cup filled with homemade blackberry jam. He was hungry and didn't care if he showed it, playing the appreciative guest.

When they were finished Benjamin cleared their plates, stacking them in the sink.

Daniel assumed someone else came in to wash up.

"So, Daniel, Are you up for a little hike?"

"I'm supposing I have no choice, so what do you really want from me?"

"I'm trying to keep this cordial. You should've figured that out by now."

"Cordial?" It came out as a shriek. "You call kidnapping me from my own home, almost asphyxiating me and tossing me into a locked trunk to take me some place in the middle of nowhere . . . cordial?"

Benjamin leaned back. "I could have killed you and left you for your nephew to find."

"All right, Benjamin. I should have known better than to engage in specious argument with you. That I do remember about you." He waited.

Benjamin blinked.

Pushing his advantage, Daniel added for good measure. "You know what we used to call you behind your back?"

"Who's 'we?'"

"Some of your fellow graduate students." He named a few. Anna's warning tried to shush him, but he couldn't back down now.

"No. What did they call me?"

"Benjamin, the Hedga Betcha Man."

"What was that supposed to mean?"

"You were always hedging your bets. Calculating the odds with your theories. You were more interested in currying favor than searching for any kind of historical truth. You pretended to care about context, but you didn't, really. Your so-called passion for your precious Confederacy is a fairytale."

Benjamin sighed. "Well, Daniel, let's analyze the truth about your situation now." He leaned into Daniel, leering. "You seem to be handcuffed to my table, eating my food under my rule. How do you like those odds?"

Daniel looked away.

"Ok, my old friend. Time to boogie." He unlocked the cuff and whapped it back on Daniel's wrist. He strapped on a backpack and ushered his guest out the door into the dark night.

The Big Dipper hung low.

Benjamin lit the way with his flashlight as they started to descend the trail to the river.

At the top of the trail that started the 45-degree descent, Daniel balked. "Ok, Benjamin. Where are you taking me? I'm not moving until you tell me. If you knock me out, I know you can't carry me and that pack. You need me up on my feet, ambulatory."

Benjamin considered this. "Ok, I'll tell you. We're going to my cabin in the woods." He pointed to the tree-line across the steep ravine. "It's located on the other side of the river. Not too far, but it's a bit of a hike. You still look fit, Daniel."

Yeah, but what are we going to do when we get there? He assumed that piece of information would not be forthcoming until they arrived at Benjamin's cabin.

He heard Anna's voice. "Remember the Twain quote you liked to use with your students when they were impatient for answers. 'To succeed in life, you need two things: Ignorance and confidence.' Right now, you've got both."

At 5:00 a.m. two figures crept across the rocks and graveled sand to the river's edge.

One bent down as if in prayer, lifting up the water, cleansing his face over and over.

The other shut off the bright beam and stood over his supplicant, enjoying the sound of the river, waiting for the first crack of dawn to light their way across the swift water to the steep chaparral that covered the other side.

CHAPTER 21

*The Civil War defined us as what we are and it opened us
to being what we became, good and bad things . . .
It was the crossroads of our being, and it was a hell of a crossroads.*

ON THE TREK UP TO THE CABIN Benjamin made Daniel lead, directing him where to go, but lack of a clear trail made trudging in a switch-back pattern slow. They entered the clearing at 9:00 a.m.

"Thirsty?" Benjamin pointed to the spring at the back of the cabin.

Although he'd provided a canteen for Daniel along the way, nothing seemed to satisfy his parched throat. In spite of the tall pines and thick undergrowth, there was little shade, and the August temperature was rising.

Daniel drank deeply, filling the cup three times. When he was sated, he turned to Benjamin who had put down his pack and using his hand for an eyeshade, gazing at the hawk riding the ethers overhead.

"Ok Benjamin, what now?"

"Well . . . allow me to introduce you to my neck of the woods." He swept his arm in an arc. "This cabin was built by one of the old timers. Did you know there was a gold rush in these mountains in the 1850's?"

"Ah . . . no . . . Then again, I'd have no way of knowing where we are since I arrived here while anesthetized in the trunk of your car."

"Well, there was. Brought a lot of people here," he looked around, "before and after the Civil War." He filled his lungs with the mountain air. "Of course, the real gold was the timber." He grinned at Daniel. "Lots of hot tubs." He wiped his sweaty forehead with a red bandana. "Yeah

. . . this was once a veritable Shangri La. Say, by the way, I didn't notice whether you and that wife of yours had a hot tub . . . Don't think so. Too bad."

He's making small talk. "So, are you going to keep me in there?" He gestured toward the cabin.

"That's very perceptive of you, Daniel." He directed him to approach the back door.

Daniel thought of Richard and his childhood tale about building a teepee fire. *He may have been more of a budding arsonist than an Eagle Scout.* The story illustrated his ingenuity. Richard was always quicker to action, but Daniel remembered that he could beat him at gin rummy, and he remembered Anna's observation:

"You're the better player. Richard loses his concentration and gives himself away, but you never do."

He'd asked her what she meant.

"I saw how you always watched what he picked up and discarded, . . . like you were calculating when to knock or go for gin. Richard doesn't play that way. For him, it's just fun being with you. He likes the action, while you watch and wait."

He also longed for his brother-in-law Billy. *Together, Richard and Billy would know what to do.* Inspired by the thought of them, he looked around and considered running. After the climb, he and Benjamin were both worn out, but the idea stagnated—no physical impulse followed. *Her voice repeated. "You're the better player."*

Inside the cabin, it was clear what Benjamin had in mind. *This was to be his prison, at least temporarily.*

Benjamin stood over him. "Take off your shoes."

He spotted the ankle cuff at the end of a six-foot chain bolted to the floor. "That for me?"

"Why, yes, it is." Once again, Benjamin reached over by the roll-top desk, tossed his shoes in the far corner, and threw him the key to his handcuffs.

He caught the key in both hands, which made him feel better, like a kid catching his first baseball. *If only I could run with it.* But he was already feeling the smaller triumphs that must become part of a captive's tenuous self-esteem. *Maybe Anna's right. I should stick to my gin rummy prowess and not make a move that doesn't come naturally.*

As he massaged his wrists, he looked up at the mighty bear pelt hanging on the wall. "Jesus, Benjamin, where'd that come from?"

"That, my friend, is Jimmy. Like him?" He grinned. "He's my pride and joy."

Daniel's eyes widened and for the first time since he'd seen Benjamin standing at his front door 15 hours earlier, he was speechless.

As he stared at the shiny molars he heard Anna's voice, "Ignorance and confidence."

After Bear received the call from Richard at 10:30 p.m., he explained the situation to Jenny. "I have another crisis on my hands. I've got to go down to the Bay Area, but I will be back as soon as I can, hopefully within 24 hours. Meanwhile, let's see what the police find. I don't want to horn in on their territory anyway. It only creates hard feelings." He got up and kissed her on the head. "Call me if she wakes up."

"Okay." She smiled.

"Call me if you learn anything at all. Susan's on her way. She'll stay with you."

"Thanks."

By 11:00 p.m. Bear headed south on the freeway. As he picked up speed, he didn't notice the black Audi passing him two lanes over heading north. He arrived at Daniel's house at 3:00 a.m.

Richard let him in. They talked for a while in low voices, not wanting to wake up Tom who had fallen asleep on the couch with Numi draped over his ankles. They decided to also get some sleep before they would all gather in the morning at 9:00 a.m.

"Will Gertrude be there?"

Richard chuckled. "Of course."

Bear knew Gertrude from a previous case involving one of Rebecca's clients. "How is that wise old owl?"

"Never better. Fit as a fiddle. She just stays the same, full of energy. I swear . . . she's a force to be reckoned with."

Bear nodded, shaking his head. "She puts us all to shame."

"That she does."

At 7:00 a.m. Jenny called Bear and told him the police had managed to find out from the Bend owner that Flora had left at noon with some old guy who was there earlier. His Audi was parked outside. He apparently left and then came back a few hours later and picked her up.

They all knew that Jenny was "car struck."

Flora speculated, "He must have offered her a ride. You know how she feels about cars."

"What kind of Audi was it?"

"They think it was an Audi W12."

"Yeah, well, that's an impressive car. Also probably never seen one like that up there in Hicksville."

"Come on, Bear. We're not hicks up here. We're just more rural."

"No offence. Remember I live there too. But since when have you seen or heard of a car like that stop at the Bend in the River Café? As in, . . . probably never? And that might be somehow the link to why Flora got into that car. If she saw it, she would have noticed it, and if she noticed it, she might have said something to the owner." He paused, thinking as he did, allowing his thoughts to free-associate. "And if she made note of it to the owner . . . he just might have not wanted it to be noticed. After all, a car like that in the Bend's parking lot would be a fish out of water."

He promised Jenny he would return as soon as he could.

At 9:00 a.m. Rebecca and Gertrude arrived together.

Twenty minutes later Tom came in with Morrigan. He'd picked her up and explained what happened on the way over.

She looked tired and pale.

Gertrude brought fresh hot cross buns and Richard made coffee.

Bear sat next to Gertrude while the others joined around the coffee table with Anna's book displayed in the middle with Samuel Adam's roving eye.

"All right," Bear started, "Daniel's filled me in on most of the background." He looked at Tom. "Zachariah . . . your great great-great-great," he calculated on his fingers, "grandfather—assuming about 25 to 30 years a generation and considering the Civil War is now 145 years old—communicates with you."

Tom agreed. Stated so matter-of-factly, it sounded perfectly normal. *As if everyone talks to their dead 4 great-grandfather who fought in the Civil War.*

"We know that Zak has warned Tom about some guy named Benjamin who's been stalking and maybe now kidnapped Daniel, and that Richard here," gesturing toward Richard, "who's known Daniel since their school days and is aware of Daniel's history with Benjamin."

Richard summarized what he knew, mentioning Daniel's friend

Ephraim Brown, that his family's letter, written by his four-great-grandfather to Frederick Douglas, that seemed to be the lightening rod at the center of their old feud. "No one knows what became of Benjamin after he was fired from the University He seems to have vanished for all these years and now . . . well, it appears he's surfaced."

"Yes," Gertrude piped up, "with some sort of revenge brewing all these years."

Bear turned to her. "What are you thinking?"

"Well . . . just that the Civil War still seems alive and well in our collective psyche. I was married for 40 years to a southern man from Charleston. I remember he read Robert Penn Warren's book "The Legacy of the Civil War "in 1961 and he liked to quote Warren. It went something like this. 'The moment General Lee handed General Grant his sword at Appomattox, the Confederacy was born, or, to put it another way,'" she paused to increase her usual dramatic flair, "that was the moment the Confederacy died and entered its immortality."

Bear stared at Gertrude and then in what appeared a moment of spontaneous chivalry he lifted her hand and kissed it.

They all watched.

Breaking the silence, Tom spoke. ' Shelby Foote said, 'Southerners are very weird about their war.'"

They laughed.

"Well put," Richard agreed. "For some reason Shelby Foote was able to talk about the South in a way that sounded neutral, even though he was a true southerner. He also said that when you grow up in a totally segregated society, where everyone around you believes segregation is proper, you can't believe how much that thinking has become a part of you."

Rebecca leaned forward. "And keep in mind the opposite is true as well. When segregation around you breeds hatred and resentment you can't believe how violent you can feel against it. Who can forget the sixties?"

"Yes," Gertrude agreed. "And that may be exactly what we're dealing with here. A man who somehow has absorbed the ideal of the Confederacy as if it were his own private religion. Only I think we must assume that this infatuation has been built largely on an idealization that has become a full-blown delusion. A delusion he acts upon that completely denies the reality of anything else."

At that moment, Bear's cell went off. He flipped it open and excused himself, heading out the front door, assuming the reception would be better outside. "What can I do for you Mr. DeWitt?"

Axel explained that his son had been missing for ten days. The police had made no real progress and he wanted to hire Bear immediately. "Your fee's no object," he added, assuming that incentive would seal the deal.

"I'm sorry, Mr. DeWitt, but right now I'm working two cases and I just don't see how I could add yours on top of the other two." He tried to give Axel other names of private detectives who might be available, but Axel was not easily put off. He increased what he would pay. Bear apologized a second time and repeated the names, looking up some phone numbers as added incentive to get rid of Axel.

Again, Axel came back with more money and added for no apparent reason, "They ran off in my Audi W12. How hard can it be to trace a car like that?"

Bear's training and life experience in the business of finding people had taught him there were no coincidences. "What kind of a car did you say?"

Axel repeated the make of car, adding, "I just bought that car. Drexel took it without my permission, and I want it back."

Bear wondered which was more important—the son or the car. As if he read his thoughts Axel quickly added, "I want my son back."

"All right, Mr. DeWitt. I'll take your case. I'll get back to you in about an hour to go over the details." He went back inside and sat next to Gertrude who smiled at his return.

Bear focused on Morrigan, who was still next to Tom. He could tell she was scared and that meant she knew something. He didn't want to press her in front of everyone, which might cause her to retreat further. He decided to let Tom find out what they really needed to know, which was, *where does Benjamin live?* He knew if the police questioned her, she wouldn't say. Their only chance was Tom . . . and Gertrude. He decided to wait and watch her as she listened to them talk, staring at the floor. *She's trying to decide something.*

He continued to go over what evidence they had. "Two coffee cups." He pointed to the couches. "They sat right here and talked." He looked at Numi peeking out from under Tom's hand stroking his head. "So, Numi, you saw it all. If only you could speak."

"Well in a way he did when I got home," Tom explained. "I've never seen him behave the way he did. He was spooked. Whoever came . . . Numi didn't like him."

"Yeah . . ." Bear drawled. He looked at Rebecca. "Too bad those Chow sisters of yours weren't here."

They all laughed, remembering how Juno and Dido helped trap another villain the year before.

"We need a plan of action." Bear looked around at all of them inviting suggestions. "Let's start with brain-storming and see what falls out." He kept one eye on Morrigan.

Rebecca leaned forward. "Do we all agree that this Benjamin we have been referring to is the same Benjamin Zak has warned Tom about and," she looked at Morrigan, "your stepfather?"

She nodded as she kept her gaze lowered.

Rebecca continued, "There are so many serendipitous moments in our hypothetical train of thought it's easy to lose track."

Gertrude took a sip of her coffee and set her mug down next to the pelican. "Then let's go through them, my Dear."

"All right," Rebecca went on, "I'll take a stab at it. Tom's mother calls her brother, Daniel, six weeks ago and asks if Tom can come and live with him—he had been accepted at the University here that both Daniel and Benjamin attended 40 years ago—a reasonable but unexpected request. Keep in mind that Daniel and his sister, Carol Ann, could not be more different and seem to have little in common." She looked at the pelican. "Contact was really maintained through Anna until she died and after that contact was initiated by Carol Ann."

Richard felt the need to speak for his friend. "Brother and sister could not be more different. He's an academic and she's . . ." the words wouldn't form.

Tom chimed in. "My mother's an intuitive. It's true her genius is not as an academic, like my uncle, but her emotional IQ is high." He looked around. "My mother is not stupid."

Gertrude spoke. "We know that, Tom. You are in a group of people who know that."

Tom sat back.

Morrigan remained quiet.

Gertrude looked back at Rebecca, gesturing for her to continue.

"Ok. Tom has a history of speaking to his great-grand father Zachariah Monroe for eight years now. And Zak has told him something recently that we all are taking seriously, which is that Daniel is in imminent danger. So, Tom's arrival here at this time and place is no accident." She looked at Tom. "You appear to be the messenger."

Tom smiled.

"And rest assured we have no intention of shooting you."

They laughed.

"Tom," Rebecca continued, "surprised Daniel with . . . I don't just want to say, his intelligence. But more to the point, that he came from his sister and brother-in-law's family. We all know that Daniel's view of his sister has been skewed by his bias toward his own small town."

She looked at Tom. "You shocked him, Tom. He never expected someone like you to show up." She thought for a moment. "And you know he should have."

They were quiet.

In their silence they all heard the front door open and close. Someone had let themselves in and stepped into the entry. They held their breath. Numi jumped down and walked out to greet her.

"Hello there, Numi." Melinda Mason peeked around the corner holding him like a gigantic muff over her folded arms.

They all stood up.

Gertrude introduced Bear, made room on the couch and summarized the situation.

Melinda looked around at all of them. "I'm very worried. I spoke with Daniel yesterday about 6:15. He sounded fine, but tired. Said he was going to eat something and go to bed early. Nothing unusual." She looked at Tom. "He said you weren't home yet and that he looked forward to a quiet evening together with me tonight."

Tom explained where he'd been.

Again, Gertrude summarized what they'd talked about at their meeting and their plan to speak with Daniel. "This very day about our concern for his safety." She looked at Melinda. "What do you think? Any thoughts?"

After a minute considering that, she spoke. "Yes . . . I think Daniel's sister should be called and asked to come out here to help."

Gertrude slapped both hands on her knees. "I heartily agree, my dear."

Rebecca agreed. "So do I."

Tom added, "Thank you."

Bear took over. "Ok. We're assuming the kidnapper is this guy you all mention by the name Benjamin. I don't want to be a wet blanket here, but how can we be sure?"

At that moment, Tom remembered that the child's pelican had been taken from the bathroom. "Could that mean something?"

Gertrude agreed. "I'm sure it does. He must have thought the pelican was special to Daniel and to Anna's memory and really her life's passion. He certainly saw the book here. Perhaps even set his coffee cup down on it. Such a personal icon would be imbued with a unique set of pneumonic associations to her specialness . . . and of course Daniel's continuing connection to her."

Gertrude's words triggered something else for Tom. He reached into his back pocket and produced the book of matches he'd found on the ground under Anna's bench the night before, just after he spoke with Zak. "Does the Bend in the River Café mean anything to you guys?"

Bear stood up. "Yes, it does."

Morrigan at last looked up and spoke. "I'll show you where he lives."

Bear went outside again to call Axel de Witt while Tom went to call his mother.

CHAPTER 22

Native tribes across North America venerated and feared grizzlies.
They felt a familial connection, calling them "grandfather" and
"great-great grandfather," "chief's son," "elder brother,"and "little uncle."

THE NIGHT BEFORE HE LEFT TO DRIVE SOUTH to pick up Daniel, and the same night he spoke to Morrigan, he had the recurring dream. In this one, Jimmy was alive, ambling beside him through the forest, heading for the river. When they came to the edge, Jimmy headed into the rapids, while he stepped back to watch the lone warrior sitting on his horse on the other side. It was Stonewall, sitting up straight, his left arm in the air, palm forward. Behind him the sky turned red as it always did in the dream. He thought it was the sunset, but the hills erupted into hungry flames, eventually consuming everything, including the old warrior.

He woke covered in sweat, heart pounding, and stepped outside the house into the crisp, clear air. "So," he announced to the sky, "this will be my ending. It was meant to be, and he waits for me on the other side."

He'd been over and over it many times, each time adding a new detail or subtracting one. The last time he visualized it he decided it was as close to perfect as it could be. The last dialog with Daniel would show him, once and for all, who he was.

Benjamin's righteousness over the years had woven a seamless web of certainty that could no longer be penetrated by any doubt whatsoever. This certainty trumped all reality so that he no longer surmised, but knew it was the truth. And like so many great truths it was simple, immediately apprehensible by anyone. He often imagined various prologues—all roads leading to the same, irrevocable ending. Like Gettysburg. Ten roads leading to a fate that could not be avoided. In his version the fact that Lee was forced to retreat after devastating casualties did not contradict this simple, obvious truth.

He played with the words over the years, taking out bigger ones, adding and subtracting clauses, putting in and taking out commas.

In the end, he wanted the perfect round number to be ten words with no commas. *Ten signifies the Divine order where nothing more is wanting. Noah completed the antediluvian age in the tenth generation after God created man. The Tenth Amendment states: "The powers not delegated to the United States by the Constitution, nor prohibited by it to the States, are reserved to the States, respectively, or to the people." Ten roads lead to Gettysburg. And last, but not least, because there are endless mystical meanings pertaining to ten—Stonewall died on May 10, 1863.*

His final notation of it looked so simple, like it was nothing. And yet it signified everything. Ten simple words that said it all:

"Freedom conceived in the Constitution equals the right to self-government."

He often pondered whether self-government was really two words. But in the end after multiple transitions, he determined that self-government was one word, the hyphenated word that embodied the whole.

There was no room for sophomoric liberals like Daniel Perry. No. The Perrys of the world would lead inevitably to a government-domination tantamount to dictatorship. He had known this long before libertarianism gained popularity. He knew it in his bones.

When he listened to his grandfather and Cal around the campfires he learned, and then knew it. He was a pilgrim carrying their legacy, and his path was lit with heavenly fire. The same fire that was in the belly of the Confederacy. *Their fight was not over slavery, but the right to self-government. They had been invaded and were simply protecting what was theirs to protect.*

He was no disgruntled actor like John Wilkes Booth. He was a soldier, unafraid to die carrying the war cry of Stonewall's Brigade born the day he was named Stonewall at the First Battle of Bull Run, or so the legend goes. "Let us determine to die here and we will conquer." *He was motivated by an inner flame that could never be put out by any reason. His truth transcended reason. There was no room for argument of the kind that Daniel Perry spawned.*

Two nights later when he drove the car north with Daniel in the trunk he thought about Anna. He had only seen her once and never met her, but Morrigan reported that Daniel still talked to her even though she was dead. He'd decided she, too, was like Stonewall. *Nothing could stop her except death.* He thought of her cavorting with the Dolphins in Heaven. He believed his possession of the child's ceramic pelican meant more to him than it did to Daniel, who never understood the mystical significance of anything, much less an object crafted by a child. He, on the other hand, respected the wisdom of children. *Their innocence transcended the stupidity of adults. Daniel's a thinker, a debater, and worst of all—a member of the radical middle. All points of view are respected, hence rendered minor in the greater scheme of things.*

Tom drove to the airport at 5:00 a.m. to pick up his parents. He looked forward to seeing them, realizing he'd missed them without knowing it. He tried to imagine what this part of the country would be, seen through their eyes, but couldn't.

He arrived at their gate 10 minutes early. The plane was on time. He watched as passengers finally began to trickle out. He stood up and maneuvered closer but didn't see them until the line thinned out.

They emerged, both looking around.

He waved, but they seemed too dazed to spot him until Carol Ann erupted with both arms out.

Billy chuckled and took his hand as if to shake it, and pulled him into a bear hug.

On the drive to Daniel's, they looked out at the awakening City and stared at the foothills. Billy sat in the back. "Is that the Pacific?"

"Yeah, Dad. It's the San Francisco Bay. That's why they call this," he waved his arm around, "the Bay Area."

Billy nodded and continued to stare out the window.

He glanced at his mother in the passenger seat. "How are you, Mom?"

She smiled and put her hand on his shoulder. "We're fine."

He wanted to say, "I asked about You," but he knew his mother. There was no "I," only "We." She was her family and she and Billy were one.

He told them what he knew so far about Daniel's disappearance. They listened quietly.

As they pulled up in front of Daniel's house Billy leaned forward and whispered, "We'll find him, Son."

Those four words brought him a kind of comfort he'd been missing. With Daniel he felt there was always some kind of intellectual competition in the air, and he'd begun to forget the soothing simplicity of his parents' world. Since coming to Daniel's he'd entered a world where relationships seemed to require more effort. Nothing, as he was learning, could be taken for granted. He liked Richard and Rebecca and Gertrude and Melinda and felt nurtured by them. But with Uncle Daniel he'd felt displaced. Or was it he who'd been displaced? After all, he and Daniel were blood relatives, but completely different. He had left his home behind. Tom knew he could never do that - move away perhaps, but never forget where he came from.

He thought about Zak. *Who could be expected to understand that he talked to a ghost? Zak might talk in riddles but somehow, he still made more sense than Daniel, who lived in a house that represented more about Anna than him. The pelican was her creature, and he hadn't understood why she named him Samuel Adams. Numi, too, was hers.*

He switched to a question that suddenly seemed the most pressing. *Who took the child's pelican from the bathroom and why?*

Benjamin left the cabin and locked the door.

Daniel heard the click of the padlock, to seal him in. He looked around. There was a rolled-up mat and blanket within reach, water, an old-fashioned urinal and a cooler. *How long is he planning to keep me here?* He opened the cooler and peered in. A couple of cheese and tomato sandwiches, jar of pickles, some granola bars, two apples and a pint of milk. He unfolded the mat and a pillow spilled up. *He's thought of every amenity. Does he want me to be comfortable or uncomfortable?*

This summarized Benjamin in his memory. *He was always conflicted. Never could tell what he was really thinking. One minute he was passionate and seemed to care and the next minute he was cold and calculating.*

After eating half a sandwich and drinking some milk he lay down and fell asleep.

In the dream he and Anna were dancing. They were young and she was laughing and teasing him because he was so clutzy, which just made him want to dance more. He hopped around trying to follow the rhythm, but he kept stumbling over his own big feet fueling her amusement.

Then they were running on the beach, and he couldn't keep up there either. The sand pulled him in. He couldn't understand how Anna could glide over it like a swooping bird. She'd look back and beckon but kept getting smaller in the distance.

Melinda appeared, taking his hand and they walked slowly, and he realized he wasn't young anymore.

He woke not knowing where he was until he saw the bear on the wall. To calm himself he began to consider his surroundings. *The chain and single ankle cuff were antique, made of wrought iron. Used for a slave before the Civil War? He probably got it on Ebay. You can get anything on there.*

He realized this whole caper of Benjamin's was symbolic of something. An enactment. *Retribution? Revenge?* He knew Benjamin wouldn't kill him until the game—whatever it meant—played out to its end. He gazed into Jimmy's dead eyes. *Who are you to Benjamin?*

He heard her voice. "He's Benjamin's 'white buffalo.'" At first, he was confused and then he remembered Anna's obsession with the Lakota Sioux. *Well . . . some omen.*

He looked around the cabin. *The bed in the corner looks new. He's begun to spend more time here. It's remote. The river's about half a mile down a steep incline. Bear country. A gold rush happened here. It's logging country . . . or was.*

He began to calculate the approximate hours from his house to that industrial kitchen where Benjamin cooked the breakfast. His watch had said 2:00 a.m. He closed his eyes to see a map of California. And then he remembered when they stood at the spring outside, Benjamin had described where they were as "Shangri La." *Why had that phrase sounded familiar?* He knew the reference from Hilton's book, "Lost Horizon," but why did it mean something about where they were? *Lots of places could be compared to a Shangri La.* And then the memory clicked in, and he traveled back 20 years.

Anna had been teaching some children about California history and the gold rush in the 1850's. One Saturday morning in July she dragged him out of bed, telling him they were taking an overnight trip to a place where you can still see what it was like in the 1850's.

They headed north and, on the way, she described the place. He could hear her voice. "It's beautiful country. Mountains, rivers, Black Bears, Golden Eagles, and it was called 'Shangri La.' It's still beautiful, but I want the children to know what happens when human greed takes over. The La Grange gold mine was one of the first to use hydraulics. They got $3,500,000 worth of gold out in 1914, before they left huge barren caverns in their wake and the loggers had already come. The town that grew up in their midst is called Weaverville. That's where we're going. You'll see what I'm talking about. It's like walking into a time warp."

They spent the day wandering around Weaverville while Anna took hundreds of pictures to show the children.

On the way back, she talked about taking them on a field trip so they could see for themselves the ravages of the LaGrange Mine and the acres of stripped forests. He remembered hoping she wouldn't rope him into chaperoning a bunch of rowdy children. She didn't. She found some helpful, enthusiastic parents and left Daniel behind "to waste your weekend as you please."

He still missed her parting shots. He knew she only half-meant whatever she said. And he remembered he did waste his time wisely by re-reading Huckleberry Finn for the fifth time and inviting Richard over for some "scotch and chatter," which is what they called their drunken Saturday night dialogs that were more like mutual diatribes.

He saw the route going up Highway 5, then turning east on 299 that took them into Weaverville. It was a six-and-half-hour drive. He remembered thinking how beautiful and remote the country was. The tourist industry seemed to have passed it by and the locals seemed conflicted about wanting to attract tourists and wanting to keep them away. Every local he talked to that day shunned the idea of more, and yet they needed it for their economy to survive after the logging industry bit the dust. *They liked their privacy and were proud of their history—the good and bad of it.* He noticed there were still lots of old timers with plenty of stories.

He was certain that they were somewhere in those Trinity Alps. *James Hilton really had labeled it "Shangri La."*

How these fun facts could help him now he had no idea. Even if he had a cell phone, what good would it do here? *In this terrain coverage would probably be less than zero. But then, of course, one never knew.*

Again, Anna's voice. "Daniel, at least you have to try. Even if it's hopeless . . . you have to try."

Figuring out that he must be in the Trinity Alps region helped him feel less vulnerable. He stood up, feeling like the Tin Man, wobbly at first but after stepping from side to side, as if in a ritual dance, the blood started to flow like oil in an engine. He bobbed up and down on his feet the way Anna used to do in the kitchen when she'd been standing too long.

He stared out the far window. Blue sky, pines at the periphery of the clearing, dry underbrush, a lazy hawk floating and gliding . . . and then he scarcely could believe what he saw. Benjamin was building a 7-foot teepee fire in the clearing about 50 feet from the cabin. *If and when . . . no . . . I mean when he sets that pyre the whole forest is going up.* He watched him step back to survey his structure, removing his baseball cap to wipe his forehead before he turned around and looked toward the cabin.

Daniel crouched down. *My God . . . what's he planning?* He tried not to panic. *Think. Think. Stay calm.* He forced himself to breath in and out. He could hear her voice. "In and out, Daniel, in and out." *Or was it Melinda's voice? He wasn't sure.* He relaxed.

He spotted the roll top desk over by the wall. The chair in front was a vintage bankers' swivel chair with a molded seat and slats on the back on a steel base with wheels. On the seat he had noticed a small black sling cloth bag. No way he could he reach it. He lay down and stretched himself across the floor as far as he could, then looked around to see if there was anything he might use to touch the chair. An old broom was next to the back door. He was about one foot shy of reaching it.

He sat up and concentrated, waiting for the light bulb to go on, which it would because it always did if he slowed down. *Count the cards. Count the cards.* He waited. Five minutes went by. And another five. Nothing. He waited.

How long it took he wasn't sure, but the light bulb finally went on. He grabbed the pillow Benjamin had so thoughtfully provided. He was an expert in pillow fights in college. His friends called him 'Pillow Shot.' He was famous in the dorm his freshman year. He sat up and gauged how far he could zap it without letting go. Sitting up, and taking aim, he could hit the chair. He didn't try because he knew he could push it farther away, but if he could sling the pillow over the back of the chair like a lever, he could pull it toward him. He practiced the shot without aiming for the chair but calculating the odds that he could make it work. If he didn't hit the chair with a hooked sling, he could push it away. He probably had one shot.

He sat up as straight as he could, held the pillow in his lap and asked himself, "Who am I?" He heard her voice. "Ahhh . . . you're Sandy Koufax." He smiled, readying himself. And then he threw the pitch.

The chair slid smoothly to him. He grabbed the bag and clutched it like Gollum with his ring, and out came a bright and shiny new cell phone. He gazed at it lovingly just as he heard the screen door pulled back and Benjamin jiggling the padlock. He tossed the bag into the chair and carefully aimed it back to the desk as he thrust the phone into his pocket.

He stood in the doorway surveying the cabin.

At first, Daniel thought, *He knows what I just did.*

"So, you're awake. That's good. We have a lot to talk about."

CHAPTER 23

Living off the grid and being kind of an outlaw brings a dangerous reality.
RON PERLMAN

SHE GOT UP AT 5:30 A.M. Outside, the trees were shrouded in the August fog that rolls in off the bay, especially in the summer.

She opened the window and leaned out to breath in the cool air.

After a quick shower she slipped out of the house. No one was up yet. Passing her landlady's bedroom, she heard the rhythmic snoring that reassured her the old lady could not be spying.

Tom was supposed to pick her up at 8:30 to return to Professor Perry's house. She hoped to be long gone by then.

After their meeting, Tom had brought her back, and she'd lain awake most of the night. They had planned to meet and form a strategy. He would be picking up his parents while she was skipping town. Her presence was essential to them, given her statement to Bear, "I'll show you where he lives."

She had bounced from one thing to another, fueled by her uncertainty and terror for her family, her mother and Hannah. She couldn't warn them. He never allowed them to use phones or have access to email or any other kind of communication. It was understood that when you joined Benjamin's family you left the outside world. Even though it was a cult, no one was allowed to mention that word or any other that might peg them for that.

She thought about Blanco, who had arrived not long before she left for college, and she knew Benjamin treated him with some specialness because of his skill on that laptop. She wondered if he could email, but realized it didn't make any difference. *He would probably tell Benjamin.* From the moment she laid eyes on Blanco she knew he would be his creature, do his bidding. Blanco was savvy and grew up on the streets rather than live in foster care. When he first came, the only real information she had about him was that he'd run away from about five foster families before he fell off the grid and out of their system, which made Benjamin Papa Cat very proud of him.

She was certain he took Professor Perry to the compound, and equally certain he would not introduce him to the others. No. He had long laid plans for the professor, and her attending the University had all along been so she could make the contact. *I'm like all of them. Just a means to some demented Armageddon that started hatching many years ago.*

As she lay in the semi-darkness, she also realized that she had not needed Beth or Sugar Pie for several weeks now. Something Gertrude said to her reverberated and she understood now it had been true.

"My dear, you have constructed these alternate personalities to protect yourself. Beth keeps you calm and applies her intellect to keep Benjamin impressed and needing you. As you've said, he admires your smarts. Indeed, he does. And Sugar Pie? Well, I'm not sure, but I think you thought you might need her to deal with any sexual encounters you might have to face with him, or any other predator along the way. But I think Sugar Pie actually betrayed you, and you must realize now she is a danger to you, not a protector."

She knew Gertrude could help her, and she wished she could let her. But the danger was too immediate. She needed to act and not think so much. *That's my skill. I'm Morrigan and I know when to act. Beth can think all she wants, but she's no good for action. And Sugar Pie? Gertrude was right about her. I should have killed her long ago.*

Her focus shifted to Benjamin. *My God, he could kill them all. He won't let them just live on without him. He can't keep it from them any longer that he's completely psychotic. I'm their only chance.*

She recalled another thing Gertrude said. "In time, my dear, I think your need for these alternate personalities will fade. As you take in gradually what you have sensed all along and needed to keep from your awareness, in order to function, you will re-absorb Beth and Sugar Pie into the real you, who is Morrigan."

Maybe so. But I can't wait around to find out. I've gotta get out a here.

It also occurred to her that something unexpected had happened this summer. For the first time she could ever remember she allowed herself to feel and care. *I love you, Tom.* The tears wet her cheeks and seeped down into her pillow, and then sleep came for several hours.

After stopping for gas, she got coffee and a pre-made sandwich from the convenience store.

At 11:00 a.m. she turned off Highway 299, heading for the place she had called home for the past ten years. If Benjamin's anything, it's unpredictable.

Tom returned to Daniel's at 9:00. "She's gone. I checked her room and then looked in the garage. Her little red VW bug was gone." He stared at everyone—Gertrude, Rebecca, Melinda, Richard, Bear and his parents sitting together on the couch with Numi draped over Carol Ann's lap.

They all could see that he was distraught.

Gertrude stood up and went over to him to guide him back to the couch.

Rebecca slid over to make room and gently placed her hand on his shoulder as he sat down. "Coffee?"

He smiled and nodded.

She poured him a cup. "Cream or milk?"

"No thanks."

She looked at Bear, who cleared his throat. "Tom, where do you think she went?"

"I'm not sure." His mind had been racing since he realized she was gone. *Was she lying to me all along? Does she work for her stepfather? How crazy is she? Have I been a stupid fool?*

Gertrude put her hand on Tom's knee. "I'm fairly certain I can guess where she's gone."

They all waited, knowing that Gertrude's guess would be their best bet.

"She will try to get to her mother and little sister as soon as possible. Certainly, before she tells us. I believe after she gets to where they are . . ." she turned to Tom, "she'll contact you."

Tom reflected on this.

Bear's phone went off. He stepped out of the room.

Rebecca spoke. "She must have a cell phone. Tom, you could try calling her?"

He shook his head. "That's just it. I don't think she does." He frowned. "I remember she said once that Benjamin didn't let any of them have phones. Wherever they live they're completely cut off."

Bear returned and sat down.

Carol Ann looked at her son. "Tom, what was the first connection between this Benjamin and Daniel?"

"Graduate school. Forty years ago."

"And Morrigan is his stepdaughter and she's a student at the University you met in Daniel's summer class?"

"Yeah . . . what are you thinking?"

"Well, I'm thinking that she must have said something. People usually do. Clues, I mean. About where they live."

Bear interrupted. "I've got some news." He told them about the connection between Flora and Benjamin and the link to Axel DeWitt. "I just got a call from Jenny, Flora's mother. Flora woke up briefly and told them the car was an Audi and that the old guy who tried to kill her resembled Benjamin. That car we think was the same one Benjamin drove west on 299, then south on 5. The Café is on the other side of Weaverville."

Tom looked up. "Omigod! I think Morrigan once said that name— Weaverville. I'm pretty sure. I don't remember the connection, and I wouldn't have remembered at all except you just mentioned it."

Carol Ann smiled all around. "You see . . . we know things we don't know we know. Why, that happens to me all the time. And you know . . . ?"

They all leaned forward, lulled by her softly sing-song voice. "I just know Daniel's trying to contact us. Since early this morning I've seen over and over in my mind's eye . . . a little silver cell phone. Itty bitty one."

No one denied the legitimacy of Carol Ann's vision.

Gertrude looked at Bear. "I think that helps, don't you?"

He nodded. "Yes."

Billy patted his wife's hand. "That's why I married this ol' girl. She wasn't just a looker. She's a seer. And what she sees is the truth."

Gertrude added, "Indeed it is." They all sat quietly until Richard broke their silence. "So, Bear . . . have we got a plan?"

"Yes, we have." He looked around the room. "A man named Axel DeWitt is flying into the local airport. He arrives in an hour and a half." He looked at his watch. "10:00 a.m. I'm meeting him there." He looked at Richard, then Billy. "I'd like you two to come with me to meet DeWitt. From there we continue in Mr. DeWitt's small private plane, and it looks like we're going to Weaverville. There's a very small airport there. DeWitt's ordered a helicopter to meet us wherever we're going."

They all looked agog.

"Just so you know . . . DeWitt's fairly rich . . . I mean really rich."

Bear announced the rest of the plan. "Tom, Rebecca and Melinda . . . you take my van to Weaverville. If you leave in the next half hour you should arrive by 3:30 or 4:00 this afternoon. We'll be in cell phone contact. Maybe Morrigan . . . or Daniel . . . will have reached out by then." He looked at Gertrude. "I think you're right . . . she wants to warn her mother and sister. She probably assumes rightly that they're in some kind of imminent danger. If we're thinking correctly, this Benjamin is a very lethal character. So, Gertrude and Carol Ann . . . you two stay here at Daniel's. You never know who might show up. And I'd like you to pick up Rebecca's chows and bring them here to keep you company. And we know what good watch dogs they are."

Gertrude and Carol Ann smiled at each other.

Carol Ann picked up Numi who had been wandering across her sandaled feet. She hugged him.

Numi turned on the purring loud enough for all to hear.

"Don't worry . . . I know you're going to catch this man."

"Hope so." But Bear was not so sure. "This guy's a silverfish."

At noon, she navigated the dirt road up to the house, carefully avoiding the potholes she knew were there.

She remembered one year when Benjamin had actually gone out to the road in the Spring, after the winter rains, to worsen what the weather had already done. At the dinner table that night he announced, "It'll take a 4-wheeler to get up that road."

But it didn't now. She could drive Ladybug up and down because she knew what to avoid. Her little car was like a Corgi puppy she'd seen dodging obstacles as if they were just playthings for his amusement.

She pulled into the clearing in front of the house. No sign of anyone. Not even their bouncy Midge, the retriever, to greet her.

She got out and walked up to the front door and turned the latch. It was locked. She stepped back and looked around. That door was never locked. She didn't even know it could be. She felt the panic start to rise.

She pounded on the door, but she knew no one was there. She raced around, peering through curtained windows, fearing the worst. *Omigod! He's killed them all.* She couldn't stop the image in her head of dead bodies strewn around. But still, no sign of life. There was no convenient window to smash so she could reach in, the way they always do in the movies to open the door.

She took a moment to try to calm down and sat on the front steps, chin resting in her hand. First, she heard the silence, then some Stellar Jays fighting over territory.

She almost didn't hear the tentative twist of the front doorknob. She jumped up and turned around, heart pounding.

Whoever was behind the door seemed to be trying to peek out without revealing themselves.

Her first thought was that it was one of the children being shy or scared. "Hey," she announced, "It's me. Morrigan."

The door opened slowly, revealing his spiked head. Blanco stood in the doorway, appearing, she thought, both pleased and apprehensive to see her. He didn't speak.

"Blanco, what's going on? Where is everyone?"

He opened the door wider, and she entered the dark interior.

They went into the dining room where she could see his laptop on the table.

He sat down in front of it and she across from him.

She waited for him to tell her what was going on.

He seemed rattled, which was unlike him. "They're gone."

"What do you mean . . . gone?" She looked around as if expecting them all to jump out shouting "Surprise!" She knew how the children like to do that.

"They left two nights ago. He came back, but didn't even check on them, so I think he doesn't know."

"What do you mean? He came back here and didn't realize they were gone?"

"Yeah."

"Ok, Blanco. You have to do better than that. Tell me what you know." She summoned as much command in her voice as she could, just in case he was lying for Benjamin. She wanted to keep the upper hand. She was the interrogator, not he. She didn't know Blanco well, since he came six months before she left, but she did know he was Benjamin's little creature. Blanco had skills Benjamin needed and that made him very valuable.

He told her that when Benjamin left in the Audi two nights ago they all got together and talked about what everyone suspected . . . that he was going over the edge, finally. "Even your mother was scared. I guess the last straw was Drexel."

"Who's Drexel?" she demanded.

He told her about Drexel. "I mean it was pretty clear that Benjamin didn't just let Drexel walk away from here. I mean we all knew."

She stared at the knot patterns on the pine table. She looked up at him, urging him to go on.

"You know he'd been stashing a bunch of cash all over. Lately more than ever. He'd go out at night and bury it under rocks, and stuff . . . like that."

Her eyes darted around trying to imagine Benjamin on one of his nocturnal wanderings. "You knew where all the money was?"

"Pretty much."

"How much was there? And who's money?"

"A lot. He likes small bills."

"How did he get it?"

He looked at her for the first time the way geeks do when someone asks a stupid, technical question. "Benjamin kept accounts all over. Never more than 50K in any one place so no one suspected how much he had. He pretty much has everyone around here believing he makes all his money from growing marijuana. Small business operation. Nothing big."

"But he didn't?"

"Well, he used to do more. But then he brought that old lady here about six years ago and she left him all her money. The one who said she was a cousin of Elvis."

"Oh my God." She stared off into the distance at nothing. "How come you know so much and the rest of us didn't?"

He was quick to explain. "I managed all the accounts after I came here and then . . ." he looked around as if there might be some one lurking, "I took all the money from Drexel's Dad."

Her eyes opened wide. She shrugged, "Like . . . how much?"

"Given what the guy's worth . . . not that much."

"Ball-park me." She watched him hesitate, but she knew he wanted to brag.

"About half a million . . . from different accounts. The guy's worth at least a billion. I doubt he's missed it."

Her mind started to reel. "So . . . where's all that money?"

"In his accounts. He keeps it there and then he withdraws cash. He makes the rounds to all his accounts. He's got cash stashed all over."

"Show me." She wanted Blanco to think she doubted him.

He looked around, considering. "Look . . . if I show you, he'll kill me."

"Trust me. He's about to get caught."

Blanco prided himself on his ability to size up anyone, and he decided to trust her. He stood up. "Follow me."

She followed him outside.

He walked fast toward the path that led to the descent to the river. Instead of heading down he veered to the left and clambered through some underbrush. He led her about 200 yards through thick Manzanita until they reached a small clearing with granite rocks strewn around. He lifted a few and then pointed to the ground.

She hesitated, suspicious. For a split second his gesture of pointing down felt like Benjamin. "Show me," she ordered again.

He pushed dirt aside that revealed a board, which he removed and pulled up a small black cash box.

"Open it."

"It's got a combination."

"Well . . . if you know everything you might know the combination."

"Yeah, it's probably the one he used for everything. It's the date of the first shot at Fort Sumpter. I told him he needed to change it, but I'm pretty sure he never did." He dialed the numbers as if he'd done it before. He produced a wad of cash.

"Count it."

"Ten thousand."

"Ok. Let's go back. Bury the box again and bring the cash."

Her commanding voice was music to his ears. For some reason, he decided to hitch his wagon to her. *This girl's my kind. I like her.*

On the way back, she held out her hand.

He gave her the cash.

She stopped, and carefully counted it, then gave him half.

Back at the house they sat back down again after she made coffee. While she was in the kitchen, she glanced into his alcove office off the kitchen. It was on his desk next to some other clay sculptures and knick-knacks the children had made for him. She recognized the pelican from

Anna's bathroom. She'd seen it once, one time when she and Tom had stopped by the house briefly and she used the bathroom. She grabbed it, and popped it into her backpack she'd set on the counter. She took the coffee out to Blanco.

"I need something from you. First, I need one of his cell phones. And second, where did my mother and sister go?"

"The first I can get you, but not the second. Everyone left separately. Your mother and sister were the last. I gave her 100K. A lot more than the others."

"How did she leave?"

"She took that old broken-down Volvo of his. You know, he has old cars stashed all over the place. She said she'd get as far away as she could and then buy herself a different car. They've been gone two days. You can get almost anywhere in two days."

CHAPTER 24

All hope abandon, ye who enter here.

DANTE ALIGHIERI, *INFERNO*

"BENJAMIN, YOU MIGHT AS WELL TELL ME NOW, what this is all about. I've seen that bonfire you've built out there."

He nodded toward the dust-caked window. "What's the point of acting so secretive now? Look where you've got me. Chained to your floor in a remote cabin in the middle of nowhere. I'd like to think that I'm in some kind of horror movie and I'm going to wake up. But this does seem rather . . ." he looked around stopping at Jimmy . . . "real." He hoped for some levity.

"I see you've awakened from your nap. Slept well I hope?"

Silence.

He approached the banker's chair, and for one split second Daniel felt panic.

Oh my God, he knows.

He started to say anything to distract him, but Benjamin took a few long steps and pulled the chair on its squeaky wheels, bumpity-bump across the old plank floor to where he came in.

Calculating the position just out of range from Daniel's chained territory, he tossed the bag into a corner and sat down, crossing his legs and arms, staring down at his prey.

Daniel relaxed into a cross-legged position, sitting on the pillow that he knew would be briefly comfortable. Even though he knew the cell phone probably would do him no good, he still felt relieved to have it hidden in his pocket. Now he was Bilbo hiding in the cave from Gollum.

"Have you finally got me where you want me?"

Benjamin uncrossed his arms as if he realized he might appear defensive. "Let's just say I've got you where I need you."

"Well, here I am. A captive audience. All ears, Benjamin."

"Yes," he grinned, "all ears after all these years."

Daniel stared. *He was always self-centered with his wit. He actually thinks that was clever.*

"Let's go back to that letter your friend forged for you."

He continued to stare him down. *He wants me to argue, be outraged at the accusation. Well, I'm not going to give him the satisfaction.*

"Oh, ok. I see. So, this is how it goes. You're silent. Well, no matter. I know it's true, so we'll just continue. The pity of it all is that even if that letter were authentic—which I know it's not—it precisely proves nothing. If—and I do mean if—that letter was actually written by your friend's relative . . . his many great grandfather or something . . . it could have been a made-up fiction back then. Let's face it, Daniel, apparently that letter never was sent. I wonder why. Could it be because it just wasn't true?" He added for good measure, "like so many stories out of that War. I mean, who knows what actually happened. Grant didn't give that Millikens Bend incident in his memoirs much notice and neither did anybody else." He leaned forward as if he just made his case to the jury. "Ever thought of that, Professor Perry?"

He knew that arguing would solve nothing, but playing along might get to the point faster. "Benjamin, I remember you forty years ago. We were young and idealistic then like all twenty-somethings of our generation. I also remember how smart you were, and I thought . . ." he paused for emphasis . . . "you cared about the research we were doing. We weren't trying to prove conclusions, but we were hoping to discover conclusions that came out of our data. And as I remember . . . correct me if I'm wrong . . . we didn't always know exactly what we were going to find."

Benjamin's eyes narrowed. "You never understood, Daniel, what I was all about. I had no interest in those picky little facts you liked to pluck out of nowhere to reinforce the horrors of slavery. If you'd paid attention, you would have known that the abolitionists were a small minority. A vocal minority I admit. But most Americans in the 1860's believed the colored races were inferior." He let that settle in.

Daniel was listening intently.

"It was a fact you hated then and a fact you still hate. You wanted to show what heroes the blacks were in that war and the aftermath, to rub it in ,that it was a moral fight. The good and almighty North against the degenerate South."

"Well, Benjamin, and you never understood what I was all about. I believed then and believe even more now . . . down to my bones . . . that if those Contraband Slave recruits had been acknowledged for their outstanding bravery—Milliken's Bend being only one example—their foothold as equal Americans after that War would have been on more solid ground." He looked down, waited, choosing his words carefully. "To your point, Benjamin, the racism was rampant in the whole country, not just the South."

"You're a fool, Daniel. You used that letter as an original source, and I knew it proved nothing. You needed to be stopped."

"I needed to be stopped?" He felt his temples pulsing.

"That War was happening between you and me. We were its microcosm. You think you won, but you didn't because look where you are now."

So that's it. He's been plotting revenge all these years. I took his life away from him. He heard her voice. "Count the cards. Count the cards." He waited. He knew if he stayed quiet Benjamin might rattle on and reveal himself. *He wants to fight, get himself worked up so he can get a hate on for me. Otherwise, whatever he's got planned will be more difficult. The trouble is . . . deep down he knows I'm not a liar. And that's going to cause a problem for him. Not a moral problem, but a motivational one. If I react, his life gets easier.*

Benjamin decided to go for the jugular. "You know, Daniel . . ." he held his hand out, palm down to inspect his fingernails. He pulled a small nail clipper out of his pocket. Snip. Snip. Snip. He let the nail bits fall on his knee, which he brushed off, flicking them at Daniel. "Say . . . that wife of yours must have been a real piece of work."

Her voice came at him, urgent. "Don't bite, Daniel." But instead of calming him down, her voice incensed him, and it flew out of his mouth like venom striking. "What do you mean?" He couldn't retrieve the words, nor could he calm down.

Benjamin lazily held up his hand to survey his handiwork. "Oh . . . you know . . . drew crazy art . . ." he glanced from his hand to Daniel, then went on. "Self-published a book of nonsense about toxins in the ocean . . . pretty trite stuff, wouldn't you say?" Back to his nails and snipped a few more edges, perfecting his work. "I mean she must have seemed pretty ridiculous pandering to all those parents who try to stop the avalanche of disinterest in their children who are now addicted to all things artificial?" He skillfully raised one eyebrow casting his gaze over Daniel, alert to the pain he felt sure he was inflicting.

Daniel stared at the floor maintaining silence, feeling defeated.

"Oh, and by the way . . . I've got that little ceramic pelican you kept in her bathroom." He let that seep in. "You know . . . that child-like psychotic bird resembling a pelican one of her kids made?"

Appalled, he ached all over and felt pounding in his temples as he shrank down into the screaming silence, crouching, slowly pulling his feet under him. Any control he thought he had was gone. All he could do was hold it together as seconds ticked by.

"Wow! Looks like I hit a nerve. Yeah . . . well, you know . . ."

He lunged. His whole body stretched as he sailed out, landing with a gigantic flop on the plank floor, but not before Benjamin was forced back in the chair against the door, hitting it so hard he lurched over and crashed down.

He knew he'd missed the mark, but Benjamin was rattled.

He had not imagined Daniel capable of anything so physical. For one second, he realized that he had not known Daniel except when they were young, back when Daniel was anything but physical.

He pulled himself together and stood up, righting the chair. He didn't speak because he knew his voice would come out hoarse and reveal his fright. It was a snake strike and it scared him. He remembered Cal and how frightened he'd been to see the swollen thumb, the bite from a dead snake. He'd reacted to Daniel's lunge by flinging the nail clipper at him—a girly gesture. He'd lost power.

Daniel sat up and held the nail clipper up, taunting him to come and get it. He knew he didn't dare take the chance now. Daniel grinned and popped it into his pocket along with the cell phone.

Benjamin opened the door and went outside to calm down. He walked to the spring and gulped the water. Adrenalin pumped through him, but instead of filling him with fools' courage it depleted him. He had to regain the ground he'd lost.

Daniel thrust his hand into his pocket and snatched the phone and flicked it open. It turned on. He was shaking and couldn't concentrate. His eyes twitched as a drop of sweat seeped into his right eye. The salt burned. He winced, trying to blink it away. The phone was a small metal blur. He heard her voice. "Slow down. Breath." He wanted to tell her to fuck off, that her fake-o calm know-it-all attitude incensed him. *Jesus, Anna. You're dead. Dead. Dead. Dead. And I'm in a bit of a pickle right now.* But, instead of resisting he heaved, taking in a balloon full of air and released it slowly, gas leaking from his lungs.

He never remembered phone numbers. Not even his own. All he knew was 911. Nothing. It immediately went to 'call ended.' He heard the footsteps returning. He stabbed the 'try later' button and jammed it back into his pocket.

Benjamin threw a pair of vintage handcuffs at him. "Cuff your wrists." He looked down at the cuffs in his lap. He looked up as if he didn't comprehend.

"Do it!"

Even Jimmy rattled on the wall.

"What's the point of this Benjamin? You've got me trapped in here."

"Shut up! I give the orders. If you don't do it, I will shoot your knee cap." He produced a revolver, a vintage one.

"That thing loaded?"

The thunderous shot shattered the window by the back screen door, splattering glass fragments all over. A small blade of glass came close to Daniel's red swollen eye. As he carefully pulled it out, he felt the trickle of blood down his cheek.

He fit one wrist into the cuff and squeezed it shut. It wasn't easy getting his second wrist in the other. His hands were shaking, but finally he heard the second one click shut. He held up his arms and pulled apart the cuffs to demonstrate how trapped he was.

Benjamin put the pistol down on the floor along with the sack that held the phone and sat back down in the banker's chair to glare at him. "Don't piss me off again."

It was not just a warning. Daniel knew it was a threat. "Ok, Benjamin. You've made your point. Let's talk about what happened 40 years ago. Where do we start?"

Now it was Benjamin's turn to be silent. His gaze bore down on Daniel as if he was trying to figure out his next move, which made him unpredictable and more dangerous than before.

Daniel stared at the floor, waiting like a penitent child not knowing what was coming next. To keep his mind steady, he yelled at Anna. *Fuck you, Anna. Fuck you. Do not presume to tell me now to calm down.* He repeated this like a mantra in order to keep her at bay. He needed his mind to be his own and not invaded by her ghostly, sanctimonious thoughts. He hunkered down.

The room seemed to have grown a little dimmer and he realized in the mountains, among the tall trees, the sun disappeared sooner. He guessed it was early evening setting in. Somewhere there was a beautiful red and violet sky as darkness was on its way. The full moon was starting to wane and there would not be moonlight until 10:00 or 11:00 when it would come up over the horizon. He wondered if outside you could hear the river below.

Benjamin got up and went outside again.

He heard his footsteps walking away from the cabin and then nothing. After a few minutes he almost convinced himself that he was gone. He lay down on his side curling up into a fetal position. Even though it was still warm he felt cold and started to shiver. Then he slept fitfully.

The screen door slammed, and he jerked up shaking his head, blinking, and trying to focus. He had no idea how long he'd slept, but it was now pitch dark outside. *Maybe an hour, . . or two?* He didn't know.

He sat back down in the banker's chair, this time with half a bottle of Jack Daniels.

Has he drunk half a bottle?

Benjamin's eyelids looked heavy, indicating he'd been calming himself down with alcohol. "That War solved nothing. It was only the beginning of the divide. You and I will never agree because we never could. Just like God and the Devil—his Fallen Angel—I am the receptacle of the truth nobody wants to acknowledge. I am in fact that Fallen Angel." He looked at Daniel leaning forward as drunks like to do when they're making a point. In a sing-song voice: "Your Avenging Angel." He took a long swig.

"What are you talking about, Benjamin? Avenging Angel of what?"

"You see . . . that's the problem with the jello-brains like you, Daniel. You think we can all just get along . . . hold hands in the middle of nowhere, kiss and make up." He blew Daniel a kiss.

"I swear to God, Benjamin. I don't know what you're talking about."

"Oh yes you do, you flaming hypocrite. When I insulted your wife a while ago you turned into a killer. And why?"

Daniel looked away.

"And why?" he bellowed getting worked up. "And why?" he leaned so far in he almost fell out of the chair.

Daniel shrank away with the fleeting question, either he was working himself up into something, or he would pass out? *Either way, Benjamin was now completely unpredictable.*

"I'll tell you why, you Moron! I invaded what was sacrosanct to you. The memory of your dear wife." Another swig.

He let the words echo around the slatted walls.

Jimmy's ancient, hollowed eyes stared vacantly.

He got up and started to pace around. "That bear . . . ," he leaned into Daniel while pointing back at Jimmy. "You invade his territory, and he will fucking rip you apart."

He didn't want to mention that probably Jimmy's death had not been a fair fight and therefore maybe he wasn't such a good example for his point. But he kept quiet, like a child who knows the adult is whipping himself into a dangerous and violent frenzy.

"Yes, of course he would. But that's the difference between us humans and the animal world. We have something called civilization."

Benjamin's face twisted itself into a montage of gnarled contempt. "Oh, my fucking God." He laughed. "You actually believe that shit, don't you!" He shook his head from side to side, guffawing. "Listen, my friend . . . I'm only going to say this once!" He shouted. "Beneath the veneer of civilization, we are killers! All of us!" He paused to calm himself for his final point, belching to clear his voice. "That War . . ." he repeated, "that War demonstrated the capacity of humans to slaughter each other at point-blank range. You have no idea the depths of human revenge." His voice sounded calm like the stillness at the center of the storm. "In that War the South showed what humans could do when what is sacred—their freedom to govern themselves, the premise upon which this country was founded—when their home territory was invaded by their own kind." He had shouted himself hoarse.

Pacing around, he went outside again, slamming the screen door.

Daniel felt a moment of relief. *He's worked himself up. Maybe he'll stumble and pass out. He got drunk pretty fast.* He tried to find a comfortable position, which was difficult with his hands cuffed. He plucked a piece of glass off his pillow and tossed it. He looked around for more. His mind wanted to escape through portals of minutiae to avoid what he knew— that Benjamin was completely psychotic now, fueled by the alcohol. *No lucid moments.*

He tried to stretch himself and thought about doing sit-ups, but he'd always hated them. In his early 50's Anna had given him a birthday present, ten passes for a gym near the campus. He tried it once. A thirty something personal trainer type had sauntered over, bulging with arm muscle and pecks through his t-shirt with a picture of Popeye on it, and casually mentioned, "Hey dude, I can help you get rid of some of that flab." He winked. "I bet your wife would like that." He wasn't so insulted by what the guy actually said. What incensed him the most was that the guy thought it was a perfectly normal, friendly gesture. And for good measure, Popeye did not belong to his generation. Needless to say, he never returned.

He did not want to think about what Benjamin's revenge would be. After an hour he fell asleep again. She was smiling. It seemed like she came from a long way off, but never quite got close enough for them to touch. Seeing her comforted him. He thought she was Melinda, but he wasn't sure. When he woke, he had no idea how long he'd been out. It was pitch dark in the cabin. He could barely make out shapes. He felt a slight breeze waft through the shot-out window. No sounds anywhere, and he wondered what time it was. *Close to midnight?* He heard the screen door open. Panic set in. *He's been planning whatever this is for a long time.*

He brought an old kerosene lantern that cast a cold light around the cabin. "Wakey, wakey, Daniel. It's time to party!"

It seemed as if he tried to sober up. His words were crisp and clear.

CHAPTER 25

*The helicopter approaches closer than any other [vehicle] to fulfillment of
mankind's ancient dreams of the flying horse and the magic carpet.*

TOM DROVE BEAR'S CHEVROLET VAN with Rebecca in the passenger seat and Melinda in the back. Most of the trip each was wrapped up in their own thoughts. They all felt anxious.

Rebecca broke the silence. "It must have been nice to see your parents."

"Yeah. It was. When I saw them just after they got off the plane this morning, I realized I'd been homesick, but didn't know it."

"I think that happens sometimes."

Both realized they could take their conversation in any direction, but their silence suggested each needed to stay within their own private thoughts.

Around 1:00 they stopped for gas, some junk food for lunch and to stretch their legs.

When they got back in the van Melinda sat in the front.

More silence, until she turned to Tom. "You know he's become very fond of you. He was really looking forward to taking you on that road trip . . . show you our mountains and coastal Redwoods that are . . ." she pointed west, "not too far from here."

He smiled, "Yeah. Uncle Daniel's an odd bird . . . but he's grown on me too."

They were both quiet.

"Do you know . . . has he always been so absent-minded? Soo . . ."

She finished the sentence. "Messy?"

"Yeah."

She thought about that. "I think so." She looked out the window at the passing countryside. "I didn't know Anna, but I'm pretty sure she learned to tolerate what she could and then just let the rest go." She thought some more and added, "He of course thinks he tolerated her."

They both laughed.

"Well, I think they became completely accepting of each other in the end. You know, he still talks to her."

"I know. He tries to pretend with me that he doesn't, but I know he does."

"Do you think it's bad to talk to a ghost?"

She looked at him, realizing he probably didn't know she knew about his great-grandfather ghost. "No, I don't think it's bad at all. In fact, I think it's good. I wish I could speak to my dead husband, but it's just never happened."

He thought about that. "I don't know . . . but you may want to just start talking to him . . . you know . . . pretend he can hear you."

She smiled approvingly. "Well . . . maybe I will. I guess I shouldn't feel so self-conscious about it. Maybe that's a barrier."

They were twenty miles from Weaverville, and it was 4:00 p.m.

Tom's cell phone rang.

"Let's pull over," Rebecca suggested.

Tom swerved into the shoulder and lurched to a stop. He grabbed the phone and leapt out of the car, flipping it open. It was Morrigan.

"Tom, listen to me. Please don't speak." She told him the directions to the property and explained that they were all gone except one. "About an hour and a half beyond Weaverville." He didn't write down the directions, so he repeated to himself as she talked. "I won't be there when you arrive. I've got something I have to do and then you won't hear from me for a while. Please don't ask. I'll contact you. Just don't know when."

Then silence.

"Morrigan?" Nothing. She was gone.

He jumped back in the van. "Write this down."

Rebecca took down the directions and then called Richard.

He answered on the first ring. "Hi. Where are you?"

"Almost there. Morrigan just called. She told Tom where the house was. They're all gone . . . except for one member." She gave Richard the directions.

"Ok. We're at the airport. Waiting for the helicopter, which may take a while to get here. Stay in touch. Be careful."

They drove for the next hour in silence.

Then Rebecca read the directions.

At 5:30 they started the bumpy, twisting climb up the mountain and pulled in front of the house at 6:00 p.m.

Blanco stood in the half-opened doorway.

Tom got out. "Hello there."

Blanco nodded.

Tom walked toward the steps, and climbed in slow motion.

The door opened a crack more, and then more. They stood three feet from one another.

"I'm looking for my Uncle, Daniel Perry."

Rebecca and Melinda stood at the bottom of the porch stairs.

"Well . . ." Blanco thrust both hands into his pockets and raised his shoulders . . . "I don't know."

"Do you know who I'm talking about?"

Blanco half-nodded, then added, "I've never met him."

"But do you have any idea where he might be?"

Blanco beckoned for all of them to come inside.

They sat around the table.

Blanco always felt more secure when his laptop was nearby. He explained that everyone had left except him. Benjamin had been there the night before but had only been in the kitchen and then he left. "I heard voices in there after midnight."

Rebecca asked, "Any idea who was in there with Benjamin?"

"Some guy, I think. At first, I thought it was friendly but then I heard the guy shout something and it wasn't friendly. Something like . . . 'kidnapping me and tossing me into a trunk' . . . something like that. Then they left through the back door. That's all I know."

They asked Blanco more questions about why everyone left, but it became apparent that he was withdrawing, so they decided to take a break.

The three went outside, leaving him alone.

Rebecca knew pressing him further might push him away entirely. She called Richard. "We're here."

"Can we land a helicopter there?"

She looked around. "There's a pretty big clearing here in front of the house. I suppose a helicopter could land here."

"Stay there outside so we can see you. We should be there within the half hour."

Earlier that afternoon it shocked her to find the pelican on his desk and in that moment, she decided to return it to Professor Perry's house. After giving Tom the directions, she told Blanco as far as she was concerned, he could have the rest of Benjamin's money and that she had no intention of blowing the whistle on him. Then she went back into his kitchen office and wrapped the other art pieces he'd plucked from the children like a greedy Stellar Jay. It enraged her that he displayed such hypocritical sentimentality. "You're such a killer and a fraud!"

She climbed into Ladybug and made her way down the bumpy road. Not wanting to pass Tom and the others, she took a circuitous route heading back. As she came into Weaverville Tom was heading up the road to the house.

So far, her plan was driven by a need for revenge. Beyond that she had no definite idea. It was important to return the pelican to where he'd stolen it. She imagined him standing in Professor Perry's bathroom staring at it. Had he already tied him up, or was he skating on that malicious, manipulative charm she knew so well, luring his prey into false hope that he intended no ill? *Taking the pelican would appeal to his phony self-image—that he felt an affinity for children.* People think if you love children, you're a good person. She felt the hatred spike through her and sensed that only Beth would stop her from killing him. She needed to see Gertrude at least one more time before she left.

At 7:00 p.m. while Tom, Rebecca and Melinda sat on the front steps, they all perked up to the sound of a low, rumbling roar as it grew incrementally louder. Waiting, not quite realizing what it was at first, it emerged over the tree line—a great red and yellow whirring primordial insect.

Tom leapt up off the steps and stood out in the clearing waving his arms, as it descended, spewing clumps of dirt, creating a dangerous vortex.

They retreated inside the house.

Blanco looked scared.

Axel DeWitt jumped down first, emerging from the settling dust cloud, head and body bowed.

Rebecca stepped outside.

He made no attempt at niceties. "Is he here?"

Bear, Richard, and Billy followed.

Rebecca explained what they knew and introduced Blanco whose eyes darted back and forth. He looked like he regretted not leaving when he had the chance.

They all congregated back inside.

The three men, except Axel, decided to reconnoiter outside.

Melinda chose to follow.

Rebecca stayed back not wishing to leave Blanco alone with Axel, who was already darting from room to room while Blanco stood looking stunned and helpless.

After 30 minutes passed, Axel calmed down, satisfied the house was empty. Finally, he focused on Blanco. "Sit down, son."

Rebecca left them alone sitting at the table and went back outside.

The black helicopter created a menacing air, now so still while poised for action.

The pilot sitting in the cockpit stared at her through his dark airplane glasses.

She tried to smile with a half-hearted wave.

He didn't move.

Rebecca walked toward the trees hoping to find the others. After 20 minutes she returned to the house to find Axel and Blanco communing like old friends pouring over the laptop.

"Ok," Blanco explained, "here's how I did this one."

Axel was riveted by Blanco's ability to hack into his accounts.

My God . . . he's not angry. He's impressed. She looked out the window and noticed the light was darkening as evening descended.

At police headquarters in Weaverville the 911 operator was still trying to locate where the call came from. "All I could hear," she reported to her supervisor, "was what sounded like scuffling and male voices . . . maybe arguing."

CHAPTER 26

Fire remains, above all, the great transmuter.

STEPHEN J. PYNE, FIRE, A BRIEF HISTORY

AT 8:00 P.M. BENJAMIN CAME INTO THE CABIN, pointing the revolver. "I'll use this if I have to." Tossing the antique key, he ordered Daniel to unlock the ankle cuff. "Stand up." He opened the door wide and ordered Daniel outside to sit in an old rickety straight-backed cane chair he positioned about fifteen feet from the teepee bonfire. "Now uncuff your hands." Another key tossed, which Daniel caught in both hands.

For a brief moment he felt relieved, forgetting he was still barefoot and couldn't go anywhere, before he realized whatever Benjamin planned for him . . . it was about to happen.

"Sit down and put your hands behind the chair." This time Benjamin used duct tape.

In his attempt to ward off panic Daniel irrationally wondered where he'd put his own duct tape back home. *In the garage? No. I think I put it in that kitchen drawer. That one I've been meaning to clean out since Anna died. How many years now?* He couldn't calculate. He looked down and realized that Benjamin was strapping his feet to the chair.

"I won't tape your mouth, old sport. Up here," he gazed around, "you can make all the noise you want. Plus, if you scream it might help keep the bears and mountain lions at bay." To demonstrate he rolled his head and howled at the sky, emitting a hollow, disembodied sound intended to terrify.

It did. He wanted her to speak. *Where is she when I really could use some comforting from the other side?*

"So, you just sit here and enjoy the twilight." He produced a red plastic grill lighter and walked around the pyre lighting it from the bottom edges, then stood back to watch the show. "Sorry, Daniel. No marshmallows tonight." He disappeared into the cabin, slamming the door.

He struggled trying to wiggle his arms and feet. *Whoever invented duct tape must have been a sadist.* Panic began to rise as he felt the warmth from the smaller flames as they started to lick up the branches. He shouted. "For God's sake, Benjamin! This solves nothing! What do you want from me? I didn't ruin your career! You did! You did!" He kept shouting, then listened.

All was silent except for the crackling of the slowly lapping flames. He was drenched in sweat, so wet he wondered if he could slither out of the tape. He wiggled his bare feet, pulling back and forth harder and harder until he became aware of the danger of tipping over. The chair was unsteady on the ground. He knew if he fell over, he would be even more helpless. He started chanting. "Stay calm. Stay calm." But he couldn't. He discovered that he could inch the chair back by rocking forward and back, but he had to be careful. Each inch could land the chair cockeyed, tipping him precariously. He had no idea if he made any progress, but in the attempt, he focused himself to avoid the panic that would surely cause the disaster he wanted to avoid—falling over still strapped to the chair.

After fifteen minutes he stopped and tried to listen. Nothing. *Has he gone? Does he just intend to leave me here to burn?*

Eventually, the flames would whip up, creating their own wind and it would be only a matter of time before they reached him.

He closed his eyes, trying to blind himself to the certainty of what was developing—Benjamin's final Armageddon. That it made no sense left him feeling more helpless than ever. Darkness was coming as the flames brightened—reds, yellows and blues flicking against the towering backdrop of silhouetted trees dry from the long hot summer.

He heard the screen door open and slam. Benjamin emerged pulling the great hide of Jimmy behind him. For a brief, macabre moment he appeared to Daniel like a young kid dragging his Halloween costume. *My God! What's he planning?*

He plopped Jimmy on the ground, a lifeless blob.

He approached the flames holding a shoebox in both hands.

Some kind of sacrificial offering?

He took off the lid and tossed it into the flames. He turned and displayed the contents to Daniel as if he were offering the contents of the dessert tray.

"This . . ." he announced, repeating for emphasis, "this is my parents. May I introduce Henry and Greta." He leered, then let loose a roar of laughter. "At long last I've found the perfect resting spot. We will all go up in flames together." He threw the box into the funeral pyre.

The flames licked hungrily at the dash of tinder.

"And now, my friend . . . the final farewell."

Daniel stared, his eyes bulging from shock as Benjamin picked up the hide, draped him over his head, turned to face Daniel holding Jimmy's glaring head over his own, then turned and flung himself at the flames.

Across the river, halfway up on the other side Bear spotted it first—the smoke rising.

They all stared.

"The helicopter!" Bear shouted. "Get back to the copter!"

Within fifteen minutes they were back at the house and got Axel to consent to commandeering the helicopter.

It rose like a great bird of prey with Bear, Richard and Billy headed out toward the smoke.

Billy bonded with the pilot. "I'm a fireman and ex-marine. I've done search and rescue. If you can put this bird over where that smoke is coming from, I can make it down if we must." He was already strapping himself into the gear with Richard and Bear's help.

They were over the smoke in a few minutes and spotted the scene below—a fire licking skyward, a cabin and a man tied to a chair flopping around in the dirt like a beached whale.

The pilot shouted. "I can't land and don't want to lower too close because it will fan those flames!"

On the ground, Daniel heard the copter's roar and assumed at last the flames were exploding all around. His lungs were filling with smoke as he coughed and choked. He knew it was the end, but rather than surrender, he continued to flop out of instinct, not to survive.

Billy ran through the forest, hoping it was the right direction. Once in the clearing he spotted Daniel and dragged him as far from the flames as he could. He pulled out his pocketknife and tore at the tape.

Uncomprehending, Daniel was no help, as he struggled even more. It wasn't until he heard Billy yelling at him to stay still so he could strap him in that he felt the strange sensation of leaving the ground.

Sailing over the trees, Richard and Bear hauled him in.

Billy would stay on the ground and find his own way back.

They had to get Daniel to the hospital.

Fifteen minutes later, the second helicopter arrived. The Forest Service was alerted that a 911 call had come from uninhabited terrain near the river. They sprayed the flames with retardant and were able to land in the clearing near the cabin, preventing it from burning altogether.

Billy found his way down to the river. He washed his face in the cool water and waited for the moon to show itself and hopefully light his way back. As he sat next to the cool water, he realized he hadn't felt so alive in years. He basked in the glow of the feeling, recognizing this had been the first chance he'd ever had to put his smug little brother-in-law in his place. He wished he'd had a snapshot of Daniel's expression as he rose above the ground staring down at Billy, recognizing his savior.

Several hours later, Tom went down to look for his father after he learned about the rescue. He found him and the two of them slowly climbed back up the other side.

At the house Rebecca informed them that Axel and Blanco had left together in the Audi. "I don't know how to say this . . ." She seemed at a loss for words. "But I think although Mr. DeWitt lost one son . . . well, I think he's gained another." It seemed that Blanco's talents perfectly fit DeWitt's needs.

They were all exhausted and decided to spend the night at the house.

Bear had called to inform them that Daniel did not suffer significant burns, but he was still in shock and covered with scrapes and bruises and would be in the hospital for a few days—and that the county sheriff would be there at the compound in the morning.

That night Tom slept on a cot out on the deck using a sleeping bag he'd found.

At 3:00 a.m. Zak showed up. "Hey Kid. How're you doing?"

The conversation was short.

Zak's message was not what he expected.

"I hate to tell you my boy, but you're not out of the woods yet."

Tom wondered if puns were a ghost thing. "Zak . . . come on. What do you mean?" He was in no mood and wanted to sleep in the secure belief that Benjamin Monroe had met his maker and Uncle Daniel was safely recovering in his cozy, warm hospital bed.

"He's not dead."

"Who?"

"Benjamin."

"Yes, he is. Uncle Daniel told everyone that he walked into his own fire."

"He did. But he's not dead. Get some sleep, my boy. Tomorrow's a big day."

He fell asleep, angry with Zak. *Why wouldn't he congratulate me instead of lying? What's he up to?* He comforted himself with the thought that maybe ghosts tell lies just to stir up trouble.

CHAPTER 27

Beware of a wolf in sheep's clothing.
AESOP

FIVE MILES OUTSIDE OF WEAVERVILLE, she ran out of gas. The meter for Ladybug had not worked reliably for years. She just knew when it was time to fill it, but today she'd been distracted and not paying attention. Even though she had a cell phone there was no one to call. Not Tom, not Blanco, not Triple A, because she didn't have roadside insurance. What she had, was cash. Calculating how long it would take her to walk back to a gas station, buy a can of gas, pay the guy to bring her back down the road to her car so she could put a few gallons in to get back and fill her tank and be on her way again—two hours.

She looked at her watch. She would be back on the road again by 8:00 and after that—six more hours to Professor Perry's house.

She started tramping down the road. Walking fast, and sometimes jogging, it took her an hour and fifteen minutes.

She had to pay the guy $40 to take her back to her car. He was nice enough about it, but when it came to the money, he knew she was stuck and would pay the price because she had no choice. No Good Samaritan country folk anywhere anymore. After 2008 it became every man for himself.

She thought of Benjamin. He liked to pretend he was country folk, doing the neighborly thing . . . and in the end he screwed everyone. She wondered if he'd bought gas from that same station. The thought popped into her mind. *He'd have killed the guy and stolen his money back . . . plus any more he could find. And no one would suspect happy-go-lucky Mr. Friendly Benjamin 'Papa Cat' Monroe. No sireee.* The itch to kill him sent ripples through her.

By 8:30 she was on her way south again.

An hour earlier he had charged into the blazing bonfire emitting his version of the Rebel Yell with Jimmy strapped over his head and draped down his back. He had no idea if the illusion would work, even though he had no intention of killing himself. What was important was that Daniel Perry's last view of the world was seeing him stride into the flames of hell.

He knew that by the time he donned Jimmy and started toward the fire Daniel would go berserk and most likely tip over if he hadn't already. *If he thinks I'll just walk into a burning cauldron to meet my maker, he will know—for a certainty—he is about to follow. He will do what anyone instinctively would do at such a moment. He will shut his eyes. Instead of going where he thinks I'm going I will sidestep the flames and be on the other side by the time he opens his eyes to see. By then I will have vanished. He will not think, but will assume the worst.*

On the other side, he threw Jimmy off and tossed him into the flames. He stood for a few seconds to watch those hollow eyes melt.

At that moment, he heard a terrible roar. He was certain it was Jimmy's ghost emitting his rage at last at what had been done to him by humans. *Shot, eviscerated, hung on a wall to gape helplessly for a hundred years . . . deprived early of his life and soul.*

He tore down the mountainside, crashing through branches, hurtling himself away as fast as he could. He had not expected to spook himself like that. He actually thought it would be a fond farewell. *Far from it. Those hollow melting eyes shot him with sheer terror that he could never erase. That terror drove him into the river.*

After calming himself in the cool water, he found the rubber boat and paddled through the swiftly flowing water trying to push that last image out of his mind. He came to the point where he knew he would be safe. On shore, he tossed the boat into the bushes and walked the mile to his trusty little Dodge pick-up. He eased himself in behind the steering wheel and rested his head on his hands. The thought that his plan had worked— except for Jimmy—buoyed him. Jimmy's hide had protected him from the flames just as he hoped it would.

Daniel, on the other hand, would be burned to a crisp by now and so would his own past. He'd imagined this new start for a long time. And now it was actually happening according to plan. Not only would he remove his nemesis from the planet, sending him to an agonizing death, he himself would be purified. *But for Daniel Perry? He is now in the lake that burns with fire and sulfur, which is the second death.* The only part of the Bible Benjamin felt spoke to him personally was Revelations.

The money was stashed under the seat. Certainly not all of it. But enough for now. He would return for the rest someday. *Blanco would keep it protected. Who knows? Maybe the next stop will be Mexico. What the hell. Lots of rich ex-pats in Mexico. Lots of lonely widows.*

But first, he had some business to take care of. He'd made up his mind after the last time he talked with Morrigan. He felt sad about it really. But resolute. *And that boyfriend of hers, too. They're a liability. I can't afford that. Loose ends can come back to bite you and she is now a loose end. He's just a casualty. But the fact that he's Daniel Perry's nephew makes my life easier. He can join his uncle in the lake of fire and sulfur.*

He started the engine and navigated the pick-up slowly out of its hiding, over the rocks and potholes until he hit the paved road where he assumed it would be smooth sailing back to where it all started just 48 hours ago. *Back to Daniel's little abode where all good things must come to an end.*

He looked at the clock. 9:00 p.m. He would get there in the wee small hours. *Perfect. Maybe that nephew will be snug as a bug in a rug in his little bed.* He thought of the cat. *I think the cat goes too. Nice big fat furry kitty kitty.* He'd never throttled a cat before. *Might be fun.*

Gertrude and Carol Ann received the good news about Daniel's rescue at 9:00 that evening. Relieved and over-joyed, they treated themselves to a simple supper and were in bed by 11:00.

Gertrude took Daniel's bed while Carol Ann slept in Tom's, with Numi for company.

The Queens were happy to stay outside on the back porch off the kitchen, gnawing on their bones until they fell asleep as the moon rose overhead.

The evening was mild with no fog. Only occasionally did they hear the sounds of the night from the neighborhood. Someone's dog barking, a night owl passing by in a car heading for home, crickets chirping at the moon.

She pulled into his driveway at 2:00 a.m. She recognized Gertrude's

Prius parked on the side. Hesitating at first to wake her or Carol Ann, she decided they would want her to. They wouldn't want her to sleep in her car and more importantly they would want to know what she knew, and she wanted to know what they knew. *Did they catch Benjamin?*

She rang the doorbell.

The Queens started to bark.

After a minute she heard Gertrude's voice. "Who's there?"

When she heard Morrigan's voice, the door swung open and she held her arms open wide.

Morrigan fell into her embrace, already sobbing convulsively as Gertrude lead her into the living room.

Carol Ann came out. "Thank God!" was all she said.

Carol Ann checked on the Queens to calm them down, then returned to the living room.

Numi peeked out from his room down the hall but did not come out right away, especially with those two frisky Chows around. He hopped back on the bed.

Carol Ann made tea, and brought some home-made oatmeal cookies and a bowl of fruit. They told Morrigan what had happened . . . that Daniel was rescued in the nick of time and that Benjamin had immolated himself.

She was stunned by this news. "Are you sure?"

"Tom and Rebecca called just before 9:00 to tell us. Daniel's in the hospital. He'll be there a few days."

Gertrude waited for the drama of it to sink in. "You're safe now. He can't hurt you, or anyone else who was in your family, ever again." But she could see . . . Morrigan would not be convinced. She put her hand on Morrigan's thigh. "Tell me . . . what are you worried about?"

"That you don't know him. Nobody knows him." She looked at both of them. "He would never kill himself." She told them about Blanco, the money stashed, her suspicions about what he'd done to Missy Tupelo, Drexel and others she suspected in the past.

Gertrude was thoughtful. "Well, we don't know exactly what happened. We understand the fire he started burned about an acre before they put it out. Until the police can go through all the ashes for the forensic evidence, we won't know for sure." She tapped her fingers together. "Daniel was certainly in shock and still is. It's possible he only thought he saw what he saw."

Carol Ann sipped her tea and then spoke. "I think it's possible this man escaped." She looked meditative. "Where do you suppose he would go?"

"Indeed," Gertrude seconded her question, "where would he go?"

At 3:00 a.m. he parked his truck a block away and walked through the shadows down the road to Daniel's driveway. He crept in and saw her little red bug parked right smack dab in front.

He felt giddy with joy. *They're here. My cup runneth over!* He saw a dim light from the living room and crept up, and stooped down under the window. He heard voices. Low, murmuring sounds. He thought he recognized Morrigan's, but not the others. They all sounded female.

He decided to creep around the side of the house where he suspected there might be an open window. *You never know. Lady Luck's been with me so far.*

Sure enough, he found a window open about six inches. He peered through the gauzy curtain and decided it was Daniel's bedroom. Someone had been sleeping in his bed. *Well it ain't Daniel* he assured himself. He pushed hard to open it further, but it wouldn't budge. After applying all his strength, he slumped down in the bushes to reconsider his entry.

In the end he decided that surprise—and with a little help from a gun—would be his best bet. He stood up, feeling the physical strain of the last few days, and hobbled back to the pick-up. He drove it back to the house. He took the gun from his glove compartment, poured himself out of the front seat, climbed the steps and rang the chimes. Hearing them he felt a sense of deja vu. *Back where I started.* He waited. Dead silence.

He let the time pass. The dogs were barking now.

He heard a voice. A deep clear soft voice.

"Who's there?"

He hadn't planned this part, but he trusted as usual in his wits. In his most upbeat but official voice he answered. "Sorry to bother you Mam, but I saw the light was on. Tom Cramer is a friend of mine and he asked me to come over even though it's very late and check on you all. I have news from him."

"Tom has a phone," Gertrude reminded him. "He's been in touch. I can't imagine he would send someone over at this hour."

"Oh . . . right . . . well something's come up." He liked these moments. He had no idea what he would come up with. He could tell this would be a challenge, and he knew Morrigan was in there. She might recognize his voice.

On the other hand, Benjamin was a master of disguise and had the uncanny ability to speak in different voices, even in different dialects. The voice he was using was a little higher pitched and he added an English accent ever so slightly to lend his words a cultured effect. He decided that might put this old lady at ease.

"What's come up?" Gertrude asked.

His mind was buzzing with some of the people Morrigan had mentioned. "It's Rebecca Calhoun. She's been in an accident. Tom's at the hospital. Can't get through on his cell." He felt like the wolf in the fairy tale about the Three Little Pigs. He wanted to giggle at his own brilliance.

The door opened a crack, and he barged in swinging the gun around, making sure they all saw it—all three of them.

He looked at Morrigan. "Well, well . . . fancy meeting you here."

He herded them into the living room. "Shut up those dogs or I will shoot them."

Carol Ann raced to the kitchen door and calmed down Juno and Dido. Too terrified to think beyond that, she meekly returned and sat down.

Benjamin had sprawled himself back on the couch where he'd been just a few days before, holding court with Daniel. He ordered them to sit across from him on the other couch. On the table Anna's book rested with the pelican's roving eye. He picked up a cookie and started to munch on it. He appraised the cookie. "Not bad." He looked at Carol Ann. "You make these?"

She blushed. "No." She nodded at Gertrude. "Dr. Lerner did."

He looked at Gertrude. "Dr. Lerner, huh! And who might you be in relation to the Professor?"

"A friend."

"Oh, ok. I suppose Daniel must have a few friends."

He turned to Carol Ann. "And who might you be?"

"His sister."

"Wow! His sister!" He thought about that. "Well, listen Darlin . . . would you mind making some coffee? I've had quite a day and it would sure hit he spot on top of these dee-licious . . ." he beamed at

Gertrude . . . "cookies." He smacked his lips and finished off the one in his hand.

Carol Ann got up to make the coffee hoping that while in the kitchen some bright idea might come her way.

He seemed to intuit this as she headed for the kitchen. "Oh . . . by the way, Sweetheart, . . . any bright idea you might have in that pretty head of yours will not sit well with yours truly here. As I've explained, it's been quite a day and I'm feeling ever so edgy about things."

As Carol Ann proceeded to the kitchen, he turned his attention to Morrigan. "My, my Little Lady. You're looking a little peeked. Hard day for you as well."

She continued to glare at him.

Gertrude was doing her best to remain calm, while sizing up the situation. *He thinks Daniel's dead. He thinks his people are still at that compound of his. He thinks he's still in control.* She went over in her mind what she thought he knew versus what they all knew.

"So . . . Mister . . ." she hesitated.

"Monroe." Morrigan piped up. Benjamin 'Papa Cat' Monroe."

"Mr. Monroe. Tell me. Why exactly are you here?"

He looked at Gertrude smiling broadly, sizing her up. "Say Ms . . ." he corrected himself, "Dr. Lerner. You strike me as quite perky for your real age, of which I am uncertain. I bet you've got money!" He leaned forward as if to expose her. "You're rich, aren't you?"

Gertrude held his gaze. "Well my, my, my. You're certainly perceptive, Mr. Monroe. I'm wondering, is that what you're here for? Money?" She shrugged as if mystified.

He chomped on another cookie. With his mouth full he responded. "Money's a side interest of mine. Never hurts to ask, I find. People never want to talk about their money, but you know . . . I think they should. I mean . . . let's face it . . . it's just a game. People take it too seriously. Like cat and mouse. The cat's hungry . . . like that one in this house somewhere . . . and the little mouse is food."

Carol Ann brought the coffee pot with cups and cream and sugar on a tray.

He smiled. "Why thank you, Darlin. I can tell, you're a nice woman." He appraised her. "But methinks you do not have much money." He turned back to Gertrude. "Not like this one."

Gertrude leaned forward. "Do you know the story about the Man

Who Outfoxed Himself?"

"Oh . . ." he looked upward as if trying to remember, "I don't believe I do."

"Would you like to hear it?"

"Well . . ." he considered, "Is it about money?" He asked like a greedy child.

"Why yes . . . it is."

He winked at Morrigan, who was seething in silence, waiting and hoping for the right moment to make a move.

"Then . . . please . . . enlighten me." He sipped his coffee and turned to Carol Ann. "I love little stories, don't you?"

Carol Ann smiled demurely, thinking it best to keep him underestimating her.

"Well . . ." Gertrude began, "there once was a man who was young and strong and intelligent. He had absolutely no weaknesses . . . except one. He was very ambitious, and he grew to understand that ambition needed money. So . . . since he had no money because his parents were poor, but hard-working, he discovered with his charm and intellect, . . . why taking other peoples' money was relatively easy. So easy in fact that he managed to gather so much money . . . I mean piles of it that he stashed everywhere . . . over a few bodies mind you . . . that he forgot where he'd hidden it all. And one day his happy, jolly family began to stumble across some of those hidden piles that the man had forgotten all about. Unlike a squirrel who never forgets, he was not blessed with those instincts. Then one day he decided to collect all his money and count it . . . and guess what?"

He stared at her, now frowning. He did not like the story.

"Guess what, Mr. Monroe?" She baited him.

"What?" he snapped.

"Why the money was all gone . . . and you know . . . so was his happy family."

He stood up. "All right. I'm getting tired of this."

Morrigan jumped up. "I have to go to the bathroom. Now!"

He stared at her. "All right. But let me tell you, Baby M. If you're not back in 5 minutes these lovely ladies will join the other. And I think you know what that means."

She walked down the hall to the bathroom. Inside she picked up the pelican that she'd already returned.

Gertrude and Carol Ann had waited while she set it down carefully knowing it was important to her.

She cupped it in her right hand. It was heavy and solid. She flushed the toilet and came back down the hall.

When she came into the living room, Gertrude knew she intended something.

So did Carol Ann.

Both focused their smiles on Benjamin who was pouring himself more coffee.

"Welcome back" he announced as he heard her come in.

She stared at his head and as he turned to the left to see her, she side-stepped to the right, and it came around in a full swinging arc, whamming him across the head.

He set down the coffee cup as if in slow motion, and with an uncomprehending look on his face he slumped over on the couch.

Gertrude saw Morrigan head in for the kill and held her hand up commanding her to "Stop!"

Carol Ann threw her arms around Morrigan reaching around for the pelican and lead her over to the chair away from him.

Gertrude swiftly let the dogs in who charged into the room. She ordered them to sit on either side of Benjamin.

He groaned.

Juno growled and Dido emitted a sharp bark, warning him not to move.

Gertrude asked, "Have we got any duct tape?"

Carol Ann was up, and, in the kitchen—in a flash returning as she pulled a wide swath of tape open. She bit off a long piece and deftly wrapped his wrists together. Then his ankles.

"Prop him up," Gertrude ordered. "He'll come to in a minute. We have a few more things to discuss with Mr. Monroe."

CHAPTER 28

"I've heard 'Uncle Tom's Cabin' read, and I tell you
Mrs. Stowe's pen hasn't begun to paint what slavery is
as I have seen it at the far South. I've seen de real thing, and
I don't want to see it on no stage, or in no theater."

HARRIOT TUBMAN

IT WAS 6:30 A.M. DANIEL PERRY WAS A LUCKY MAN, and he knew it. Propped up in his hospital bed, hooked up to drips and monitors keeping track of his vital signs, with a splint on his wrist and a bandaged head, he beamed at his audience: Melinda, Rebecca, Tom, Billy, Bear and Richard. He was not only grateful to be alive, he was equally grateful that he had no serious burns.

His brother-in-law was being modest about his heroism.

"Billy, you saved my life. I don't know how you did it, but you did." He wanted to say more but started to choke up. They all knew that sentimental gratitude was not his strong suit.

Billy patted him on his shoulder. "Just doing what I do best."

"No," Daniel corrected him. "You are the best."

To recover his equilibrium, he changed the subject. "He's dead . . . right? It was horrible. He put that ghastly old bear skin over himself and just ran into the flames. I mean . . ." he started to choke up again . . . "it was horrible."

Silence.

He looked around at all of them while their expressions remained unchanged. He added, "What an ending."

After a few seconds he realized they weren't responding with sympathetic horror. He looked at them one by one. Their faces showed no understandable expression. "Bear . . ." he demanded. "He's dead . . . right?"

Bear shifted his feet. "Well, Daniel . . . here's the problem. They've combed through the ashes, and . . ." he hesitated.

"Yeah . . . right . . . and?" His euphoria was draining fast.

"They found no remains of Benjamin. Nothing. Nada. They'd gotten the flames out pretty quickly . . . soon enough for there to be some evidence. I mean, they found charred bits of the bearskin. But no evidence of human remains."

Daniel looked horrified. "I don't believe it. I saw him go in."

Richard stepped forward. "You think you saw him."

"No! I saw him. I was there. You weren't." He glowered at Richard.

Rebecca spoke. "Daniel, listen to me. You were in a state of great shock and panic. When anyone's in a state of extreme trauma our minds play tricks on us."

He looked at her as if she, too, had betrayed him. He glared at all of them. *They're all against me. My best friends. My own flesh and blood. They're all against me.*

"I know what I saw."

Bear's cell phone played the marimba. He left the room and headed outside, knowing there would be little to no reception within the hospital. He listened to the message.

Gertrude's voice. "Please call immediately."

She answered mid-ring, and explained the situation, that Benjamin Monroe sat tied up on Daniel's couch with the Queens on either side, carefully guarding his every move. "I wanted to alert you first. I suppose we better call the police."

His thoughts jumped around, intuitively landing on a decision. "If you call the local police there's really nothing but circumstantial evidence to hold him on. He'll lie and say Morrigan attacked him. Remember, he's a consummate liar. They won't know whom to believe and he might somehow get away. But the County Sheriff up here will be more than happy to arrest him for kidnapping and attempted murder."

He instructed Gertrude to photograph Benjamin with her phone and send it to him.

"I'll get it to the Sheriff so Flora can identify him as the man who tried to kill her. We're in the same hospital as Daniel and Flora both. I can get to her right away. Daniel's story will take some time for them to comprehend. Flora's our best bet to get him in custody for long enough to dig up the other evidence."

"All right," she agreed. "How soon can you get here? Carol Ann and I are fine for now, but you must imagine he's not the most charming person I've ever met, and I must admit . . . he's quite devious, even tied up and guarded by the Queens."

He laughed. "Gertrude, I think Mr. Monroe has met his match. Give me a couple of hours. I think DeWitt will let us use his plane."

He called Axel DeWitt.

"Yeah?"

Bear explained the situation.

Axel agreed.

Bear asked, "Is that spikey-haired kid with you?

Axel hesitated. "Yeah.

"He stole a lot of money from you."

"I know."

"Well, what're you gonna do about it?"

"Haven't decided, but for now he's more valuable to me under my wing than he is in jail."

"What about your son?"

Silence.

He heard Axel breathing. "I'm quite certain he's dead."

"I think we've got the killer. We may need that kid to testify later."

"He'll do it." DeWitt looked across the room at Blanco tapping away at his laptop. "Trust me. He'll do what I tell him."

Bear went back to Daniel's room to report what had happened.

Richard and Billy went to the airport with Bear.

Tom, Rebecca and Melinda stayed behind with Daniel.

After talking with Bear, Gertrude returned to the living room.

Carol Ann had made another pot of coffee.

Benjamin cupped it in his bound hands, slurping and spilling it as he stared at her sitting quietly staring back at him.

Earlier, after Benjamin was bound and guarded, Gertrude and Carol Ann talked with Morrigan, beyond Benjamin's hearing, about what she wanted to do. They agreed to let her go.

Gertrude knew if she remained near Benjamin, she would have

difficulty controlling herself. It was better to set her free. She was exhausted, but she was young, and they knew she could drive far enough to get away before she stopped to rest. Gertrude asked only for one condition—that she keep in touch once she knew where she was going, and she promised she would.

"Please tell Tom someday I'll let him know where I am."
Gertrude picked up her backpack. "Do you have enough funds?"

"Yeah. Enough."

"Do you know where you'll go?"

"Sort of." Morrigan had a hunch about where her mother and little sister might go. Several times over the years her mother mentioned Michigan, where she said she was born in a small rural town. Before she had called Tom the day before she and Blanco split some more cash. She had enough to live on for a year if she was careful. She left at 5:30, exactly 24 hours after she'd left the previous morning heading for the compound.

At 7:00 a.m. Gertrude held her cell phone up. "Say cheese, Mr. Monroe."

He winced. "Do you think you could call off your dogs? I mean . . . they're making me nervous. They seem jumpy. If I even twitch, that one," he glanced at Juno, "starts to growl and show her pointy little molars."

"Oh please, don't worry about them. They're quite well trained and perfectly harmless, if you remain calm. I'd like to have a little chat if you don't mind."

"Chat? About what?"

"Well, it would seem you've led quite an . . . how shall I put it . . . unorthodox life, Mr. Monroe. I understand you've maintained an interest, . . . or should I say obsession . . . with the Civil War with quite an affinity for the Confederacy?"

His eyes narrowed to slits. "What would a rich old lady like you know about the Civil War?"

"Well . . . my late husband was a southerner from South Carolina."

He continued to glower. "So? I suppose you think you have something to tell me."

"No. I wouldn't presume to try to tell you anything, Mr. Monroe. But I would like to ask you a question."

He stared, waiting, poised for the kill. If he couldn't physically attack her, at least he could annihilate her with his contempt for her puny attempts to outwit him. He eagerly awaited his chance to put this arrogant dame in her place.

She interpreted his silence for permission to continue. "Tell me. What is the source of your hatred and revenge? I'm not referring to what you think Mr. Perry did to you forty years ago, because I believe this hatred started long before that."

This was not what he expected. "Don't try to psychoanalyze me, lady."

"Oh, of course not. I'll re-phrase the question. What could be important enough for you . . . or anyone I suppose . . . to sacrifice human lives for?"

"Who says I killed anybody?"

"I said sacrifice, not kill."

"What's the difference?"

"Not all sacrifices are human beings."

He looked away, then back at her. "All right. You wanna know?"

"Yes."

"You won't understand this. Nobody does. But since we're sitting here with nothing better to do . . . I'll tell you." He waited. The ten words fell into place. "Freedom conceived in the Constitution equals the right to self-government."

She let that sit, knowing that somehow in those words resided his moral compass, or more to the point, the lack thereof. "My husband did say something about freedom you might be interested to hear."

"What was that?" He felt more than ready for whatever thought rattled around in her head that she believed could counter this simple, over-riding truth.

He said, "Unless you were born a slave and later set free, you can't possibly understand real freedom." She looked around the room as if she'd just stated the boringly obvious. "So you see . . . when you talk about freedom to govern ourselves from my husband's point of view . . . you couldn't possibly know what you're talking about, and I suppose that's the reason there was so much bravery in that war coming from those contraband soldiers. They really were fighting for their freedom. I think that may have been Daniel Perry's point forty years ago, and why he went to such lengths to discredit your lies about him and his friend's letter— Mr. Ephraim Brown's four-great- Grandfather's letter to Mr. Frederick Douglass."

"The letter was never sent."

"Well I understand for good reason. Mr. Brown's ancestor was hung by an angry white mob during the race riots in New York City in July 1863. The Battle of Milliken's Bend occurred only one month earlier on June 7, 1863. So, you see, Mr. Brown may have written the letter and not had time to send it to Mr. Douglass. However, the letter survived and was handed down in Mr. Brown's family as a valuable family heirloom."

"He and Daniel forged it."

"No, Mr. Monroe, the letter was not forged."

He wriggled the tape and ground his teeth. Staring into her was not enough. He willed himself to be Superman. To break free of his bonds and lunge for her. He would hack those dogs to pieces and rape the other woman before he throttled this arrogant old bitch.

Sensing his hostility the Queens stood, fur bristling, curling lips, in unison emitting a low, steady growl

He hissed at her. "You know nothing."

"Maybe not," she chirped, "but I wonder if you've read Uncle Tom's Cabin lately." His eyes rolled. "Well, for some reason I'm reminded of Simon Legree's ending. He was haunted by a ghost. Do you remember?" He plopped his head down as if she was boring him to death.

"Well, I'm reminded of a quote from that book when Ms. Stowe speaks of the ghost who haunts Legree. She says something like "What a fool is he who locks his door to keep out spirits, who has in his own bosom a spirit he dares not meet alone, whose voice, smothered far down, and piled over with mountains of earthliness, is yet like the forewarning trumpet of doom!"

"What the hell has that got to do with me?"

"Oh, I think you know, Mr. Monroe. After all, you are a haunted man.

"I'm tired of this conversation." He looked at Carol Ann. "I'm hungry."

"You can have some breakfast, Mr. Monroe, but just bear with me one little bit longer. My husband liked to quote Shelby Foote, whom he admired, who said that it was the Civil War that defined us Americans— for better and for worse."

"Is that it?" He tried to sound exasperated.

"Oh, yes . . . just one more little bit of information. That young woman you think you strangled and think you left for dead in the bushes? Well, she's alive and will recover. Also Mr. Perry is alive and doing just fine. They're both in the same hospital."

"You're lying."

"No, Mr. Monroe, I happen to be deadly serious."

It seemed that he suddenly noticed that Morrigan was not present. "Where is she?"

"Where is who?"

"You know fucking well who I mean."

"You mean Morrigan?"

"Of course, I mean Morrigan. She's my daughter."

"I don't think so, Mr. Monroe." Gertrude held his stare. "She's gone and left a message for you."

He looked around the room as if she might reappear.

"She said to tell you, 'I know where some of them are. It didn't make sense when I was younger, but now it does.' I assume you might know what she meant."

At 9:30 a.m. Bear, Richard and Billy arrived.

For the first time in his life Benjamin felt overwhelmed.

Several hours later the County Sheriff arrived as well, to take him into custody on charges of murder, attempted murder, kidnapping, arson, embezzlement, drug trafficking, and whatever else they thought might stick.

Already the police were combing Benjamin's property for more evidence of possible homicides. They found some human bones and were having them tested for DNA.

Axel DeWitt promised to keep Blanco in his custody pending trial.

CHAPTER 29

"He was never a man-eater. He's indebted for his character for ferocity almost entirely to tradition, but, in some degree, to the female bear when seeking to protect her young." (Joaquin) Miller witnessed firsthand how the great grizzly, who had lived so long and well with indigenous tribes, "went out as the American rifle came in."

G. A. BRADSHAW, *CARNIVORE MINDS, WHO THESE FEARSOME ANIMALS REALLY ARE*

EIGHT HOURS LATER HE SAT IN THE BACK SEAT of the sheriff's 4-wheel jeep, hands cuffed behind him, watching, and waiting for them to turn down 299. The plan had been hatching in his head while he pretended to doze, and by the time they turned he knew it would work.

The sheriff was a friendly man, and the much younger woman with him was clearly still in training. She didn't come across as a rookie. In fact, she impressed him as being overly zealous. Nevertheless, she was the unpredictable one, not like the sixty-year-old county sheriff who'd seen it all. Between the two, he felt far more wary of her

He knew they would stop before Weaverville at a coffee shop twenty miles short. Not the Bend Café, which was on the other side, but the favorite old truck stop for loggers who were on their way up and down the coast with their deliveries, called Nellie's Place.

Inside, it was dark and crowded around 5:00 p.m.—the time everyone congregated to have a beer and watch whatever game was on. It was filled with the heads of dead animals and the plank walls were covered with old photographs and business cards of all kinds. Anyone who owned a business within a hundred miles had left their card. Many were defunct, but that wasn't the point to begin with. It was probable that no one went to Nellie's to look up someone's business. And these days, just as in the old days, everyone knew everyone who needed work, and few were spending.

"Hey, Sheriff . . . I wonder if you're stopping at Nellie's. I'd sure appreciate a visit to the head if you know what I mean."

Sheriff Reynolds looked over at his sidekick. "What do ya think? You hungry?"

The sidekick, Sandi, looked wary, but she wanted to please her boss. "Yeah, sure. I could eat something. What about him?"

"Oh, don't worry about him. We've got him on a leash. I'll cuff him to me. No problem."

They walked inside and found a table. It was awkward, but no one seemed to notice.

They ordered some food and coffee and then Benjamin leaned over to the Sheriff. "Hey, man, I hate to bother, but I really gotta go."

"Oh, yeah . . . sure. All right. Here's how we do this. You'll have a little company."

He turned to Sandi who looked uneasy. "Don't worry. We'll be back. He's just gotta take a leak."

She accepted this.

They got up in unison, and Benjamin walked shoulder to shoulder over to the bathroom that was out the back. He knew it was a big open room and that the sheriff would insist on coming in with him. They got to the door where he stopped. "Listen, I have to confess . . . I've got stomach problems and well . . . you know . . . it's not very pleasant. I'm pretty embarrassed about it." He described in detail what his bouts of colitis were like. "Not pretty, sir. Look . . . you would probably hear me in there moaning and groaning and well . . . it can get pretty bad smell-wise if you know what I mean." He was certain he'd already spoiled the sheriff's appetite by the look on his face. *What great luck! A sheriff who hated bad smells.*

"Ok, ok. But if you aren't out in five I'm comin' in."

"Sure thing. Thanks." He bent over as he went in holding his stomach, causing the sheriff to turn away.

Inside, he knew exactly what to do. He'd been there many times and knew about the back door. It was used by all the druggies. In the last stall, down low, it was a dog door, only reasonably small humans could crawl through. Benjamin wasn't small, but he knew how to tunnel. He knew how to turn himself into mouse bones.

Within three minutes, he had wiggled out and was running through the trees to the river. He made it to the river just as he heard the screech of the wheels and the siren blaring.

They were out of the car, shouting at each other, flicking their guns.

He was already immersed in the water up to his neck, with his head under the embankment. They'd called for backup, and he heard the sheriff tell her confidently, "He won't get far. There's nowhere for him to go."

What the sheriff didn't know was that Benjamin knew all the growers in these woods. He'd done favors at one time or another for all of them. They were a secret underground.

He made it to one house where he knew he could get a car and within two hours he was on the back roads heading past his own place farther north and then he turned into the river. This was the point where he'd hidden his best stash. Money, canned food, a backpack with down bag, hiking boots, a change of clothes and a revolver. Everything he needed for a few days' trek in the woods.

By 2:00 a.m. he was far up in the pines, settling in for the night. He didn't dare make a make a fire, but he opened some health bars and snuggled under the brush for the rest of the night. He didn't think he could sleep, but he did. He was exhausted. As he fell asleep, he thought about tomorrow. *He would find her. No . . . he would find all of them. And then he'd be on his merry way.*

When he opened his eyes, he felt the warmth of sunlight. He realized he'd slept late. He sat up and started to peel himself out of the sleeping bag when he heard the rustling sounds about fifteen feet away.

They were so cute, actually playing with the cans, pushing them with their over-sized paws they would someday grow into. One jumped on the other and they tumbled over rolly-polly, growling, squeaking . . . like puppies. He couldn't help smiling.

Then he was seized with reality. *Omigod! Where's the mother?* He eyed his revolver about five feet away on top of his jacket. Slowly, he crept out of the bag, never taking his eye off the cubs. They were too involved in their play to notice him. He crept a few feet on all fours and then froze.

She came out of the trees like thunder barreling down on him. He stared at her fierce eyes like bullets. He screamed "Oh my God it's Jimmy!" as she ripped him from stem to stern.

One month later on a Sunday morning, Daniel sat at his breakfast table in his plaid flannel bathrobe eating the whole grain oatmeal Tom left for him on the stove.

Numi sat up straight on the chair across from him craning his neck, sniffing the air.

Daniel eyed him. "He spoils you. Just like Anna. In fact," he spoke to Numi in a conversational tone, "it's like having a little male Anna around."

Numi tentatively rose, about to slide onto the table, but thought better of it, humped his back to stretch and settled back down.

"Let's face it," he continued, as if Numi perfectly understood, "he's gone to the grocery store, just like she used to, and he's cooking dinner tonight for everyone." Richard, Rebecca, Melinda and Gertrude were coming. "He even got the recipe from Gertrude for her southern fried chicken."

He looked around as if he had a sympathetic audience all around. "Where do I fit in?" Whiney tone. "He cleans, he shops, cooks, sends me to yoga, we eat fresh vegetables," he wrinkled his nose, "and he organizes my stuff behind my back with Melinda. Professors brag to me about how smart he is. And . . . if all that weren't bad enough . . . he tells me what I should teach!" Shrieky tone.

The hall landline rang. He pushed his chair back and plodded into the hall while Numi slithered onto the table and headed for the cereal bowl to taste the creamy leftover porridge with his paw. He licked lazily knowing the sound of Daniel's voice meant he was predisposed.

"How are you, Daniel?" Carol Ann's nurturing, melodious voice drifted into his ear.

He slumped down on the hall rug against the wall. A child hearing the maternal, sweet voice. "Ok. I'm much better." He gave her a detailed run down of his aching, healing parts. His wrist. Ankle. Back pain. Bruises. Minor burns.

Her voice was like salve. Then it changed. Not her tone, but the topic. "How's Tom?"

He shifted his weight, groaned. The streak of envy he worked full time to submerge raised its ugly head. "He's fine!" He winced, knowing how that sounded. *Too chirpy. No feeling.*

"Well, I know he's fine. But Daniel, tell me how he's really doing?"

He felt the resistance to answer. *Your son is a well-behaved, talented, kind genius . . . and how am I supposed to tolerate that!? And . . . the salt on the wound is that he relates to all my best friends better than I do and . . . if things couldn't get any worse than that . . . how about this? He now talks to my dead wife more than I do.*

He heard his own voice answer. "No seriously . . . you and Billy should feel extremely proud. He's a wonderful young man."

"Oh, my goodness Daniel," she paused, "that must be difficult for you."

"Difficult?" He felt the lump in his throat like a stone he couldn't swallow. He cleared his throat. "No . . . not at all." He waited, pretending not to know what she was getting at, but fearing she was about to tell him.

"Well Daniel, I remember when we were young. You know, in middle school. Remember? I won that award for best essay in the school? I wrote a silly little story about making friends with a family of opossums? Mama, Papa and Baby opossums? You were quite young but that was difficult for you. I announced to you and our parents at the dinner table that I wanted to grow up and write stories for children?"

He didn't remember. But he was wiping the tears on his flannel sleeve.

"You were so smart and . . . well, I really wasn't. So, it was hard for you. I mean it was hard for you to maybe think I could be smart too. So, I wonder if living with my son isn't a bit like that?"

He choked. And then came the tears.

She listened.

"Daniel? Are you ok?"

He wasn't. "Yeah, of course."

"Well look, give my love to Tom. Billy sends hugs. And love from all of us to all of you California folks. We're off to Church, and then you know . . . Sunday dinner as usual with everyone. We hope someday before Billy and I are too old, or God forbid in our graves, you'll come for a visit.

He choked and managed to squeak, "I will."

Dinner that night was a challenge.

Tom and Gertrude giggling and clucking in the kitchen. Richard and Rebecca talking about Tom's virtues while Melinda beamed at him as if he were the luckiest man in the world. He knew it was all too true.

That night in bed she came to him. "Listen, Daniel. You are blessed. You must see that. Grow up. Tom's an extension of you."

He wanted to defend but managed to calm himself. "I know."

That night at 2:00 a.m. he woke to the whisper that was always like a wind in his ear. "Hey, kid. Meet me out back."

He forced himself up, waking Numi, pulled on his t-shirt and trudged down the hall toward the kitchen and out the back sliding glass doors. He sat on her bench.

"Son, I won't be seeing you for some time."

"What do you mean by that?"

"Well . . ." he looked up at the moon . . . "Time means nothing to me, but it might to you."

"Oh," Tom thought about that. "I guess I can understand that."

"Nope. Not really. But you will someday."

"So, Zak. Did I do what you wanted? Help save Uncle Daniel?"

"Listen, Son, that wasn't the main point."

"All right, Zak. What was the point? You knew about the danger. Uncle Daniel would be dead if you hadn't warned me. And I warned them."

"First of all . . . dead's not so bad. But I don't wish to dwell on that. Daniel and Benjamin represented a divide that's still gathering momentum. It just changes with the generations. That war was never quite over."

Tom was thoughtful. "You know Zak . . . I think I know what you mean, but could you just spell that out for me?"

"What I mean by the divide?"

"Yes. Your Uncle Daniel straddles two worlds—the ephemeral now, this physical universe on one side, and the endless ethereal on the other. What has happened in the past—history—becomes the now, into the future. He understands we are all part of a continuum."

"I get that. In his first class this summer he quoted a piece of the Lucretius poem Anna had written to him in a card just before she died. He wanted us to see ourselves as connected to all living and dying—he called it 'the great swirling, chaotic oneness of it all!'"

Zak nodded. "And Benjamin? He was caught in a web of his own making. The idea that there is one truth that supersedes all others only creates conflict and death. No continuum."

"Zak, is the divide what we call death?"

"Yes, you've got it. Death is not nothing, because there is no nothing. It's what you believe when you look up at the sky that matters."

Tom looked up. "You're talking about loss of faith. Not religious faith, but faith in the oneness."

"You're learning, Kid."

"You know, Zak, I think Mark Twain believed, and then he lost it. He got stuck and lost his way. I guess you'd say he lost his faith."

He turned to Zak and saw only the empty space where he'd been. In that moment Tom saw the invisible being of it all.

He looked across the lawn and noticed Numi's head and tail swishing back and forth like a flag beckoning him to return to bed.

He got up and went in.

Numi followed Tom down the hall and hopped on the bed.

Tom patted his head and turned out the light.

SELECTED BIBLIOGRAPHY

Beckwith, Martha. *Hawaiian Mythology*, University of Hawaii Press, Honolulu, 1970.

Bordewich, Fergus M. *Bound for Canaan, The Underground Railroad and the War for he Soul of America*. New York: Amistad Books, 2005.

Faust, Drew Gilpin. *This Republic of Suffering, Death and the American Civil War*. New York: Alfred A. Knopf, 2008.

Foote, Shelby. *The Civil War, A Narrative*. 3 Volumes. New York: Random House, Modern Library Edition, 2011.

Garrison, Webb with Garrison, Cheryl. *The Encyclopedia of Civil War Usages, An Illustrated Compendium of the Everyday Language of Soldiers and Civilians*. Nashville: Cumberland House, 2001.

Holton, Woody. *Unruly Americans, and the Origens of the Constitution*. New York: Hill and Wang, 2007.

Jackson, Lawrence P. *My Father's Name, A Black Virginia Family After the Civil War*. Chicago: The University of Chicago Press, 2012.

Konstam, Angus. *Civil War Ghost Stories*. San Diego: Thunder Bay Press, 2005.

Lee, General Fitzhugh. *Introduction by Gary W. Gallagher. A Biography of Robert E. Lee*. Wilmington, NC: Da Capo Press, 1994.

Lapore, Jill. *The Whites of Their Eyes, The Tea Party's Revolution and the Battle for American History*. Princeton: Princeton University Press, 2010.

Lucretius. *The Nature of Things*. Translated and With Notes by A.E. Stallings. Introduction by Richard Jenkyns. London: Penguin Classics, 2007.

McGrath, Thomas A. *Shepherdstown: Last Clash of the Antietam Campaign, September 19-20, 1862*. Lynchburg, VA: Shroeder Publications, 2012.

Nesbitt, Mark V. *Ghosts of Gettysburg, Spirits, Apparitions and Haunted Places of the Battlefield*. Second Chance Publications, 2012.

Paine, Thomas. *Common Sense, On the Origen and Design of Government in General; with Concise Remarks as the English Constitution*. Together with The American Crisis 1776-1783. Introduction by W. Stitt Robinson. Norwalk, Connecticut: The Easton Press, 1994.

Petruzzi, J. David and Stanley, Steven. *The New Gettysburg Campaign Handbook. June 9—July 14, 1863. Facts, Photos, and Artwork for Readers of All Ages*. New York: Savas Beatie LLC, 2011.

Quarles, Benjamin. *The Negro in the Civil War*. Boston: Da Capo Press, 1989.

Robertson, James. Editor: Neil Kagan. T*he Untold Civil War, Exploring the Human Side of War*. Washington D.C.: National Geographic Society, 2011.

Savas, Theodore P. *Brady's Civil War Journal, Photographing the War 1861-65*. New York: Skyhorse Publishing, 2012.

Sears, Stephen W. *George B. McClellan, The Young Napoleon*. New York: Da Capo Press, 1999.

Seton, Ernest Thompson. *Woodcraft and Indian Lore. A Classic Guide from a Founding Father of the Boy Scouts of America*. New York: Skyhorse Publishing, 2007.

Shaara, Jeff. *Gods and Generals*. New York: Ballentine Books, 1998.

Spaeth, Frank, Editor. *Phantom Army of the Civil War, and other Southern Ghost Stories.* St Paul Minn: Llewellyn Publications, 1997.

Stowe, Harriet Beacher. *The Annotated Uncle Tom's Cabin.* Edited with an introduction and notes by Henry Laws Gates, Jr. and Hollis Robbins. New York: W.W. Norton & Company, 2007.

Ward, Geoffrey C. with Ric Burns and Ken Burns. *The Civil War, An Illustrated History,* with a new Preface by Ken Burns. Alfred A Knopf, Inc., Thirteenth Paperback Printing, 2010.

Williams, Robert L. *The Old West, The Loggers.* Canada: Time-Life Books, 1976.

Woodfield, Stephanie. *Priestess of the Morrigan, Prayers & Devotional Work to The Great Queen.* Llewellyn Publications, Woodbury, Minnesota, 2021.

Wright, John D. *The Language of the Civil War.* Westport, Connecticut: Oryx Press, 2001.

BIO

Born in Pennsylvania and raised in California, Jan Thorpe grew up on the grounds of a hospital. Her father was medical director and she and her brother had the run of the place. People would say, "There go Doc's kids on their bikes!" On their vacations with their father, an avid fly-fisherman, they camped throughout the western Sierras, cooking trout over a campfire next to rivers and lakes. Jan's mother, while braiding her hair, told her about a flea named Skeezix that bothered everyone, an early influence that inspired her to make up her own stories.

In childhood Jan was a contradiction to most of the adults—too dreamy and a bit wild. She graduated from Vassar College with a degree in English literature, then married Larry Thorpe. Living in the San Francisco Bay area they bought a cabin at 7400 feet on a small lake where they spent summers with their two sons and many beloved dogs. After ten years of creating limited edition serigraphs, Jan found her way to earning a master's degree and later Ph.D. in clinical psychology. In her Jungian-oriented psychotherapy practice, specializing in dreams, she began to write novels that weave the strange and elusive dimension of dreams into her psychological thrillers.

Coming soon the new psychological thriller
by Jan C. Thorpe

MOTHERBOARD. Copyright © 2022 Jan C. Thorpe.

CHAPTER ONE

*Motherboard—(mobo) The main printed circuit
board in an electronic device, particularly a
computer, which may contain sockets that
accept additional boards ("daughter-boards").*

THE FREE ON-LINE DICTIONARY OF COMPUTING, DENIS HOWE, 2010

IT WAS A MOMENT OF RARE PRIVACY in her office cubicle after she'd snagged her left middle finger in the file drawer. As usual, she was moving too quickly, and now she leaned back and studied the broken nail. The Monday morning staff meeting with her boss was in 40 minutes. *OK, so I screwed up.* Now she blamed her entire industry. *Why isn't there a really useful App like "Instant Nail Repair On The Go," or something?*

She texted her friend, Molly, at the Google office a few blocks away: "Got extra nails?"

Molly's response was instant, as she knew it would be—her job was beyond boring. "No. Walgrns on 4th?"

She answered. "No time."

Response: "Sorreee. Drinks still at 5?"

Answer: "Gesso. Depends on Nelson. Not sure."

Response: "K. Let me know."

She rummaged in her drawer for the China Glaze Ruby Pumps glitter polish and started filing. This was going to be slow work. The break was jagged, straight across like a sandstone cliff. She would have to take it down to the nub. Her landline rang. The caller ID displayed: Social Services, Albuquerque. It must be a mistake. After it rang three times, curiosity got the best of her and she picked it up, cradling it between her ear and shoulder as she continued to file, frowning at how bad the shortened nail was going to look no matter what she did.

"Claire Hamilton speaking."

"Ms. Hamilton, my name is Roberta Thompson." The caller sounded a little out of breath. Slight southern accent with a lilt—warm, inviting and professional.

"Yes, well, just so you know, you've called a business number. We're a software start-up in the Bay Area . . . California. I'm an executive assistant in marketing." *This should clarify things quickly.*

"Yes. I understand. My business with you is of a personal nature. I'm calling from the office of Social Services in Albuquerque, New Mexico?"

"Yeess?" Now she knew it was a wrong number. *But, oh well, it was turning into one of those days filled with little screw-ups.* Before the nail fiasco it started with spilling her latte on her new white rayon blouse from Anthropologie. She looked down to see if it had dried after she'd dabbed it with wet paper towels and saw the stained water outline. *Another damn cleaning bill—the last one was over $200.* One of those costs of working in corporate headquarters. She had to look the part at all times. Unlike Nelson Longstreet, her live-in partner, who had one outfit: jeans, tee shirt and Converse slims.

"I'm calling on a matter regarding your older sister, Rowena Cooper."

The pink nail file flipped up and froze in midair. "Whoo?"

"Your older sister, Rowena Cooper?"

"Ahhh . . . just a sec here. Ms . . . ?"

"Thompson."

"Yeah . . . ah . . . Ms. Thompson, I'm afraid there's been a mistake." Summoning her peremptory, professional tone that served her when she needed to cut things short, she continued, "I'm sorry to inform you . . . but you see I don't have a sister." She let that sit a few seconds before she added the coup de grace. "In fact, I'm the only child of Matthew and Elizabeth Hamilton . . . both of whom are now deceased." The lump rose in her throat. "My mother passed six months ago."

Silence. She heard Roberta sigh. "Yes . . . I'm so sorry and well . . . I suspected as much."

Claire pitched forward. "What do you mean . . . 'suspected as much?'" When in high dudgeon she employed her favorite management technique —throwing the opponent's words back at them. She prided herself on being able to summon bits of dialog like hard evidence from past conversations to set the record straight. It worked well with everyone, except Nelson. Nothing persuaded him. He lived in a universe apart from average mortals because . . . well . . . Nelson was a geek's geek. He and his laptop were merged into one personality, which meant that nothing pronounced by any human, an automatically unreliable source, went unsearched.

Roberta remained calm. "Let me explain."

Claire looked at her mother's platinum diamond Bulova. Her meeting was in twenty minutes. She put Roberta on speaker and continued to file vigorously, rounding the edges as best she could to match the other nails. Impossible, but she had to keep going. "Please do." Her nail was dwindling down to a nub among red spikes.

"I would prefer to do this in person."

"Where are you again?" She looked at the phone that indicated Albuquerque.

"As I mentioned, right now I'm in Albuquerque, but I could be there in San Francisco tomorrow morning."

"Ahh . . . you better explain quickly, Ms. Thompson. For one thing, I have an important meeting in less than ten minutes." Unaware until this moment how rattled this woman was making her, she blurted, "And I've broken my Goddamn nail!"

Silence. *Wow! Maybe that did it. Where'd she go?* "Ms. Thompson?"

"I'm here. I'm going to tell you in a nutshell, so please pay attention. Before your mother married your father, Matthew Hamilton, in December 1974 she gave birth to a daughter, Rowena Cooper. The father was a Native American named John Cooper, a member of the Chiricahua Apache. Your mother met John Cooper at the Pine Ridge Reservation protest in 1973. Your mother gave up the baby, your sister, to be raised by the father's family. Mr. Cooper was killed in 1978 while serving a nine-month prison sentence for political conspiracy related to counterculture protests. Your mother never saw Rowena, but she did send money to the family when she could, and she was in touch with Social Services. Then in 2009, Rowena had a child. Your niece. She's five years old now. Her name is Blossom Hunt. Your sister did not marry the father, but his name was William Hunt. Both parents are recently deceased."

She stared at her hand realizing she'd been holding up her fingers splayed, willing the nail to grow. She collapsed forward and grabbed the receiver. "I don't know who you are or what any of this has got to do with me, Ms. Thompson, but I must inform you . . . her voice petered out . . . "I must inform you . . ." her words lurched and squeaked . . . "my mother was the soul of propriety . . . she never went out without her lipstick . . . we belonged to the Country Club . . ." Her throat constricted, the precondition for a flood of tears. Snot oozed down her upper lip. She plundered the drawer for Kleenex. "My mother was a devout Catholic. She went to mass every Sunday and I grew up with Sunday dinners at my grandparents' home in Highland Park—that's Chicago." She hiccupped, but managed to add, "My mother was funny and popular. She was a housewife and a happy person. What you're saying just could not have happened."

Roberta took over. "I know this is a shock . . . your niece is five. Her parents . . . ah . . . your sister and her partner were murdered we think."

She let that sit.

Claire stared at the cubicle wall covered with scraps of paper, notes pinned in disarrayed patterns, a photograph of Nelson at his 36th birthday last year in the snow wearing his furry wolf hat she'd gotten him on Etsy, his cheeks inflated, mocking eyes at the camera, blowing out his 36 candles.

"Are you there, Ms. Hamilton?"

She blew her nose hoping it popped in Roberta's ear. "Yes. What do you mean murdered?"

Roberta went on. "This happened a month ago. Of course, it was a terrible trauma for the child. We think she may have witnessed what happened. But she doesn't remember."

"Stop!" She shrieked. "This is crazy! I have to go."

She told Roberta if any of what she said was true she would have to come and meet her in person. Claire hoped that would put an end to this, that Roberta would not show, and all of this insanity would just disappear and later become a hilarious story to tell her friends over cocktails.

"I will be there. What time and where?"

Claire gave her the address of the old rundown 1904 Victorian in the lower Haight neighborhood that she had bought with a down payment from her maternal grandmother's inheritance. She and Nelson lived there with their teacup poodle "Lulu" and large orange cat "Lion," a neighborhood denizen who had adopted them after they'd moved in.

They hung up.

She was five minutes late for the meeting.

Her boss, Dennis, noticed immediately that she wasn't all there. He asked in front of the five others, "What's wrong?" His favorite phrase was "We're a team," and his second favorite word was "transparency." This gave him carte blanche to humiliate anyone any time in front of everyone present, which Claire believed to be a loophole in the whole ideal of "we're a family here," giving the bosses permission to humiliate lesser staff in front of everyone, rationalizing it as transparency.

She looked at him blankly. "I don't feel well."

"Yeah. You don't look well." His gaze bore into her.

He's playing his little game again. She could not forget how, over lunch two years ago, in their first tete-a-tete meeting while she was still being considered for her current job, Dennis leaned over the table across from her and asked why she chose his company. *How many times have you asked this? You expect me to say something earth-shaking? How about: the money you jerk!* As she delayed delivering her cosmic revelation, Dennis grabbed the plastic ketchup bottle and squirted red globs all over his $10 fries while holding her eye. Claire answered, "I believe what your company offers will make the world a better place and I want to be part of that." She could still see him picking up a fry, guiding it slowly into his mouth, chewing and smiling. It was then she realized she hated him.

She took a deep breath. "I was up all night with food poisoning. I probably shouldn't be here."

"Go home," he ordered. "See you tomorrow."

Dismissed, relieved and still angry, she grabbed her iPad and ran for the bathroom. *I bet he even saw my nail.* The cold water on her face helped, and as she leaned into the mirror, pulling her lower eyelid down to study its redness, Rita, her co-worker came in.

Rita looked concerned. "What's up?"

As Claire headed out the swinging door, she tossed Rita the only truth she could muster: "I wish I knew."

The bus home staggered along with passengers piling in and out as she looked out the window at all the people moving fast, most staring or talking into a small screen. The only possibility she could tolerate, the only one that made any sense, was that this was all a horrible misunderstanding. This Roberta person obviously had tracked her down and somewhere along the way had gotten her facts wrong.

A teenager wearing earbuds and dressed in her Catholic school uniform sat down next to her, plunking her bulging backpack between her legs, leaning back lost in her music. Claire heard snatches of the lyrics.

You don't know oh oh . . .

That's what makes you beautiful . . .
    Baby you light up my world like nobody else . . .

The girl was in another universe. The young male voices sounded so innocent. She felt old and jaded as the bobbing teenager rocked the seat.

Elizabeth Hamilton, her mother, had once more occupied center stage. Claire could still see her, that last time on a visit to Chicago before her cancer diagnosis. Elizabeth had gathered her friends, all women, in her large living room, laughing, gossiping and trading stories. As usual Elizabeth was funnier and louder than the others, the Queen Bee of the group. She was always very proper, but she knew how to have fun. It was a diverse group, all ages, different ethnicities, some professional, others were housewives, some married, some single—all cried at Elizabeth's funeral and vowed to meet every year to remember their friend.

After her father died Claire's mother partially lost her moorings. Claire, too, missed his steady presence, his ability to make light of any difficult situation. He may have been a bit boring to some, but to Claire he was the tiller in their lives. Now she missed them both all the time. After her mother died, she entered psychotherapy with Rebecca Calhoun and that was helping her manage the loss. Even after two years, she still told Rebecca, "I can't believe they're both gone. When will I feel better?"

Rebecca's response never varied: "You'll feel better when you do."

This sounded like no answer at all, and yet that's not how it came across to Claire. For her, it was calming because it gave her permission to continue to feel her grief, which she knew she needed to do. Nelson's attitude was the opposite. He'd make her laugh about something entirely unrelated to distract her and that also worked. Both helped.

After forty minutes the bus, now filled with noisy school children, belched upward as breaks hissed at her stop. She hopped down almost snagging her heel on the step and headed down the sidewalk. She stopped to see if she'd scraped the leather and with relief thought, "That's something to be grateful for." She stopped at the corner market and bought flowers. They were expensive, but she needed them. As she climbed the stairs to the front stoop, she had no idea how she would break this latest news to Nelson.